5105 7361

P9-CAD-564

BRISTOL HOUSE

BRISTOL HOUSE

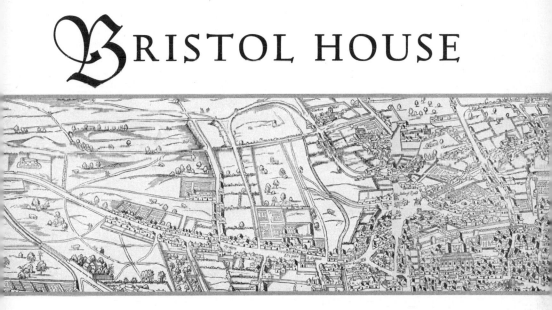

Beverly Swerling

VIKING

VIKING
Published by the Penguin Group
Penguin Group (USA) Inc., 375 Hudson Street,
New York, New York 10014, U.S.A.
Penguin Group (Canada), 90 Eglinton Avenue East, Suite 700, Toronto,
Ontario, Canada M4P 2Y3 (a division of Pearson Penguin Canada Inc.)
Penguin Books Ltd, 80 Strand, London WC2R 0RL, England
Penguin Ireland, 25 St. Stephen's Green, Dublin 2, Ireland
(a division of Penguin Books Ltd)
Penguin Group (Australia), 707 Collins Street, Melbourne,
Victoria 3008, Australia (a division of Pearson Australia Group Pty Ltd)
Penguin Books India Pvt Ltd, 11 Community Centre,
Panchsheel Park, New Delhi–110 017, India
Penguin Group (NZ), 67 Apollo Drive, Rosedale, Auckland 0632,
New Zealand (a division of Pearson New Zealand Ltd)
Penguin Books (South Africa), Rosebank Office Park, 181 Jan Smuts Avenue,
Parktown North 2193, South Africa
Penguin China, B7 Jiaming Center, 27 East Third Ring Road North,
Chaoyang District, Beijing 100020, China

Penguin Books Ltd, Registered Offices: 80 Strand, London WC2R 0RL, England

First published in 2013 by Viking Penguin, a member of Penguin Group (USA) Inc.

1 3 5 7 9 10 8 6 4 2

"Agas" map (detail), City of London, London Metropolitan Archives

Floorplan illustration by Jeffrey L.Ward

Publisher's Note: This is a work of fiction. Names, characters, places, and incidents
either are the product of the author's imagination or are used fictitiously, and
any resemblance to actual persons, living or dead, business establishments,
events, or locales is entirely coincidental.

LIBRARY OF CONGRESS CATALOGING-IN-PUBLICATION DATA
Swerling, Beverly.
Bristol house / Beverly Swerling.
p. cm.
ISBN 978-0-670-02593-0
1. Women historians—Fiction. 2. Architectural historians—Fiction.
3. Americans—England—London—Fiction. I. Title.
PS3619.W47B75 2013
813'.6—dc23   2012029009

Printed in the United States of America
Set in Adobe Garamond Pro and Brioso Pro
Designed by Francesca Belanger

For Bill, as always.

And for Michael, our forever darling boy. R.I.P.

BRISTOL HOUSE

Bristol House is a tale set simultaneously in the sixteenth century and the twenty-first, wherein a monk and a historian, each battered by love and terror, meet "as through a glass darkly" and hurtle toward destinies five hundred years apart yet on a collision course.

❖

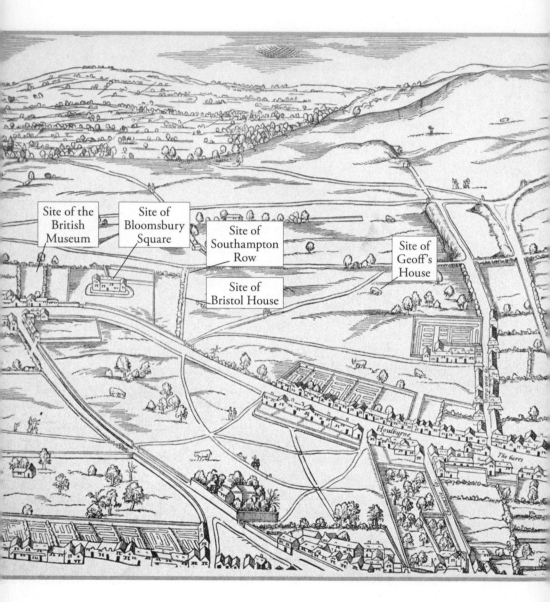

Site of the British Museum

Site of Bloomsbury Square

Site of Southampton Row

Site of Bristol House

Site of Geoff's House

Houlburne

The fares

CIVITAS LONDINIUM

Templar Church

Charterhouse

Cottage of the
Jew of Holborn

Smithfield

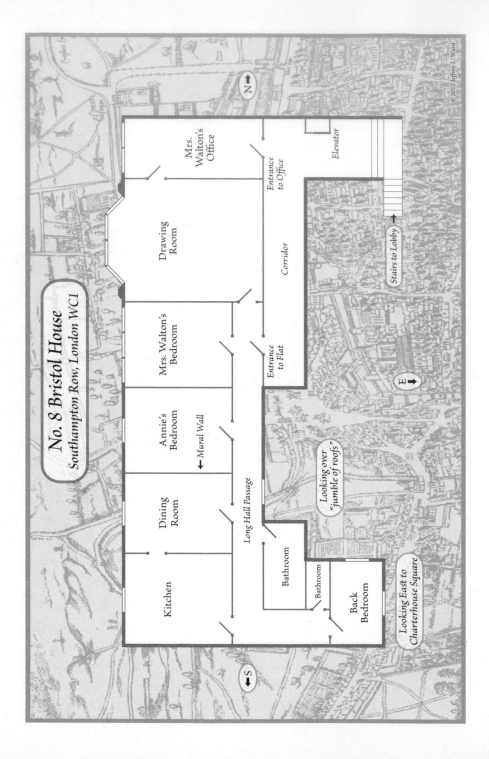

No. 8 Bristol House
Southampton Row, London WC1

N

Kitchen

Dining Room

Annie's Bedroom

← Mural Wall

Mrs. Walton's Bedroom

Drawing Room

Mrs. Walton's Office

Long Hall Passage

Bathroom

Bathroom

Back Bedroom

Entrance to Flat

Entrance to Office

Corridor

Elevator

Stairs to Lobby →

E →

"Looking over "jumble of roofs""

"Looking East to Charterhouse Square"

S ←

© 2012 Jeffrey L. Ward

1

The apartment was seven rooms, much bigger than Annie needed. But it was a four-minute walk to the British Museum, where she would be working frequently, and in the heart of Holborn, the London district that was the focus of much of her research. Not to mention the appeal of high ceilings and fireplaces and tall windows that overlooked busy Southampton Row, where double-decker buses went north and south to places called Chalk Farm and Covent Garden.

"I suggest," Mrs. Walton said, "you have a wander on your own. You must have been too jet-lagged to see it properly yesterday."

In her sixties, Annie thought. Fair, still pretty—no doubt an English rose in her day. Possibly a family resemblance to her niece, Sheila MacPherson, secretary to the director of the Shalom Foundation, the organization that had sent Annie Kendall to England. *My Auntie Bea's off to Singapore to visit her son, Dr. Kendall, just when you arrive, as it happens. I know she'd love to let her flat and have that bit of extra income, as long as she was sure the tenant would look after her things.*

There was a certified check drawn on Shalom's account in the bag slung over Annie's shoulder. She was here to sign the furnishings inventory, hand over the payment, collect the receipt, and pick up the keys. Mrs. Walton was leaving early the next morning, Tuesday, the first of May. It was agreed Annie could move in as soon after as she liked.

"Go on." Her soon-to-be landlady pressed into Annie's hand the list of the contents of each room. "Take this with you and have a look round without me peering over your shoulder."

"Well, if you don't mind . . ."

"I do not. Off you go. I'll be in my office if you have any questions." According to her niece, Bea Walton managed property for absentee owners. Her office was at the far end of the apartment and could be reached by a separate door from the outside corridor—lofty ceiling, broad stairs, and a creaking old elevator—or from what she referred to as the drawing room. Imagine, Annie Kendall from Brooklyn living in a place with a drawing room. Not that there was anything particularly grand about the flat. Shabby chic, more like, with an air of things having been in place for many years. Settled. Sturdy. Comfortable. In other words, perfect. She took the papers from the onetime English rose and turned left, starting down the long hall that formed the apartment's spine.

Old sketches and drawings lined the walls, along with two nineteenth-century gilt-framed mirrors that reflected wavy, mercurous images. A mahogany half-moon table held a vase of vivid yellow tulips; another, a few feet farther along, a lighted lamp. Each formed a small oasis of brightness in the dim passage. Annie's trained eye—she was an architectural historian—made it fifty-two feet, give or take six inches. Except for a big old-fashioned bathroom, all the rooms opened off the Southampton Row side. The first door led to Mrs. Walton's bedroom. Annie peeked inside. Two suitcases were open on the bed, and an ironing board had been set up in front of a small TV.

Next came the second bedroom, the one that would be hers. The day before—fresh off the plane from New York—she'd registered little other than a remarkable black and white mural made up of tiny overlapping pen and ink scenes of London, a helter-skelter riot that covered one entire wall. "Painted by a man named Stephen Fox," Mrs. Walton said. "He lived here alone until he died. Got run over in one of London's last pea-souper fogs, poor thing. I know his art is a bit odd, but we liked it, so we always decorated around it." Annie liked it too, but the amount of detail was dizzying, like a *Where's Waldo?* illustration.

She turned her back on the mural and looked at the rest of the bedroom. There was a bed covered in an old-fashioned crewelwork spread, a night table, a chest of drawers, an armoire, and a chair. Everything was pleasant and comfortable and inviting. Soothing enough, she decided, so she should be able to sleep despite facing the frenzied mural. She stepped back into the hall, closing the door firmly behind her.

A small dining room came next, and off it, a recently modernized kitchen. The apartment's long passage then made a sharply angled left turn and extended another eight or so feet to a small bedroom that had probably originally been intended as a maid's room.

She really must still be jet-lagged. She'd been wandering and gawking, trying to imagine herself living in these spaces, and forgotten she was meant to be checking the inventory. She'd have to do a second pass.

Annie opened the door to the small back bedroom. Double bed, six-drawer chest, desk, two lamps, and assorted books and decorative objects, according to the list.

She was looking at none of that.

"*Gloria Patri, et Filio, et Spiritui Sancto.*" A monk intoned the words while bent over in profound reverence. "*Sicut erat in principio,*" he chanted as he stood upright and looked, not at the book in his hands, but at the crucifix on the wall in front of him. "*Et nunc, et semper, et in saecula saeculorum. Amen.*" Bright sun shone through the window at his side, illuminating him in a broad shaft of light. His habit was pure white; everything around him neutral. The only contrast was the ruff of dark hair that circled his shaved head in the ancient cut known as tonsure.

The monk closed the book and swung around to face her. He smiled.

Annie slammed the door.

She turned, instinctively searching for a witness. The short length of hall was empty. She walked to the corner and looked down the long corridor all the way to the drawing room, or living room, or whatever it was to be called. Nothing. No one. The only sound was a radio playing softly, apparently from Bea Walton's office at the flat's far end.

Annie turned, walked back to the little bedroom, and pressed her ear against the door. Total silence. She reached for the doorknob.

Double bed, six-drawer chest, desk, two lamps, and assorted books and decorative objects—precisely as promised. Small, but two windows, so nice cross ventilation. The light they afforded was dim. It was late afternoon, cloudy, threatening rain, as it had been when she arrived. No sunlight.

And no monk.

For a fleeting moment, she considered backing out of everything. The job, the apartment. The whole deal.

Absurd. This assignment was—at least for her—the chance of a lifetime. Besides, she didn't believe in ghosts.

Mrs. Walton took the check. Both women signed the inventory and the rental agreement. The keys to number eight Bristol House changed hands. As of the next day, the flat was Annie's for three months.

The Two Princes Hotel on Gower Street was a stone's throw from Bristol House on Southampton Row. It boasted charming and tasteful rooms designed to appeal to the sort of tourists who wanted to be close to nearby London University or the British Museum. In New York, looking at the pictures on the hotel's Web site, Annie had thought the rooms likely to be claustrophobically small, but it hadn't seemed to matter, since she was only going to be there for two nights. Now, given that her two large bags took up much of the tiny amount of floor space, there was no room to dispel her nervous energy by pacing. She stood instead in the narrow gap between the bed and her luggage, hearing still the ancient Latin words, and her heart seemed to be beating in time to rhythms she'd first heard kneeling beside her father in some monastery he'd taken his family to visit.

Such excursions were a feature of her childhood. John Kendall had been a noted scholar of church history. Maybe that's why Annie's academic specialty became late Renaissance England, specifically the vernacular buildings of London in the time of the Tudors. Her doctoral dissertation had been titled *The Effect of Protestant Iconoclasm on Sacred Doorway Decoration in Tudor England, 1537–1559*. It was an investigation of the almost-instant disappearance of crucifixes and pictures of saints and the Virgin Mary from outside private houses after Henry VIII broke with Rome. The examining committee had accepted her work with "special commendation."

Gloria Patri, et Filio . . .

She remembered pressing her face against the scratchy tweed of her father's jacket, and the way he always smelled of tobacco. And she was quite sure he was the first person ever to put a pencil in her hand. "Draw something, Annie. Draw whatever you see."

She unzipped the outside pocket of one of the cases, withdrew a pad of paper and a pencil, and began to sketch. As a historian of architecture rather than a practitioner, Annie didn't require meticulous draftsman's skills. Her talent was for quick sketches, workmanlike and accurate. They conveyed the whole picture, mood rather than infinite detail of cornices and lintels. And as so often happened, once she began to draw, she remembered more than she recalled having observed.

In quick, sure strokes, a world took shape on the page—three views of the white-robed monk bathed in sunshine. In the first, he bowed before the crucifix; in the second, she drew what she'd seen after he stood up. His back was to her in both of those. The third sketch was her last sight of him, the most unsettling, the one where he turned to face her and beamed a smile of welcome. The background was the same in all three, a room simple to the point of austerity. A prie-dieu—one of those individual kneelers frequently seen in churches—stood beneath the crucifix. To the monk's left was a small stool, beside a table holding an open book, as if he'd been studying before he broke off to say his prayers. His cowl, the hood typical of so many monastic habits, was thrown back, and he was bare-headed.

Then, in another series of quick sketches on a separate page, where once more her pencil seemed to know more than she did, Annie caught his features. In profile first, so the shaved top of his head, the tonsure, showed. Another, straight on. Thin face, high chiseled cheekbones, the nose maybe a bit too large. Definitely good-looking, but kept from being too much the pretty boy by a strong chin with a sharp cleft.

She finished the last drawing and flipped through all of them, trying to see what exactly she had created. Pictures of a monk who appeared, then disappeared, in a place that did not look in the least like where she'd seen him.

She shivered. The commonsense explanation, that she'd imagined the entire episode, that her mind manufactured the details in her drawings, was terrifying.

Annie put down the pencil and returned the sketchbook to the suitcase. Four hours later—when according to her internal clock it was eight p.m., though it was one in the morning London time—she got up, dug out the sketchbook, and put the date and time on each drawing.

2

Annie woke at the Two Princes a few minutes before six to bright sun coming in the window and a sense of rising excitement.

For six weeks she had thought of little besides this stay in London, visualized the shining future that would be so much better than the immediate past. She had tasted it, nurtured it, striven for it. But now here, on the brink, her stomach was in knots, and turmoil lurked in the corners of her mind.

There was a shower of sorts, not much pressure but plenty of hot water. She was quick about it. Her hair—red, very curly, chin length—could survive another twenty-four hours without being washed. She'd done almost no unpacking, but she found an emerald-green knit shirt that shook out unwrinkled. Enough, she decided, to take the curse off the black pantsuit she'd been wearing for the past three days.

Downstairs she could smell coffee, though the dining room wasn't open—not until seven, according to the sign. Half an hour was too long to wait. Annie went outside.

There were few pedestrians at this hour, but even without them, Southampton Row was a purposeful sort of place. The traffic, mostly a mix of lumbering red buses and square black taxis, moved steadily in either direction. Annie stood across the road from Bristol House and studied the building, its little piece of the world. Every once in a while a gap gave her a clear view of its unassuming entrance. It was sandwiched between what the British called an off-license, a liquor store, and a shop where a man was arranging newspapers on an outside rack. A large commercial hotel stood a little farther up the road.

After a few minutes she saw a car stop in front of Bristol House. A mini-cab Annie surmised when she saw Mrs. Walton come out of the building dragging a couple of suitcases. The driver stowed the cases in the trunk. Mrs. Walton got in. The car eased into the traffic and sped away.

The flat was all hers now.

Mrs. Walton's scent lingered in the rooms. Freesia by Fragonard, according to a box of dusting powder in the bathroom, left open in the last-minute rush of making an early flight. Annie closed it and carried it to her landlady's bedroom. She left it on the old-fashioned dressing table—everything looked much as it had the day before, except the ironing board and the suitcases were gone—and closed the door behind her.

Silence. And the long corridor stretched ahead.

Annie took a few steps, then a few more. Past the yellow tulips and the table with the lamp, unlit at this hour, when bright daylight came in the single window. She reached the place where the hall made the left-hand turn, paused long enough to take a deep breath, then went around the corner.

The door to the back bedroom was open. There was nothing to see. Annie walked forward. When she reached the threshold, she stopped and whispered aloud, "*Gloria Patri, et Filio, et Spiritui Sancto.*" The response, *Sicut erat in principio, et nunc, et semper, et in saecula saeculorum,* came only in her imagination.

Shaking, she pulled the door shut and fled.

Annie was a runner. She exulted in the pounding of her feet on pavement, in sweat that slicked her skin. She loved the way every inch of her felt alive when she was able to lengthen her stride and cover a decent distance. She would have liked to clear her head with a run when she left Bristol House, but she wasn't dressed for it. Instead she retreated to a café called the Brew Hut, a few doors down the road.

No monk today, where there had been one the day before, might well mean she had imagined the whole business. No, call it by its name. It might mean she'd been hallucinating. *You're a drunk, Annie my girl. You're strong and beautiful, and you've run yourself clean, but you'll always be a drunk.* The voice in her head was not her own but that of Sidney O'Toole, her AA buddy, the guy who had taken her under his wing at the second meeting she'd attended, and one way or another had stayed by her side ever since.

But Annie had not hallucinated when she stopped drinking. Not everyone does. So why now, after four years of strict sobriety?

Perhaps she had a brain tumor. Or worse, perhaps she was losing her mind.

After she had walked through hell and somehow, stripped naked though she was, come out the other side. Now. Madness.

A clock on the wall said it was ten to nine. Work, she had long since learned, is the great, sometimes the only, salvation. Time to begin. First stop: the Tudor London Documents Collection, which, as luck would have it, was at this moment at the British Museum.

London institutions did not post staff résumés or pictures on their Web sites. Since her appearance had been left to Annie's imagination, she had decided the archivist she'd corresponded with before coming to England was old and slightly stooped and wore her gray hair in a bun. But Mrs. Franklin, who ten minutes after they met insisted on being called Jennifer, was tall, blond, and gorgeous. From the vantage point of five-two, with the freckles that went with her red hair, and around the same age—Annie would be thirty-three in a few months—it would have been easy to feel inadequate in Jennifer's shadow. Except the archivist was also friendly and helpful. She stayed with Annie for something close to three hours, patiently pulling ancient papers out of floor-to-ceiling chests of wide, shallow drawers and discussing such mysteries of sixteenth-century Holborn as whether Crooked Bone Alley might have run between Red Lion and Great Ormond streets.

Annie began to feel guilty. "You're being enormously helpful, but I think I shouldn't be keeping you so long."

"Not to worry," Jennifer said, "I'm delighted. I don't get many chances to talk about exciting stuff like this these days. Everyone here turns up their noses at anything that didn't happen before Caesar conquered Gaul."

Jennifer was actually on the staff of the London Archives, but parts of the documents and maps section of that institution was currently closed for remodeling. It was sheer good fortune that the specific collection that interested Annie, along with its archivist, was being housed temporarily in a basement room of the British Museum, a four-minute walk from Bristol House.

"Given the name," Jennifer said, "I take it this Shalom Foundation is Jewish. Israelis?"

"No. American Jews interested in the European Diaspora. Particularly the Ashkenazim of northern Europe in the fifteen hundreds. Someone known as the Jew of Holborn."

The archivist raised a well-shaped eyebrow. "I'm sorry, that's highly unlikely. If you'd asked, I would have told you that no one would be publicly identified as a Jew in Tudor times."

Annie was startled by the other woman's assumption she didn't know that English Jews were massacred in the twelfth century and officially expelled in the thirteenth. "Unlikely, not impossible," she said. "A few Jewish merchants found their way back into London over the years."

"I suppose," Jennifer agreed. "But using that name, announcing himself as it were—I think you've got your work cut out for you. I've never seen an official reference to any Jews in Holborn in Tudor times."

"Nor have I," Annie admitted. Then, carefully considering her words: "But there is some material that's recently come to light."

It was impossible to miss the way Jennifer's eyes narrowed. "Truly? New material from the Tudor period? How fascinating. I've seen nothing in any of the journals."

"Nothing's been published yet," Annie said.

The archivist turned away, busying herself with putting some of the books they'd been consulting back on the shelves. "I take it you're planning to fill that void." Her voice betrayed nothing of the calculation that had momentarily shown in her face. When she turned back, she was smiling. What Annie took to be unguarded professional jealousy no longer showed. "How about lunch? There's a quite good restaurant here in the museum. Too good, perhaps. We may not be able to get a table. But there's a café as backup. Unless you'd prefer the more casual option to begin with."

Annie glanced at her watch. Two o'clock. Already past checkout time at the Two Princes. If she hurried, maybe she could get them to bend the rule. She put her hand in her pocket and fingered the key to number eight Bristol House.

What the hell. An extra night at a hotel without a ghost wasn't such a bad thing. Lunch. "Let's try the restaurant first," Annie said.

It was late enough that there were a number of empty tables, and the remaining diners were mostly settling up and getting ready to leave. Jennifer and her guest were shown to a choice spot by the glass wall overlooking what for a couple of centuries had been the famous round reading room and was now once more a central courtyard beneath a soaring glass dome. "I get a ten percent staff discount," Jennifer said. "Shall we treat ourselves to a bottle of something decent?"

"Sorry, I don't drink," Annie said. "You go ahead, however."

"I'll do just a glass, then." And after the waiter had come and gone: "You mentioned you're here on your own. Maybe you'd like to come out with my husband and me sometime. See a bit of—oh, hello! What are you doing here?"

A man had come up behind Jennifer and leaned forward to kiss her cheek. "I should say I was hoping to catch a glimpse of you. Truth is, I'm showing some visitors the glories of London."

Annie knew her jaw had dropped and that she was staring. If Jennifer noticed, she didn't let on. "Annie, this is the famous Geoffrey Harris, who chews up politicians and spits them out on prime-time TV. Geoff, this is Dr. Annie Kendall. She's an architectural historian from New York. Over here for a bit doing research for the Shalom Foundation. Definitely much too clever for you."

Annie mumbled something, all the while continuing to stare.

Geoffrey Harris was quite good-looking: dark hair, high cheekbones, and a strong chin with a pronounced cleft. He didn't have a tonsure, not even a bald spot; otherwise he looked exactly like the monk she'd seen in the back bedroom of number eight Bristol House.

3

Wednesday morning Annie wrestled her luggage into the flat, closed the door behind her, and stood for a moment in the long hall.

Listening to silence.

Her suitcases were on wheels, but stuffed so full, they were difficult to maneuver. She jockeyed both of them and her tote bag and handbag into what was to be her bedroom. This time, at least at first sight, the unusual art wasn't quite so overwhelming. Maybe because it was ten a.m. and the light was slanted toward the wall with the bed and its charming crewelwork coverlet, not the imposing black and white mural.

The spread was much too nice to use as a platform for unpacking. Annie folded it and put it in the chest's bottom drawer, then hoisted the first of her suitcases onto the bed. Half an hour later all her things were hung up or folded away, and she reached for the tote bag.

It was large and roomy and blazoned with the name Davis School, the last place she'd worked before coming to London. Her laptop was in it, along with a number of other things, including the sketchbook with the drawings of what she'd seen in those few extraordinary moments on Monday afternoon. Annie pulled out the sketchbook, found the drawing that showed the monk's head and face from a number of angles, and propped it against the pillows. Next she retrieved her laptop.

She'd Googled Geoffrey Harris the previous afternoon, as soon as she'd left Jennifer Franklin and gone back to the Two Princes. There were dozens of hits. He was, as Jennifer said, quite well-known. His program seemed to be a kind of exposé, like *Dateline* or *60 Minutes* back home, but focused on elected officials and their activities. She'd found a number of magazine and newspaper articles written by or about him, and transcripts of at least three dozen interviews he'd conducted with every notable politician and statesman of the last half-dozen years, mostly skewering them for something they had or hadn't done. The only personal information she uncovered was a story from four years earlier saying Harris's wife had been killed in a car accident.

Annie had captured a head shot from his Web site. She sat on the bed with the laptop on her knees and pulled it up. He looked slick, supremely assured, and not just good-looking but magnetic. Dark hair, light-colored eyes—maybe gray, maybe blue—and a cleft in the chin. She looked again at the sketchbook. No doubt whatever. The man she'd met at the British Museum didn't just look like the monk she'd drawn before she'd ever seen him. The man was a dead ringer for the ghost.

She had spent a fruitless hour imagining Harris had impersonated the monk, thinking she'd been thrust into the middle of some elaborate scam that involved both him and Mrs. Walton—otherwise how had he gotten into the apartment? If so, she had to be the mark, as it were, the person being scammed. Why? She had neither money nor influence, nothing anyone could possibly want. Like most conspiracy theories, it was absurd.

Maybe Geoffrey Harris had an identical twin. But why then no mention of such an interesting tidbit online? And even if he did, it simply shifted the parameters of the conspiracy, without making it any less farcical. The same objection negated the possibility of a true double who wasn't a relation. Besides, Annie didn't think the degree of resemblance that passed for an unrelated look-alike could fool her artist's eye, much less her hand. She knew exactly what she'd seen, both at Bristol House and in the British Museum.

She was left with only one logical conclusion. Geoffrey Harris looked as he did because the monk was his ancestor. Meaning, however extraordinary, that the monk had once been real and that Annie Kendall had seen a ghost. Never mind that she didn't believe in them.

That wasn't all she had to process. Meeting Harris fewer than twenty-four hours after she saw the ghost was unlikely to be a coincidence. The monk was sending her a message, declaring his intentions. Very well, she would make hers equally clear.

Annie set the laptop on the bed, grabbed the sketchbook and her tote, and headed for the back bedroom. The door was still shut, exactly as she'd left it yesterday morning when she fled in a panic. There would be no more of that. She squared her shoulders, reached for the knob, turned it, pushed the door open, and went inside. The little bedroom felt musty, unused. The ghost was not there. Neither was the crucifix, nor the prie-dieu, nor the rest of the monkish paraphernalia. Instead she was once more looking at the items detailed in the inventory: a bed, a six-drawer chest, a desk, two lamps, and assorted books and decorative objects.

Her tote bag felt heavy in her hands, weighed down with her impulse buys of the previous day. She had a plan, but it seemed as insane as the ghost idea itself, belied by the total ordinariness of her surroundings.

Annie reached out a hand and touched the wall. It was unquestionably real. She knocked and was rewarded with the thud of solid plaster. There was no hollow ring, no suggestion of a sliding something-or-other that could be used to produce a Houdini-like illusion. What remained, the only conclusion that fit the data, was the same conviction she'd reached yesterday. The ghost existed. She had truly seen what she saw and what she drew.

That was remarkable, maybe earth-shaking, but she had neither the background nor the wherewithal to tackle the investigation of something so extraordinary. She had three months to do what the Shalom Foundation was paying her to do, and she had gambled everything on her ability to do it. A haunting, however real, was a distraction she could not afford. And there was another argument against investigating: she didn't have credibility. Even if she came up with some kind of proof of her ghostly sighting—and it was hard to imagine what that proof might be—she'd still be dismissed as a crackpot, one more promising academic who'd destroyed her brain with alcohol.

Annie put the sketchbook and her tote on the bed and crossed to the window. It opened more easily than she expected, flying up almost as soon as she touched it. She leaned out. There was no vista. She was peering into a jumble of bricks and mortar, mostly the rear of other buildings.

What about the fact that the ghost had a living, breathing double? And that double was somebody really well-known who was walking around modern London? Nothing about it. There was no way she could conclusively prove she'd made the drawings before she met Geoffrey Harris.

Annie closed the window and returned to the bed. She opened the sketchbook to the first of her drawings, the one of the monk as she'd initially seen him, praying before the crucifix. She laid the picture on the bed. "Object of the exercise," she said aloud, then paused for a long moment, listening for a response that did not come. After a few seconds, she took from her tote the three items she'd bought the day before and placed them in a careful row on the desk.

A small brass handbell.

A Bible.

A tall white candle.

She'd remembered seeing a candlestick among the decorative items in the room. In fact there were two. She chose the one made of carved wood. It stood about a foot high, and while it might not be old, it looked as if it were. When she inserted the candle, the assembly seemed both classic and imposing.

Bell, book, and candle.

She was, after all, John Kendall's daughter. Small wonder she knew the tools of excommunication, and that no threat would be more horrifying to the ghost of a Catholic monk.

Annie put a small box of matches beside the candle, then added a copy of the official dictum of spiritual banishment and consignment to hell. She'd found the text, along with directions for conducting the ceremony, in a book called *The Roman Ritual,* the authoritative source on all Catholic rites, however arcane. Back when she was a student, she'd have had to visit a specialist library to consult the *Ritual.* These days it was available online.

"Now," she said into the quiet, "you can't say I haven't given you fair warning."

* * *

When she first saw the flat, Annie had thought she'd use the back bedroom as an office. Under the circumstances, that no longer seemed practical. Instead she set up the tools of her trade in the dining room: her
laptop, of course, along with a few notebooks, pens and pencils, a stack
of sketchbooks, and—relics of a bygone age, in these days of smart-
phones with cameras—another of picture postcards. She chose one of
the postcards and sat down to write. The sunshine of late morning was
streaming through the window by then, illuminating the bracelet that
was always on her wrist, even when she slept, even in the shower. As a
piece of jewelry it was unimpressive and very simple, a thin gold chain
that held in place a free-form script of three letters: *ARI.* As for what it
represented—call it wearing her heart on her sleeve, or at least on her
wrist.

Ari was short for Aaron. It had been her twin brother's name. Also
her son's. She couldn't send her twin postcards—he'd died of AIDS
when they were seventeen. Her thirteen-year-old son, her twin's name-
sake, was alive and in Chicago, though she hadn't seen him since he was
three.

The postcard she chose was a shot of Big Ben as seen from a Whitehall street. There was a red double-decker bus in the foreground, and
next to it, really tiny, a guy on a motorbike. *If you look close, the bike could
be an old Triumph, a T120,* she wrote, knowing—given who his father
was—that Ari would find the historic bike more impressive than the
famous clock. *Maybe 1960. What do you think? Love you, Mom.* Beneath
it she added the postal address and the notation *Staying here for three
months.*

She'd started trying to reach Ari four years before, when he was nine,
as soon as she'd emerged from the alcoholic fog and faced the wreckage
she'd made of her life. Finding him hadn't been difficult. She'd been
separated from his father when Ari was born, but it hadn't occurred to
her not to put Zak's name on Ari's birth certificate. Aaron Johnson, son
of Zachary Johnson. So once she sobered up, it hadn't been hard to find

the pair of them. They were living in Chicago, where Zak had a radio show about biking, and wrote on the subject for a number of specialist magazines. Of course, the birth certificate had also made it easier for Zak to take Ari away.

Not that she didn't deserve to lose him.

She hadn't tried to explain any of that to Ari. There was no way to make a child understand such things, much less forgive them. Instead she'd tried to find some common ground with the boy she believed he was growing up to be. His father's boy, bound to be more interested in motorcycles than in history. Letters at first; then, when they were consistently returned unopened, postcards. She'd never had a word in reply, but she refused to give up hope.

She took a stamp from the supply she'd bought as soon as she stepped off the plane at Heathrow and went out and dropped the postcard in the mailbox on the corner.

It was noon by the time she got back and sat down at the laptop and opened the digital copy of the documents Shalom had sent with her to London. Her brief was written at the top, succinct and almost word for word as Philip Weinraub, head of the Shalom Foundation, had stated it during one of their early meetings.

> We believe, Dr. Kendall, that in the year 1535 or thereabouts a man known as the Jew of Holborn uncovered a remarkable trove of ancient Judaica, possibly from the time of the Second Temple in Jerusalem. We would like you to corroborate that fact and possibly even locate the source of the treasure. We realize nothing is likely to be left, but simply proving that such things found their way to England will be a remarkable coup.

Annie did not disagree. Indeed, it would be a coup capable of putting an academic career—even one as moribund as hers—in the fast lane. Which was why finding the Jew of Holborn trumped investigating a ghost, and why she had to resist the urge to keep running to the back bedroom to check the status of the things she'd left behind. In the matter of historical research, three months was not very long. It was time to get to work.

The previous month, when it looked as if she were going to get this job, she'd set herself a crash course, studying the artifacts of Jewish practice, what Weinraub had called Judaica. The first thing she'd learned was that according to the book of Genesis, Jewish identity was formed at the time of the covenant between God and Abraham, to be solemnly marked by the circumcision of all males. The worship Jews were to offer God was also described in biblical texts, and eventually those rites were carried out in the ancient Temple of Jerusalem.

The theological significance of Temple practice was beyond Annie's brief or her expertise, but the historical and archaeological facts of the acutal structure were relatively simple.

According to the book of Kings, Solomon built the First Temple in the tenth century B.C. There was no documentation of this structure outside biblical sources, but scripture said it stood for four hundred years, until it was destroyed by the Babylonian army, who then took the surviving Israelites into captivity. In 538 B.C. the Jews were released and returned to Jerusalem and began building in the ancient city a second Temple on the site of the first, a man-made hill called the Temple Mount. Eventually the turbulent history of the Holy Land contrived to produce a single site that contained both the remains of this ancient place of Jewish worship—the famous Western wailing wall—and two of the most sacred of Muslim shrines.

The Second Temple, however, predated the pair of mosques by almost five hundred years, and was well documented in sources other than the Bible. It had existed until seventy years after the crucifixion of Christ, when Roman soldiers razed the Temple, forbade its rebuilding, and said no Jew might live in Jerusalem or practice circumcision. Then the conquerors took their Jewish prisoners and the most precious objects of Temple worship to Rome and paraded them in triumph. The period of the modern diaspora had begun.

As far as the Temple went, Annie needed no more background than that for her current assignment. Her focus was on a list of transliterated Hebrew words, none of which she would have recognized a month earlier, though she knew them now.

She ran her cursor down the screen. There were five items: *makhtah, bazekh, kaf, ma'akhelet, mizrak*. A *makhtah* was a pan used to carry burning coals, and a *bazekh* was a smaller pan. The *kaf* was meant to hold incense during a ritual slaughter. The *ma'akhelet* was the knife the priest used to slit the animal's throat—a sheep or a goat usually, sometimes a calf. The *mizrak* was the basin meant to catch the blood of the offering so it could be sprinkled on the altar.

No such sacrifice had taken place in almost two thousand years.

She'd read about fringe groups of modern Jews who were desperate to rebuild the Temple and resume the ritual sacrifice of sheep and goats and birds. They were following the instructions in Genesis and Deuteronomy and re-creating things like those on Annie's list, using copper alloys made according to ancient formulae. Annie had no knowledge of whether the artifacts on her list were authentic, only that each was described as being fashioned in bronze (an imprecise term for various combinations of tin and copper), and that though each belonged to a different congregation, all claimed the same provenance. Everyone reported that their treasure had come to them in 1535, as a gift from the Jew of Holborn.

Philip Weinraub himself had put the list in Annie's hands, and he had no doubts as to the origin of the artifacts. "Just think, Dr. Kendall, of what you are holding." Weinraub was not a physically imposing man, but when he'd said that, his eyes had seemed to bore into her skull. "*Kaf, ma'akhelet, mizrak* . . . for such things to have existed in 1535, they had to have come from the ancient Temple in Jerusalem."

However charismatic Weinraub could be, on this point Annie resisted. The task was already Herculean; she couldn't allow him to make it impossible. "That leaves a fifteen-hundred-year gap in the traceable history, Mr. Weinraub. I don't think I can expect to find documentation of a provenance that old, not if I had three years rather than three months."

"No, of course not." Weinraub had waved away her concern. "I'm sending you to London to look for the man. Find the Jew of Holborn, Dr. Kendall. Tell us who he was, what he did. Do that, and you'll discover the source of his treasures. I am convinced of it."

Maybe. But even if she did not get exactly what Weinraub wanted, an investigation based on the Shalom documents should yield enough to write a knock-your-socks-off article for a prestigious professional journal. In the academic world she so desperately longed to reenter, that was the way in. Finding the man was, however, a—

The sound wasn't particularly loud, only a dull thud she might have missed, except that for every moment since she'd left the back bedroom, part of her had been waiting for just such a signal.

Annie jumped up and reached the bend in the corridor in three long strides. She peered down the short length of hallway leading to the back bedroom. The door was still shut. She sprang forward and yanked it open. The sun had disappeared, and she felt a rush of damp, cold air. The window was up, and the curtain waved in the breeze. She was quite certain she'd closed the window, but she couldn't swear she'd locked it. It slid up very easily, she'd already noted that.

The candlestick lay on the floor by the door, obviously blown off the desk. That must have been the thud she'd heard. The candle had come loose as a result. Annie found it, stuck it back in the holder, and restored the assembly to its previous position. Then she closed the window, and this time she made absolutely sure it was locked.

4

Running, Annie had learned, could supply her with a measure of control when little else did. Nothing would better buttress her resolve to ignore the phenomenon in the back bedroom at Bristol House.

She used Google Maps to work out a basic route that took her northwest along Southampton Row to Russell Square. The distance there and back was less than half a mile, but she could extend the workout to her preferred two miles by adding a zigzag course along the paths that wandered among the square's extensive gardens. She tested the route a little past dawn the morning after she moved into Bristol House, and it was glorious. The air was fresh and sweet, and once she was in the gardens, she had birdsong as a counterpoint to the muted traffic. Her sense of infinite possibility grew with each step.

Afterward she showered, did her laundry, and got the apartment organized for her stay. On the grounds that the best defense is a good offense, she located the flat's many radios—blessings on Mrs. Walton, there were four of them—and tuned each one to BBC Radio 4, news and world affairs around the clock. With a bit of programming of the universal remote she'd found in her bedroom, she was able to turn three on simultaneously.

She placed the remote on the hall table nearest the front door. It was of course silly to think she could fend off a ghost with a radio, but it was disquieting to wonder, every time she walked into the flat, if she was alone. Sane English voices saying sensible things as soon as she crossed the threshold couldn't hurt and might help.

It would take more than disquiet, however, to entirely smother her essential curiosity. After she came back from that first run, Annie walked to where she could see the closed door of the little bedroom, then strode the rest of the distance and opened it. She saw nothing and no one, and the bell, the book, and the candle were exactly as she'd left them. She left the door open this time and headed back to the drawing room—she loved calling it that—gathering up dusty and drooping flowers on her way.

It was still early when she went to the nearby supermarket and stocked up on staples. At the last minute, she added two bunches of fresh tulips to her cart, bright red this time. At home she'd shared a Brooklyn apartment with two people she barely knew and seldom saw. They lived together so they could afford the astronomical rent of any place within commuting distance of Manhattan. The refrigerator was divided into shelves marked with each of their names, and the only other common space was a living room as impersonal as a dentist's office. She'd loathed those bleak living arrangements almost as much as teaching at the Davis School. She gave up the apartment along with the job.

There were enough red tulips for a third vase, and she found one in a cupboard in the kitchen and carried it into the dining room. She was still arranging the flowers when her cell phone rang. It was Jennifer Franklin. "I've thought of something I think you should see. Could you come by?"

Annie said she could.

The archivist was prepared for Annie's visit. She had two pairs of white cotton gloves at the ready. Annie felt a surge of excitement as soon as she saw them—they meant she and Jennifer would be handling something particularly old and rare.

Jennifer unlocked a cupboard at the rear of her basement office and produced what looked like an ordinary cardboard tube, though Annie knew it was not. Like the gloves, the tube was made from specially treated nonacid fibers, one of the tools of the museum trade. What the archivist extracted from this highly specialized storage container was a document some eighteen inches square, a hand-drawn parchment map labeled in the lower right, in the distinctive Tudor script that both women could read without difficulty: "Richard Scranton, By His Own Hand An. Dom. 1535."

Jennifer spread the map on a large gray cushion, also made of specially treated nonacid, nonlinting fibers, and each woman used a gloved finger to hold down two of the corners. Jennifer let go of one long enough to move the magnification lamp a bit nearer, careful not to allow any part of the brass lamp to come remotely close to touching the cushion, much less the document it supported. "I thought of this map after you left the other day," she said while adjusting the lamp. "I've also been wondering if there would be anything about your Jew of Holborn in the papers associated with the master of the rolls."

One of the oldest offices in English law, the second-most important judge after the lord chief justice. Annie considered for a moment. "By 1535," she said, "Cromwell had become Henry's master of the rolls." No prize for coming up with his name. Thomas Cromwell loomed large in Tudor London.

"The thing is, all the Cromwell papers are in a separate archive that's been sequestered during the remodeling. I suppose I could—"

Annie shook her head. "Don't worry about it. I'm told the Cromwell papers have already been examined. Nothing related to the Jew of Holborn showed up."

"I thought that might be the case. And I don't believe there's anything specific here either"—she nodded toward the map—"but it's a unique piece, and it seems you should see it. It was drawn to identify the king's opposition."

Annie was studying the square of parchment on the gray cushion. "I take it these marks"—she indicated a series of triangles superimposed with a cross—"are where this fellow Scranton claims there were people resisting Henry's claim to the right of primacy?"

"Exactly. The map has twenty-two such symbols, and every one corresponds to the location of someone eventually executed for treason. Because he or she refused to swear it was lawful for Henry, not the pope, to be head of the English Church. Richard Scranton was the double-oh-seven of his day. Licensed to kill."

"He was also a damned fine draftsman," Annie said. "Look at the

Fleet." In Scranton's drawing, the river Fleet was wide and obviously navigable. Later, after the swill of countless generations of Londoners filled it with so much sludge it was reduced to a polluted trickle, it had been built over. These days it traveled from Hampstead Heath to the Thames through a series of underground storm and sewer drains. Now as then, it passed through the section once called Olde Bourne. "The way he's drawn the river makes you want to stand on the banks and whistle up a boatman. Has anyone superimposed today's Holborn on this map?"

"Not officially. But we're just about here." Jennifer's hovering finger indicated the left lower corner of the document.

Annie bent closer. "Right between a pig and an ox."

Richard Scranton, cartographer of death, had scattered little pictures of domestic animals here and there on his map, indicating that the Holborn of his day was mostly farmland, with a few clustered houses hugging the riverbank. A few more were close to the Holborn Bar, the western tollgate in the wall around the square-mile City of London. So this Jew of Holborn might be a needle in a haystack, but the haystack wasn't all that big.

She kept searching Scranton's map for something that might point to the man she was looking for, but Annie suspected the document, however fascinating, would be of no use to her. Why should a Jew care if the pope or the king was to be the highest Christian authority in England? But given that it was the consuming issue of the day, anyone could get sucked in. She spotted one of Scranton's crossed triangles by itself on the upper-right-hand corner of his map, amid what he had clearly indicated as open land dotted with small areas of woods.

Annie felt it first as a tingling, a buzz somewhere in the back of her mind, something important she knew but was forgetting. She pointed to the mark. "Any idea who or what this is?"

"The monastery known as the Charterhouse," Jennifer said immediately. "First blood, if you will. Henry sent a few of the monks to Tyburn, starting in May 1535. Theirs was the first execution of the primacy debate, though God knows not the last."

Tyburn meant death by hanging, drawing, and quartering. Not the most awful of Tudor execution methods, but right up there in the roster of—

Annie drew a breath and held it. Of course. The London Charterhouse. Home to Carthusian monks, who as it happened wore white habits and had tonsures—and were up to their ears in the bloody drama of Henry VIII and Anne Boleyn. Henry had set off on what became wholesale butchery with those monks living a ten-minute walk from Bristol House. So perhaps, given that she'd already been forced into admitting that ghosts existed, it was one of the Carthusians she'd seen. Annie exhaled.

"I won't be here next week," the archivist was saying as she rerolled the Scranton map. "We're off to the Canaries for a short break. I get six weeks holiday a year, but I'm not allowed to take it all at once, and this was arranged before I knew you were coming."

"Nothing to worry about," Annie said. "I understand perfectly." Really she did not. It seemed odd for Jennifer not to have mentioned a long-planned vacation in the e-mails they exchanged before Annie arrived in London. She could not, of course, say so.

Jennifer put a pass with an orange border on the table. The one she'd given Annie previously was edged in green. "This new one will get you in on your own. You'll be able to access most of this material, but the goodies in that cupboard"—she pointed to the place where she'd locked away Richard Scranton's map—"won't be available until I come back. I'm not permitted to leave the keys with anyone who's not a member of the London Archives staff. Since the collection is only visiting here, there isn't anyone I can delegate."

Annie said not to worry and added her thanks, then gathered up the pass with the orange edge. The one clipped to the other woman's blouse was rimmed in purple. Color-coded bureaucracy.

Jennifer was making neat piles of the papers on her desk. "Did you want to see anything else today?"

"No thanks. I've decided to take an afternoon off. Maybe do some sightseeing."

"Sounds like fun. Where are you headed?"

"The National Portrait Gallery." Annie was almost out the door, her head filled with portraits of monks, quite possibly one who looked like her ghost among them. "Have a great vacation. See you when you get back."

It occurred to Annie, while she made her way to Trafalgar Square, that her initial hope was probably misplaced. Unless a monk came from a wealthy family and his picture was painted before he entered a monastery, the Portrait Gallery would have no record of him. The collection did not chronicle the important events of the day, only the important people—and only those wealthy enough to have sat for a formal painting. Still, she had to start somewhere.

As it turned out, the Gallery had an entire section devoted to the Tudors, including three rooms given over to Henry VIII and his times. Fully eighty-seven portraits of the king, seventeen of Anne Boleyn, and twenty-four of Thomas Cromwell were on display, among a great many others. But of the monks of the London Charterhouse, there was not so much as a sketch.

She'd taken the tube to get to the Gallery, but when she came up empty, she decided it would be more fun to go home by bus. A man feeding pigeons at the foot of Nelson's Column told her she wanted the number ninety-one. "Just over there, love. Goes straight up Southampton Row to Euston Station."

She was on the top deck, lost in the scenery, when her cell phone rang.

"Hi, glad I got you. It's Geoff Harris. I hope you remember me. Jenny Franklin introduced us the other day at the museum. I threatened mayhem, and she gave me your number."

He wanted to ask her something, he said. Might be important, though he wasn't sure. Would she meet him for a drink? "I don't drink," she countered. "Coffee?"

"Of course." Then, after she said where she was—on a bus heading north on Kingsway—"Get off at the Holborn tube station and turn left.

You'll see a short little street called Sicilian Avenue. Chloe's. You can't miss it."

She did not. And Chloe's wasn't simply easy to find, it was delightful, a candy box. The walls were covered in flocked red velvet, and there were gilt sconces, fresh flowers on the half-dozen tiny marble tables, and a showcase full of delicious-looking chocolates and sinfully rich pastries. She ordered a *citron pressé*—fresh lemon juice in sparkling water—with very little sugar and sat where she could see the door. Five minutes maybe. Then he arrived.

When she met him at the museum, Geoff Harris had had on a suit and tie. Today he was dressed casually in cords and an open-necked shirt with a sweater tied over his shoulders. Nonetheless, he looked exactly as he did when she first saw him: tall, dark, incredibly good-looking, and unquestionably related to the monk she'd seen at Bristol House.

"I really appreciate your meeting me on such short notice," he said. "Good of you."

"You made it sound mysterious. I'm a pushover for mysteries. Particularly when they're important."

"Maybe only important to me." He looked slightly embarrassed. "I hope I haven't lured you here on false pretenses."

The waitress appeared. Annie's glass was still half full. Geoff ordered an espresso. It came in moments, dense and black and frothy with foam. He added some sugar and took a sip. "Annie, forgive me if this seems incredibly pushy, but the head of the organization you work for, this Shalom Foundation. What—"

"I don't actually work for them. Not on any regular basis. I'm here on a research assignment."

"Yes, so Jenny said. Doesn't matter. It's the head of the outfit who interests me."

"Philip J. Weinraub."

"That's him. What do you know about him?"

Annie shook her head. "Not much. He's . . . I guess the word is *insistent*."

"Overbearing," Geoff supplied.

"That too."

"I presume you know Weinraub's a billionaire. And that he's deeply involved in Middle Eastern affairs, Israeli affairs to be precise. Any bearing on your research?"

"Not exactly."

He smiled. "The cautious academic. I promise I'm not trying to beat you to some kind of punch."

"I didn't think you were. But I'm an architectural historian. What I'm doing for Shalom concerns Tudor London. That's my period."

"And that, I take it, is the connection to Jenny Franklin. All the same, your foundation is supposed to be concerned with Jewish affairs."

"In this instance, European Jewry," Annie said. "Nothing to do with Israel, or Palestine as it was then."

"Hard to separate Jews from the so-called Holy Land," he said stubbornly, "in any period."

Annie had to work to keep herself from concentrating on the cleft in his chin. It was for some reason very attractive. "Are you going to tell me why this all matters to you?"

They had both finished their drinks. Geoff looked around. Every one of the little tables was occupied. He put a bill on the table. "Let's get out of here."

"Hope you don't mind," he said, once they were sitting on a bench in Bloomsbury Square. "This isn't a conversation I'd like to have overheard."

Annie said she didn't mind in the least. Then she waited.

"Yitzhak Rabin," Geoff said. "Remember him?"

"Of course. Prime minister of Israel during the Clinton presidency. Actively involved in the peace process."

"That's the one. Assassinated in 1995 by an Israeli who despised the idea of a Palestinian homeland on the West Bank."

She'd been a freshman at Wellesley College in 1995. Not yet what

Sidney O'Toole would call a fully fledged lush. She studied—grades were never her problem—and was reasonably aware of the world around her. But she'd also sneaked off campus to hang out with bikers. That was how she met Zak and learned to do vodka with a beer chaser. "What does Rabin have to do with Weinraub?"

"The kind of money Weinraub has, the nature of his interests—it's provocative."

"Provocative how? A great many American Jews, wealthy or not, share Weinraub's interests."

"I know. I'm being vague because I don't have proof. Usually when I set out to nail someone, I have my facts thoroughly documented."

"And nailing people," Annie said, "is what you do." She hadn't meant it to sound accusatory, but that was how it came out.

His reaction was matter-of-fact. "Nailing people is my job. At least my regular job. I'm on leave just now. Writing a book on the Middle East."

"Does Weinraub have a role in your book?"

"He might." Geoff hesitated, then apparently decided to trust her. "Rabin's death was seismic in his part of the world. It left a hole that's not been filled since. And right after he was killed, I came across a considerable number of unusual leads involving New York, Strasbourg, London, and Jerusalem, and possibly tying Philip Jeremiah Weinraub to the planning of the assassination."

"I take it you didn't say so at the time."

"I couldn't. I was working for the BBC back then. On the research staff. I had no show of my own and no clout. So given that I had no proof, the Weinraub story never went anywhere."

"Maybe there isn't any proof. Maybe you were wrong." His eyes, she decided, were neither gray nor blue. They were hazel. "In any event, I don't see how I can help you."

"Probably you can't. Still . . . will you tell me what kind of research you're involved in?"

Annie shrugged. "Ancient Judaica. Someone called the Jew of Holborn. All to do with the sixteenth century, so it can't have much bearing on your story."

She knew she sounded defensive. She also knew why. She had tied herself and her future so thoroughly to Shalom's goals that anything that threatened Weinraub threatened her.

Suddenly, without warning, a breeze came up. Annie had on jeans and a T-shirt. She shivered. Geoff untied the sweater from his shoulders and put it over hers. It was camel-colored, so soft it had to be cashmere. "You need to be a Londoner," he said, "to know never to trust hot and sunny. Even in May."

"I'll bear it in mind," Annie said.

"Look, I don't think you—" He was interrupted by a sudden burst of music. James Brown's "Soul Power," Annie thought, but she didn't hear enough to be sure. Geoff whisked an iPhone out of his pocket and glanced at it. "Sorry, I've got to take this." He got up, took a few steps away from the bench, spoke softly for a moment or two, then returned. "Sorry," he said again. "I have to run. I've been trying to get this interview for a month. People aren't as anxious to talk to you if they're not going to be on the telly as a result. Bloody Blair will only see me if I can be there in twenty minutes. I've got your number." Waving the phone, he backed away. "I'll call you."

5

On Monday, four days after her meeting with Geoff Harris, following an early-morning run through cold and rainy gloom, Annie felt the need for coffee before she showered. She went into the kitchen and made a cup, then carried it into the dining room she'd turned into an office. Without actually sitting down at the laptop, she idly clicked the list of ritual implements onto the screen, looking yet again for a pattern that might shed some light on—

"*Ut inimicos sanctae Ecclesiae humiliare digneris . . .*"

A single male voice was petitioning heaven. It betrayed the slight tremulousness of old age, but still it filled the apartment, echoed down the hall, and bounced off the dining room walls.

Annie stood frozen, the mug of coffee still in her hand.

"*Te rogamus, audi nos.*"

The monk had brought reinforcements. The response—*Te rogamus, audi nos*, "We beg Thee to hear us"—came from a chorus of male voices, vigorous and young.

"*Ut cuncto populo Christiano, pacem et unitatem largiri digneris.*"

"*Te rogamus, audi nos.*"

The ebb and flow, call-and-answer, was strong, insistent. She almost felt compelled to join in the responses.

She put down her mug and went into the hall. The chant surrounded her, seeming to come from everywhere. Not so. She knew its source. She walked toward the back bedroom.

"*Ut fructus terrae dare . . .*"

"*Te rogamus, audi nos.*"

Annie flung open the door.

The chant ended abruptly.

The room was empty of ghosts, whether one or many.

Everything was exactly as it had been, and the things she had put on the desk were where she'd left them. She heard nothing. Not an echo of the litany, not the traffic of busy Southampton Row, not a few notes of birdsong. Number eight Bristol House was deathly quiet.

She wondered if opening and closing the door was some sort of switch. She stood just inside the door and pulled it shut behind her, then opened it again. The chant did not resume.

Annie approached the desk. Her hands were shaking, but she managed to strike a match and light the candle. She picked up the brass bell with her left hand and rang it—tentatively at first, then with more vigor—and put her right hand on the Bible. She only had to bend her head to be able to see the words she'd copied out of *The Roman Ritual*. It occurred to her that she should have translated the excommunication into Latin. Too late now. "'I separate him,'" she read, beginning very softly, the words coming with difficulty through an almost-closed throat, "'together with his accomplices and abettors.'" Stronger now, with determination, and something like the conviction that had propelled her into her first AA meeting years before. *I will not continue to live like this. I will not be a victim.* "'I separate him from the precious body and blood of the Lord and—'"

She heard the noise before she sensed the movement; rather like a giant inhale, then an exhale. The sound took shape. It became a floor-to-ceiling cone spinning toward her, seeming to travel a great distance despite how small the room was. The candle flickered, then went out, and the brass bell was yanked from her hand. It chattered madly before it disappeared. Annie was caught in the whirling mist, her body constantly turning as it was drawn into the vortex. For an instant it seemed as if she were revolving in one direction and the room in another. Then everything was gone, and there was darkness.

Dom Justin
From the Waiting Place

It is easy on the other side to dismiss this bleak but blessed antechamber to eternity known as purgatory, but since all must die, all will come to understand this place between before and after. For my part, here is where I find myself in this time out of time where yesterday, today, and tomorrow have no meaning. Bliss, they tell me, is assured, but only when I have made atonement.

To that end I am required to tell my story as it happened whilst yet I was in that state men call living, though it is but a shadow of real life. The telling is not difficult, since here one remembers in perfect detail each choice made during the testing time. But for the rest . . . how to atone for such sins as mine, I know not.

I am told I will find a way. Also that the woman has been brought to me to serve both my ends and her own. I am given to understand we go on together. Also, that there is for her true peril in the journey. Not as to the disposition of her soul, for that is a matter in which no mortal can have influence save her own conscience. Rather it is the length of her time on earth that has been put in my care.

Her danger grows. I must begin the telling.

I was barely sixteen in the year 1531 when my master, Thomas Cromwell, commanded I become a monk of the Charterhouse. There, he said, I might be his eyes in a place he could not go. I shall tell more of that, but my true adventure, and the source of my most grievous sin, began four years later, on the occasion of the mighty wind which was a portent of terrible things to come, though none yet knew the extent to which all England would struggle and suffer.

The day of the great circular wind was a May Thursday, a day when the custom of our order demanded we chant together the litanies that beg Almighty God for all manner of good. Thus, well before dawn, we hermit monks had left our individual cells, as Carthusians call the little houses wherein each lives alone with God, and assembled in the courtyard outside the great church of the monastery. Our prior was not with us that day (an absence of which I will later have more to say), so it fell to old Dom Hilary to lead the prayers. His voice occasionally betrayed the shiver of age, but the rest of us sang out the responses with force and enthusiasm. Indeed, those were times so troubled as to make every man know how grave was our need for divine aid.

It was whilst Dom Hilary petitioned heaven on behalf of all of us that the strange and violent wind came out of the sky and rushed toward earth. So strong it was that a man might actually see it with his own eyes, a visible wind in the form of a funnel-shaped cloud.

This thing, which the moment it appeared was so extraordinary that every monk in the courtyard fell silent and signed himself with the cross of the Savior, touched down near where we stood. In that instant when the wind met the earth, I felt myself threatened with something that could hurl me into total darkness, where I should forget even the memory of light. I resisted with all my might, clinging to the thought of Jesus Christ crucified for my sins, and in the flash of an eye I had escaped the most terrible of judgments, and the thing lifted itself up again into the heavens and disappeared.

In the place where the tip of the funnel-shaped wind had struck, the cobbles were shattered into dust, which two of the brothers who live with us priest-monks immediately swept into a neat pile. Yet, wondrous to report, despite that evidence of the wind's immense power, no one of us was in any way harmed, and the monastery church was untouched.

It is only among the silent monks of the Charterhouse that such an event could remain a secret for all history, but I tell it here, and my testimony from this Waiting Place is true.

The great funnel wind was a sign from heaven of the trials to come. In the illusion of passing time with which men live before each faces judgment, it occurred in the year of Our Lord 1535, in the twenty-third year of the reign of Henry VIII, the second Tudor king of England, in the twenty-seventh year of his marriage to Queen Catherine of Aragon, and the fourth year of his illicit liaison—though Henry and most of his ministers insisted it was a true and heaven-blessed union—with Anne Boleyn.

Many then believed we had come to the end of what was called the King's Great Matter, his annulment and remarriage. We had, however, only begun the greatest matter of all: whether king or pope should be head of the Christian church in England. As for me, the monk known in the Charterhouse as Dom Justin, the day of the visible wind began a passage of many months during which love and lust would entwine to endanger my soul and the souls of others then unborn.

❖

Annie opened her eyes. She was lying on the floor, but she was unhurt. The room seemed undisturbed. The Bible was exactly where she'd put it originally. The candle, however, had been extinguished, and the brass bell was shattered into tiny bits. They formed a neat pile on the desk, as if someone had been tidying up after the tumult and swept them all together.

She used the side of the bed to pull herself upright. Her sketchbook was where she'd left it as well. Annie took it with her when she left the room, pulling the door shut behind her.

She put the sketchbook in the dining room and went across the hall into the bathroom and turned on the shower, stripping off her running clothes while she waited for the water to get hot, struggling to believe that what she'd experienced had really happened.

It wasn't until she was standing under the comforting spray, feeling the heat begin to revive her, that she noticed the scrapes. They occurred only on the left side of her body, a series of consecutive scratches that went from her rib cage to just above her knee, as if someone had drawn an oversize fork across her flesh, pressing just hard enough to break the skin but not tear it.

Annie spent the rest of the day at her laptop, so intent she forgot to eat. She was looking for information about the old London Charterhouse, because the symbol Richard Scranton had drawn on his sixteenth-century map, identifying the monks with opposition to Henry's plans, was the only link she had to what was occurring in number eight Bristol House.

The fact that she'd been shown Scranton's map while doing her job, trying to find out about the Jew of Holborn and his ancient treasures, was one more indication that there was nothing coincidental about this haunting. Somehow the two mysteries were related.

A little before six her phone rang. It lay beside her on the dining room table, and Annie picked it up without looking at it. "Annie Kendall here." She remained intent on the laptop screen and a nineteenth-century out-of-print history of the monks of the London Charterhouse she'd found among the millions scanned by Google.

"Geoffrey Harris. How are you?"

"I'm . . . I'm fine."

"That doesn't sound too sure."

"No, it is sure. I am fine." The scrapes on her left side had stopped stinging about an hour earlier. She had to touch them every once in a while to provoke a reaction and remind herself they truly existed. "I was working. You caught me by surprise."

"The sun's over the yardarm. Time to stop work. I know it's short notice, but will you have dinner with me? If you don't have other plans."

"No other plans," Annie admitted. "I don't know anyone in London."

He chuckled. "In that case, perhaps you won't mind settling for me."

She was glad he could not see her blush.

Most of the Monday-night crowd in the pub in Cosmo Place, a small and busy pedestrian passage between Southampton Row and Queen Street, were still drinking, not yet eating. Geoff, however, insisted they order immediately when Annie confided she'd had no lunch and was really hungry.

Their first course arrived. Duck spring rolls for him; mackerel pâté with mint salsa for her. The food looked good and smelled better. Their waiter, a sullen young man with bad skin and worse teeth, asked if they wanted fresh drinks. "Two more," Geoff said, nodding toward the small green bottles of Perrier. "Lime for me. Lemon for the lady." Too much wine with his agent at lunch, he'd said. He was teetotal for the night. And he'd remembered her saying she didn't drink.

"How was your meeting with Tony Blair?" Annie asked, starting on what turned out to be delicious pâté. "That is who you meant, isn't it?"

He looked puzzled. "Meant how?"

"When you left me the other day, you said bloody Blair would only see you if you got there in twenty minutes. Since you only talk to politicians, I presumed Tony Blair."

"On the evidence," he said, "politicians and curly ginger-heads with green eyes." He held out his fork, offering her a bite of spring roll.

Annie shook her head and felt the chin-length curls brush against her cheek. She'd been letting her hair grow lately. When she was drinking, she'd kept it as short as a man's, cutting it herself with a pair of old barber's shears, sometimes without even looking in a mirror. In all that time it was the only thing in her life about which she had been consistent. Last fall, when she passed the fourth anniversary of being sober and ran the New York Marathon—it took her five hours, twenty-seven minutes, but she'd finished—she realized that whatever statement she'd been making with her hair was no longer relevant. She threw the shears away.

"Tony Blair it was," Geoff said. "But not in his capacity as the unlamented former prime minister. My book's about modern Britain's relationship to the Middle East. Lawrence of Arabia to now. Blair's important because, having landed us with that god-awful cock-up called the Iraq War, the EU rewarded him by making him envoy to the place he'd left in a worse mess than he found it."

The boy with the bad skin reappeared with their main courses. Steak for Geoff, lamb chops for her. "To be fair," Geoff said when the boy was gone, "Blair put me in touch with a couple of Syrians I'm very glad to have met. They were only in London for two days, so it was fortuitous."

Was that meant as an apology? He had not called her in the last few days because he had been pursuing two Syrians who would not long be available. But why should three days of not calling a woman you've only just met require an apology? "I still have your sweater," she said. "The one you lent me—"

"—the other evening in Bloomsbury Square," he finished for her. "Not to worry."

"Are you always so gallant?"

He took a moment over the answer. "I think probably not. But despite the title and the expertise, you rather invite gallantry, Dr. Annie Kendall."

"I do? Why?"

He laughed. "I wish I knew. But frankly, I find the role of Sir Galahad novel. And enjoyable."

"Can I ask you something?"

"If you like."

She hadn't found anything about another marriage online, but that didn't mean it hadn't happened. And she wasn't entirely certain if this was a "date" or some sort of extension of their previous meeting. "Are you married?"

"Was," he said. "My wife died four years ago. What about you?"

"Also was."

He nodded toward her bracelet. "To someone called Ari?"

"No, Ari was my twin." She never talked about her son. It was too painful a wound and, even after ten years, still much too raw. "I'm divorced, by the way, not widowed." She said nothing more. The silence between them lasted a few seconds.

"Change of subject," he said, apparently picking up the go-no-further vibe. "Why do you keep staring at me the way you do? As if you thought we'd met before. We haven't, have we?"

She turned bright red. "No. At least I don't think so. But there's something . . . I don't think I should . . ." Yes, she did think she should. That's why she'd brought the drawings.

He seemed to have read her mind. "I'm betting you want to show me something. And that it's in that satchel you're lugging around."

Another blush. She couldn't control them, and she'd long since given up trying.

An upscale pub, he'd said, with better-than-average grub. She'd worn skinny jeans, dressed up with a truly gorgeous black chiffon blouse—and despite the fact that it didn't go with her outfit, she'd carried her unfashionable Davis School tote so she could bring the sketchbook. She'd pictured them in a booth that provided some privacy. Instead the pub had only tiny tables shoved almost up against one another. "You're right," she said. "I do want to show you something. But . . ." She nodded, indicating their surroundings.

As before, Geoff didn't bother asking for a check. He put a few bills on the table and stood up. "My place," he said. "It's not far."

He lived at 29 Orde Hall Street, about five minutes from Southampton Row, in what the English called a terrace, a string of houses sharing party walls on either side. Only one party wall in Geoff's case—his house was on the corner. "Fabulous High Victorian," Annie said, glancing up at the facade. "Built around 1855."

"Eighteen fifty-six," Geoff said as he fished for his key. "I'm impressed."

"Don't be. The shape of that pediment over the doorway is a dead giveaway."

"Hope you're not disappointed with the inside," he said. "The facade's the only thing original about the place. The interior had pretty much been gutted when I bought it, and I ripped out whatever remained of the old layout."

He did something with what appeared to be the keypad of an alarm system, then flicked a switch by the door. Subdued lights came on in various places, revealing what looked to be an acre of shiny oak flooring, and an open plan layout with a sleek kitchen at one end and other living spaces delineated by groups of furnishings. Everything was stainless steel, black leather, or polished wood. "Now I'm impressed," Annie said.

"No, you're not. You hate it."

"I do not."

"I'm betting you do. Nothing particularly English about it. No sagging springs or faded old velvets. Nothing to do with theme park Britain. It's perfectly all right. Horses for courses."

"I don't know what that means."

"It's a quaint British way of saying everyone's entitled to their own taste. Coffee? I can offer espresso or cafetière."

Geoff Harris's was apparently one of the few British households that didn't use instant, and cafetière she knew to be what she thought of as French press. "Cafetière, please. And I don't hate your house. Obviously you have exquisite taste." She followed him to the kitchen. Everything that wasn't granite was marble or copper or brass.

Geoff activated the switch on the electric kettle and another beside it. The house was filled with Mozart's Flute Concerto no. 1.

Annie smiled. "Sometimes I think that's my all-time favorite piece of classical music. Is it the Galway recording?"

"Yes, and I love it too. I'm glad our tastes aren't so entirely different. Now, let's see what's in that bag. The thing you wanted to show me."

"Not one thing," Annie said, as she took out her sketchbook and laid it on his granite kitchen counter. "A series of drawings."

She had deliberately left the sketch of the monk's face on top. She covered the date with her hand and waited.

Geoff leaned forward and took a long look. "Am I to understand you drew this?"

"Yes."

"I see. Well, except for the strange buzz cut, it looks like me."

"It's the spitting image of you," Annie said. "And the haircut is called tonsure. In the early Middle Ages, all Western clerics shaved the center of their heads. By the fifteen hundreds, only monks did it." Annie moved her hand and revealed the date at the bottom of the sketch. "I drew this a week ago Monday night. I'd never seen you before Jennifer introduced us that Tuesday."

"I hate sounding like a conceited jackass, but my face is pretty well-known."

"It is in England. But I arrived here a week ago Sunday. And I haven't been in London since I spent a few months studying here six years ago. I remember a man called Jeremy somebody who grilled politicians on television, but I had never heard of you."

"Jeremy Paxman," Geoff said. "*Newsnight* on the BBC. In fact, I was researching for his show when I stumbled on the Weinraub material. As I said, I didn't have my own program back then."

"So I couldn't have seen you when I was here. And I'm afraid no one knows who you are in America." She blushed. "I mean at least I don't. Didn't."

He didn't say any more.

She'd heard someone label TV talking heads "egos with legs." Based on what she'd read, Geoff Harris was a cut above, cast in an older, more serious mold, but with sharp twenty-first-century teeth. Still, there was no way to know that for sure. If she told him her whole story, by tomorrow she could be a feature in some notorious English tabloid: crop circles and a visiting American seeing British ghosts.

Her instincts said he would not treat her that way.

He was looking directly at her. "Annie," he said. "I'm waiting for the other shoe to drop." His voice contained no judgment, no intimidation. That ease of manner, implying endless patience, was no doubt a technique he'd developed for wheedling information out of politicians. It was effective with her as well.

Annie flipped the pages of the sketchbook and let him see the rest of the drawings. "As I said," she began, "it started that Monday. When I was checking out the apartment I'm renting while I'm in London . . ."

He listened without comment, occasionally turning the pages of the sketchbook, studying the different views of his doppelgänger.

"The thing is," she finished up, pointing to the monk in the drawing, "I think I know who the ghost is—or rather was."

"That's interesting. Who?"

"I mean I know in a general sort of way. I think he was one of the Carthusian monks from the London Charterhouse. In 1535 Henry VIII began executing anyone who didn't agree that the king should replace the pope as head of the English church. He started with the Charterhouse monks."

Geoff raised a single eyebrow. "And according to your theory, one of them is my ancestor?"

"That's right."

"Unlikely," he said.

"But it could be, couldn't it?"

"Pretty much anything 'could be.' But in this case . . . I grew up in a solid working-class neighborhood in Portsmouth, down on the south coast. My dad had a small grocer's shop that his granddad had started and his dad had run before him. As far as I know, no Harris was religious, much less Catholic. My mother is a German Jew whose family managed to get her to England in '39 as part of the Kindertransport. Some holy monk from God knows when or where doesn't sound like part of my lineage, does he?"

"Particularly," Annie said with resignation, "a monk who may be a figment of the imagination of an overwrought American."

"There is that," Geoff agreed, "though I didn't want to say."

"I'm not insane, Geoff. And I'm not making this up. Really." She couldn't very well strip off her jeans and show him the scrape marks. She settled for the next best thing. "There's a picture of some of the monks from the London Charterhouse in an out-of-print nineteenth-century book I found online. Can I show you?"

"Have a go," he said, nodding toward a large rosewood desk positioned in front of a massive bookcase suspended from the ceiling on steel wires so it acted as a room divider. "Let's see if one of them looks like me."

There were, Annie noted, no pictures of the dead wife on his desk. Nothing particularly personal, come to that. Only a small stack of books and maps, a notebook, and a PC with a lightning-fast chip. She downloaded the book in seconds, and because she knew exactly what she was looking for, she had the drawing on the screen almost immediately. It was described as three of the monks enduring the first part of their punishment. They were strapped feetfirst to a horse-drawn hurdle, a board flat on the ground, and were being dragged over the cobblestones to their execution. Tudor custom encouraged the watching crowds to pelt such prisoners with every kind of filth.

In the picture the monks were lying faceup, so it should have been possible to enlarge the image, print it, and get a decent look at their features. Geoff's printer was a floor-model Xerox with all the bells and whistles, but however advanced its enlarging capacities, it produced only a blur.

Geoff brought their coffees to the desk, a mug for her, a small cup of espresso for him. They spent the next forty minutes trying to Photoshop the drawing. "Above my pay grade," he said finally, "but I know who to ask."

"Who?"

"Bloke at the studio. Clary Colbert. World's best techie. If it can be done, he can do it. Is it okay to send him this?"

"Sure. The whole thing's in the public domain. Though I'd prefer we didn't tell him why we're interested."

Geoff wrote a quick note, then punched a few keys. "Done."

Maybe, Annie thought, but I'm due for some luck. Maybe it's just beginning.

6

Annie spent most of the next day at the Jewish Museum. It was a base she had to touch, but she had not expected to find anything there and she was correct. The collection was fine, but it concentrated on the great nineteenth- and twentieth-century waves of immigration and on British Jews of the modern era. It offered nothing about Holborn in 1535, much less any Jews who may have lived there. She could return to focusing on the things that might move her forward.

She spent the bus ride back to the flat adding up what she knew, and what she only surmised. For one thing, she was sure the Scranton map was somehow related to her quest. It wasn't obvious how, but her gut told her it mattered. Every researcher alive learns never to ignore the all-important gut. So although she wanted to separate the ghostly goings-on at the flat from the quest for the Jew of Holborn, her gut told her not to, and she obeyed it. She also had to admit to a similar instinct about the book she'd found online. The nineteenth-century history of the London Carthusians had a number of illustrations, among them a series of drawings identifying the location of the old Charterhouse.

According to Annie's calculations, a direct line of sight had run between the monastery and Bristol House. You could stand at the window in her flat's back bedroom—the window that seemed to have flown open of its own accord—and, presuming no buildings in between, look directly into the world of the Carthusian monks. Never mind that Henry drove them out in 1538, or that Bristol House wasn't built until 1901. In terms of the phenomena she'd experienced at the flat and nowhere else, that sight line seemed to her to be of major importance. And the persecution of the Charterhouse monks had begun in 1535—the same year her Jew of Holborn was supposed to be distributing his treasures. How coincidental was that likely to be? she asked herself as the bus stopped and started its way through the traffic of modern London.

Returning to the apartment after spending hours away had evolved into a set routine, a series of checks. Turn the key. Open the door. Hold her breath while she reached for the remote on the hall table. Holding her breath should not have anything to do with whether the ghost appeared. Still, Annie always drew in that first long gulp of air and did not exhale until she clicked on the radio.

"The Foreign Office has said there is no doubt that the United Nations vote will come in the next few days. As previously announced, Britain will abstain because . . ."

Annie was unaware of the issue, or whether she should approve or disapprove Britain's abstention. The discussion moved on to a cricket match in Jaipur. She had no idea what that was about either, but it didn't matter. It was the announcer's voice that gave her both comfort and courage. Annie waltzed confidently into number eight on a wave of inexplicable talk of overs and declarations and wickets.

She dropped her bag in the drawing room, taking a minute to note that the lilacs she'd bought the day before were already wilting, but all else was as it should be. She walked down the hall to the kitchen with, thank God, no extraordinary incident and stopped to squeeze a lemon into some soda water, add a bit of sugar, then take a sip. Finally, with her heart beating at a furious rate despite the soothing drone of the BBC, she turned and looked down the short leg of hall toward the back bedroom.

The door was closed, which was how she'd left it earlier in the day, and there was nothing to see.

In the dining room her laptop was open—also as she'd left it—but idling in sleep mode. She struck a couple of keys and waited for the screen to light up, then clicked open her mail and ran her eye down the list of senders. Most of what had come in while she was away was advertising. There was, however, an e-mail from Geoff Harris. He'd written one word, "Bollocks," and attached a picture from the old book. It was the drawing of three Carthusians being dragged on a hurdle to their execution at Tyburn, enlarged so every detail was sharp and clear. None of the monks even slightly resembled either Geoff or the man she'd seen in the back bedroom.

Annie hit reply and typed, "Whatever bollocks means, I agree."

Moments later her phone rang at the other end of the apartment. She had to dash down the hall to grab it from the bag she'd left in the drawing room. Geoff was on the line. "I want to talk about this. May I come by?"

Annie said he could.

"Clary said he had to add pixels to make it this clear, but that he didn't change any of the parameters. The way he explains it, this is the picture from the book, adjusted to how it would appear if the artist had been working to a larger scale."

"It looks right," Annie said. "Exactly like the original, just bigger."

"But none of these blokes look like me."

"No," she admitted. "They do not." It was indisputably true and made her wonder what exactly he'd wanted to come rushing over to talk about.

They were sitting side by side on Mrs. Walton's slightly faded blue sofa. The printouts of the enlarged drawings were spread out on the coffee table. Geoff leaned in to look more closely at one of them. She could feel his body heat. "Do you think the artist was drawing from life?" He pointed to the picture of the three men strapped to a hurdle. "The attribution says the original is in the motherhouse in France. Maybe this drawing has nothing to do with the Charterhouse here in London."

Annie shook her head. "Drawings like this were made on the spot by itinerant artists. They were the newspaper shots of their day. My bet is someone in the crowd sympathized with the monks and got one of the drawings to them. They preserved it and passed it on."

"They all have beards," Geoff said. He waved his hand at the assortment of drawings. "None of the other monks do."

"That also feels accurate," Annie said. "In 1535 Henry was still cautious. The population mostly supported the monks and the pope. This is a picture of the Carthusian prior, the Venerable Father as they called him, and two of his fellow monks. They were the first victims, and they were imprisoned for months—probably without shaving gear—because no jury would convict them, until Thomas Cromwell said the jurors would die traitors' deaths unless they did. After that the trials became pro forma and very quick. From the Tower to Tyburn in a few days." She started to say that was barely enough time to grow designer stubble. Like his. But Geoff's grim expression put her off.

" 'To be hung by the neck,' " he quoted, " 'cut down whilst yet alive, sliced open and gutted, and cut into four pieces.' "

"That's what the judge said," Annie agreed.

"Jesus God Almighty, we were a bloodthirsty lot. And all because Anne Boleyn was hot stuff and Henry wanted a new wife."

"And there was no such thing as divorce, meaning Henry had to get the pope to annul his marriage to Catherine. The pope wouldn't do it."

"So Henry declared himself head of the Church in England."

"Exactly. The pope became simply the bishop of Rome, and the king made the rules for every Christian in England. The monks wouldn't swear to that being legit, so they were condemned."

Geoff was still bent over the picture of the monks on the hurdle. "I have interviewed a fair percentage of the most important people around. I can't think of one of them who would likely endure that for a principle. Religious or otherwise."

"You're a cynic. Besides, these guys were Carthusian monks. They ate nothing but bread and water two days a week, no meat ever, and they wore hair shirts beneath their habits and almost never spoke. Religious principle is what they were about. Are about."

"You're joking. They're still around?"

"Absolutely. Priest-monks—they call them Dom-somebody, not father—who live in solitude, and brothers who do the daily work. I looked them up a couple of days ago."

"Online? Hair shirts, but also Web sites?"

"Yup. Turns out there are at this moment eighteen charterhouses in a dozen countries. Including one in Vermont and one here in England. Someplace called Parkminster."

"Holy shit."

"Well, I don't think they'd claim . . ."

He laughed. "Parkminster is in Buckinghamshire, in Milton Keynes. There is no place less exotic on God's green earth."

"They don't think of themselves as exotics. Only a minority option."

"I interviewed a Trappist once. He'd been a Labour backbencher. After he became a monk, he wrote a book of poetry that was sixty-six weeks on the best-seller lists. He was fat and jolly. Didn't look as if he lived on bread and water. Though he did tell me they ate no meat."

"The Trappists are thought to be one of the strictest orders in the church, but compared with the Carthusians, they're playboys. A char-terhouse is a collection of small houses, each occupied by one hermit monk who mostly does all his praying on his own and even grows much of his own food in a small garden. They only leave the monastery once a week. Every Thursday the hermits come out of their little houses and take a walk."

"Now you are joking."

"I'm not. It's true. They stroll along two by two and talk. Every fif-teen minutes they change partners. The weekly walk was started by Saint Bruno when he founded the order in the eleventh century. Five thousand feet up a French mountain, incidentally, at La Grande Char-treuse. In the mouths of English speakers, *Chartreuse* became *Charter-house,* so today that's what their monasteries are all called." Annie stood up. "More coffee?"

"Yes, thanks."

She took his empty mug and started down the hall toward the kitchen. The radios were playing softly as she passed, murmuring in unison about the death of a prominent Roman Catholic cardinal in Hol-land who as a young man survived imprisonment by the Gestapo but at eighty-eight choked to death in a bizarre accident involving a quail egg.

It occurred to Annie that she'd never seen a quail egg. Or a live quail, for that matter.

It was after seven. She should probably offer to make something to eat. But not only did she have nothing so gourmet as quail, her shopping had not anticipated dinner for two. She had one pork chop and one chicken breast. Maybe he'd like a cheese sandwich.

It was deep dusk outside—a bit early for such a blueberry sky. Perhaps a storm was coming. The kitchen was dim and full of shadows. Annie turned and reached for the light switch. The movement gave her a direct view down the short leg of the hall.

Her heart accelerated until it was a drum thudding in her chest. "Geoff, come here."

Her voice sounded—even to her—far away, distant, and apparently not loud enough. She tried again. "Geoff, I'm in the kitchen. Come. Right now, please."

She heard him running down the hall in the semidarkness.

"Look." Annie pointed to an intense bright light shining from under the closed door of the back bedroom.

Dom Justin
From the Waiting Place

We walked and talked as if that May afternoon in the year of Our Lord 1535 were an ordinary Thursday. Instead it was the day the man we Carthusians call the Venerable Father, our prior, had been most cruelly martyred and went to paradise. Also the day when the funnel of wind had come down and pulverized the cobbles outside our monastery church. Looking back, I have no doubt many thought that remarkable phenomenon a sign of heaven's displeasure with the actions of the king, but even among ourselves such was our caution in those times that no one gave voice to the idea.

Dom Casper, however, could not hold back his tears when he spoke of the martyrdom of the Venerable Father, but the others—and I myself, who had certainly the least right to do so—talked more of the glory than the suffering. Dom Hilary, who always knew more than the rest (as if God himself spoke to Hilary on account of his superior virtue) told what he'd heard from Fra Herman, one of the brothers of our order who got about the countryside, unlike us monks who are vowed to almost total silence and solitude.

Dom Hilary said that, according to Herman, immediately the deed was done, a woman of the town ran straight to the house of the lay brothers and told them she'd been near enough to hear the Venerable Father's last words. It was after he had been hanged and cut down, and after his belly was slit and his entrails pulled out, and while the knife was poised to enter his chest. According to this woman, he said, "Good Jesu, what will ye do with my heart?" Then, so the woman said, his heart was cut apart from him, and he gave up his spirit.

Dom Augustine, who was always a bit simple as well as contrary, said it was an odd thing to say. But I pointed out it was a mark of the Venerable Father's certainty that his heart was going to Our Blessed Lord, since he had offered it so many years ago when first he entered the Charterhouse.

It was astonishing how easy it was for an imposter like myself to sound like a pious Carthusian. Meanwhile, as we walked and talked of paradise and martyrdom, I thought of how earlier that day, though to my knowledge there were no quails kept anywhere in the monastery, another of the creature's eggs found its way to my cell. As always, the appearance of the speckled quail's egg meant I was that very night commanded to visit the Jew of Holborn.

❖

"Tell me again what you saw," Geoff said.

"A bright light." Minutes had gone by, but Annie's voice still quivered. "White. Shining from under this door."

Geoff opened it. Nothing in the small bedroom looked disturbed. "What do you mean by a white light?"

"Not ordinary. As if . . . phosphorescent." It was a relief to find the right word.

He stepped across the threshold and flicked the light switch. A desk lamp went on. "Not even a fingerprint in the dust," he said.

Annie stayed where she was, leaning against the wall. Her heart was no longer racing, and she could breathe, but there was a rushing sound in her head. Everything seemed to come through a filter between herself and the known universe. "You're sure you didn't see it?"

Geoff shook his head. "Sorry, I really didn't."

The white glow had still been there when he joined her in the doorway to the kitchen. It had faded while they walked toward it. "Maybe it was a lightning flash," Annie said. It was pouring now. They could see the rain beating against the bedroom windows.

"This is English rain," Geoff said. "It's polite and quiet. No thunder and no lightning. At least not usually."

Anyway, a flash of lightning would not have produced a sustained glow, and she had seen the light for many seconds. But she couldn't let it go. "It could have been," she insisted.

"I suppose."

He sounded as if he were indulging a frightened and unreasonable child.

Annie turned and walked down the hall, putting on all the lights as she passed. She heard Geoff close the back bedroom door and come after her. In the drawing room she sat on the sofa, facing into the corner, her shoulders hunched over. The springs gave when he sat next to her. Annie clenched her hands in her lap.

"You can't stay here, Annie. Come back to my place tonight. Tomorrow we'll see about finding you somewhere else to live while you're in London."

"No."

"You're being ridiculous. How can you stay here? You're trembling."

"I'll be fine." She had four radios and a universal remote. What better defense against visits from the beyond? The rain looked to be coming in the open window. Annie got up and closed it.

"Annie, I want to help you."

"Why?"

"Why not? And why are you being so stubborn?"

"I'm not stubborn, just practical." The sense of everything being distant was dissolving. And the rushing sound in her head was gone.

"How is it practical to stay in a flat that scares you out of your wits?"

"It's not the flat." She turned. "And I'm scared, but not the way you mean. I can't run away. There's something I'm supposed to find out or . . ."—she hesitated—"accomplish. Some connection."

"With what?"

"My job, what I came here to do. A connection with the Jew of Holborn. I would rather that were not true because it complicates things, but I'm convinced it is."

"I take it you mean the job Weinraub sent you here to do." His expression changed, got harder.

"Weinraub's got nothing to do with this. Okay, he's the one who gave me the assignment. But that only makes him the—I don't know, the proximate cause. The instrument."

"I still can't see how staying here is—"

"Look," Annie said, "maybe you're smarter than I am. Or luckier. Or you had better judgment. Whatever—my life hasn't gone the way yours has. I don't have a fabulous career or live in a gorgeous house where everything is exactly the way I want it to be. But what I do know is how to hang tough. I know about that."

The words were pulled out of her. She had certainly not meant to say that much. And if she told him more—if she tried to explain how booze had been first a lover whose embrace made the pain go away, then a scourge that robbed her of herself, but in the end left a place where she could pour molten steel—what were the chances he would understand? *It's not that civilians don't want to get it, Annie my girl. Only that they can't.* Sidney O'Toole was usually right about stuff like that.

Annie made her choice and took a deep breath. "I've already been through the worst that can happen to me, Geoff. I'm an alcoholic. A recovering alcoholic," she amended. "I've been sober for four years."

"I know."

"What?"

"I know you're a recovering alcoholic. I'd pretty much figured it out by the time we had coffee at Chloe's."

The mark of Cain. The word *drunk* tattooed on her forehead. "How? Because I don't drink?"

"That was one of the clues. Also, before you went to work for Weinraub, you were teaching in a third-rate girls' school, despite the fact that by the time they made you Dr. Kendall, you'd gone through half a dozen professional journals in a blaze of peer-reviewed glory."

She had Googled him, and he had Googled her. Only he'd done so with a great deal more efficiency. Her life wasn't on display online the way his was. He'd had to dig deep.

He waited, probably until he was sure she'd figured it out. "I checked you out," he admitted after a few seconds. "It's what I do."

" 'Chew them up and spit them out,' as Jennifer put it."

"Not usually people I meet socially. But Jenny mentioned the Shalom Foundation, so I knew you worked for Weinraub. That meant you had my full attention."

"For God's sake, Geoff—that business with Philip Weinraub and Rabin was, what—twenty or so years ago? And you're still chasing his shadow? Who are you, Inspector Javert?"

"Weinraub made billions from those hedge funds he used to manage. He retired a few years back, but he remains active in some deeply suspect groups involved in Israeli affairs."

"Sorry to belabor the point," she said quietly, "but you have no proof."

"You're right," Geoff said. "I have none. That's my problem. I thought we were discussing yours. Staying here despite how the place makes you feel—that seems mad to me."

"I know it's a cliché, but you just don't understand. I don't know that you ever could."

"Try me," he said quietly.

She hesitated, gathered herself. "Everything that's happened to me . . . No, that's not right. Everything I did to myself, I had to undo. Piece by little piece. Publicly and out loud. Making myself totally naked. I cannot tell you what that kind of seeing, that kind of nakedness, does. AA thins you, it hollows you out, but it does not leave you more fragile. It leaves a kind of tensile strength. Am I making any sense?"

"Quite a bit of sense."

"The strength," she insisted, feeling still the need to persuade, "that's the takeaway. It's why however I feel about what's happening here—and I admit it's scary—I cannot quit."

"I'm not asking you to quit. Simply to choose a different venue for the engagement."

Annie shook her head. "Shalom has paid three months' rent in advance. What would I tell them? A ghost chased me out? As you said before, in professional terms this assignment is the best thing that's happened to me in ten years. If I can pull it off, I can write up my findings and publish. And that may set me on the way to better things. So I'm not going anywhere."

Annie turned so he wouldn't see the flush that stained her cheeks and busied herself with Mrs. Walton's CDs, choosing one at random and shoving it into the player. John Coltrane's unmistakable tenor sax competed with the sound of pelting rain beating on the windows.

Geoff stood up. "I think I'd best be on my way. Annie, you're sure?"

"I'm sure."

"Fair enough, I'll let myself out." He started for the door, then turned back. "Annie—"

She looked at him expectantly.

"I think you're very brave."

Something about the way he said it—rather like the end of a story. She perceived a considerable amount of finality in the sound of the door closing behind him.

7

Most of Wednesday she didn't get out of bed. The white light shining beneath the door had been vivid and completely apparent to her, but Geoffrey Harris, who had appeared seconds later and while it was still bright, had not seen it.

The only conclusion was that the ghost was speaking—or appearing, or chanting, or shining—directly to Annie Kendall. Whatever the monk wanted, and regardless of whether the direct line of sight between his ancient Charterhouse and the back bedroom of this flat was what made his visitations possible, his intention was to communicate with her. Moreover, in the past week he'd proven he was in charge. He came and went as he pleased. The phenomena that accompanied him could open windows and fling solid candlesticks across the room, even whirl her around until she lost consciousness, then leave his calling card in the form of red scrape marks on her body. This ghostly monk was not something she could study, not something or someone she could tame with her intelligence or the power of scholarship. Rather he had so far managed to control their encounters. If she gave in, followed wherever the ghost wanted to lead her, where would she end up? Not, she suspected, with the solution to the mystery she'd come to London to solve. Not with anything she could publish in a scholarly journal and thereby earn the renewed respect of her peers.

Days like this she always went back to the custody hearing, to Zachary Johnson's statement to the judge, the words that ever since were permanently entwined in the double helix that was the Annie-ness of Annie. "Her apartment reeked of urine and feces. There was no food in the kitchen, and the only bottle of milk in the refrigerator was sour. My son was wet and hungry and alone, crying in a crib he shared with one tattered blanket."

They'd never lived together, almost no one knew they were married, and she hadn't seen him in months when their son was born; nonetheless she couldn't bear to write "father unknown" on Ari's birth certificate. She told the truth. So Zak had standing and the court granted him custody. It was an absolutely logical thing to do.

"Kick the booze, Annie," Zak said on the courtroom steps. "Find a program. Go into detox. Whatever works." The social worker was waiting for him, holding in her stranger's arms a three-year-old Ari who struggled to escape and cried for his mother. "Straighten up," Zak said, before he turned away, "then get in touch. We'll work something out."

She had tried, a little bit at least. Nothing took. Instead she had used that searing, unspeakable loss as an excuse for six more years of drunken havoc. Then four years ago she had walked into an AA meeting in Boston, and by some miraculous gift of undeserved grace she was saved. But by then what Ari wanted mattered as much as any arrangement she and Zak might make. And what he wanted was not her.

Never again, she had promised herself, absolutely never again would she lose herself in that way, cede control of her life. She was not about to break that vow because of a ghost.

Around four she got up to make herself a sandwich. That's when she closed the kitchen door facing the back hall. From now on she'd only go into the kitchen from the dining room.

She carried the sandwich back to the bedroom and ate it while walking up and down in front of the remarkable black and white mural with its jumble of tiny, detailed London scenes. If she focused on just one, she could sometimes identify a corner of Trafalgar Square or a bit of Piccadilly Circus. The scenes, however, occurred in no order and with no discernible pattern, making it impossible to maintain concentration on the mural for any length of time. Moreover, she was, she realized, acutely aware of the chest in the drawing room that contained two bottles of scotch, one of gin, one of sherry, and three of wine.

"Do feel free," Mrs. Walton had said.

Annie went into the dining room and sat down at her laptop. She'd looked up a schedule of Holborn AA meetings before she left New York. There was one at 7:45 p.m. on Wednesdays. It was a short walk away on Emerald Street, which, according to Google Maps, was closer to Geoff's place than hers. She worked out a route that bypassed his house.

Thursday morning she wrote another postcard to Ari and took it out to mail when she went for a run. South to Covent Garden this time, as if a new route might intensify the endorphins and deliver a more potent sense of well-being. When she got back, she showered and changed and headed for the British Museum. She'd be working on her own since Jennifer was on vacation, but the Shalom Foundation had recommended the archivist only as a resource.

Annie didn't actually need her.

Weinraub had been full of praise for Annie's skills the last time she saw him. She'd been scheduled to leave for London that evening, and gone to Shalom's Lower Manhattan office to pick up the hard copy documents and her ticket.

In New York terms, the building was plain vanilla—no prestige and no glamour—but from where Annie was sitting, she had a fantastic view of the harbor. The Statue of Liberty had loomed over Weinraub's shoulder while he spoke. "I have no doubt you're going to do great things for us, Dr. Kendall. The academic world will be set on its ear. Judaica from the Second Temple! Who would imagine we might be able to confirm the existence of such things?"

She'd started to protest again that such a provenance was bound to be impossible to prove, but he'd waved away her concern. "No, no, I understand. A connection of that sort would be only a bonus, and we're unlikely ever to document it." He'd shrugged. "That doesn't matter for our purposes, Dr. Kendall. It's the source of the Jew of Holborn's gifts we're after. A clue as to where he found his treasures. The items we've discovered, the links between them, went unnoticed for centuries. Who's to say there isn't still more ancient Judaica to be located?" The words were accompanied by another shrug. "Perhaps other types of pans they used for carrying the coals for burnt offerings. There's one called a *seer* in Hebrew. And there are other basins and bowls connected to the sacrifice. Or why not some ancient mezuzah? That's the case with the parchment inside. Jews fix them to their doorways. Like that one." He gestured to the mezuzah on the door frame of his office.

Annie had turned to look, but only to be polite. "I'm familiar with them, Mr. Weinraub."

"Yes, of course. I'd forgotten. Your doctoral dissertation was about religious symbols on doors and doorways, wasn't it?"

Annie hadn't made that association. It surprised her that he did. "Christian symbols," she said.

"That doesn't matter. You'll be sensitive to the possibility. *Mezuzot* have been part of Jewish life since the time of Exodus. And they are small, easy to transport. Also easy to overlook."

"I take your point." She didn't really. Discovering some actual ancient artifact seemed to Annie extremely unlikely. Finding out something about the man himself, the improbable Jew of Holborn—that she believed she might do.

They had sat for a few seconds without speaking, Weinraub seeming to look through her. The sun was going down over the harbor meanwhile, turning the Lady's crown to gold. "I'll do my best, Mr. Weinraub," she said when the silence was becoming uncomfortable. "I promise you that."

He nodded, still pinning her with his dark-eyed gaze. "I have no doubt, Dr. Kendall. I am sure you will not fail me."

As promised, Annie's orange-bordered pass got her into the staff sections of the British Museum, no questions asked. After she let herself into Jennifer's temporary domain in the subbasement bowels, things became more difficult.

She knew she had to locate her mysterious Jew if she were to have any hope of unearthing his secrets, and that meant starting with Holborn in the 1530s. Back then it was pretty much all fields and meadows, but according to the Scranton map, a few houses hugged the banks of the now-covered-over River Fleet. With Jennifer away, she couldn't see Scranton's drawing again, so she spread a large-scale modern map on the table, then—painstakingly, using a number of different reference books—drew in the river as if it still traveled aboveground. A little before noon she went out to try to walk along the banks of the Fleet as it flowed through Holborn.

She never got a decent start. Her cell was in the pocket of her jeans, and it vibrated against her hip while she was passing Russell Square tube station. Geoff had sent her a text: "Why boiling pot?" She texted back a series of question marks while she waited to cross Bernard Street. The phone rang in her hand. When she answered, he said, "I've been looking at the other enlargements my techie mate sent back. Next to the Tyburn gallows there's a huge cauldron sort of thing with a fire under it. What's it for?"

"Oh, that." She looked the wrong way before stepping off the curb. A cabbie leaned on his horn. Annie jumped back. "It's for parboiling the parts of the bodies after they're hacked up. Human flesh lasts longer if it's not entirely raw." The jaw of the woman standing beside her dropped about three inches. Annie grinned at her. The woman turned and ran.

"Jesus," Geoff said. "Where are you?"

She told him.

"Head up Guilford Street toward the entrance to Coram's Fields. I'll find you."

She didn't see him coming, didn't know he was there until minutes later he slipped his arm through hers. "Good morning. Look, it's a miracle."

"What is?"

He nodded toward the entrance to the park on their left. "There's no gatekeeper on duty. C'mon."

"Why should there be—"

"Don't talk. Hurry." They ducked into the park.

* * *

It was perfect weather, sunny and warm. The park was filled with children playing. Geoff, however, looked grim. And everything she told him about Tudor justice seemed to make it worse. "After they cut out the heart," she said, "the victim was dead."

"I suppose," he said.

"Then they cut off the head, to be displayed on the city walls, and divided what was left into four parts. That was the quartering. It was those four parts they parboiled in the cauldron. Before they tacked them up around the town."

"You keep saying parboiled. As if it were a recipe."

"It sort of was," she agreed. "You're a cook." He'd said he bought the house after his wife died—he wouldn't have put in a kitchen like that if he didn't cook. "You must know what happens to flesh if you boil it for too long."

"Falls apart."

"Exactly. They only wanted the body parts not to be bloody. Semi-preserved."

"So they'd last longer."

Annie nodded. "Making a public show of the victim in as many places as possible was very important. The entire operation was about deterrence."

"When I first saw the pot, I thought they were boiling people alive. Like cannibals."

"Not at Tyburn."

"Jesus fucking Christ. You mean sometimes they did?"

"Sometimes. How come you didn't know? I thought English schoolboys took all this in with mother's milk."

"Not this schoolboy. And it was no part of Maggie's milk."

Maggie must be his German mother. Annie remembered him explaining his thoroughly nonmonkish Portsmouth background, and how his mother had been sent to England at age nine to escape the Nazis. "Boiling alive was not a regular Tudor thing," she said, "but there are a few instances. If I tell you how they did it, I'll really freak you out. It

was a punishment reserved for the most heinous crimes. Poisoning no-
bles at their own tables, that sort of thing."

Geoff started to say something. A soccer ball flew toward their heads.
Annie ducked. The ball missed her and bounced a few times on the
pavement a short distance away. A small boy shouted an apology and ran
to get it. Geoff stood up and got there first. Annie thought he'd pick the
thing up and throw it to the boy, but instead he dribbled it back onto
the grass, the ball dancing at his toes as if it were attached with strings.
After a few seconds he called out, "Yo! You there, blondie," and kicked
the ball straight to the feet of one little boy. The child shouted something, obviously delighted, and passed the ball back to Geoff. Another
boy, dark and considerably bigger, tried to take it away. Geoff put the
ball through the second kid's legs, took control of it again behind his
back, then kicked it some twenty feet into the goal. There were more
shouts. A number of the boys raised their hands above their heads and
clapped in appreciation.

Geoff came back and sat beside Annie on the bench. "I suppose like
most Americans you don't know the first thing about football, so you're
not in the least impressed."

"I'm sorry." She felt the flush crawl up her neck to her cheeks.

"I love the way you blush."

"I can't help it. Redheads do. Are you very good at the game?"

He laughed. "At my age? Not on your life. I was pretty good once upon
a time, and I can still come up with a couple of flash moves"—he nodded
to where the kids were again playing intently—"but only if the competition's nine years old." He put his arm along the back of the bench and
twisted one of her curls around his finger. Their hands had met a few times
when they passed things back and forth, and earlier today he'd taken her
arm to guide her along the street. This was the first time he had touched
her for no reason except, apparently, that he wanted to. "How are you,
Annie? Since the other night, I mean."

"Fine."

"No more bright white lights?"

"None. But I saw it, Geoff. It was not my imagination."

"As I said before, I believe you."

"You do?"

"Yes."

"Why?"

He grinned. "Is that an alternative to just saying thank you?" And before she could reply: "Look, in my business I meet a lot of very bright women, some of them almost as pretty as you"—his fingers were still tangled in her curls—"but with most, even socially, it's a constant contest. They never stop being warriors. You, on the other hand . . ." He stopped speaking and took his hand away. "Will you understand if I say that, despite how tough you must have had to be to overcome devil booze, you strike me as being tender at the bone?"

"I'm not sure. I am tough, Geoff. A warrior if you will. I've had to be."

"Let it lie," he said. "I like being with you. That's enough."

More than enough. But she didn't say so. "I do want to say thank you. For believing me."

"Don't mention it. Now can I ask a personal question? All the details you know, about the things these folks did, the Charterhouse and the monks—I realize it's professional expertise, but are you a Catholic?"

"Ah," she said, "a gap in the Annie file. My parents were committed Catholics. In fact my father was John Kendall. You're probably not familiar with him, but he was a well-known church historian. And my mother taught Latin at a Catholic college in Boston."

"That sounds like they're both gone."

She nodded. "Killed in a plane crash when I was eleven. Afterward I was sent to live with an aunt in New York."

"Tough," he said. Then, taking her hand so her bracelet caught the sunlight: "What about your twin?"

"Aunt Sybil, the New York aunt, was supposed to take us both, but after a few weeks she decided two were too many. She sent Ari to our other aunt in Los Angeles. The one my parents hadn't put in their will because they thought she was a flake."

"So first you lose your parents, then your twin. Doesn't sound like fun."

"It was not." Sybil kept a bottle of sherry in the kitchen and usually had a glass before dinner. Eleven-year-old Annie began taking sips just to spite her. "But it's not an excuse, Geoff. If there's anything you learn at AA, it's not to make excuses. And in answer to your original question about my religious beliefs, AA is all the church I need."

"I get that."

No, he did not. Because unless you've been there, walked the walk, you have no idea. People on the outside, civilians as Sidney called them, always thought if you were intelligent and well educated—as well as being a drunken bum—you put up with the slogans and the hand hold- ing and all the rest. Took what you needed and discarded the kitschy rigmarole. That was not so. "I believe in it all," she said. "Passionately. With my whole being. One day at a time. Accepting the things I cannot change. Asking a Higher Power to grant me serenity. I drank every drop of the Kool-Aid, and I keep going back for more. It keeps me alive. And sober. Which for me is the same thing. I'm sunk otherwise."

Dom Justin
From the Waiting Place

When I first went to the Charterhouse, I intended only to pretend to fol- low the ritual. Four years later doing as Carthusians do had come to seem the natural way of things. Except that I was certain no Carthusian in all the centuries of the Order had done as I did at least once each week and sometimes more often.

Master Cromwell had used his power as privy councillor to the king to arrange that my cell be the one on the corner of the Great Cloister, a short distance from the trades entrance used by laypeople who had business with the monastery. That gate had no purpose private to the monks and was never barred.

On the day of the Venerable Father's martyrdom, having been earlier sent the signal of the speckled quail's egg, I waited until the shadows lengthened. Then, keeping close to the walls, I crept out of the Charterhouse using my customary route. Soon I was hurrying across the fields looking sometimes toward the nearby monastery of the soldier monks, the Knights Hospitaller of St. John. That monastery had once belonged to the Knights Templar, as was still obvious by its distinctive round church, but in 1312 the Holy Inquisition said the Templars confessed to heresy, and the pope suppressed them and gave all their property to the St. Johns. What would I confess, I wondered, after the rack and the thumbscrews? Whatever I was told to confess. Worse perhaps than ceremonies involving an obscene kiss and spitting on the cross, but that had been enough to smoke the skies over Europe with burnt Templar flesh. I shuddered, thinking that I too lived under the threat of the stake, and walked on beside the Fleet until I saw the small copse of trees that separated the Jew's house from the river.

I had just gathered up the skirt of my habit to run toward it when I noticed a white glow hanging above the water. It shimmered and shone in the night, and I put my hand to my mouth to muffle my terror and signed myself with the cross of Christ, but I could not command my legs to move. Perhaps the Venerable Father himself waited to accuse me. He was surely by then in that place where all things are known. How would he repay me for the terrible betrayal I had practiced these four years?

"At last you are here," a voice said, "I have made every excuse I could think of to come out and look for you. You must hurry."

Rebecca, the Jew's daughter and the reason, apart from Thomas Cromwell's command, that I was a monk of the Charterhouse, emerged from the copse. "Why do you stand there? Come quickly." She held out her hand and whispered, "We can steal a few seconds if you waste no more time."

God knows it was not the first time she had found an opportunity to meet me on the darkened path, but surely, I thought, she would not be so brazen as to thrust herself against me in the presence of the glowing spirit. "We dare not," I whispered. "Do you not see the Venerable Father there behind me?"

"The Venerable Father?" Her voice had that teasing undertone that was so much a part of Rebecca's character. "Even the silent monks of the Charterhouse must know their prior died today at Tyburn."

"His body perhaps. His spirit is here. Look!" I turned to point to the white light rising from the river, but it was gone.

"You are mad as well as late. Come at once. Master Cromwell waits inside."

"The master himself?"

I was astonished, since usually he sent his secretary to take my report, but Rebecca was unlikely to mistake one for the other. The secretary was a man whose face was horribly marked by the pox, and who carried about him a dead rodent stink which announced his presence before any sight of him.

"The master himself," she repeated. "Hurry. He is impatient for you, and I have left him alone."

This could portend no good. It was Thomas Cromwell's habit always to keep himself at many removes from his schemes and strategies. He was far too clever not to know that in Henry's England he might himself one day need to profess an innocence he truly possessed. I was sure, for instance, that the speckled egg which on occasion appeared in the basket of food delivered at midday to my door and meant I must visit the Jew, was put there by someone who received the instruction from someone else. That someone would have had the order by way of a signal from yet another— and none would know precisely what the egg commanded, or whether indeed I was the last in the chain to act on its authority. All was no doubt put in train by a murmured word from the master to his foul-smelling secretary, but neither would have had any knowledge of quails, their eggs, or indeed what device was chosen to summon me. Master Cromwell had placed me in the Charterhouse, but I did not imagine myself his only spy within its walls. None of this was the business of any woman, even one as clever as Rebecca. I asked only, "Where is your father?"

"Out doing Master Cromwell's business," she said.

I knew well the nature of that business. Like everyone, Master Cromwell believed the Templars had brought wondrous things back to England from Jerusalem, then hidden them with such cunning, they were unfound these two hundred years since the old knights' disgrace. Somehow Master Cromwell had discovered that the man known to all London as Giacomo the Lombard was a Jew. As payment for keeping his secret, Giacomo was ordered to live outside the city wall and search the Holborn countryside for the Templars' treasure, things he would recognize more readily than most, being a goldsmith of some renown.

"Why do you dally?" Rebecca demanded. "Already he has waited too long." She motioned me forward, but she herself did not move. To avoid the thorns of the barberry bushes either side, I must pass so close as to touch her body with my own.

Her smell overwhelmed me.

She rose on her toes to reach my height and for a moment pushed her breasts against me. "Do not forget me," she whispered into my ear.

Would to God that I could have done so, and thus perhaps secured forgiveness of my many sins.

I pushed past her without speaking, grateful for the loose white robe that hid the sign of how strongly Adam responded to Eve's sinful provocation, and went into the modest little house.

Master Cromwell demanded to know everything that was said when the word of the Venerable Father's death reached the monastery. I must tell him, he said, who wept and who cursed, and if any of the monks seemed to think justice had not been done.

I dared not tell him that none thought justice done. It was Thomas Cromwell's intention to have the property of the Charterhouse in his possession once he made all England Protestant. He had told me so himself back in the days when I was his bound servant, but I had proof of neither the man's heresy nor his greed. If I took such information to the king, he would believe Cromwell's word over mine, and my end would be the same, burning or quartering. So I told the man whom I still thought of as my master—as indeed he was, if a master is one who has power over another—as much of the truth as I could manage without piling still more sin on my soul. "Even Dom Hilary spoke only of the glory of heaven," I said, "not the means of the Venerable Father's getting there."

Cromwell smiled at that. "Ah yes," he said. "Dom Hilary. He is known to be the holiest monk in the Charterhouse, is he not?"

"So it is said, master. And not just by the monks. Many people from the town come to the monastery gates to beg for Dom Hilary's prayers. Before becoming a Carthusian, he was an ordinary priest in London, a bishop in fact, so many knew him."

"Priests and bishops," Cromwell said with one of those smiles that in any other man might appear to be a grimace. "We shall see how long they are important in this kingdom." Then he dropped any pretense of good humor and grabbed the front of my habit and put his face close to mine and asked, "Did this Dom Hilary who is also a bishop not call down a curse on the king for ordering a traitor's death for your prior?"

"Absolutely not." My master looked hard at me, but I did not change my story.

"And since these Carthusians have made you a priest after their detestable custom"—he whispered the words though there were none to hear him, Rebecca having remained outside and left us to our business—"we know you cannot lie. Is that not so, Dom Justin?"

He spoke the name assigned to me in religion in the same manner as he said everything else, with contempt. But I answered as if his question held no guile. "That is true, master."

After a time he released his grip and looked away, so dismissing the subject of my ordination. Easy for him, but not for me.

When Master Cromwell first sent me to the Charterhouse, I believed he would release me from my charge before the time of my priesting should arrive. Even after I had been some three years among them, he still had not. Then, six months before, the holy Dom Hilary had himself laid his hands on my head and anointed me with holy oil and proclaimed me priest. So priest I truly was. As well as a Carthusian monk, vowed never to depart the monastery and to be always poor and chaste and obedient.

Almighty God, I thank you for the great mercy you have shown in assigning me to this place in Purgatory where I might atone for my many sins.

But I must go on, for as yet I have not told the worst of them, and I sense that on the other side time grows short and the woman's danger increases . . .

When I left the Jew's house, Rebecca was again waiting in the stand of trees beside the river. But this time when she pressed against me, the hair shirt of the Carthusian rule, a garment we wear always beneath our habits, scraped against my skin, and I was reminded of the suffering of eternal damnation. It was enough to overcome the carnal heat that burned my flesh, though my cock stiffened at the mere thought of the sin to which I had not as yet succumbed.

I returned quickly to the Charterhouse, but despite the urgency to be back in my cell before the bell rang for the midnight office, I was forced to pause when I saw nailed above the great doors the quarter part of the carcass of the Venerable Father. It had been put there since I left, and below it was a notice saying the thing must not be removed, "on pain of an even more terrible death for he who did the action and all who encouraged him therein."

Giacomo the Lombard, known also as the Jew of Holborn
From the Waiting Place

I do not know why I am commanded to tell my story, nor who it is who listens. But I am grateful to be in this place that is neither earth nor Gehenna, where the eternal fire burns. I have, I know, much for which to atone, and I am promised that to tell what happened between me and my daughter and he who was known in the Charterhouse as Dom Justin will help erase their stain. So be it.

I am not required to tell everything: not how I came to leave Lombardy and smuggle myself into London to seek greater fortune, nor of the sweet young maiden I married there, a Lombard who was secretly a Jew like myself and a number of others, nor of her death hours after she gave birth to our only child, a daughter. What matters to the story I must tell is that when he was still at the beginning of his rise to the great power he was to wield, the man known as Thomas Cromwell learned my secret. Even with such vision as is granted me here, I do not know if it was his lackey, the draftsman Richard Scranton, who somehow exposed me, though I suspected that to be the case. Such details are of no importance now. It is enough to say that Thomas Cromwell commanded me to leave the town and live in the rural fastness of Holborn, there to seek on his behalf the rumored treasures of the disgraced Templars.

From the very moment I was assigned the task, I knew that if it was the will of Boré Olam that I should discover such Jewish treasures, I would never give them into the hands of any gentile. When, after a year in the Holborn countryside, I did indeed stumble on such treasures as had come from ancient Jerusalem, defiance was already rooted in my heart.

In this place where neither past nor present has meaning, it all seems of such little import . . . But I am given to understand I must begin my story at a specific point in earthly time, the night when the monk came to my cottage beside the river Fleet, and contrary to the many previous occasions, I was not there waiting for him.

Great peril had been my constant companion during the Holborn years, but I did not know how much it increased when I chose that particular evening to go to the pit. I could not anticipate that Master Cromwell would on that occasion not send his usual vassal but instead would come himself to meet his treacherous Carthusian. Even if I'd known, I might have done nothing different.

I found the pit irresistible. Since I discovered the place, it had infected my mind and churned in my belly and demanded my speedy return. So that evening I left Rebecca to receive the stinking lackey I expected Cromwell to send, a small, dark man with the mark of the pox on his face and always a stench of dead rat about him. He was an unwelcome guest, but Rebecca and I were accustomed to him. The strange trysts between him and the Carthusian had gone on for nearly four years, since my daughter was eleven and just beginning to show her womanliness and the uncommon beauty that was so much like her mother's. Rebecca looked unhappy at the prospect of the meeting—I had seen how the poxed man eyed her and so, no doubt, had she—but she saw that I had made up my mind and did not argue.

That same day I had been testing different compounds to make new things appear old—a necessary part of the great deception I practiced on Thomas Cromwell. When the latest such experiment proved unsatisfactory I threw the mixture into the river. The result was first a bright blue flame, then a ghostly white glow that lingered above the water for many hours. I had long been a goldsmith, but I had never seen such a thing before. It entered my mind that perhaps the days the ancient rabbis promised were near, the end times when Boré Olam would send the Chosen One to judge the world and bring peace and justice to all who were worthy and cast the rest into Gehenna.

I had sins enough to feel no confidence about how I would fare in that reckoning, but I reasoned it might go better with me if I had at least saved some of what the gentiles had taken from the Holy City, and from me and my fellow Jews. That hope—divine forgiveness—is why I had the audacity to give no true treasure to Master Cromwell but only the occasional copy of one of the remarkable things I found. My forgeries were so cleverly crafted, he believed them to be genuine and kept me in place to continue to search on his behalf. I did not, however, fool myself about what would happen if he ever discovered the ruse, or for any reason became convinced he had no further need of me. In those days agony beyond description lurked always just over my shoulder.

❖

8

It had clouded over in Coram's Fields. Annie thought that's what Geoff meant when he said, "Here comes trouble."

"I brought an umbrella." She reached for her tote bag.

"Not that. We're nobbled." He nodded toward a uniformed security guard approaching them with a look of purpose.

"I don't understand," Annie said.

"No adults," Geoff explained, "are supposed to be in Coram's Fields unless accompanied by a child."

The guard was a few steps away. The boy with the white-blond hair, the one Geoff had originally kicked the soccer ball to, appeared at Geoff's shoulder. "Can I play a bit longer, Dad?"

"Sure, as long as Mum here doesn't mind."

"Not a bit," Annie said.

The guard hesitated, then turned away. Geoff and the boy slapped a high five. The boy left. "Better get away while we can," Geoff said. "Who knows, they may bring back hanging."

"And drawing and quartering." Annie gathered up her things and they headed for the exit.

Geoff turned to wave at the kids playing soccer, but they'd gone back to their game and didn't notice. He wrested her Davis School tote bag from her grip, then pretended to stumble under its weight. "What do you have in here besides an umbrella, bricks?"

"Sketchbooks," Annie said, "and lots of maps. I was planning a stroll along the banks of the Fleet."

About then the heavens opened. They dashed for the nearest pub, a rather dingy place on Lambs Conduit Street. "I expect this one dates from around merry old 1972," Geoff said.

"Doesn't matter as long as the roof doesn't leak."

Annie slid into a booth, and he went up to the bar and came back with a squat, fat bottle of Schweppes Bitter Lemon, a pint of ale, and a plate of anemic-looking crustless sandwiches. "They don't do *citron presse*. This is the best I could manage." He handed over the soda and nodded toward his beer. "Okay?"

"Of course okay." When she was drinking, one of her coping mechanisms was to tuck a few bills in various pockets. That way wherever she was when she sobered up, she'd maybe have enough cash to get somewhere else. The habit lingered. She found a ten-pound note in her jeans and offered it to him.

Geoff waved the money away and picked up one of the sandwiches. "Cheese and pickle. The only thing on offer. You do know the Fleet's an underground sewage ditch these days, don't you?"

"Yes, but it was a major waterway in 1535. That's when the man I'm trying to trace, the one called the Jew of Holborn, lived here. I think he was a craftsman, perhaps a goldsmith who needed to plunge his finished pieces into water to cool them quickly. He'd probably live close to the riverbank, where he'd have access."

"I take it he really was a Jew—it wasn't only a nickname?"

"Apparently so," Annie said. "Though it was illegal for Jews to be in England in the early fifteen hundreds." She reached for a sandwich. It looked like supermarket cheddar smeared with dark brown relish, and the bread hadn't been fresh for two days. She put it back and dug into the depths of her tote. "The Shalom people have collected a number of 1535 references to him."

Geoff took the papers, riffled through a few, then gave them back. "German," he said. "Maggie tried, but I can't read it." He picked up one of the sandwiches, made a face but started eating.

"I can't read it either." Annie flipped a few of the sheets and offered the documents a second time. "Everything's been translated." Geoff ignored the papers and kept looking at her. She put them on the table and reached for the soda. Then, after a long swallow: "The papers are a collection of letters—answers to a questionnaire—from synagogues in cities that are in France or Germany today but in 1535 were part of the old Rhenish Palatinate."

Geoff took another sandwich. "These are terrible."

"I thought they must be. Why are you eating them?"

"I'm ravenous. It's too miserable out there to leave and look for something better. About that translation." He indicated her papers. "Who did you get to do it?"

"No one. Shalom arranged—" She saw his expression and broke off. "They sent me the digital copy first. The German wasn't translated then. And I know what you think, but—"

"I don't think anything yet. Go on."

"As you probably know, the Shalom Foundation was set up to study Northern European Jewry from the Middle Ages to the Second World War."

"I know that's Weinraub's story," he said.

"It's true," Annie insisted, tapping the sheaf of papers to make her point. "This is documentation of a study conducted over the last couple of years. They went looking for Jewish memorabilia that might still be in the hands of congregations that survived the Nazis."

There was half a sandwich left. "Last chance," he said. Annie shook her head. He picked it up. "I take it some things were found."

"Yes, some remarkable Judaica. Often old and rare, because that's what people took the greatest care to hide."

"That part makes sense."

"It all does," she insisted. "When the questionnaires they sent out came back, there were five stories with a remarkable commonality. In each case, the item was identified as a gift from a man living in London in 1535."

"Your Jew of Holborn," Geoff said.

"Exactly. Two of the synagogues have contemporary proof of provenance, sixteenth-century inventories. The other items show up in later documentation but still pretty early. And in every case the attribution is the same. A gift received in 1535 from the Jew of Holborn. The same wording passed down through each congregation's history."

"In German."

"Of course. Old German, obviously, given the dates."

"Which you can't read, but not to worry, your Shalom Foundation took care of that and had a translation done for you."

"Yes."

He took a few seconds, then nodded toward her papers. "Seems odd Weinraub would give someone without German a research assignment based on the information in those documents."

Annie put everything back into her bag. "I read Latin," she said. "And I'm fluent in Italian."

"Fair enough. It just seems—" He broke off.

"Go on. Say it."

"Okay, it seems Weinraub is taking advantage of the fact that you're a lovely and highly intelligent female who happens to be particularly . . . fragile."

"*Fragile* being code for a drunk."

"That's not what I meant." And when she didn't respond: "Look, connecting the dots is part of my job. I've learned not to jump to conclusions, but sometimes the obvious answer is the right one. If Philip Jeremiah Weinraub picked an architectural historian who for ten years has done nothing in her field, and who doesn't speak the language of his source documents, he has a reason. He's a nutter, but he can afford to hire anyone he wants for this task."

"So why choose the deeply flawed Annie Kendall?"

This time he didn't contradict her. "I take it you replied to an advert he ran somewhere. What do you know about the other applicants?"

"Nothing," she said. Then before he could comment: "I thought you were after Weinraub for plotting an assassination. What makes him a nutter? To use your term."

"*Extremist* is probably a better word. I know he's given money to various Israeli groups who want to restore the worship of biblical times. Rebuild the Second Temple and Jew it the old way. Sacrifice sheep and goats and the occasional cow."

"And," she said quietly, "given that the ruins of the Second Temple are under one or another of two of Islam's holiest sites . . ."

"Exactly. How the Israelis are supposed to get control of the place to do their 'rebuilding' doesn't bear thinking about." He swallowed the last of his ale and pushed the glass away. "Look, I'm not religious. I couldn't care less how anyone wants to worship. Stare at the sun, dance beneath the full moon, drink chicken blood—it's all the same to me. But none of that applies in the Middle East. It's a tinderbox, and I think Weinraub is playing with matches."

Annie took a long drink of her soda. A tinderbox capable of setting fires all over the world, forcing people to jump out of hundred-story windows, getting them blown up on the commute home from work. "You were asking about my job with Shalom," she said. "I didn't answer any ad. Last March the foundation wrote and invited me to talk to them about a project. A month later I was told I could have the job, but I had to start immediately. So I walked out of the Davis School and pretty much straight onto a plane."

Sidney's voice played in her head. *You have a contract, Annie my girl. A sober citizen does not leave her employer in the lurch. Say you'll do it, but in June, not May.*

Weinraub had insisted she be in London by May 1. The time, he'd said, was right. She hadn't asked right for what. Philip Weinraub said jump, and she said how high.

Geoff put his hand over hers. She tingled, acutely sensitive to his touch. The more he touched her, the more she responded.

"Annie," he said, "look at it from their point of view. Whatever they sent you here to find, it's been waiting five hundred years. The urgency doesn't make much sense, does it? Unless the point was to make you more . . . vulnerable."

"You mean more easily manipulated."

"Something like that."

"All I could concentrate on," she admitted, "was that the assignment seemed tailor-made for me."

"Exactly," he said. "Tailor-made." He reached for his phone. "There's someone I'd like you to meet. Will tomorrow be okay?"

9

"Sit down, darlings. Geoffrey, tell me why you brought me this gorgeous creature."

"Her name's Annie Kendall. Annie, this is Maggie Harris née Silber, who among her many distinctions is my mother."

They were in a section of North London called Primrose Hill. Trendy, Geoff had explained on the way over. People like Jamie Oliver and Kate Moss and Jude Law regularly moved in and out of Primrose Hill. "Maggie bought her flat in the nineties when it was a hell of a lot less expensive. It went through the roof in the early 2000s, then cratered with the rest of London property. Now it's a gold mine again."

The gold mine—five rooms on two floors—was in a short street off Regent's Park Road and crammed with overstuffed, chintz-covered furniture. And books. And vases full of flowers. "Don't be fooled by all this," Geoff said. "Maggie's posh flat used to be a grocer's shop. So my dad had the last laugh."

"He means because Jack Harris, my husband and Geoffrey's father, also had a grocer's shop, and I worked there until the day he died. I hated it. Sit near me, Annie." Maggie patted a wing chair upholstered in a riotous assortment of roses. Geoff chose a pink-and-white-striped love seat. The cushions were so plump, they seemed to envelop him.

"I really and truly loathed that shop," Maggie said. She was busy with delicate flowered cups and saucers and a matching fat-bellied teapot. "So when poor Jack dropped dead behind the counter, I put up the closed sign and telephoned the estate agents before I rang Geoffrey, who was up at Cambridge at the time. The property was sold within five minutes of Jack going into the ground. I went from the graveyard to the solicitor's to sign the papers. Milk and sugar, Annie?"

"Just milk, thanks, Mrs. Harris."

"Call me Maggie. Everyone does, even Geoffrey. You've seen that mausoleum he lives in? Imagine doing that to a nice Victorian terrace house. I think women are happy to go upstairs to his bedroom because at least it has walls. Sorry, am I being indiscreet?"

"Of course you are," her son said. "When are you not?"

Maggie sat back and put her feet on a tasseled velvet hassock. She was nearly eighty-two, according to Geoff, white haired, not as tall as her son, and very thin, wearing pearls and a silk caftan of an intense sea blue that matched her eyes. "I am indiscreet when it suits me," Maggie said. "And you are an American, Annie Kendall. I like that. Tell me about yourself."

"In due time," Geoff said. "I brought Annie to hear your story." Then, turning to her: "Maggie was shanghaied in 1945 by the WAC, the American women's army corps as it was then. She wasn't yet sixteen."

"That's because it was the Americans who found me," Maggie explained. "Bill Donovan ran the American OSS in World War Two—you call it the CIA today. He got the idea of testing the older children of the Kindertransport, the Jewish children Britain managed to rescue shortly before the actual start of the war. Geoffrey told you about my being part of that?"

Annie nodded.

"In 1944 the Yanks started looking for the *Kinder* who had been a bit older when they were brought to England, so they might actually read and write German. If they had retained those skills, along with the English they must have learned in the years since they arrived, they could be extremely useful."

"I'm guessing as spies," Annie said, looking with a certain amount of incredulity at the elegant woman opposite.

"Of course," Maggie said with a chuckle. "But perhaps not the sort you're thinking of. Admiral Sir Hugh Sinclair had set up what they called the Government Code and Cypher School at Bletchley Park in Buckinghamshire. That's where they broke the Enigma code in '39. Do you know about that?"

"I think so," Annie said. "It was the code that, once they broke it, let them know everything the Germans were doing."

Maggie smiled. "Almost everything. Anyway, Sir Hugh wasn't convinced the idea would work, but he agreed to give it a chance. I was nine years old when I came to England, so naturally I was on Colonel Donovan's list."

"What did the Americans think of your German?" Annie could detect only the faintest traces of a non-English accent in Maggie's speech.

"That it was fine, but they were also looking for code-breaking skills. Usually mathematicians and musicians score the highest. Donovan's people figured if you could find Jewish children who spoke both English and German and also had natural puzzle-solving ability, you would have the complete package."

"And you fit the bill."

"Yes. I had in fact some musical ability, and unlike many of the *Kinder,* I was fortunate in my placement in '39. I was taken in by a wonderful woman, a spinster as we called them back then. She helped me learn English and encouraged me to keep up my German. Also, she was a piano teacher and gave me lessons." Maggie nodded to an upright piano in the corner. It was surrounded by so much furniture, Annie hadn't noticed it. "That was hers. She died after Jack and I were married, and I've had it ever since. Geoffrey was seriously good when he was a boy, but his father insisted no footballer could play the piano. 'It will make him a nancy boy,' Jack said. So now my son is not a footballer, and he is also not a concert pianist."

"I'm sorry I turned out such a useless good-for-nothing. You're getting ahead of your story, Maggie. Forget about Portsmouth. Tell Annie more about Bletchley."

"It was the most uncomfortable drafty barn you can imagine, but what was happening there was . . . marvelous. A few hundred people had worked on Enigma. When I arrived in January of '45, I was one of nine thousand drones, all of us doing grueling, painstaking work, even boring sometimes, but desperately important. We monitored every word the Germans spoke over the airwaves, as well as all the data from the radio operators the Allies had behind Nazi lines. The Y stations, the listening posts, sent it all to Bletchley to be processed."

Maggie turned away, ostensibly to put her teacup and saucer onto one of the room's many tiny tables. Really, Annie thought, to drag herself out of the past. When she turned back to them, she was smiling brightly. "Why are we talking about this? Geoffrey darling, I don't believe you brought Annie here to listen to an old woman's stories. Tell me the real reason."

"Annie's seen a monk," Geoff said. "In the back bedroom of the flat she's renting in Southampton Row."

Maggie's eyebrows shot up, then settled back down. "I take it," she said, "he's not simply a lodger someone forgot to mention?"

Annie shook her head. "I know it sounds incredible, but—"

Maggie held up a hand. "Let me tell you the three things I took away from Bletchley. I can curse like a sailor in seven different languages. I know a fine claret when I taste one because we regularly raided Sir Hugh's prewar cellar. And most of all I know that very often things are not what they seem. So what else do we know about your lodger?"

"Annie has only seen him once, but she made a sketch, and he looks exactly like me."

"Annie, my son is a prize beyond price, at least in my view. But even I do not believe he's a monk."

Geoff did not rise to the bait. "We think Annie's monk was alive in the early fifteen hundreds. Tudor London. That's her period. Annie has letters after her name. She's Dr. Kendall, and she's an architectural historian over here looking for someone called the Jew of Holborn."

"No Jews could officially be in London at the period," Annie said, "but a few passed as Lombard traders and craftsmen. The one I'm after appears to have been identified but somehow managed to remain. And he had access to magnificent things. Ancient Jewish artifacts. I'm trying to locate the man, place him in history."

"And the connection between this Jew and your monk?" Maggie asked.

"I don't know," Annie said. "I think there is one, but sometimes I'm not sure."

Maggie had been sitting forward, listening intently. Now she leaned back. "I know nothing about monks and less about Tudor London. But puzzles? Those I know. There is always a connection."

"Perfect segue," Geoff said. The sheaf of translated German documents was sticking out of Annie's tote bag. "May I?" he asked, and when she nodded, he passed them to his mother. "This is what we came to ask you about. I want to know how accurate the translations are. I think things may be left out, if not actually changed."

Maggie took the documents and turned to Annie. "I take it you also want to know how accurate the translations are? This isn't just my son thinking he knows everything and no woman can possibly have a valid opinion?"

Annie had gone for a run earlier. The Covent Garden route. A kid—hair as bright red as her own, maybe seventeen or eighteen—had fallen into step beside her on Kingsway. They ran in tandem for some ten yards, then he flashed her a grin, sprinted ahead, and got lost in the crowd. Back at the flat Annie filled three pages of a sketchbook with drawings of his retreating back. The images became smaller and smaller and he got younger and younger. Eventually it was a three-year-old Ari toddling in front of her, barely able to keep his footing but determined to try. She knew what it cost not to face up to the tough choices. "I want to know the truth," she said.

Maggie looked at her intently and nodded, as if she were pleased by the answer. "Then I'll see if I can tell you." She put on narrow, rimless glasses and bent her head over the pages, quickly turning them, once or twice going back to look at an earlier entry.

Annie carried the tea things into the small kitchen at the back of the flat. It took no more than five minutes to wash the dishes—she couldn't see a dishwasher—and leave them to drain beside the sink. When she returned, Maggie's eyes were closed, the papers were on her lap, and the rimless glasses dangled from her hand. Geoff was sitting quietly, watching his mother. Annie took her place in the rose-strewn chair.

"Play something, Geoffrey," Maggie said with her eyes still closed.

"I'm way out of practice."

"Doesn't matter. It's only to help me think. My Bletchley music."

Geoff shoved a chair out of the way so he could pull out the piano bench, then flipped back the cover on the keys. He played a few notes of a 1940s standard, singing the lyrics softly in a pleasant if unremarkable voice: " 'Lovely, never, ever change . . . love you . . . Just the way you look tonight.' " He riffed a couple of more bars, then stopped. "More?"

"Not now," Maggie said. "And you're right, you are way out of practice. That was terrible, but never mind." Then to Annie: "Sometimes it helps to hear the music of the old days, to remember how we did it then. In this case"—she shrugged—"I can't say much about your papers on such a quick reading. Except . . . You've noticed that the numbers are all written out?" Annie nodded. "Well, they're a little peculiar. But much of this is in very old German. You'll have to leave it with me if you want more. One thing I can tell you, however. About your puzzle . . . you need a learned rabbi."

"Don't tell me you know one," her son said.

"Of course I do." Maggie was reaching for the phone as she spoke.

"Simon can see you Monday," she said when she hung up. "Two in the afternoon. Don't be late—he's a busy man. One of the foremost Jewish scholars in Europe."

"How in God's name," her son asked, "are you on first-name terms with a Jewish scholar?"

"Because when I met him in '45," Maggie said, "he wasn't a scholar. He wasn't even sure he was Jewish. Not the way he is now. Religion he got after the war. The brains he always had. Simon was a top-level code breaker, one of the clever blokes in what we called hut three. Their job was to look at the whole picture while the rest of us slaved over tiny details. If I tell you he was not quite twenty-one, you can guess how remark-able that was."

"I think," Geoff said, "it's better if I don't ask how a barely sixteen-year-old *Mädchen* drone got to know a top-level code breaker."

"Not unless you want me to tell you," Maggie said. "Now you must go home. All this talk has exhausted me."

"I am so sorry!"

"My dear Annie, I have not had this much fun in years." Maggie tapped the sheaf of papers. "Something to think about besides whether I remembered to take my pills, or should I have fish or chicken for my lunch. You can be sorry if you wish—I'm ecstatic."

Then, with only a token attempt not to be overheard: "I like this one, Geoffrey. And I'm sure Emma would as well."

Maggie's flat was on Sharpleshall Street, a few steps from Regent's Park Road. They turned left, then left again. Because according to Geoff, their best chance to find a cab was at the edge of Primrose Hill, a steep grassy rise he said they must someday climb. "There's an astonishing view of London from the top."

Her heart gave a little bounce at the casual assurance they would spend other times together. She thought of saying that Henry VIII had hunted deer and wild boar in what was now Primrose Hill and Regent's Park. Instead she blurted, "I take it Emma was your wife."

"Yes. Entirely too good for me, as she and everyone else agreed. But Emma and Maggie—now there was a match made in heaven. Sometimes I think Emma only married me so the indomitable Maggie could be her mother-in-law."

"Maggie is lovely," Annie said when they were in the cab Geoff had hailed, heading up Regent's Park Road. "Tell me what happened to her after the war."

"Pretty much what happened to so many who had been dragged out of childhood into Armageddon. When it was over, Maggie was just another young woman in a place where too many young men were dead."

"Did she move back in with the piano teacher?"

He shook his head. "No, she was demobbed in London, and she stayed. But code breaking wasn't much in demand in peacetime. For a while she played piano in a variety of Soho clubs."

"Is that where she met your father?"

"No chance of that. He wasn't a Soho type. The way she tells it, the gigs dried up as she got older. When she met Jack Harris, she was working in a souvenir shop on Brighton Pier, and he'd come for a day at the seaside."

"Oh dear," Annie said.

"Oh dear indeed. She says she figured by then she was too old to get pregnant, so they weren't cautious. Next thing you know, I was on the way. Enter grubby old Portsmouth and the grocer's shop. She hated it from the first minute, but as she saw it, she had no choice."

They pulled up in front of Bristol House. It was in Annie's mind to ask him to come up. They were, after all, consenting adults who obviously liked each other. A little no-strings-attached sex would be good for them. Hell, it might even be terrific.

They got out of the cab, and Geoff leaned into the window of the front seat and handed over the fare. Annie pulled a five-pound note out of a pocket. As usual, Geoff refused to take it. "I'm on three hundred a year. You've spent the last four years teaching in a girls' school." Then: "I'll come up with you. Just to make sure everything's okay."

She opened her mouth to say she'd like that. What came out was: "No need. I'll be fine. You're sure you want to go with me on Monday?"

She thought she saw a flash of disappointment, but he recovered quickly. "Are you mad, woman? A chance to meet one of the many who knew Maggie in the old days? A learned rabbi, no less. Wild horses couldn't keep me away."

He leaned a bit forward, and it seemed he might kiss her, even if just on the cheek, but it didn't happen. "See you Monday," he said. Was she only imagining a new coolness? "I'll call that morning so we can set it up."

Annie watched until he turned the corner into Cosmo Place, then she went into the newsagent's next door. Among their postcards was a view of the gigantic Ferris wheel on the Thames known as the London Eye. According to the tiny print below the picture, it had been taken from the top of Primrose Hill. She bought two the same and wrote them at the counter. The first was for Ari. *Isn't this the biggest Ferris wheel you've ever seen? Love, Mom.*

The second card was for Sidney O'Toole. *Miss you. Hope you're not still angry with me. I am really truly fine. Annie xxxxx.* She had to fish in her bag to come up with Sidney's snail-mail address, near MIT in Massachusetts. Usually they communicated by e-mail, though since she'd quit her job—Sidney had put his own painstakingly rebuilt reputation on the line to get the Davis School to hire her—they weren't communicating at all.

After she'd dropped both cards into the mailbox on the corner, Annie allowed the obvious question to surface in her mind: Why had she let Geoff leave like that?

It was, she decided, the no-strings-attached part she wasn't sure of. She had a feeling strings were sprouting from every inch of her.

Among the many tomes on church history her father had published, there was one small thin volume called *On Scholarship.* It had originally been written as a magazine article, but it had proved so popular, it was reissued in hardcover. Today, Annie thought, it would simply have been put online, or published as an e-book single. Essentially *On Scholarship* was a love poem to the joy and exhilaration of leaving no stone unturned.

Maggie Harris's story had made her think of it. Maggie had called what she and thousands of others did during the war "grueling, painstaking work, even boring sometimes, but desperately important." Her eyes had been alight when she'd said that. John Kendall would have understood.

Annie was sitting at the dining room table. In the background the

BBC was murmuring about the Vatican denying the pope's failing health. Duplicate copies of the documents she'd left with Maggie were spread out on the table in front of her. She picked up a pencil and underlined the names of each of the congregations that had one of the Jew of Holborn's treasures. She hadn't been given street addresses, only the names of the towns in which the congregations were located.

Before she left for London, she had made a copy of a map of the Rhenish Palatinate as it was in the early 1500s and circled the places where the gifts were found. They formed a slightly rippling north-south chain between Strasbourg, which was today in France, and Freiburg, across the river Rhine in the foothills of the Black Forest mountains of southwestern Germany. The distance between them was some sixty miles, and using modern roads and bridges, you could drive it in a little over an hour. In the early sixteenth century it would have been a treacherous journey across rivers and through forests involving many perilous days, perhaps weeks.

Annie pushed aside the papers and pulled her laptop closer. After twenty minutes she had located mailing addresses for three of the five congregations, those in Offenburg, Metz, and Breisach.

10

"You're sure, Dr. Kendall," Simon Cohen said, "it was a Carthusian you saw?"

"Annie, please, Rabbi. And yes, I'm sure." Cohen was holding her sketchbook. Annie pointed to the drawing of the Bristol House monk bowing before the crucifix. "The bit of material here toward the bottom of the habit is unique to Carthusians. It's called a band. I didn't realize I'd noticed it until I sketched it. That sometimes happens when I draw."

"Ah yes," Cohen said. "I understand. Memory is one of the most unpredictable of human accomplishments."

Well, at least that much was easy. Maggie's scholarly rabbi hadn't yet written her off as crazy—a nutter, as Geoff might say.

The three of them—Annie, Geoff, and Rabbi Cohen—were in his study at the front of a redbrick, single-family house in a leafy, suburban-feeling part of London called Hampstead. The room was lined with books, and there were piles of papers and folders and stacks of more books covering most surfaces. Their host must be a widower or a bachelor, Annie decided. Maybe it wasn't too late for Maggie and her rabbi. Cohen looked a lot younger than the mid-eighties that Maggie's story made him.

"Please understand," he said, "I have little to offer on the question of your . . ." He hesitated. "Your sightings. Understanding mysticism, explaining it, that's not one of my strengths. And as you can imagine, I know very little about monks. So Maggie didn't send you to me for that. But your 1535 Jew of Holborn, and the possibility that there may be a very sophisticated code hidden in your documents—on those topics I may be of some use."

Cohen had dark hair, no gray, and a small, carefully trimmed goatee, plus a habit of stroking it when he spoke. His knuckles, Annie noticed, were swollen and the skin reddened and rough, a contrast to the scholarly image. "These gifts from your Jew of Holborn, Annie, they are not unrelated."

"I know. They're all to do with ritual sacrifice, aren't they?"

"With *korbanot*. Precisely. Moreover, *kaf, ma'akhelet, mizrak*—these are very old words. Rare even."

"I believe *mizrak* occurs in Exodus," Annie said. "And *ma'akhelet* in Genesis."

"Exactly so. I am impressed," Cohen added with a small smile. He turned to Geoff. "I'm guessing you have no idea what we're talking about. Maggie is wonderful, but about being a Jew I don't think she taught you much."

"Rabbi, I don't want to fly false colors. I have an interest in certain political aspects of this situation, and of course I'm fascinated that the monk Annie saw looked just like me, but personally—I don't consider myself a Jew in any religious sense, and I haven't come for spiritual instruction."

"That's as may be, but make no mistake, if, God forbid, there should come along more people who want to put Jews in ovens, for them you will be a Jew. You are for us as well. Your mother was a Jew because her mother was. You are therefore also a Jew. Nonobservant, yes, but still a member of the tribe."

"Fair enough," Geoff said. "But that's not Annie's concern just now."

"I agree, it is not." Cohen turned to Annie. "And I doubt the specifics of *korbanot* are your focus either."

"What I'm trying to do," she said, "is locate this Jew of Holborn, see if I can discover who he was and place him in history. At this point all we know from the documents the Shalom Foundation has collected is that he lived in 1535."

"And do you think he has something to do with your monk?"

"I'm not sure. So far the only connection I can find is that it was in May 1535 that the first monks from the London Charterhouse were executed at Tyburn."

"But according to Maggie, you have uncovered some drawings of the executed monks, and they don't look like this one"—he nodded at the sketchbook—"nor like Geoffrey."

"Not remotely."

Cohen shook his head. "This seems then to get us nowhere. Let us leave aside your ghostly visitor and concentrate on matters I may be able to help with, your documents." He put on a pair of glasses and turned to his computer, keying in a few commands with sure, quick strokes.

"Maggie mentioned peculiar numbers," Annie said, "but she didn't explain."

"They are scattered throughout. In parentheses, as if they were simply giving in numeric symbols a value spelled out in words. Sometimes, however, numbers appear in one string—the words or the symbols—that do not occur or are different in the English translation."

Geoff stood up and went to stand behind Cohen, so he could see the screen. "A code," he said.

"We think so, yes."

"I take it," Annie said, "by 'we' you mean you and Maggie."

"Indeed." The rabbi smiled. "Maybe we are simply having a second childhood. A pair of has-beens remembering when they were hot-blooded young geniuses pursuing evil." The words were accompanied by a derisive laugh. "Only I don't think so. Because it seems . . ." He entered a few more keystrokes. The screen was filled with obscure numbers and signs and symbols.

Annie leaned forward. "Kabbalah," she said. A few of the teachers at the Davis School had been taking lessons. Some of the students as well. Kabbalah was right up there with Wicca in the New Age spiritual hit parade.

"Yes," the rabbi said, "but remember, mysticism isn't my line. I can't explain the ins and outs of kabbalah. The numerology that accompanies it, however—that's something else." He hit a couple of keys, and the kabbalah site disappeared and was replaced with an e-mail from Maggie. Annie couldn't read it from where she sat, but she saw it included strings of numbers.

"Some years after we all left Bletchley," Cohen said, "in the fifties, I was living with my family deciding about whether to become a rabbi, and I got a letter from what I thought was the Foreign Office requesting I come to Whitehall for a meeting. It was not the sort of summons you could refuse. Turned out someone from Special Branch wanted to see me. I had already declined an invitation to become a career spook, but they had a code they couldn't break, and they thought maybe I could. Maggie was in London then, performing in a gentlemen's club."

Annie heard the sound of a small snort. Apparently Cohen did as well. He did not turn around. "Your mother, Geoffrey, was playing piano in an entirely respectable place. And in case you do not know, she was beautiful. And marvelous. Anyway, we got together over this code."

"Did you break it?" Annie asked.

"Yes, though I was not always sure we should have done. Britain was no longer administering the Palestinian Mandate, and in large measure their former enemy the Irgun—today we would call them terrorists—had been absorbed into the Mossad. But back then Whitehall still thought it ruled the world, and certain elements of the old guard were never going to side with Jews. Maggie and I had no doubt that whatever information we gave them would be used to play off the Arabs against the Israelis, and not to the advantage of the latter."

He removed his glasses and held them up to the light, wiping them carefully and with concentration. Neither Annie nor Geoff spoke. Cohen replaced the glasses and went on. "In the end we were English Jews. England, not Israel, was and is our country." He waved a dismissive hand. "An old argument. We broke Mossad's code for our Whitehall masters, exactly as we'd been asked to do. It was, as it happened, based on the numerology of kabbalah, which is one of the reasons it was so very difficult. As soon as she saw your papers, Maggie remembered the lessons we'd learned back then, and thought maybe your documents contained a similar code. Now"—he tapped a few more numbers into the computer—"I think I am sure."

Annie realized her hands were clenched into fists. "What does it say?"

Cohen guffawed. "I have no idea. Neither, I assure you, does Maggie. It takes a great deal of time and effort, almost mind-boggling persistence, to break a sophisticated code. At Bletchley we had the first practical computer, the Colossus. It filled a room. This"—he nodded at his desktop PC—"is a true miracle. So it's easier. But easy? Never. For now, we're saying only that we think the Shalom documents contain a code, and it is somewhat reminiscent of a code we worked on before. So we're willing to try and break it. But there's one thing I should tell you. I don't—"

A soft knock, then the door of the study opened. A woman in a nurse's uniform poked her head into the room. "It's three, Rabbi Cohen. I have to leave. She's sleeping, but . . ."

"Yes, of course. Just a moment more."

The nurse withdrew and closed the door. Cohen stood up. "I must go. My wife can't be alone. Alzheimer's." He rushed on, not giving them a chance to speak. "You have my card, and we will surely be in touch. Only I must tell you, Annie, that I have grave doubts about Mr. Weinraub's judgment. If I should find anything here that indicates—"

"What? What do you think you'll find?"

"I don't know. I simply wish to be clear. It is possible, my dear, that our interests may diverge. You are looking for an historical truth. I have no interest in suppressing such truths, whatever they may be. But if Weinraub and the *meshuggeners* around him, many of whom intend—unilaterally, with no prior agreement—to rebuild the Temple on a site that millions of Arabs consider holy to Islam were to get their way . . . in my view such a scheme would destabilize the Middle East and truly threaten the existence of Israel. I cannot speak for your mother"—a nod to Geoff—"but this time my conscience may point me unequivocally in a direction that puts British government interests above those of fellow Jews whose wisdom I strongly question. Which, my dear, will put you in direct conflict with the people who are paying you to seek facts that to them may not be merely academic."

Annie hesitated.

"I understand conflicts of interest, my dear. As I explained." Cohen went to the door of his office but didn't immediately open it. "Moreover, these documents belong to you. If you choose to close the matter right now, that is that, so far as I'm concerned. Do you wish me to continue?"

Annie held her breath for a few seconds. She looked at Geoff. He was watching her. Measuring her, she thought. Simon Cohen as well. She exhaled. "Between my professional concerns and blowing up the Middle East—no contest, Rabbi. And no real conflict of interest. Please continue."

Cohen beamed, but it was Geoff's barely perceptible nod of approval that warmed her.

That evening, when she was cleaning up after a late supper—over the soft sound of the radio telling her that the Vatican insisted the pope would resume his duties shortly—Annie heard the singing.

"*Salve Regina, Mater misericordiae, vita, dulcedo, et spes nostra, salve.*"

She had sworn she wouldn't open the door between the kitchen and the back hall, but she could not help herself. She peered into the dimness. The door to the little room was closed and there was nothing to see, but the singing was louder. "*Ad te clamamus, exsules filii Hevae . . .*"

Louder still as she walked down the passageway. "*Ad te suspiramus, gementes et flentes in hac lacrimarum valle.*"

Annie stopped a few inches from the bedroom door. The sound was all around her. "*O clemens, O pia, O dulcis Virgo Maria.*"

The flat had been chilly when she came home. She'd pulled on a thick sweatshirt. But standing in front of the door that led to some vision or place or thing beyond her imagining, it was not just warm but oppressively hot.

She stretched out her hand and turned the knob.

The door opened to complete quiet and the familiar, ordinary furniture. If anything, the little room was colder than the hall. The veil of sweat she had generated a few seconds earlier cooled to a shiver-making slick. "Who are you?" She whispered the words at first, then shouted them. "Who are you, and what do you want with me? If you've got some kind of message, just tell me."

The silence mocked her. Annie pressed her forehead to the wall and punched it repeatedly in frustration.

Dom Justin
From the Waiting Place

Danger! Beware you are in danger!

I call out to the woman, but I cannot make her hear me. I understand it is frequently thus, that breaking through is very difficult, usually impossible. Go on with your story, I am told. A way to reach her may present itself . . .

On one night soon after the martyrdom of the Venerable Father and the visit of my master to the Jew's cottage, and though I saw no speckled quail's egg, I determined to go to the house of the Jew of Holborn.

In truth I went because my dreams were tormented by the Jew's daughter. I woke each morning drowning in her smell, my carnal nature evident in my twisted habit and sodden bedclothes. Though I took the discipline every day, using the knotted cord on my bare shoulders until I drew blood, it did not calm my lust. But though I admit now that I went merely to have a sight of Rebecca, I insisted to myself that my excuse for leaving the monastery that night was that I had a real and important errand to perform. So on the night of which I speak, I did as was my custom when summoned by the speckled egg. I slipped from my cell and out the tradesman's gate as soon as evening fell.

The walk to the Jew's was uneventful, and I spent the time thinking on the events that had brought both him and me to this place.

When first I met him, I did not know the goldsmith was descended from Christ killers; he was to me only Giacomo the Lombard. Thomas Cromwell sent me many times to the smith's workshop on errands to do with the seals of office the man beat out on his anvil, and never did I bring back intelligence that would reveal him as anything but a good Christian.

In truth, I told my master as little as I could about the Lombard's household, because by then I had seen Rebecca.

She was not quite eleven, but her beauty already showed in budding breasts and narrow waist and hips that seemed more round and appealing each time we met. These four years later her body was more luscious still, her black hair longer and more lustrous. As for her eyes, they remained the intense blue of the sea.

Immediately I saw her, I wanted Rebecca for myself, and I was careful to tell Thomas Cromwell nothing about her. King Henry's taste for beautiful virgins was well-known. If my master saw the Jew's daughter, he would surely bring her to the court with an eye to putting her in the king's bed, thus gaining more favor for himself. So whoever revealed that Rebecca and her father were Jews, it was not me. In truth, I never suspected their perfidy.

My master discovered it nonetheless, though I knew not how. Soon after that Giacomo the Lombard was forced to move from the city of London to Holborn, and set to find the treasure so many believed the once-mighty Knights Templar had hidden thereabouts. The Jew's wanderings in the countryside soon produced results, and he gave Master Cromwell one exquisite bauble after another, each appearing to have come from ancient Jerusalem. I suspected the smith might be using his skills to create these things, and some Jews' alchemy to make them look old, but if so, he played a risky game. Why, I wondered, would this Lombard toy with a man who had the power to make him suffer indescribable torment? It seemed to me a certitude that he would not—unless he had discovered the real hoard.

Rebecca once told me her father had let slip the phrase "the pit," and that she had tried to follow him and failed. I could not risk traipsing about the countryside in the Jew's shadow, so we had no clue where this mysterious pit might be, but I was sure it existed and—I admit—consumed by curiosity as to where it was and what it might contain.

That night a bright half-moon lit my way from the Charterhouse to the Jew's cottage, and I arrived swiftly at my destination. Rebecca came to answer my knock, but the Jew her father was right behind her. He had pure white hair and an enormous bushy beard, and from the first both seemed to bristle whenever he looked at me. Indeed, he knew the heat that passed between his daughter and myself.

Before I was sent to play at being a Carthusian, he had one day called me to the back of his workshop. "As of last month, she bleeds," he said. "So know this, if I catch you near her with a stiff cock, my face will be the last thing you see." Then he grabbed my head and bent it so close to his anvil, I could feel the heat from the sheet of precious metal he'd been working. "You will be just as blind if I burn out your eyes with a piece of white-hot gold as would be the result with the iron poker they use in the Tower." He told me he meant to marry his daughter to one of his fellow Lombards as soon as she was fifteen, the marriage age customary among them. "It will be someone rich enough to keep her properly," he added.

I understood that he planned to wed his only child well enough so in his old age he could rely on her husband's purse. As a bound servant, I was a poor prospect. If, I thought then, after my time in the Charterhouse the master did as he promised and rewarded me with my freedom and a siz-able sum, everything would be different. The Jew's daughter was for sale. If I was clever, I might be able to buy her.

On the night of which I speak, when—though not summoned by a speckled quail's egg—I went to his dwelling, the Jew came to the door and shoved his daughter out of the way and spoke to me directly. "What are you doing here? I had no notice you would be coming."

"I come not on the master's errand but on that of the monks."

"They know you come here?"

"Are you mad? Of course they do not know. But they need something I have suggested you could provide, and tomorrow they will send one of the brothers to make the request. I come tonight only to be sure you will agree to do what they ask."

Then I told how the quarter part of the Venerable Father's mortal re-mains was hanging above our door, the bones mostly picked clean by the birds. "The thing is yet in place, but it is suspended only by a scrap of flesh and will fall within a day. The lay brothers keep watch and will catch it, but if we are known to preserve it as a holy relic, we will be accused of disloyalty to the king, and Cromwell's men will come to arrest us all. I have told the other monks that you will find a hiding place for those precious bones."

"Me? Am I not as likely to run afoul of the king and his Cromwell as are you and your monks?"

The monks had raised the same objection when I suggested the smith be asked to perform this mercy for us. I had convinced them that I had known Giacomo the Lombard before I entered the Charterhouse, and that he was a man of such great Christian virtue, he would count it a blessing to risk his life for our sakes. I repeated none of this pious nonsense to the Jew. Instead I said, "It is only a small chest. It will easily fit in that place you have found."

At that he grabbed the front of my habit, pulling me so close, I felt the heat of his breath when he spoke. "I have found nothing. Nothing."

"The treasures you give the master," I murmured, "say otherwise."

The Jew let me go and turned and spat on the floor. "You think they are treasures? Baubles only. Shadows of the real—" At once he sensed he'd gone too far. "Such things as I find and give to Master Cromwell come to my hand during my wanderings in various fields and meadows," he said firmly. "If such a place as people speak of exists, surely it is inside the walls of that round church and monastery that once belonged to the Templar Knights."

"Leave that aside," I said, pretending to believe his protests. "Will you not help us for pity's sake?"

Finally, I think as much as anything to cause me to go, he said he would look out a secret place in the countryside. "Nothing to do with any treasury once known to the Templars," he insisted. "But as you say, for pity's sake."

As for the other and truer reason for my excursion, that night Giacomo waited until I turned to go, then barred the door after me. I had not even a moment alone with Rebecca.

I returned to the Charterhouse in time to join my brother monks for the midnight prayers, which were the only ones we Carthusians chanted together in the church. Each monk had his hood pulled forward to shade his face, as was our custom, but all knew Dom Hilary was not in his place even after the last toll of the bell echoed in the night. Then, when silence prevailed, we heard his shuffling steps approach.

The saintly old man walked slowly toward the rest of us, then stopped beside me, youngest in vows and so at the very end of the line. For some moments he stood at my shoulder. I did not turn my head and neither did he, but I was sure that somehow Dom Hilary knew of my secret wanderings and intended to denounce me to everyone present for being the imposter I was. I quaked with fear, but after some moments he moved on.

When two hours later we processed back to our cells singing the Salve Regina, the night had became unnaturally warm. Though perhaps it was the heat of my sins that drenched my habit in sweat . . ..

❖

11

The envelope had been pushed through the mail flap and lay on the floor just inside the flat. Annie saw it as soon as she opened the door after a run. It was small and square and looked rather like an invitation, or at least something personal. Mrs. Walton had redirected all her bills and correspondence before she left; until now the only mail to arrive had been advertising circulars. Annie could make out her name from where she stood, but before she stooped to pick up the letter, she grabbed the remote and turned on the radios: ". . . the banks remain underfunded despite the many reforms since 2011, but . . ."

Just Dr. Kendall, no first name. The handwriting was spidery—done with a fountain pen, she guessed immediately—and the return address said it had come from a Frau Wolfe who lived in Breisach am Rhine, Deutschland. The paper was lovely, thick and cream colored. It demanded to be opened properly, not ripped apart. She carried it into the dining room, feeling a little tingle of excitement. According to her documents, the Jewish synagogue in Breisach had the *kaf,* the ritual incense burner. Her hand was trembling slightly when she slit the envelope and withdrew a folded note embossed with initials, the sort of stationery she remembered her mother having. *My dear Frau Doktor Kendall, first I must apologize for my poor English . . .* The note went on to say in perfectly correct English that the Hebrew congregation the Frau Doktor had addressed had not existed since 1938, when the Nazis destroyed their synagogue and sent most of the congregants to the gas chambers. Frau Wolfe, whose father had been the last president of the Breisach congregation before he died at Dachau, was now ninety years old and the official custodian of the site, which the government preserved *in memoriam,* though of course she no longer did the physical work. So while she remembered hearing the story of the *kaf* that had been a 1535 gift from the Jew of Holborn, after the war whatever treasures had survived had been sent to Israel. She had not, Frau Wolfe said, thought about them in years. Certainly she had received no correspondence concerning the treasures in recent times.

Annie sat down hard.

She had written to the three congregations for which she'd found postal addresses, asking in each case if there was more information to be had, if perhaps the recent inquiry from the Shalom Foundation hadn't posed all the possible questions. She had known it was a long shot, particularly since she had to write in English, but she'd been thinking of her father's dictum to leave no stone unturned. He was obviously correct, but what had she uncovered? If she believed Frau Wolfe's letter, Weinraub's foundation had not within the last few months written to Breisach asking about ancient treasures that had survived the Nazis. If they had, they would have learned that the *kaf,* which indeed the congregation once had and which was reputed to be a 1535 gift from the Jew of Holborn, had been sent to Israel after the war.

So Frau Wolfe's note called into question how Weinraub learned about the *kaf;* it didn't contradict the essential facts. But it made no sense for Philip Weinraub to lie to Annie about how he got his information. On the other hand, a ninety-year-old woman might easily be mistaken. She would, Annie decided, wait and see what responses she got from Offenburg and Metz before coming to any conclusions.

About then the alarm on her cell phone went off, alerting her to the fact that she had an hour and a half to shower and dress and get to South London.

Annie had applied for an appointment to visit the Bastianich Archive, a private collection in a house in totally ordinary Clapham, before she left New York. The archive was available only to scholars and only one day each month. After writing a letter sent in triplicate—the Bastianich did not deal in e-mail—and filling out numerous forms, Dr. Kendall had been granted access at 2:45 on this particular May afternoon.

The collection represented the world's most complete assembly of architectural drawings of buildings influenced by a Germanic tribe called the Langobards who invaded northern Italy in 568 and eventually controlled territory that included Mantua and Milan and Venice and Verona. Their kingdom was called Lombardy and the inhabitants were known as Lombards, the Latinized form of their original name. By the early 1500s, when the Lombards were providing cover for a handful of illicit London Jews, they were the most successful seagoing traders of their time, and their cities were poetry in stone, wonders of soaring beauty and grace.

The man who let Annie into the redbrick house adjacent to Clapham Common looked at least as old as the things he guarded. He was stooped and walked with a shuffle, and his glasses were so thick, they made his eyes look like a bug's. "In here," he said, opening a door to a large room lined with shelves and bookcases and chests. The only other furniture was one long table and three straight-backed chairs, one of which was drawn up in front of a large square of soft, midnight-blue, nonacid velvet and a pair of white cotton archivist's gloves. "I took the liberty of assembling the same sort of material you were looking at six years ago."

That trip had been Annie's reward to herself the first time she got sober, something to beef up her résumé so maybe she could get started again in her profession. But a month spent penny-pinching in London hadn't led to any kind of steady work, and she hadn't stayed sober until two more years went by and she found AA and then, with Sidney's help, a job. None of which could possibly be known to the keeper of the Bastianich Archive. "I'm astonished you remember me," Annie said.

Bug-eyes smiled and went to a shelf on the other side of the room, returning with a black cardboard portfolio tied with frayed cotton ribbon. "Remembering is my job," he said. "Besides, I don't see many Americans."

"Thank you for doing all this preparation, Mr. Clemenza." For her part, if it weren't for the recent correspondence, she'd not have been able to produce his name.

"My job," he said again, putting the portfolio to the right of the place he'd made for her. "The plans of the four London churches that show Lombard architectural influence are in here. You were looking at them last time. But as I recall, you said it was vernacular buildings that were your primary interest."

"That's right. Vernacular buildings of Tudor London. Doorways particularly."

The bug eyes lit up with pleasure. "That's what I thought I remembered, but I wasn't absolutely sure." He scurried off to another corner of the room and began busily opening first one drawer and then another. "In here I believe . . . yes! Here they are. The archive has only recently acquired these drawings, Dr. Kendall. They appeared in someone's attic, and we bought them at auction. I'm afraid we have no satisfactory provenance prior to the early part of the twentieth century." He looked grim enough to be announcing the advance of the plague. "But these small treasures have a safe home here." He laid a thin folder to the left of the square of velvet.

Annie's right hand was now gloved. Mr. Clemenza nodded approvingly. "Do look at the new acquisitions first. I think you will find them interesting."

Annie opened the folder. It contained two drawings, about eight inches by twelve, each dated 1530. Both were done in pen and ink on paper, and both had undoubtedly been drawn by the same hand. That the bold black ink had not faded to sepia was remarkable, but not as surprising as the way the artist had labeled his work. The script was the curlicued Tudor writing common to the period that Annie read with customary ease. The words, however, puzzled her. *Domus contineo acqua Fleet.* While she could guess the meaning, the Latin was crude to the point of incoherence.

As for the drawing, it showed a string of two-story houses on a riverbank, built cheek by jowl in the manner that long before the sixteenth century had become common in cities. Annie reached into her tote for the jeweler's loupe she always carried, screwed it into her eye, bent closer, and read the Latin words again. She turned to the archivist. "Do you see—"

"The Lombardic pattern? Of course. It's unmistakable. If you look at the first and last house in the row," he said, "you can easily make out the way the brick and stone have been alternated in the quoins. The same pattern is repeated in the lancet arches above the windows. I've seen such stonework nowhere else in Tudor London."

"Nor have I," Annie agreed. "Do you have any idea who the artist was?"

Clemenza looked unhappy. "No idea at all. The drawings are labeled, as you can see, but not signed, and as I said, the provenance goes back only as far as the early nineteen hundreds. The ink, however, is definitely iron gall with an addition of carbon black."

Iron gall ink had been in use for centuries. It was a mixture of ferrous sulfate and a tannin made from oak acorns called galls. The mixture resulted in a pale gray solution that got blacker over time. The addition of carbon black—essentially soot—made it darker still. Nothing written or drawn with iron gall ink could be erased, only scraped off either paper or parchment. It had been enormously popular throughout the Renaissance and was frequently used by the old masters. These drawings, however, were not masterpieces; rather their charm was that they exhibited a draftsman's accuracy, the buildings as vivid as if they had been photographed in sharp, revealing light.

The quoins, the corners of the buildings that Clemenza called to her attention, were mounted in precise courses of three stone to one brick. The relative uniformity of the bricks was depicted with cross-hatching. The rough texture of the stones presented a greater challenge. Working with graphite or charcoal, the artist could have used a finger to blend the strokes and create light and shadow, indicating the rough surface of dressed stone. Iron gall ink made that impossible. Stippling, marks made with uncountable small specks of ink, had been used instead. It was a technique that required patience as well as skill.

"Do look at the other drawing," Mr. Clemenza said. "It is most mysterious."

"This one also raises questions. For instance—"

"Questions about the Lombard influence?" Clemenza looked ready to snatch away his precious drawings and banish her to the outer darkness of Clapham Common.

"No, absolutely not," Annie said. "You are entirely correct." A lioness with her cubs had nothing on an archivist with his collection. Annie moved on to the second drawing. It appeared to be the same houses, this time seen from the rear. In the lower-left corner, in print so tiny she had to rely on the loupe to make out the words, was the same date, 1530. In this case the label said "*Domus Judaeorum.*"

"You won't believe what I have found." Annie was standing on the street, at the entrance to the Clapham South tube station, with her cell jammed against her ear.

"Try me," Geoff said.

"Can't. I'm on my way down to the subway."

"Underground," he said.

"Whatever. I'll lose the signal." She wanted to see his face when she told him.

"Where are you going?"

"Back to Southampton Row." Maybe he'd suggest she come to his place instead. She'd definitely agree if he did.

"Tell you what—it's a super day. Go to Russell Square. One stop beyond Holborn on the Piccadilly Line. I think you'll have to change at King's Cross. I'll meet you there in forty minutes. Northeast corner of the gardens. Closest to the tube station."

Another missed opportunity to see the upstairs bedroom. "You're on," she said.

"Why is a collection like that located in Clapham, of all places?"

"Because that's where the billionaire who created it lived. When he died, he endowed the archive and created a foundation to look after it. The archivist is called Mr. Clemenza."

"You're kidding me. As in *The Godfather*. Clemenza sleeps with the fishes?"

"That was Luca Brasi." Annie said. "'Luca sleeps with the fishes.' Clemenza was a different bad guy."

"You are an absolutely amazing woman."

"I absolutely am. Anyway, I don't think my Mr. Clemenza's a mafioso. He's sweet, really. Looks like a grasshopper. I visited when I was here six years ago, and after all this time he went straight to those particular two drawings because he recalled my interest in vernacular buildings."

"Why would he not remember you? How often can he have seen red curls like this?" He was twisting one around his finger.

That was becoming a habit. Nice. "My hair was much shorter then," she said.

Geoff pulled back and studied her with exaggerated attention. "I don't think I'd like shorter nearly as much."

"There's a lot about the short-hair period you wouldn't have liked. A lot I didn't like either." She changed the subject. "These drawings are a real lead, Geoff. More proof of Jews in London in 1530, living somewhere on the banks of the Fleet."

"In Holborn you think?"

"No. The sketch was a cityscape, four houses sharing party walls. Today you'd call it a terrace. Holborn was totally rural at that time. But it's a start, and I'm much further along than I was before I found it." She'd told him only what the inscriptions said—houses near the Fleet and Jews' houses—and not about the anomalies. She needed to think more about the fact that the Latin was not only clumsy and incorrect but seemingly inappropriate in the context. Something else was nagging at her as well, though she couldn't put her finger on it.

"Well done, Annie," he said. "Give the girl a prize."

"None deserved. It was sheer luck. Listen, last night—" She stopped speaking in favor of nibbling on her lip.

"Another sighting?" he prompted. "To use Rabbi Cohen's apt term."

"Not exactly." She told him about the singing. "It was the Salve Regina. It's a Latin hymn to the Virgin Mary. Men's voices. And when I got close to the bedroom door, it was hot as—" She broke off. "I was about to say hot as hell. That's not the best analogy, is it?"

He laughed with his eyes, she noticed. And today he had on jeans and a black leather jacket over a starched white shirt. Open at the neck, no tie. Gorgeous, Annie thought. There was no other word for him.

"Not the best," he agreed. Then: "Tell me something—do you think hell exists?"

"I've no idea." She was fingering her bracelet. "But I don't think anyone I've ever known would be sent there."

Geoff took her hand. "I'm guessing your twin is dead."

"Yes. Since we were seventeen. AIDS. Ari liked living on the edge. I doubt he'd have accepted treatment after he was diagnosed. Even as a little child he knew he was gay. So did I. Probably before I knew what it meant. I think my folks knew as well."

The super day had clouded over. Annie shivered. Geoff started to take off his jacket. She reached into her tote. "Keep your clothes on, Sir Galahad. I'm becoming a Londoner." She pulled out a plaid scarf large enough to pass for a shawl.

"Ach, the Black Watch tartan," he said with an exaggerated Scots burr. "It suits you, lassie. The green matches your eyes."

Annie pulled the shawl close, seeking its warmth. "Remember I told you my aunts separated us when we were eleven. I never knew Ari was sick, and when he died, I didn't know about it for a week. I was at college in Boston at the time and they didn't tell me."

"Stuff happens, Annie."

He still had hold of her hand. Neither of them moved to break the contact. "It does," she agreed. "But I've got good memories as well. Like that song you played at your mother's the other day . . . Ari used to do Fred Astaire imitations. My folks bought him a top hat and a cane for our ninth birthday."

"What did you get, high heels and swirling chiffon?"

"A sketchbook and crayons. Two left feet. I was never going to be

Ginger. By the way, your mother said your playing was terrible, but I thought you were great."

Another chuckle. "Coming from a woman who can recognize James Galway on the flute, and keep the characters in *The Godfather* straight, that's high praise. Even if undeserved." He still hadn't let go of her hand, and he leaned in. Annie leaned closer as well. "I can't believe I haven't kissed you yet," he said.

"I like 'yet,'" she said. "And can you tell me, kind sir, how the English feel about public displays of affection?"

"Screw 'em," he said before he kissed her.

Nice, nice, nice. Apparently he thought so too. He pulled back, but not very far, stroked her cheek with one finger, and kept looking at her. "Can we," Annie said, "try that again? I want to see if it's as good as I thought it was."

Even better.

"Listen," he said when the second kiss ended, "there's something I have to tell you. Rotten timing, I'm afraid."

She could still taste him. She'd done some fucking in the last few years, probably more in the years she mostly couldn't remember. That's what it had been—just fucking. The greater intimacy of a kiss? Years and years. "I am an expert on rotten timing," she said. "Fire away."

"I'm going to be gone for a bit. In Syria, doing some interviews for my book. The blokes I met through Blair—they've set up a meeting with some of the earliest architects of the so-called Arab Spring."

"That's great."

"I think it may be. Useful anyway. But being away for a week . . . I'm leaving in a few hours. I'll miss you."

"Me too."

"I want you to have a couple of things." He pulled a card and a key out of his pocket. "The key is to my house. In case you need a bolt-hole." She started to say something, but he hurried on. "The card's got directions about using the alarm system. Maggie's e-mail and phone number are on the reverse. I talked to her this morning, and she says they're not even close to breaking the code, but in case you want an update, or think of something that might help, that's how you find her."

He said he had to leave then, that he was already cutting it close. Annie remembered that she hadn't told him about the note she'd gotten that morning from Frau Wolfe in Breisach. One reason, she realized, was that she didn't want to feed Geoff's suspicions about Philip Weinraub. They raised too many questions about the academic worth of whatever she might discover in London. That particular revelation could wait for a better time.

Annie unlocked the door to number eight, holding her breath as always, and reached for the remote. The radios came on. The BBC was talking about a meeting of the G-20. She went into the drawing room. She flicked a switch. The radio went off and the TV came on.

She was looking at a soccer game. The announcer was discussing the likelihood of Portsmouth avoiding something he called relegation, which Annie gathered to be a demotion of sorts. Geoff was a big Portsmouth fan. She wondered if he'd found somewhere at the airport to watch the game.

She left the television on—it served the same purpose as the radio— and went looking for a piece of string or ribbon, eventually turning up a length of narrow red satin in one of the kitchen drawers. Annie threaded it through the key to 29 Orde Hall Street, then hung the ribbon around her neck and tucked the key into her bra. In case she needed what Geoff called a bolt-hole. She'd already memorized the instructions for getting into his place without setting off the alarm.

She went into the dining room and switched on her laptop. A quick supper of canned soup and toast, then work.

Artifacts five hundred years old could not be subjected to a photocopy machine, but Mr. Clemenza had allowed Annie to take photographs of the two drawings. She uploaded them to her laptop and enlarged each one until it filled about two-thirds of the screen—anything bigger turned the images into blurs—and spent the next hour examining both, inch by careful inch. Leaving aside the bad Latin, something else was bothering her about the inscriptions, a memory she knew was there but could not access.

After an hour she needed a break and went into the kitchen to get a bottle of Schweppes Bitter Lemon, now her London go-to drink. For one heart-stopping moment, she thought she heard something other than the radio and walked closer to the once-more-closed kitchen door that opened onto the back hall. She listened carefully for a few seconds. Nothing.

In the dining room, the second drawing was on the screen, the one that showed the houses from the rear and was marked "*Domus Judaeo-rum*." She had been looking at it so long, she almost couldn't see it. Time for a new perspective. Annie rotated the image counterclockwise, then sat back to study the upside-down view. Nothing new to be seen. Why should there be? It was a drawing, the Tudor equivalent of a snapshot, and there was no reason to think—Jesus. Yes, there was. Plenty of reason to think.

Some of the tiny dots that composed the stippling were slightly lighter colored than the rest. They had been done, she surmised, with iron gall ink to which no carbon black had been added. And some, she realized as she cocked her head and squinted at the screen, were simply missing. The result—looking at this drawing from this particular angle, if she managed to focus in exactly the right way—was a strip of difference running through the intricate work. That strip formed a series of letters.

She reached for her sketchbook and pencil.

12

"I sketched it," Annie said. "But it's more authentic if you can see it in the picture of the drawing."

Rabbi Cohen slipped on his glasses and leaned forward so his face was a few inches from his computer screen. The image was upside down, which was how she'd sent him the attachment. "I am to look at it like this?"

"Yes. That's the only way you can see the letters. They're in the stippling. That's the device the artist used to indicate shading on the stone. He was working in iron gall ink, so he couldn't use his finger to do it."

Cohen turned to look at her. "That's interesting. Torah scrolls are frequently written in iron gall ink, because it doesn't fade but can be scraped off. During their use in a synagogue, the scrolls are unrolled and rolled all the time, so sometimes a letter cracks. That makes the Torah not *kosher,* ritually pure. So the *sofer,* the scribe, must scrape it off and replace it. The scrolls are vellum. Your drawings . . . ?"

"Rag paper. Most likely produced in the Rhineland. Commercial papermaking didn't get started in England until the 1580s. Considerably later than these drawings."

"Fifteen thirty." Cohen peered again at the computer image. "Why do you think an artist would date his work but not sign it?"

"I can't be sure, but I think an effort was made to keep these documents from looking like what they were."

"Which is?"

"I suspect they were indictments."

Cohen sighed. "Of Jews," he said. "*Domus Judaeorum.* I should have guessed."

"In Tudor times," Annie said, "Latin was reserved for a small segment of official documents. These drawings were clearly not official, and their Latin inscriptions are crude and incorrect. *Acqua Fleet* for 'river Fleet' is nonsense. The word for 'river' is *flumen*—*acqua* simply means 'water.' I think the artist was a fine draftsman but not educated. Working for someone else. Maybe fulfilling a commission to identify the homes of Jews, some of those you were talking about the other day, who lived here secretly."

Cohen turned back to the computer. "Tell me again what I'm supposed to see."

"Letters. Marked out in the stippling as long as you're looking at it upside down. Some of the dots are lighter than the rest, and some are missing."

"Ah, I understand. Like one of those tests for color blindness," he said. "I'm color-blind, I can't distinguish purple from red, and on the test paper they show me, everything looks the same. I can't identify a number picked out in purple."

"Exactly like that," Annie said. "But in this case, it's tone, not color. What you're looking for is a strip that's lighter than the rest."

"That I should be able to see."

Her sketchbook was in her lap, and she had written out the letters hidden in the drawing, but she waited to see if he would see them for himself. "It's like looking at an optical illusion," she said. "Sometimes you have to consciously switch your focus for it to work."

Cohen sat forward, then pulled back. Annie saw him close one eye, then both, then look again. Finally, "Aha! Of course. You are absolutely correct . . . c-n-d-l-s," he spelled out. "Then a space followed by g-t-r-n-g. Finally f-r and n-t." He paused and took off his glasses and wiped his eyes.

"I have the whole thing right here," Annie said. "I just wanted you to see the technique for yourself." She passed him the sketchbook. "I'm not at all sure what it's supposed to mean, but this is what's written in the drawings."

"An example of graphic code making," he said, still focusing on the screen. "I've never seen anything exactly like it." He turned to her sketchbook, then reached for a pencil and paper and began making notes of his own. "However, once you get to what we used to call pay dirt . . . As codes go, this one is very crude. It's the way it was hidden that was clever."

"Yes," Annie agreed. "I think the first word is *candles*. The second I don't know. The third could be *from* or anything else, but—"

Rabbi Cohen held up his hand for silence. He made a few more notations. "Not *from*," he said. "F-r stands for *Friday*."

Annie leaned forward so she could see her sketchbook, still on his desk. "Yes, I see that. Then n-t . . . perhaps it means *night*. But what's g-t-r-n-g?"

Cohen didn't answer. He'd moved on to the message contained in the second drawing. "The next sequence is possibly even more damning. T-h-d-y is *Thursday* and I'm betting s-l-d is *soiled*. Could k-r-t-l be that old word *kirtle*? An undergarment of some sort?"

Annie's eyes opened very wide. "Yes, of course it could. A kirtle was either a tunic a man wore under his outer shirt, or a woman's top petticoat. But what can be damning about a kirtle?"

"You believe the artist to be offering proof of the claim that Jews lived in these houses, correct?"

Annie nodded. It was why she'd contacted him rather than Maggie; the history mattered as much as the code.

"Well, my dear, since you're an expert—tell me. In households such as these look to be, in Tudor times, how would most candles have been put out?"

"With a candle snuffer."

"That was my guess. But if you light ritual candles on a Friday night to usher in Shabbat, the Jewish Sabbath, you would not snuff them out. That would be contrary to *Halakah*, Jewish law and jurisprudence. On Shabbat you must allow the ritual candles to burn out on their own."

"To sputter and spark," Annie said quietly. "To gutter. G-t-r-n-g stands for *guttering*."

"Yes. So one proof that the people living in the house were Jews was candles guttering on Friday night. He's watching from outside, and he sees them flicker, then die rather than go out suddenly. And, he says in the other drawing, the residents wash their kirtles on Thursday. Something he also sees from outside, because most of the time they would be hung out a window to dry. These people want a clean kirtle on Friday, when at sundown Shabbat begins. Christians were likely to want clean undergarments on Sunday, the Christian Sabbath. So to wash your underwear on Thursday rather than Saturday is proof positive that you're a Jew. In Spain the Inquisition frequently cited such evidence to prove that Marranos, forced converts, had reverted to Jewish practice. It inevitably meant the stake."

"Good God," she whispered.

"Sometimes," Cohen said, "we can be forgiven for wondering."

Giacomo the Lombard, known also as the Jew of Holborn
From the Waiting Place

Word came that I was to go to Master Cromwell's apartments in the Palace of Westminster. "Why does he want to see you?" my daughter asked.

"I don't know. Perhaps he is disturbed that I have not lately presented him with any treasure." Which was true only because I had not recently managed to make anything approaching the level of craftsmanship of the treasures in the pit, but that I did not say.

"It cannot be your fault," Rebecca said, "if you do not find what is not there."

"With Master Cromwell," I said, "fault and virtue are whatever he wants them to be."

After that Rebecca helped me into my city finery and hung around my neck the pendant that said I belonged to the Worshipful Company of Goldsmiths. Wearing it not only granted me the freedom of the city, it forgave the toll for passing through the Holborn Bar.

I set out from my simple country dwelling with calm, but once through the bar, my composure deserted me and I all but staggered through the

London streets. After four years of living outside the town, I felt confused by the din and the incessant press of people. I managed to keep some control of my senses by following the Fleet and finally found enough wit to summon a boatman and ask to be taken to the palace.

It was a short journey down the Fleet to the Thames, and having come to the confluence of both rivers, we turned left and headed upstream. The tide ran with us, and I was in good time deposited at that entrance to the palace reserved for those who were members of the Livery Companies, my pendant again being the pass required. Finally I was in the antechamber of Master Cromwell's most private reception room, and I could smell the dead rodent stink I had come to loathe as much for what it represented as for its propensity to make a man gag.

The pox-faced secretary appeared soon after and motioned me forward. I followed him into the chamber, where Master Cromwell was standing by an open window, holding a pomander to his nose. He did not move from that spot when he bade me good day and told the stinker he could leave us. Pox Face bowed himself out of our presence.

"It's not the poor fellow's fault," the master said when the door shut behind his stinking secretary, all the while wafting his hand in the air to drive the stench out the window. "He has a disease of the skin that no doctor has been able to cure."

Finally, the smell having dissipated, the master pulled the window shut and seated himself behind his table, only then putting down the pomander. He bade me to sit as well, pointing to the seat opposite him and remarking that I should be comfortable and smile. "Do not look so glum, Giacomo. We are met on a happy affair."

My stomach churned. I had anticipated trouble since the summons to Westminster arrived. Now I was sure it would be truly terrible. For Thomas Cromwell to display such good humor was a thing that boded ill.

"Your daughter," he said, when I had managed to stretch my face into something approaching the smile he demanded, "she is well?"

"She is." I could barely keep from shitting myself like a napkined babe. My bowels had become water, and I feared now that I knew too well the purpose of this meeting. Henry's taste for beautiful virgins was well-known. She would be worth nothing when he was through with her.

"Tell me," Master Cromwell asked, "I'm not mistaken, am I? Mistress Rebecca will be fifteen her next birthday." He added that he knew that to be the marrying age of Lombard women.

I was thrown into a panic. Henry would fuck her, not marry her. "Forgive me, master, you are mistaken. She will be fourteen." It was not particularly clever, but it was the first thing that came into my head.

"No, Giacomo. Fifteen. I am quite sure of it. I have in fact a statement from the midwife who delivered Rebecca. She swears the date of the child's birth to be July of the year 1519."

It was true I had lied, but it did not matter. Nor did he actually need to produce any such oath from a midwife I myself could barely remember. In the matter of Thomas Cromwell, truth was what he said it was. "Possibly I am mistaken." I spoke the words into my beard, thinking he might not hear them, though what difference that might make was unclear.

"Indeed, Giacomo, I am sure you are. Or perhaps you bend the truth because of your great affection for your only child. Don't worry, old friend. Rejoice. You will be delighted to know I have agreed that Timothy Faircross may marry her."

Timothy Faircross was the name of the pox-faced stinker.

I had long puzzled over the fact that Cromwell kept the creature in his employ. At last I had the answer. The stinker was a weapon in Master Cromwell's arsenal. In this circumstance, he was more to be feared than any crossbow.

"You will be happy to know," Cromwell said, "that Faircross has a fine future as my trusted secretary. What more could you wish in a son-in-law?"

"Nothing," I said. "Nothing at all."

Master Cromwell smiled and we talked some more, but I do not remember what we said. I was so sick at my stomach that I wanted only to get out of that room and find a place where I could relieve my bowels. As for what I would tell Rebecca, I did not think words would convey the message. Rather, I knew the leather strap with which I belted my winter tunic would be required. Ultimately she must accept that she had no choice but to comply, and nor had I.

Even as I reached that conclusion, her mother's sweet voice seemed to echo in my mind, and I fancied the tears that wet my cheeks were not mine but hers.

Dom Justin
From the Waiting Place

As we expected, the Venerable Father's carcass fell from the place above the gate where it had been nailed, and two lay brothers carried the precious burden into the monastery. Then they threw on the ground outside the disjointed bones of the carcass of a sheep, that any who passed by might believe the prior's remains to lie where they had fallen.

We monks now had possession of our treasure.

We packed the bones (picked clean of mortal flesh by the birds of the air and whitened by the sun and the wind and the rain) into a small chest that the brother blacksmith had been preparing for the purpose—it was forged metal covered in horsehide and would defy all moisture and rot.

What to do with it after that?

We found a temporary hiding place beneath the St. Joseph altar in the church, a place where two stone walls meet. When the chest was shoved all the way to the back of that corner, it was in some measure invisible. But not even the most unworldly among us thought it to be sufficiently safe for such times as those were in England.

Dom Hilary asked if I remained convinced the man known as Giacomo the Lombard could be trusted to guard this great treasure on our behalf. I assured him that was so. My opinion, I repeated, was based on my having known him before I entered the Charterhouse.

The old man looked at me for some time without speaking, and once again I felt his eyes boring into my soul. "If you are certain," he said at last.

My blood chilled. If Dom Hilary was aware of my perfidy, Thomas

Cromwell would soon have cause to think I had failed him, and I should burn or mount the Tyburn steps, or perhaps even be dipped repeatedly into boiling water until one by one my appendages fell cooked into the cauldron, and finally my torso was lowered and death came.

❖

Annie could not stop thinking about the meaning of the code in the Bastianich drawings, the sheer wickedness of such bigotry. She called Maggie and, as she'd hoped, was invited to Sharpleshall Street.

"I was jealous when I heard you went first to Simon with this business, Annie darling." Maggie was wearing her rimless glasses and peering at the screen of a small laptop. "But of course you were right. He pointed out that they changed their underwear on Thursday, so they were Jews. I would never have thought of such madness."

"Who would?" Annie asked.

"Apparently many people in the sixteenth century. But the way the artist hid the code, that's really clever. I've never seen anything like it."

"That's what Rabbi Cohen said."

"And as usual, Simon was right. Now, tell me, do you like him?"

"I like Rabbi Cohen a lot. I've never known a rabbi before, and he—"

Maggie chuckled. "You know I didn't mean Simon. I'm asking about Geoffrey, and you are politely telling me to mind my own business."

Annie blushed.

"It's all right, darling. You are entirely correct, and I should mind my own business, but that's never been my style. So tell me, have you heard from my boy?"

"A couple of e-mails," Annie said. "He says he's pleased with the interviews. Good material for his book."

"Hmm. To me he sends e-mails asking if I have invited Annie to tea, but"—Maggie gestured to the books and papers that covered every surface—"there's not room just now for any kind of tea party. Don't tell Geoffrey, the gourmet cook, that I had you get fish and chips on your way here. He'll tear me a strip off."

Maggie wore gray pants and a soft blue angora sweater. The clothes hung on her thin frame, as if, Annie thought, they needed to be a couple of sizes smaller. Which, given how much Maggie clearly liked pretty things, made it seem they had probably fit better when she bought them. She probably missed meals, as older people often did. Annie was glad her presence meant that Geoff's mother was getting a decent meal, even if they were eating it straight from the paper wrappings.

"Authentic East End style," Maggie said, wiping her fingers on a paper napkin. "Now, since you won't tell me indiscreet things about my son, I will tell you what's bothering me about these drawings."

She took off her glasses and began tapping the frame on the table in a rhythm that punctuated her words. "Why would a Jew passing as a Lombard necessarily live in a house built in the Lombard style?"

"Because small houses like these"—Annie nodded toward the coded drawings on the laptop—"were mostly built by the people who lived in them. So if the occupants were Lombards—and even more so, I suppose, if they were using that identity to obscure the fact that they were also Jews—they might have deliberately built in the Lombard pattern."

Maggie nodded. "I see. Geoffrey did say you were clever."

"The inscriptions, however, are really odd." Annie explained about the bastardized Latin.

"Interesting," Maggie said. Then she nodded toward the bottles of beer occupying one corner of a table piled high with papers and books. "You're sure you won't have one of those?"

"Quite sure, thank you." Annie finished the last of her fish and made up her mind as she tidied the remains of the meal. "I don't drink, Maggie." She looked directly at the other woman as she spoke. "I'm a recovering alcoholic. I thought Geoff might have told you."

"I see." Maggie did not smile, but neither did she frown. "No, he didn't tell me. At least not in so many words."

"I've been sober for four years. I'm sorry if that makes you worry about your son and me, but we're not—"

"Not yet," Maggie said firmly. "I guessed that much. And you and

Geoffrey do not worry me." She reached to touch Annie's hand as she spoke. "It was his marriage to Emma that worried me."

Annie was startled. "But Geoffrey said you and Emma adored each other."

"Indeed we did. Emma was beautiful and brilliant, and I loved being with her. Everyone did. It was like being warmed by the sun. But she was entirely the wrong wife for Geoffrey."

"Why?"

"Too much a golden girl," Maggie said. "Too strong, and much too independent. Of course my son needs someone as smart as he is, else he'd be bored silly. But . . ." She hesitated. "Geoffrey thrives on righting wrongs. It's not simply his professional persona—it's who he is. He requires someone he can enfold and protect, because that's what steadies him. Someone who's not just intelligent but strong enough to need him. I'm not sure if you are, but I always knew Emma was not."

Before Annie could come up with any response to this possible vision of herself and her future, her cell rang. She started to say she'd let the call go to voice mail, but when she looked at the caller ID, it said "P. J. Weinraub."

13

The Connaught Hotel was a small and polished gem in the heart of Mayfair on Carlos Place, near Grosvenor Square and the U.S. embassy. Americans who could afford it frequently stayed there. "They know me well here, and my suite is exceedingly comfortable," Weinraub said. "I hope you can say the same about Mrs. Walton's apartment."

Annie told herself it was a perfectly natural question, and that Mr. Weinraub was not looking at her with any particular intensity. "The apartment's very comfortable, thank you."

"And so convenient for your work. Since it's near the British Museum, and the Tudor documents archive is there for the moment. The archivist . . . what's her name?"

"Jennifer Franklin."

"Yes, I remember now. This Mrs. Franklin, is she being cooperative?"

"Entirely. Very helpful."

"Good. Tell me then, Dr. Kendall, how matters are progressing. Have you uncovered the secrets of our Jew of Holborn?"

"I've had three weeks, Mr. Weinraub. This was meant to be a three-month assignment. I can't—"

"No, of course you can't be definitive yet. I entirely understand. But are there any signs of progress, any reason to hope?"

She'd come directly from Maggie's. Her tote—the one that said Davis School—was on the floor near her feet. Between them, actually. Safe but out of sight. It did not measure up to the bags of the women around her marked Gucci and Fendi and Vuitton, but in it were hard-copy prints of the digital photographs of the drawings of the Lombard houses, including one that enlarged the stippled section containing the code. She could produce the pictures and make Philip Weinraub a happy man.

What was it the woman from the synagogue in Breisach had

written . . . *I remember the story of the 1535 gift from the Jew of Holborn. But no one has seen the famous* kaf *since the war, and certainly no one has asked about it in years.*

Which statement added to the increasing body of evidence proving that Geoff had it right all along. Philip Weinraub had picked Annie Kendall for this investigation because he could manipulate her. Because she was vulnerable. Annie was conscious of squaring her shoulders. It wasn't going to be quite that easy for him, she decided. Academia, even at the level of a third-rate private school for girls, was excellent training for collegial infighting. She left the drawings where they were. "I'm close, Mr. Weinraub. I may have some exciting information very soon."

"That is good news. Can I presume it relates to the source of the ancient Judaica?"

"Indirectly perhaps. My approach is to physically locate the Jew of Holborn, prove his existence, then—"

"We are absolutely convinced of his existence," Weinraub interrupted. "Shalom has been following this thread for a few years now."

"Yes, I understand," Annie said. "But for the information to stand up to the scrutiny of scholars, you must document every step and prove each assertion."

"The Judaica is the issue." Weinraub sounded not simply annoyed but truculent. "If we can discover where the Jew of Holborn found his treasures, the whole world will take notice. Surely you realize how much that will enhance your professional reputation, Dr. Kendall."

"I do, Mr. Weinraub. And as I said, I expect to have more information for you shortly."

"Very well. I shall try to be patient. I also have a bit more information. A few days ago I heard from the synagogue in Gerstheim. You remember, they have the *ma'akhelet.*"

"I remember," she said. She had not found an address for the synagogue in Gerstheim. Originally she'd simply thought they had no Internet presence; now she was beginning to think they might not exist. It was, however, too soon to confront Weinraub. She still hadn't heard from Metz or Offenburg.

"I wrote to ask them about *mezuzot*," Weinraub said. "We are particularly interested in *mezuzot*. Did I tell you?"

Annie said he had. She did not add that she'd forgotten, because like so many of the detailed instructions Philip Weinraub delivered during their New York meetings, his arguments sounded obscure and circular and his expectations unrealistic. Now she suspected he might also be a flat-out liar. There was only one response to that: Fuck you, P. J. Weinraub. Under the table she nudged the tote bag a little closer to her leg, beyond any possibility of being accidentally overturned and spilling out the evidence she was withholding.

"Especially *mezuzot* made from silver or gold," he was saying. "Such things could actually have come from the Temple. And it seems at least possible that such a mezuzah might still exist. They're small, easy to hide . . . You could come across a silver mezuzah from the Temple right here in London today. That would be an enormous coup, Dr. Kendall."

Annie let that pass. "May I ask what the Gerstheim synagogue told you?"

"They do not have any unusual or particularly old *mezuzot*. But I can assure you there is a legend that such a thing exists. A silver mezuzah from the Holy Temple itself that will one day show up in London. So why not now?"

And pigs, Annie thought, might fly. But not anytime soon. "History is full of legends, Mr. Weinraub. Some of them are only that. Magical stories we wish were true."

Her employer stared at her, waiting for more.

According to Geoff, Weinraub was fifty-nine. In addition to being short and thin with narrow shoulders, he had a shiny bald head over which he arranged a few strands of black hair. A skinny, wrong-side-of-middle-age guy with an obvious comb-over. He should have seemed utterly ordinary, even boring. But in the elegant bar of the Connaught, where everything reeked of money, Annie was conscious of just how much power the eccentric billionaire had over her future.

Dom Justin
From the Waiting Place

I must accept that I cannot reach the woman unless she is where I may have been able to see her from the Charterhouse. Such rules, I have learned, are not arbitrary; they are built into the design of this universe. They are immutable as well as logical and cannot change, as the nature of Almighty God does not change. So though here peacefulness prevails in the knowledge that salvation is assured, I know a great and disturbing urgency. I cannot find her, and on her side of the divide the danger grows.

❖

Jennifer Franklin had returned from her vacation in the Canary Islands. On Wednesday morning Annie was to meet her at the museum. Wednesday was also the day Geoff was due home, but not until late in the afternoon. He'd e-mailed to say he'd call her when he landed.

Mr. Weinraub was still at the Connaught. When they'd met on Monday in the hotel bar, he'd said certain business interests would keep him in London for a time. "In the light of that, Dr. Kendall, perhaps you will keep me regularly informed of any new developments in the search for the Jew of Holborn and his secrets."

She'd promised she would. Apparently that wasn't enough for him. He'd called her twice that same evening and three times on Tuesday. The question was the same on each occasion: "Anything new, Dr. Kendall?"

"Not really, Mr. Weinraub." She still hadn't told him about the drawings, or the coded words in the stippling. Annie considered it each time they spoke, but the revelation stuck in her throat.

A little after ten p.m., while she was watching the news—some royal had been photographed in Genoa with a woman not his wife, the viability of a single-currency euro zone was once again under intense scrutiny, the pope had been taken to the hospital, and Annie Kendall realized how much she missed Jon Stewart—her cell rang. Weinraub again. "Nothing at all?" he asked. And when she didn't immediately answer: "I am disappointed, Dr. Kendall. Perhaps I will have to close down this inquiry."

"You gave me three months, Mr. Weinraub. I'm not a third of the way through that time yet."

"Almost a month," Weinraub insisted. "And if you don't have anything to tell me now, why should I think the next two months will produce results? I must see some progress, Dr. Kendall, or you will have to go home. A pity, since I know you were planning to publish the results of this study."

"I expect to have something interesting for you very soon, Mr. Weinraub."

"I'm looking forward to that, Dr. Kendall."

When she hung up, Annie caught herself staring at the cabinet full of booze an arm's length away.

The next morning she went to a sunrise AA meeting at the Y on Great Russell Street.

Different but the same, everywhere. These folding chairs were wood, scarred and battered with age, but they were arranged in the customary circle. She was a couple of minutes early. Everyone smiled at her. She smiled back. At precisely six a.m. a silver-haired woman with a surprisingly young face read the customary preamble. "Alcoholics Anonymous is a fellowship of men and women who share their experience, strength and hope with each other that they may solve their common problem and help others to recover from alcoholism . . ." Then the moment of silence, followed by the famous serenity prayer. And soon the stories. She was the third speaker. "Hello, my name is Annie, and I'm an alcoholic . . ." Finally the hugs. As far as she knew, they weren't prescribed, but she'd never been to a meeting that didn't include them. *Nobody really knows why it works, Annie my girl. Maybe it's the hugs.* Sidney had said that years ago. Annie thought it was true.

Precisely an hour, and it was over.

Maybe the universe figured she deserved a reward. Annie followed the meeting with a run. Then—after she'd showered and changed, while she was walking to the museum—she finally nailed down the elusive something that had been bothering her about the drawings of the houses. The Tudor script in the pseudo-Latin inscriptions was written in a hand she had seen before. She was pretty sure she knew where.

Jennifer said she'd had a lovely time; they'd had wonderful weather, and the place they'd stayed had remarkable views. "Lanzarote is entirely black, covered in volcanic ash. Quite extraordinary really. And all the Spanish wines are a third the price they are here." The food, she said, had just been so-so.

She must have eaten a lot of it nonetheless. She looked as if she'd gained weight while she was away. Great tan, though. She looked sensational. "Jennifer, could I see the Scranton map again?"

"Yes, certainly." The archivist pawed through the keys on a crowded ring. "May I ask why?"

"I want to see the inscription. I think the handwriting's the same as on some other documents I've found."

"In this collection?" Jennifer sounded annoyed as well as astonished. "What have I missed?"

"Nothing. There are a couple of drawings in the Bastianich Archive . . . I'm not sure. It's just a hunch."

Jennifer took Richard Scranton's map of death out of the cupboard. "The Bastianich in Clapham? Lombardy architecture?"

"That's the one."

"I don't think there's any record of Scranton ever being in Italy. Of course, that doesn't mean he never was, only—"

"The sketches show two houses," Annie said, "both here in London. Made with pen and ink, unsigned, but dated 1530." She reached into her tote and pulled out the pictures of the drawings. She did not include the one that magnified the stippling and gave the game away.

Jennifer meanwhile had set out the velvet cushion and a couple pairs of white cotton gloves. She left the archivist gear on the table and moved over to study Annie's pictures. Her finger hovered over the inscription on the second drawing, "*Domus Judaeorum*," and moved to the air above the first, "*Domus contineo acqua Fleet.*" "Shocking Latin," she said.

"Yes, I know. Can we . . ." Annie nodded toward Scranton's map of death, still rolled up in its cardboard tube.

Minutes later they were comparing not just the inscriptions—Richard Scranton's signature on the old map, and the Latin notations on the drawings—but something more, a feel for the drawing style. "It's the same," Jennifer said. "We'd need a lot of tests to prove it, which neither the Bastianich Archive nor my directors at the museum are likely to sanction for documents this old. But even without them, I'd bet anything the same person drew the Scranton map and your Lombard houses."

"Richard Scranton," Annie said. "It has to be him, doesn't it?"

"Hard to imagine it would be anyone else, since he signed the map flat out. Which raises the question, why the atrocious Latin in the Bastianich drawings? Why didn't he just write in English? And since he signed the map, which in its way was much more damning, why not the drawings?"

Annie nodded. "I've been thinking about that. In 1530, when Scranton, presuming it was he, drew the houses, ordinary Londoners were still hostile to the idea of Henry divorcing Catherine of Aragon so he could marry Anne Boleyn."

"God yes," Jennifer agreed. "Catherine was enormously popular."

"And Anne," Annie said, "was 'the King's Whore.' Plus, in 1530 it was still all about getting the pope to annul Henry's marriage. No one was talking about Henry naming himself head of the Church in England."

"Agreed, but so what?" Jennifer started to roll up the map. "According to the inscription, the artist thought the people who lived in the houses were secret Jews. What did that have to do with whether or not

Henry could get an annulment? And do you know what evidence the artist had for his claim?"

Annie reached for her tote. Her hand paused at the picture that exposed the encoded stippling. She passed it by and pulled out her camera. Even if Weinraub sent her home, if she got nothing more from this whole project, she still would have a terrific article in the graphic code. A prestigious journal would be interested, as long as she honored the first and greatest principle of academic scholarship: publish first.

Jennifer ignored the camera in Annie's hand. "Furthermore," she said, "what difference did it make to what, as you say, was the burning issue of the day? How did the presence of Jews in London affect the argument about Henry's divorce?"

"Here's my theory," Annie said. "I think Scranton was Cromwell's lackey, probably for years. We know Cromwell was up to his eyeballs in intrigue. Isn't it likely he'd see proof of Jews living in London as useful knowledge?"

Jennifer nodded. "Probably. The way to thrive in Henry's court was to accumulate bits of information you could barter later for more bits of information. Thomas Cromwell was an expert at that game."

"Exactly. But in 1530, when the pictures of the houses were drawn, Cromwell had only just been appointed a king's councillor. He had nothing like the power he'd accumulate five years later in 1535, which is when Scranton drew your map and signed it." Annie still had her camera in hand, and Jennifer was still ignoring it. Time to be direct. "Would you consider allowing me to photograph the Scranton map? Only for my records, as part of the case for the presence of Jews in London."

"I think you may be right," Jennifer said, "about why the drawings weren't signed, but the map was. It's clever, and it makes sense. Though as I'm sure you know, in terms of publication, the theory would be seen purely as speculation." She inserted the map into the cardboard tube with, Annie thought, a hint of impatience. "You really need to come up with more if you're going to get any serious academic attention. As for

photos, I daren't. It's against museum policy. I can submit a formal request, if you like."

"Please do," Annie said. The camera disappeared back into her tote.
Actually, she wasn't that unhappy about being refused. It had been in
her mind to feed Weinraub both sets of photographs. First she'd show
him the house sketches, without pointing out the code in the stippling
and counting on him not to spot it for himself. Later—in a few days, a
week, depending on how long she could spin it out—she'd produce the
pictures of the Scranton map, with an explanation of what the two
things had in common.

The point was to buy a little time. She'd had no word yet from the
congregations in Offenburg and Metz. She had, of course, to face the
fact that her letters might be ignored, tossed aside by someone who
didn't speak English. In which case she would have to determine whether
to confront Weinraub with the statements of the old woman in Breisach.
Annie was not at all sure how she was going to come down on that, and
not yet having pictures of the Scranton map was a convenient excuse to
postpone the decision.

Annie went back to Bristol House and spent a couple of hours sitting at
her laptop and writing up her theories about the draftsman who she
thought created both the Scranton map and the Bastianich drawings.
Then she checked on the arrival schedules of flights from Damascus.
Syrian Airways had one that got in at 5:00. Qatar Airways involved a
change of flight at Doha and arrived at Heathrow at 5:55. There was
every reason to think Geoff would take the direct flight. So allowing
time for passport control and customs . . . she should hear from him
around six.

At 4:30 she decided to go to Chloe's, the candy-box pastry shop on
nearby Sicilian Avenue. She'd get something delicious to have later.
Maybe she and Geoff would meet somewhere for dinner—then she
could suggest he come back to Bristol House for coffee. So she could
show him the code in the drawings and Frau Wolfe's letter.

She was leaving the shop with a maroon and gold box of thumbnail-size chocolate truffles when her cell vibrated. Geoff had sent her a text. His flight had made an emergency landing in Madrid—trouble with the cabin pressure. The delay would be at least four hours, and he'd be in touch again when they got to Heathrow.

Three hours later she'd had no further communication. And according to the arrival information for both Syrian and Qatar airways, each of the flights she'd identified as likely had landed without incident and without substantial delay.

Two kisses, she told herself, do not a romance make. Only they were such great kisses. And he'd said he would miss her, and he'd e-mailed three times, then sent the text.

Which told maybe not the exact, unvarnished truth.

But why?

Because a week away from her had given him the opportunity to consider more carefully the wisdom of becoming romantically entangled with a drunk.

She'd put clean sheets on the bed that afternoon and laid out white satin pajamas. Not much point now. Annie went to bed a little after ten, wearing the old gray T-shirt she usually slept in. The fresh sheets were no aid to falling asleep. The last time she remembered glancing at the luminous readout of the bedside clock, it said 12:07:47 a.m. When she saw it next, it said 3:59:59 a.m. And she realized she'd heard footsteps.

Very soft and slow and deliberate, and right outside her open bedroom door.

14

Annie strained every sense to probe the shadowy dark. She never closed the curtains—there was an office building across the road, and no one was there after business hours, so she felt no need for privacy. The reflection of ground-level neon and streetlights faded to a pale grayness by the time it reached her third-story window, but it was enough to show her an empty room. The monk had not come to sit beside her bed.

Because, something screamed in her head, it was not the monk. The Carthusian meant her no harm. She was convinced of that. This . . . whatever . . . was a malevolent something.

The footsteps receded, presumably heading toward the back bedroom.

She consciously made herself move first one leg, then the other. She sat up. The jeans and sweatshirt she'd been wearing earlier were on a nearby chair. Annie pulled both on over the gray T-shirt. Her running shoes, all her shoes, were in the armoire across the room, but a pair of flip-flops did duty as slippers, and they were beside the bed. She started to put them on, then thought better of it and shoved them into the front pocket of the sweatshirt. Finally she stood up and grabbed her cell phone from the night table.

She could hear her own breathing. Whatever was out there would—

The footsteps were coming back.

Annie pressed herself against the wall beside the door.

The footsteps paused.

She held her breath and put her hand over her heart as if that would somehow stop its frantic beating. She could feel the key to Geoff's house digging into the skin between her breasts.

A few more footsteps. Silence. Then a few more. Not coming toward her anymore. Whatever the creature was, she-he-it had gone into the dining room.

This was the only chance she was likely to have. She had to take it.

She glided a few steps out of the bedroom and into the hall. The front door was double-bolted. How silently could she unfasten it, particularly when her hands were trembling? The flat had another door out, in the office beyond the drawing room. If she could get to it, any noise she made fumbling with the lock was less likely to be overheard.

You are insane, Annie. How can you know what whatever it is in the flat hears or doesn't hear, or sees or doesn't see?

I don't know. I don't know!

Shouting it the second time, but only in her mind.

I only know I have to get out of here.

She moved down the hall, her bare feet making no sound on the Oriental runner. Then just as she reached the door to the drawing room, she felt whatever it was looking at her. She spun around.

The intruder was standing in the door to the dining room, watching her.

She screamed. He disappeared. Annie ran into the drawing room, slammed the door, and ran to the office and its door to the outside corridor. She got the chain off quickly, but her hands were slick with sweat, and the bolt wouldn't turn. She kept trying. A few seconds later she threw open the door, dashed past the ancient elevator, and started down the stairs.

In the lobby she paused long enough to put on the flip-flops, then ran into the street.

It was the dead of night, and almost no one was around; if anyone paid her any mind, Annie didn't notice.

She had no idea how long it took her to run to Geoff's house. Minutes, no more. When she got there, every window was dark. Maybe he'd gone to sleep. Maybe he wasn't alone.

I don't care!

Another scream, heard only in her mind.

Annie dragged the key from around her neck, started to put it in the lock, and then remembered about the alarm. The pad was on her left. She squeezed her eyes shut and concentrated as hard as she could. *Zero-seven-two.* She punched in the numbers. *Then wait five seconds. Then key in seven-six-seven-eight. Now you have twenty seconds to unlock the door.* She was in.

Annie slammed and locked the door behind her.

It was over. She was safe. Her body knew it before her mind did. Her legs turned to rubber. She slid down the wall and sat on the floor, knees drawn up to a chest that was rising and falling at frantic speed. Never mind that she ran longer distances four or five times a week. The terror-induced adrenaline faded, but she was overcome by the sensation that she would never get enough oxygen, would never breathe normally again.

She heard noises outside. Geoff's voice. "Thanks, mate. Keep the change." A taxi—no mistaking the sound of a London black cab—revved up and pulled away.

A few seconds passed. A key turned in the lock. "What the hell? Why isn't the alarm—"

"Geoff"—a loud whisper, all she could manage—"it's me."

She heard the flat-hand slap against a switch beside the front door, and every first-floor light blazed on. The sound system as well. *"In the morning I sleep alone, sweep the streets I used to roam . . ."* The dark had been her friend; the sudden illumination increased her panic. Annie hunched over and covered her face with her still-trembling hands.

"Jesus bloody Christ. What—never mind. Don't try and tell me now."

"Never, never an honest word . . . that was when I ruled the world . . ."

He tossed his bag onto a nearby sofa and leaned down and picked her up. "It's okay," he murmured, holding her close, pressing his cheek against her hair. Coldplay still sang in the background: *"Be my mirror, my sword and shield . . ."* "I'm here," he whispered. "Everything's fine."

* * *

Sun was coming through the window.

Annie did not know where she was.

Yes, she did. She was in Geoff's bedroom, the one room in the house with walls. There was a picture on the nightstand, positioned so it would be the first thing you saw when you opened your eyes: Geoff standing behind a woman, his arms around her waist, her hands clasped over his. She was almost as tall as he and every bit as good to look at. The remarkable Emma.

Annie tried to brush the cobwebs from her mind. It did not work. She had no idea how she'd come to be in Geoff Harris's bed. A few seconds later common sense asserted itself. She turned her head, expecting to find him lying beside her. He wasn't there. She was alone and wearing the gray T-shirt, not the satin pajamas she'd laid out when she changed the sheets at Bristol—

Oh God. The rush of memory was so intense, she broke into a sweat.

The bedroom door opened. "Morning tea," Geoff said. "One of our more civilized English customs." He held a steaming mug. "Breakfast is under way. The bathroom's through there"—he nodded toward a door on the right—"and I've left a robe for you."

"Geoff, last night I saw—"

"Not now." He leaned down and kissed her, lightly, just enough to stop her words. "Let's get some food into you first. Then you can tell me everything."

"Okay. But Geoff . . . I don't remember . . . did we . . ." She made a gesture that took in the bed.

He chuckled. "We did not. And when we do, I promise you'll remember."

When, not if. She smiled for what felt like the first time in days.

"I don't think," he said, "this is an occasion for muesli and yogurt. A proper British breakfast is called for. Stick-to-your-ribs food."

His movements were deft and practiced, pans moving across the stove in differing constellations as the meal came together. And what he made, despite what he'd said, was not your typical fry-up from the local caff, as Brit-speak had it. Instead, it was a delicate omelet rolled around a filling of sautéed mushrooms, and on the side cherry tomatoes cooked briefly in olive oil. He'd been away for a week yet somehow managed to produce fresh eggs and vegetables. Annie watched the magic happen from a stool at the kitchen counter, wrapped in the sumptuous robe he'd provided, thick white terry cloth that was as smooth and soft as velvet. With a monogram of course. "What's the *M* for?" she asked.

He looked puzzled.

"The *M* in the monogram." She'd checked the initials carefully, thinking for one panicky moment he'd given her a robe that had belonged to his dead wife. "The monogram says *G.M.H.*"

"Michel." He pronounced it with a soft rather than hard *ch*. "No *a*. German form."

"But you spell Geoffrey the English way."

"Yes, thank God. I was named for Maggie's father. He was Gottfried, but my dad wasn't having it. Apparently they reached one of their rare accommodations. White toast or brown?"

"Brown, please." As in what she knew as whole wheat.

"I tried to get croissants, but the good ones were already gone. Only the packaged sort left. Not worth buying."

The mystery of the fresh food was solved. He'd gone out to shop while she slept. Annie glanced at the digital clock on the oven control panel. It was nearly one. She was astonished. "I had no idea it was so late."

"Anything you need to cancel or apologize for?"

She shook her head.

"Nor have I. Eat up." He slid a couple of plates of food across the counter and poured coffee. Cafetière for both of them, because, he said, you had to be a Mediterranean type to drink espresso for breakfast. Then he came to sit beside her.

Perfect. Perfect. Perfect. Geoffrey Michel—German spelling and pronunciation—Harris and his perfect life. Far too good for Annie no-middle-name Kendall. She got the food down, but she couldn't taste it.

"Let's go somewhere more comfortable," he said when their plates were empty.

He carried the coffeepot to the table in front of the black leather sofa. His luggage, one of those folded-over garment bags that men somehow managed to pack with enough for a week's trip, lay in the corner where he'd tossed it the night before. Annie glanced at the airline tag. It was written in English and, below that, in a script she couldn't read. Presumably Arabic. No, it had to be Hebrew because the English said El Al. So much for flights from Damascus. "You were in Israel?"

"Jerusalem for two days at the end of the trip. Which reminds me." He hauled the garment bag closer and unzipped one compartment. "I brought you something."

He handed her a folded scrap of blue tissue paper that, when un- wrapped, yielded a delicate crystal heart molded around the thinnest pos- sible gold chain. "An old woman made it. She holds the chain in both hands and blows the glass around it. In a street stall in one of the markets."

There was a large lump in her throat, maybe because she was still so shaky inside. "Thank you," she murmured while trying to put it on. She fumbled, maybe because she was still shaky outside as well.

"Let me." Geoff fastened the necklace in place. "I chose gold, not silver, so it wouldn't clash with your bracelet."

The lovely Emma had trained him well.

"Suits you," he said when she'd turned to face him. "I thought it would."

"Do you mean suits me because it's glass and fragile?" She wanted to bite her tongue.

"No," he said. "Suits you because it's beautiful."

"Thank you," she repeated. "For thinking of me. And for choosing something so lovely. I didn't know you were going to Jerusalem."

"Last-minute decision. I'll tell you about it later. First . . . are you ready to talk about what happened last night?"

"Yes, I think so."

But when she tried to speak, the words wouldn't come, only the remembered terror. She opened her mouth, then closed it again. Opened it a second time. Nothing came out. Geoff sat quietly and watched her. The perfect interviewer.

"I was asleep and I heard footsteps and I woke up," she said finally. "He was walking up and down the hall."

"The monk, I presume."

Annie shook her head. "No. I'm not afraid of the monk."

"Then who . . . ?" And when she didn't answer: "Annie, did whoever it was come into your bedroom?"

She shook her head. "No. The door was open, but he didn't come in."

"Then where did you see him?"

"Standing in the door of the dining room. I was trying to get away, and—"

"What is it?"

"I'm not sure . . ." Annie pressed her fingers to her temples.

He waited a few moments more and, when she still didn't speak, got up and went to his desk and came back with some pencils and a sheet of paper attached to a clipboard. "Draw what you saw."

Three minutes later they were both staring at the sketch she'd made. A man was standing in the doorway of what was obviously the dining room at number eight Bristol House. He wore a knit hat pulled down over his forehead and a zip-front jacket, maybe fleece, with one detail she hadn't known she'd seen until she drew it, a zipper pull in the shape of the letter z. Jeans and sneakers as well. Nothing distinctive about either.

"Well, you're right," Geoff said. "He's certainly not a monk, Carthusian or otherwise."

"I knew it from the first," Annie said. "That it wasn't the monk, I mean. I knew it was something that meant me no good."

Geoff was still looking at the sketch. "Something about this guy is familiar," he said.

"Familiar how?"

"I don't know. Not important. Half of Britain has exactly the same jeans and jacket."

"And wears a ski hat in May?"

"Absolutely. De rigueur for breaking and entering. Listen, the way you've drawn him—he doesn't have a face."

"I don't remember what he looked like." She made a few more pencil marks on the paper. "His features won't come," she said.

"Never mind. But there's something else. He doesn't look as if he's in hot pursuit."

"Of me?"

"Or anything else. He didn't chase you down the hall?"

Annie shook her head. "I went out the office door. So he could have gone out the front door and cut me off before I could reach the stairs, or—I forgot."

"What?"

She didn't answer, simply began to sketch furiously. "In the outside corridor," she said, holding out the drawing so he could see it, "I ran past the elevator and down the stairs. The door to the elevator was in this position." In her picture both the door and the metal accordion gate were open. "The thing is older than Methuselah. I only take it if I've got a ton of bundles. But if you don't shut it carefully when you get out, no one else can call it. There's only one other flat on my floor. Mrs. Walton said her neighbor was elderly and seldom went out. I've never seen her. I didn't use the elevator anytime yesterday."

"An ordinary thief," Geoff said, speaking softly and without much conviction, "who uses the lift, not the stairs, and walks up and down the hall enough times to get you to wake up and run out."

"Then doesn't chase me," she said quietly.

"Stupid bastard," Geoff said, putting his hand below her chin to tilt her face up for a kiss.

"Annie, this is my friend the geek genius, Clarence Colbert."

"Genius, yes. Geek, no. Geeks aren't cool, whereas I, my man, am the epitome of coolness. Thoroughly chilled." And to Annie, "Pleased to meet you. Call me Clary."

He had dark chocolate skin, with liquid brown eyes, and spoke in a smooth, mid-Atlantic sort of unaccented English that belied what Geoff had earlier told her was a Caribbean boyhood. Followed, according to Clary, by a number of years in New Orleans, where he had met and married an Englishwoman. Which was why he'd spent the last five years working in Britain. "The Clary Colbert Story," he finished up. "Soon not to be appearing anywhere."

"Thank you so much for coming," Annie said. "I really appreciate it."

"Anything for my main man here." Clary nodded in Geoff's direction. "Maybe get him to stop pretending to write a book and return to jawing at our fearless leaders."

"Won't be so good for you when I do," Geoff said. "You'll have to get some real work done."

"Plenty of work without you, man. They're still putting stuff on the air, and Franklin's still busting my balls."

"Rob Franklin," Annie said. Because she remembered that Jennifer's husband had been Geoff's producer before Geoff took time off, and she knew Clary Colbert had been part of the production team of Geoff's show. Which was how it happened that Clary was now sitting in Mrs. Walton's dining room looking at Annie's laptop. Neither she nor Geoff had touched it since they entered the apartment a couple of hours before. She'd started to, but Geoff stopped her and said he knew who to call to check it out. "I know Rob's wife, Jennifer Franklin," Annie said. "We've been working together."

"Jennifer's okay," Clary said. "You work at the museum?"

"Not exactly. I'm an architectural historian. Over here doing a special project. Some of the documents I'm interested in are at the museum."

"Right," Colbert said. "The old picture of the three monks I worked on. Definitely museum-type stuff. Got it. So what's happening here?"

"Annie's renting this flat while she's in London," Geoff said. "Someone broke in last night. She heard him and managed to run out and come to my place. We came back a while ago, and absolutely nothing seems to have been taken or disturbed. Her wallet was in a tote bag in the lounge—not touched. The only thing Annie thinks isn't exactly how she left it is her laptop."

"It may have been moved," she said. "Just a little." She always left it on the small side table, between a pair of brass candlesticks. Her instinct for artistic balance meant she invariably centered it, automatically, without thinking about it. Now it was a little bit closer to the candlestick on the right. Enough so she'd noticed first thing.

"And neither of you have touched it?"

"Not since before I went to bed last night," Annie said.

"What time was that?"

"Early. Around ten. I heard footsteps at four a.m. That's what woke me up."

"You call the police?" Colbert asked.

Annie shook her head.

"Not a good idea," Geoff said. "Annie's working for a New York outfit that would take a dim view of any publicity. And since nothing's missing . . ." He shrugged.

They had not seriously entertained the idea of calling the police. The story had too many wrinkles, too much they couldn't explain. And as Geoff had said, nothing was missing. *They'll think I imagined the whole thing.* She had said that, but not the rest of it, not that back home she had a rap sheet. She'd been drunk and disorderly a few times, and once she'd been picked up for soliciting. She hadn't been, the cop just wanted . . . Maybe the London police could get at stuff like that. Maybe Geoff would see it all, nasty and degrading and spelled out.

"All the same," Colbert said, "I shouldn't touch any evidence without gloves." He nodded toward the laptop. "In case later the cops get involved. Forensics. You know."

"Clary," Geoff said, "really wants to go back to the States and work on something like *24*."

"Not like them," Colbert said. "Too commercial. Maybe some version of *CSI*."

"Ah," Geoff said, "that fine example of thoughtful, highbrow drama."

"I can give you gloves," Annie said. She went into the bedroom and came back with a pair of white cotton archivist's gloves. "Not a fashion statement," she explained. "Standard equipment for anyone who regularly handles old documents."

Colbert put on the gloves—they were snug, but they stretched sufficiently so he could fit into them—and lifted the laptop onto the dining room table. "You usually leave it on or shut it off?"

"Depends," Annie said. "But I know I shut it off last night." She'd done so quickly, in a mix of anger and disappointment, after she'd seen that both flights from Damascus had landed close to their scheduled arrival times.

"Okay," Colbert said, "it's off now." He turned it on. Blue lights flickered, and Annie's screen saver appeared, geese flying across a pond in a scene of infinite tranquillity. "This will take a while," he said.

"Coffee or tea?" Annie asked.

"Coffee, thanks." Then, apologetically, "Except if it's instant I'll have tea. Sorry, but—"

She smiled. "The Yanks have landed. It's not instant."

"And I'll bet you've got ice."

"Of course," she said.

"There is a God. Coffee over ice then. Three sugars. Splash of cream if you've got it."

"Nothing yet." Clary Colbert had spent the better part of twenty minutes fiddling with the laptop while Geoff and Annie sat quietly nearby.

"Have to reboot," Colbert said. This time when he turned it back on, he hit a few function keys as soon as the laptop activated. No geese appeared, only a black screen headed by some lines of white machine code. DOS, Annie realized, the gobbledygook that once upon a time had been the ordinary way for human and machine to communicate.

Geoff was apparently thinking the same thing. "Give it up for Bill Gates," he said.

"You hear that, Annie?" Colbert asked. "My man Geoff here's been infected. No more hip, hip rubbish. Been hanging around me for a while, and now he says 'give it up.' Like a homeboy, a brother from the 'hood." He was keying in various commands as he spoke, producing a stream of unreadable data that continuously crawled up the screen and disappeared into cyberspace. "In a just world," Clary said, "Steve Jobs would have cleaned Gates's clock because—oh baby . . ." He leaned in close and hit a button that froze the current screen in place. "Baby, baby, baby, what have we here?"

15

Clary Colbert's face was a few inches from the DOS gibberish on Annie's laptop screen. "Son of a bitch," he said softly. "Nice, simple, effective. Might have been perfect, except at the last minute our intruder fucked up."

He sat back, turning the laptop slightly so Geoff and Annie could better see the text. "See that? Right there." He pointed a white-gloved finger at the last few lines.

Annie shook her head. "No, sorry. What are we looking at?"

"We're idiots," Geoff said. "You've got to spell it out, Clary."

"Whoever came in here last night was after what's on your computer, Annie. No doubt about that. And he had a smart way to get it. Just plug in a stick—a USB data key, a flash drive—and download the works. It's an obvious choice. I thought of it first thing. If you do it right, there's no way to prove it. So it could have been perfect. Except it takes a while. You've got a three-hundred-and-twenty-five gigabyte hard drive on this machine, and a hell of a lot of your stuff is graphics."

Annie nodded. "I deal in historical architecture, old pictures, JPEGs of ancient documents. I've been thinking I need a bigger-capacity drive."

"You can wait awhile if you want," Colbert said. "Your disk is only sixty percent full. But that's still a shitload of data. Your visitor"—he peered more closely at the screen—"must have needed multiple keys and better than half an hour to get everything uploaded. I can't identify previous switches because he did them right. But—and bear in mind I'm guessing here—the last upload must have seemed like it was taking ages. And after so much time, he was feeling antsy. Probably figured any minute you'd come back with the cops. So he fucked up."

"Fucked up how?" Geoff asked.

"Soon as he was done, he yanked the last stick out of the USB port right here." Colbert pointed to a connection portal on the side of the laptop. "Normally that shoots a dialogue to the screen. 'Unmount USB key?' The first few times he responded, and everything was fine. On the last go-round, the sucker didn't wait to see the question and hit Enter. My guess is he was shitting himself by then. He just yanked the stick and turned the machine off because that's how he found it. Only Annie's running Windows 7, so that slam-bang shutoff triggered an entry in the events log." The gloved finger indicated a line of text. "'At 4:29:06,'" Colbert read aloud, "'Sony flash drive blah, blah, blah'"—indicating a long string of numbers—"'disappeared from the system without first being prepared for removal.' And that is that. Proof positive. Annie's been screwed over."

"It's got to be Weinraub. Who else would give a damn what's on your computer?"

Clary had gone back to work. It was Geoff who posed the question.

"No one else. But why? Why did Philip Weinraub send me here, then send some thug to scare me half to death so I'd run out? The thug could have simply stolen the computer. Why didn't he do that?"

"I'm guessing," Geoff said slowly, "because then you'd know something had happened. Weinraub suspects you of stringing him along, which is what you said you were doing, right?" Annie nodded glumly. "But he doesn't want to tip his hand all the way, let you know something's up and maybe he already has the stuff you're not giving him. So he hires some thug to get what's on your computer without your knowing he has it."

"Then why all the walking up and down the hall? Why did Weinraub's thug make enough noise to wake me up? He even left the elevator so I could conveniently take it. What was all that about?"

"No idea," Geoff admitted. "But I'm guessing he wanted you out so you wouldn't catch him while he was fooling around with your laptop. A wrinkle of his own, something he maybe didn't tell Weinraub about before or after."

Annie looked doubtful. "It doesn't sound—"

"Tell me a better idea."

"I haven't got one."

"Okay, let's leave that," Geoff said. "More to the point, what does Weinraub have now that he didn't have before? Exactly."

"The Bastianich drawings," she said. She felt sick, violated even.

"Okay, now he knows about the 'Jews' houses.' What does that give him really?"

"It's more than just the houses. I wrote up an explanation of the code." Geoff looked blank. Annie realized she hadn't filled him in. That was supposed to have happened over dinner the previous evening, before things got romantic. "While you were gone, I figured out that both drawings are hiding a secret." She brought them up on the screen and launched into an explanation about the code in the stippling, and what she suspected about Richard Scranton, the probable artist.

"So now," Geoff said when she was finished, "Weinraub's got the pictures and an explanation of the code. Rabbi Cohen's analysis as well?"

She nodded. "I'm well trained. I always write up my notes while they're fresh. Shit."

"Okay, but what does all that really give him?"

"I'm not sure. I don't know where the drawings fit in the big picture. They prove there was a clandestine Jew or Jews in London in exactly the period we're interested in, but that's something historians have long suspected. And Weinraub's already convinced it's true. What he knows now—his new information—is that I deliberately kept information from him, despite the fact that he was pressuring me." She had mentioned that pressure when she told him about the meeting at the Connaught and Weinraub's subsequent phone calls.

"I've been meaning to ask you about that. Why didn't you tell Weinraub about the drawings when he first asked for a progress report."

"Hang on," she said, "I'll show you."

Annie went into the drawing room and returned with her bag. The letter from Frau Wolfe was in it. "The only reason this wasn't on my computer," she explained, passing him the envelope, "is because the only contact data I could find for three of the five congregations that have the ancient Judaica are postal addresses."

His eyebrows shot up in a gesture exactly like Maggie's.

"I thought I was going over ground that had already been covered," she said. "Doing academic due diligence. But it seems I've been opening a whole new can of worms. Read it. That's better than my explaining."

"Crazy," Geoff said when he'd read Frau Wolfe's note. "Why would he lie about the source of the information? She says they did once have this *kaf* thing, and it came from the Jew of Holborn. So she's backing up what have to be the most important points of the story as far as Weinraub's concerned."

"I'd have thought so," Annie agreed. "But I haven't yet heard from the other two synagogues. Meaning it has to be possible that Frau Wolfe's memory isn't accurate."

Geoff nodded. "Definitely possible."

"But even if that's true," she added, "Weinraub is paying my salary. That's his real leverage, and I'm sure he knows it. If he thought I was holding out on him, he could simply deliver an ultimatum. Come clean, or he makes good on his threat and fires me. Why arrange a break-in? It's insane."

"For most people maybe. Not for Philip J. Weinraub. Devious is what he does. How many times has he called you today?"

She had checked the messages on her cell a short time before. "Five times. Geoff, last night—how do you think the guy in the ski cap got in here?"

They had examined the front door as soon as they arrived. There was no sign of breaking and entering. And though Annie was sure that when she fled, she'd left open the door from the office to the outside corridor, they had found it closed and locked. Even the chain was back in place. "Has to have had a key," Geoff said quietly.

"A key! Where would he get a key?"

"You can't have any idea who Mrs. Walton may have given keys to."

She nodded in misery as much as agreement. "That's true." Then: "Oh—"

"What?"

"This flat, the way I found it—"

"Jesus," he said quietly. "I forgot. Your Mrs. Walton is the aunt of Weinraub's PA."

"His personal assistant, yes. Sheila MacPherson arranged everything. So that's one more way I've been their patsy from the beginning."

Geoff's answer was to leave the room. Annie followed him. "Where are you going?"

"One other possibility has occurred to me." He headed down the hall.

"The back bedroom," she said.

"Yes. It's the only room in the flat that has a rear-facing window. Let's presume a cat burglar, just for a moment, to cover all the possibilities. Even at four in the morning, no one would climb up the front of a building in full view of Southampton Row."

"Climb up—Geoff, that's crazy. We're three stories above the ground."

"A lot of things are crazy," he said. "Doesn't mean they don't happen."

She couldn't argue with that.

Geoff put his hand on the doorknob. Annie shut her eyes. Not knowing was worse. She opened them.

There was nothing to see but a perfectly ordinary little bedroom, obviously not in daily use. Geoff went over to the window. "Locked from the inside." He drew a finger along the sill. "Dust. Undisturbed for at least the three weeks you've been living here. Maybe longer. Your monk isn't very tidy."

"Don't."

"Sorry. C'mon, let's get out of here."

"Wait."

"He's here? The monk?"

Annie shook her head. "No. I was just thinking . . . That window looks east, doesn't it?"

He took a moment to orient himself. "Yes, it does."

She had been spending a great deal of time with London maps of late. "Charterhouse Square is due east of Southampton Row," she said.

Geoff nodded. "So it is. But there haven't been any monks there for five hundred years."

"I know. I was just . . . sight lines, that sort of thing."

"C'mon," he said again. And once back in the dining room: "You've got to have the locks changed. We'll call a locksmith, but it's after four now. Probably won't happen until tomorrow, unless you pay a fair bit extra. You can stay at my place tonight."

She didn't argue the practicalities. They were not what was troubling her. "Geoff, presuming it's Weinraub, why is he bothering? I'm here, I'm doing what he wants. It's all so . . . extreme."

"That's his MO. Extreme means something different to Weinraub than it does to you and me." Then, after a few seconds: "Look, I probably overstepped, but the reason I went to Jerusalem . . ."

"Yes?"

"I've got a number of contacts there. I made some inquiries. There's a group called the Temple Institute who are getting together all the stuff you're supposed to need to perform the official rites of worship in the Jewish Temple. They have, for example, people growing special sorts of plants from which they can extract special sorts of fibers to make into thread, out of which they will weave special sorts of cloth to make the correct robes for the priests. Who can't enter the Temple without them."

Annie shook her head. "There was nothing on my laptop about special cloth or priests. Weinraub wouldn't expect there to be."

"I know. That's my point. The Temple Institute people want nothing to do with the Shalom Foundation. They say Weinraub's ideas go too far. Even for them, Annie. Even for people using ancient methods to weave cloth for garments in which to dress a priest who is going to conduct ritual sacrifice at an altar that hasn't existed for two thousand years. For them, Philip Weinraub is too extreme."

Giacomo the Lombard, known also as the Jew of Holborn
From the Waiting Place

Three days running I closed my mind to what I imagined as the entreaties of the girl's mother, and took the leather strap to Rebecca, and put a leash around her neck and chained her like a dog to a post. Still my daughter refused to swear on her soul to do what she was bidden, marry Timothy Faircross. Finally, thinking she must surely have had enough to break her to my will, I set her free to clean up the mess she had made for reason of not having access to the outdoors for so long (the stench being as offensive to me as to her). Rebecca at once lunged for the hearth, screaming that the stinker would not want a blind wife, and I stopped her just in time from grabbing up a smoldering ember and burning out her own eyes.

I held her by the hair of her head and made her look at me. "You think you are not afraid of pain, my daughter? Let us see."

I knew it was in her mind that I would beat her again more fiercely than before, but that was not what I planned.

For some time the smell of smoke had drifted downriver from Smithfield, where there is some days a market for meat. At such times many set up braziers and scurry around among the butchers, collecting the offcuts that fall to the ground. The smell of them roasting causes the stomach to growl, and the tidbits, though mostly gristle, can be sold for a farthing, sometimes even a ha'penny. So it was that day when, using the leash with which I'd fixed her to the post, I dragged my daughter from the house. The smell of cooked meat was everywhere.

But it was people they burned on Smithfield that day.

I had heard there were three heretics to go to the stake, and the business was under way when we got there, but it was not finished. As usual, they burned them one at a time. That way those waiting for punishment were given a plentitude of time to watch and ponder what was to come.

Rebecca hung back as soon as she heard the screams. "No, no, no," she protested when I dragged her up the hill and onto the meadow. "Why have you brought me here?"

"So you will know exactly what will happen if we defy the master."

We arrived at the very moment when one victim finally shuddered and screamed his last agonies. Those who tended the fire had thrown on enough fuel to cause the flames to leap up and engulf him, not crawl slowly up his flesh so as to cause suffering but not death. Which was the custom for the first hour.

The last victim was a woman, a witch they said, and they stripped her naked, then tied her to the stake. People in the crowd, mainly children, were given long tongs and encouraged to pick up embers from the earlier fires and run toward her and burn all parts of her body. The woman cried out at the pain of those fiery kisses as if she did not know how meek they were, and how much more she would soon have to lament. Then the tenders built a small fire and lit it, and the flames devoured her feet and her ankles and her legs, and the smoke turned black and scented the air with the burning grease of her flesh, and she screamed and screamed and screamed until it seemed there could be no other sound in all the world. After that the tenders fueled the fire higher, though not yet high enough for mercy.

It took at least an hour for the poor wretch to die, and I made my daughter watch and listen and smell until the end. When I took Rebecca home, she was covered with the blown ash of the witch's hair because I had thrust her forward as it took the flames. I knew her will was bent to mine, and I would have no further need of strap or leash or chains or anything else.

But the lesson was, perhaps, better learned by me than by my daughter. That very night I witnessed her defiance in a way that, had it occurred prior to the command from Master Cromwell concerning whose wife she was to be, would have caused me to send her into the street exactly as she was, there to whore or beg, while I would mourn the daughter dead to me. Instead it happened after Cromwell told us our fate and while I yet had imprinted on my eyes the vision of the witch burning in agony, and in my heart deep hatred for the man who had so upended my life.

It was because Cromwell had made himself my master that I had become custodian of a patrimony that prevented my simply leaving this bitter land and seeking a better place. Before I uncovered the pit, that was surely what I would have done, rather than give my daughter in marriage to the most repulsive man in all the kingdom.

After sundown, when Rebecca and I had both gone to our beds, there was a soft tap on the door. I was sure it was the brother whom Dom Hilary, the monk of the Charterhouse, had recently sent to make arrangements for the collection of a chest such as "you will know what to do with." The message struck me as coming from one who had little understanding of conspiracy. Who would not overhear it and have his suspicions aroused? The plan, however, was sensible enough.

The brother would come again when the time was right to send Rebecca to the Charterhouse. There her cart would be loaded with honey to take into the town to sell. She had done this before, and always the arrangement had proved itself profitable both for us and for the monks. Only on this occasion, according to the plan, there would be a small chest beneath the honey and well concealed by it. I was to hide the chest in a secure place until the monks wished to claim it.

That evening when the knock at the door came, I was sure it was the brother who had come before, this time with a firm date for the collection of the honey, and I rolled over and ignored it. I was reluctant to quit my warm bed behind the hearth, so heavy did my body feel after the rigors of the last three days, particularly that afternoon at the Smithfield fires. Let her deal with him, I thought. She must be the one to collect the honey.

I think I may have fallen asleep in the moments after I heard them whispering in the door of my house, but only for the space of a few short breaths. Then I woke with a start, sitting bolt upright and not knowing at first why, though the explanation of what troubled me came quickly enough. I had not heard Rebecca's footsteps returning to her bed.

I was at once certain my daughter was no longer under my roof.

I knew I had to find her. More, I admit, for fear of Master Cromwell than for the loss of my child. Rebecca had become a burden to me, and I wanted to be rid of her, though I did regret the necessity to give her to a husband who was with good cause repugnant to her.

It was a balmy evening, full dark by then, but lit by a quarter moon. I took no overtunic, only a sturdy staff from its place beside the door, and went into the night.

The path to the right led to the few other houses that made up the small hamlet where we lived, then to the hill leading to the Holborn Bar and the city beyond. Rebecca would not go that way. I went left, toward the stand of alder and birch that came between my holding and the river. I was only a short way into the trees when I heard them rutting. In a few steps I could see them.

My daughter lay on the ground, her skirts pulled up to her waist, and her arms wrapped tight around a figure wearing the white robe that marked him as vowed to chastity. There was moonlight enough for me to see that the one lying on top of her was not the humble brother who had first brought the note (I had not truly imagined it would be) but Dom Justin, as he is known now he's vowed and priested.

I raised my staff and started forward. My rage was boundless. I intended to beat them about their heads, even maybe to kill one or the other or both.

I cannot say what damped my righteous anger. Perhaps it was the echoes of my dead wife's cries as she birthed the child, or perhaps the thought of Master Cromwell and his disgusting acolyte; perhaps simply because the entire drama tired me. All that had transpired these days since Cromwell called me to Westminster—no, even much earlier—was for exactly what I saw before me. The lust for one particular cunny, when so many others might be made to serve the same purpose, drove the poxed stinker and this supposed monk both to strive and connive and quite possibly pave their same but separate ways to Gehenna.

I had a patrimony to protect. If I were brought before the bailiff on a charge of murder, it would not help that cause. Besides, what did I care if the stinker took soiled linen to his bed rather than fresh? Did he deserve better? Was his noxious affliction not already a mark of how Boré Olam disfavored him? As for her, let her find her own way to explain that the blood she should have shed in her marriage bed she now poured willingly on the ground.

I turned and left them to their pleasure, quite certain they did not know they had been observed.

❖

16

At number eight Bristol House the locksmith came and went, taking wax castings and promising to come back the following day and fit new locks with keys that were harder to copy. "How hard?" Annie asked. The locksmith shrugged.

After he left, Geoff suggested an early dinner at a nearby Italian restaurant. "Not great," he said, "but above average." Annie barely tasted the food. When she only picked at the chocolate mousse he'd ordered to cheer her up, he decided it was time to go. "My place," he said. "You need an early night."

As soon as they got through the door, while she was wondering if there was a second bedroom upstairs and she simply hadn't noticed, he said, "Mind if we catch the news?"

"No, of course not."

She hadn't noticed a television either. She was still looking for it when he aimed a remote, and a large flat screen descended to eye level near the black leather couch. She might have guessed.

". . . was buried today in Jerusalem," a woman's voice said. "A celebrated scholar, Cardinal Luigi Falcone, was ninety-two and had retired to the Holy Land after years of being in charge of the Vatican Secret Archives." The pictures on the screen were of a casket draped in red being carried into what looked like the crypt of a church.

Geoff leaned forward. "They didn't waste any time getting him out of the way. He died a few days ago while I was in Jerusalem." He pulled out his iPhone and began keying in something. "Texting Fiona," he said. "Maybe she's got something more."

"Who's Fiona?"

Geoff nodded toward the TV. "Fiona Bruce. That's her."

The picture on the screen had switched to an attractive young woman sitting behind a news desk. A dead-wife-Emma type, Annie noted, with the sort of straight dark hair that had to be cut every few weeks to keep its perfect shape. She wondered if Fiona had visited the upstairs bedroom. "I take it," she said, "what you find interesting about the death of a ninety-two-year-old cardinal is the Secret Archives connection."

"Only partly," Geoff said. On the screen someone was going on about an EU directive concerning cabbages. "It's how he died that's intriguing."

"How?"

"Choked to death on six quail eggs. All of which were still in the shell and lodged in his throat."

"Wow! And they're not telling that story on television?"

"Exactly my point. Do you think an old guy would willingly swallow half a dozen unshelled quail eggs?"

"Maybe he had some kind of dementia."

"Not according to everyone who knew him. He was physically frail, but he still had all his much-admired marbles."

Annie thought for a moment. "There are said to be fifty-six miles of shelves in the Secret Archives. And the collection has never had a public catalog."

The woman on the television was saying, "This is Fiona Bruce, and—"

Geoff clicked her off. "In practical terms, what does it mean not to have a catalog?"

"That the only way to get hold of a document is to request it by name. You have to already know it exists and that it's there. What you ask for may or may not be produced even so, but the absence of a public catalog means you can't try and prove a thesis by following a number of different leads until you find one that works."

"Would the archivist of such a collection know everything that's in it?"

"That's not possible with something as extensive as what we're talking about," Annie said. "But he might remember something specific, and if that was precisely what someone didn't want discussed . . ." She shrugged.

Geoff's iPhone vibrated. "Text from Fiona," he said. "She doesn't have anything more. The story only made the cut because of Falcone's influence, and the Secret Archives, and because not a lot happened today."

"Sounds to me as if the Jerusalem authorities kept quiet about the quail eggs."

"It does," he said.

"How did you find out about them?"

"Pretty much by accident. The day Falcone died, I was having dinner with an old friend, a reporter on an English-language paper, and he mentioned it. Because of the oddity factor. But I remember looking for the story in his paper the next day, and it wasn't there."

"So who quashed it?" Annie asked. "The Vatican or the Jerusalem authorities?"

"That's exactly what I'd like to know."

Annie sat up straighter. "Oh my God."

"What?"

"You know I have the news on all the time when I'm at Bristol House?" He nodded. "A while back there was something about another cardinal who'd just died. I'm sure they said he'd choked on a quail egg. Damn. I can't think which cardinal it was or where he was from."

"Forget about it," he said. "We'll check it out later. You're beautiful."

"That's a whopping non sequitur," she said. "But I don't think I mind."

Finally another real kiss.

"I was planning to sleep down here on the couch," he said. "Honest."

Annie smiled and shook her head. "I don't think so."

She was too tense, in country too unfamiliar. She knew about casual sex but not this. At least not this as she perceived it to be. The feel of his skin against hers, his breath warm on her neck—there was a glory here she had not known before. It terrified her, and she could not let go.

When it seemed he'd been holding back and waiting for her forever, she faked it.

Annie thought she'd gotten away with it, but a few moments later he rolled her on top. "Nice and slow and easy," he murmured. "There's plenty of time."

There was.

"Okay?" Geoff asked afterward.

"Much more than okay," Annie said. "Wonderful." And because the splendor seemed too much, she retreated to humor. "As they say in the business world, thank you for your patience."

He chuckled. "I didn't feel as if I'd been put on hold."

"You weren't."

"I know."

By then she lay next to him, and he was hovering over her, leaning on one elbow and looking at her. He bent his head and kissed her forehead. "You're so beautiful," he said again, his finger tracing the outline of the glass heart that was still around her neck. "All my life I've heard of green-eyed redheads, but until now I've never actually met one."

"I thought your taste ran to tall brunettes." Annie nodded toward the picture on the nightstand, the one of him with Emma, the dead wife.

"Oops. That shouldn't be there just now, should it? I hadn't planned—"

Her laugh cut off his words. "Don't apologize," she said. "Not planning speaks well of you."

"Well, it did occur to me that if I could arrange to have your flat burgled and it was necessary to change the locks, you'd have no choice but to come sleep at my place. Then perhaps I could inveigle you into my bed."

"Clever thinking," Annie said, "but entirely unnecessary. All you had to do was ask."

After that they didn't say anything for a time, until about half an hour later, when Annie picked up the conversational thread as if it had not been on pause. "I like it that you keep her picture here."

"Why's that?"

"For one thing, it makes it special. It's not downstairs on public view. Up here it's just for you. Besides, I was curious about what she looked like." Emma, Maggie had said, was too much a golden girl for her son, too large a personality, not someone who would admit, much less display, her need, not someone he could enfold. Was Annie, on the other hand, being too vulnerable to him?

Her hands were on top of the sheets, her bracelet in full view. Geoff touched it. "When were you divorced?" he asked.

"Ten years ago."

"You had to have been pretty young."

"Twenty-three," she said. "If I tell you we'd been married five years by then, you'll pretty much get the picture."

"Way too young," he said. "Stacked deck."

"How old was Emma when she died?"

"Thirty-four. Two years younger than I. She was twenty-eight when we married."

"Older and wiser."

"Older certainly."

"Geoff, I know she died in a car accident. I saw that online. But . . . who was driving?"

"Not me, if that's what you're thinking. Emma was alone. Which if you knew her wouldn't sound particularly unusual. Anyway, seems a bloke on a motorbike pulled out to pass her. She swerved to avoid him and was broadsided by a lorry full of Christmas trees. Turned out the driver had been stopping periodically to imbibe holiday cheer."

There was a rote quality to the explanation. It sounded like a practiced way to avoid what he didn't want to say. Annie did not feel she had any right to probe further. "Awful," she said.

"Yes, but in the past." He kissed her again. On the lips this time, but softly, with no demands.

It made her want to give him more.

"When I was a kid," she said, "I lived and breathed bikes and bikers.

The speed, the noise, the craziness of it all, that's what drew me. Bikers live in their own world and follow their own rules. Later they became my escape from my horrible Aunt Sybil, and the fact that my mom and dad were dead and my twin was three thousand miles away in California. Enter Zak Johnson. He was the toughest and the baddest among a very tough and bad group. And I," she added, in a voice so low she almost could not hear her own words, "was an adoring groupie."

"Groupies don't usually marry the objects of their fascination," Geoff said.

"Sometimes they do."

"You had to have been what, eighteen?"

"Barely. And I was a sophomore at Wellesley College near Boston, on a scholarship that would have been canceled if I acquired a husband. We eloped and kept it secret. I stayed in school, and no one knew. It was fun at first, but you won't be surprised to hear the novelty soon lost its charm. He left when I was twenty-one and just starting on my postgraduate work at BU." Her right hand was clasped around the bracelet on her left wrist. She had gone right up to the edge, like a kid flirting with danger. There were tears prickling behind her eyes. Hopefully he hadn't noticed.

Geoff had stopped hovering over her. His hands were clasped behind his head, and he was leaning against the headboard staring at the ceiling. "I suspect," he said, "my baggage is heavier than yours."

Okay, he had noticed. "I doubt it," she said.

"Yeah, it is. Emma and I had a huge argument the day she was killed. Certainly not the first. I'd prepared what was supposed to be a festive pre-Christmas lunch. If it hadn't turned into a shouting match, she wouldn't have stormed out of the house and driven away, or been cut off by a motorbike and intersected with a drunken lorry driver."

She did not ask what they'd been fighting about. Too many emotions this night, coming too fast. Her hand was still clasping her bracelet when she said, "I'm sorry. About Emma, the biker—all of it."

"So am I. We're all sorry, Annie. It goes with the territory."

* * *

The next day at Bristol House, while they were waiting for the locksmith to finish fitting the new locks, they tied together the quail egg stories. "Bingo," Annie said when the information flashed up on her computer screen. "Radio Netherlands English service, review of Dutch newspapers. Tuesday, May eighth, this year. From *De Telegraaf.* The byline is Harlingen."

"In the Frisian Islands," he said.

" 'His Eminence Cardinal Ruud de Boer,' " Annie read aloud, " 'was found dead early this morning in the farmhouse he'd been living in since retiring from his post as Archbishop of Utrecht. As a young man, De Boer was active in the Dutch Resistance and was captured and tortured by the Gestapo.' There's a lot of stuff about his career," she said, quickly scanning the words. "And they say his was one of the most respected voices in the post–Vatican II church. Wait, here it is. 'It appeared that Cardinal de Boer may have choked to death on the egg of one of the quails he had raised since retiring to this isolated community. Neighbors found his body after the birds became unnaturally noisy, presumably because they had been without food for three days.' " She looked up. "What do you think?"

"I'm not sure. I have some Dutch contacts. I'll get them to check, and I'll ask my mate in Jerusalem why his paper didn't run with the quail egg part of the story."

Both excellent ideas. So how come at that exact moment the only thing Annie wanted to analyze was the shape of his hairline, and the way he looked at her every once in a while with a special, secret grin? And whether she was mad to think maybe this might last? Cue Sidney. *Everyone talks about living in the moment, Annie my girl. For us it's more than talk, it's survival.*

Three days later her cell phone rang while she was on the last lap of her morning run. She might have let it go to voice mail, but it was Geoff. "Maggie has summoned us to dinner tonight," he said. "Early, because that's when Rabbi Cohen can get away."

Annie stopped running, forgetting even to jog in place. "He's coming too? They must have broken the code."

"I think they have. Sort of."

"What does that mean? How can you sort of break a code?"

"I'm not sure. But Maggie said not to get your hopes too high."

Annie didn't think she had any hopes. Or if she had, exactly what they were. She definitely had, however, a supersize quotient of curiosity. The rest of the day passed in what felt like slow motion.

Finally it was six p.m., and they were seated at Maggie's round table eating Chinese takeaway, and Simon Cohen was explaining his menu choices. "It's a modern interpretation of *kashrut,* 'keeping kosher,' as people call it. I eat no pork or shellfish, and I don't mix meat and milk. The rest of it, the business about different dishes and such . . ." He waved a dismissive hand.

"Are quail eggs kosher?" Annie asked. Geoff had told the quail egg story while he was helping his mother in the kitchen. Maggie tossed out the restaurant's foil containers and insisted on arranging their dinner in pretty serving dishes.

"Quail eggs," Cohen said, "are *pareveh,* neutral, neither dairy nor meat. I don't think any of the ancient rabbis thought of them as a lethal weapon."

Maggie made a small circle of her thumb and forefinger. "No bigger than a small walnut," she said. "How many would it take?"

"To choke," Geoff said, "only one." He gestured to the remains of their dinner. "Hell, you can choke on a bite of General Tsao's chicken if it goes down the wrong way. But the cardinal in Jerusalem had six of those little spotted eggs lodged in his throat. According to my reporter friend, the autopsy indicated death by suffocation. The quail eggs were shoved down his throat after he was dead."

"So," Cohen said, "a sign of some sort?"

"Has to be," Annie said, "but of what or who . . ." She looked pensive.

"The official Israeli word," Geoff said, "is that the story got bumped from the next day's paper for space reasons. Unofficially, it appears some Vatican higher-up requested it be killed. Something about the dignity of a prince of the church."

"And this particular prince," Cohen said, "had been connected to the notorious Secret Archive?"

Annie nodded. "But De Boer, the Dutch cardinal, never held any Vatican post, wasn't a scholar, and had nothing whatever to do with any of their archives, secret or otherwise."

"But he was in the Resistance and captured by the Gestapo." Maggie shivered.

"My contact in The Hague," Geoff said, "tells me he was missing the middle and ring fingers of both hands. And that before the war he'd aspired to be a concert pianist. Gave him a great deal of cred with his peers."

"But," Annie said, "so far I find nothing like that in the background of Cardinal Falcone, though it appears he was also an influential man."

"So, many mysteries remain," Cohen said, looking at his watch. "But just now we do not have time for the quail eggs. Only the code." He reached for his briefcase. Geoff began to clear the table. Maggie put on her rimless glasses. Annie waited.

"The Torah," Cohen began, "contains six hundred and three *mitzvoth,* commandments to righteous behavior. Rabbinic stipulations have been added for a total of six hundred and thirteen. In English we translate *mitzvoth* as 'laws,' but in Jewish thinking they are not restrictions but enhancements of Jewish life. The first hundred and sixty *mitzvoth* relate to the manner of the Divine service in the Temple."

"*Korbanot,*" Annie said.

"Ritual sacrifice, yes. Which, as you know, no longer exists. Some of the Orthodox say the Temple cannot be rebuilt until the Messiah comes. Others insist we are obligated to rebuild as soon as we can. A small but vocal minority are making active preparations for that rebuilding, getting ready to restore the ancient forms of worship. Your Shalom Foundation, Annie, is in that latter group."

"On the outermost fringes of it." Geoff had returned from the kitchen with a tray containing four mugs. "Has to be tea," he said, "because the only coffee available is instant. My German-born mother has been corrupted by her English upbringing." He leaned down and kissed Maggie's cheek. "Weinraub and his crowd are considered total nutters even by most of the 'rebuild the Temple' crowd."

The papers Annie had delivered to Geoff's mother the first day they met were now spread on the table. Maggie reached for one of them. "Maybe, but in terms of the papers the Shalom Foundation gave Annie, they provided an accurate translation from the German. These documents are exactly as advertised, information about five rare pieces of Judaica that are reportedly gifts from the Jew of Holborn, given in 1535 to synagogues in Offenburg, Metz, Gerstheim, Breisach, and"—she hesitated—"and Freiburg."

Annie was about to explain about the note from Frau Wolfe in Breisach, the old woman who didn't remember any questionnaire from the Shalom Foundation, but Geoff spoke before she had a chance. "Hang on, Maggie," he said. "That's where you always told me you were from. Freiburg im Breisgau. Capital of the Black Forest."

"Yes," Maggie replied. And to Annie and Rabbi Cohen, quietly: "I've never been back and never taken Geoff for a visit." She shivered. "They destroyed everything. I never wanted to see it like that." Her voice became more matter-of-fact. "There were Jews in Freiburg since at least the thirteenth century. I don't know exactly when our family came, but I know my father's business went back hundreds of years. They shipped decorative silver pieces all over the world. In 1936 the Nazis took over our factory. Papa wasn't allowed to work there or anywhere else. Two years later, during Kristallnacht, the old Freiburg synagogue was blown up by the storm troopers. I was eight years old and I could see the flames from my bedroom window. A few minutes later a gentile friend came and got me. I remember my father holding me and saying good-bye and whispering in my ear."

"You never told me that," Geoff said. "What did he whisper?"

"It was a long time ago, Geoffrey." Maggie shook her head. "A little later the Gestapo came for my parents and took them away. I never saw them again."

"On that one night," Simon Cohen said, "ninety thousand German Jews were arrested and sent to concentration camps. Immediately afterward Britain inaugurated the Kindertransport." He put his hand over Maggie's.

Geoff's face was dark with fury. This, Annie realized, was the origin of his interest in current affairs. Politicians had screwed his family. He'd devote his life to making the bastards give an accounting of themselves. It was as Maggie had said—righting wrongs was part of Geoff's DNA. She looked from him to his mother. Maggie was studying Annie, not her son. *See,* her eyes said. *What did I tell you?*

Geoff leaned forward and tapped the papers. "I'm not getting something here. Weren't virtually all the synagogues of Europe destroyed by the Nazis?"

"Not all," Annie said. "For one or another reason, some of the old buildings escaped. But anyway, that wasn't the issue in terms of survival of the treasures. By the time of Kristallnacht, Hitler had been chancellor for five years. Plenty of Jews had seen what was coming and had hidden their most precious things, ancient Torahs and things like the items mentioned here." She pointed to the documents.

"That," Cohen said, "is definitely in the Jewish DNA. There's a legend that King Solomon, who built the First Temple, created numerous secret tunnels and passageways in the bowels of the earth. Now the original Torah and Ark of the Covenant are supposed to be hidden there, waiting to be reclaimed when the Temple is restored."

"Indiana Jones," Geoff said.

Cohen smiled. "Without the jungle." He looked at his watch again. "There's a further point that shouldn't be forgotten. The items these congregations possess"—he tapped the stack of documents—"are all valuable in and of themselves. Even if they're ancient forgeries made in the sixteenth century—which has to be a possibility—they are exquisitely made according to the descriptions, and now at least five hundred plus years old."

"So they're worth a fortune today," Geoff said. "You're thinking perhaps that's what Philip Weinraub is after? Some museum-quality artifacts."

"Rubbish," Maggie said. "He's a billionaire. Gold and silver are available without this enormous carry-on."

"He can also afford to finance the rebuilding of the Temple," Cohen said. "Or at least make a good start. And if he could not, others could."

"But money isn't the sticking point," Annie said. "They have to rebuild on the Temple Mount."

Cohen nodded. "Exactly. Which raises two problems. For one thing, Jews hold that the Holy Temple was literally the home of God on earth, and the location is described in great detail in the Torah. It must be there and nowhere else."

"Except," Geoff said, "apparently they don't know where 'there' is."

"The exact location is in dispute," Rabbi Cohen agreed. "But it's either under the Dome of the Rock or under the mosque known as the Al Aqsa."

"And if the Israelis try to make the Arabs leave the top of the Temple Mount so they can find out . . ." Maggie shuddered.

"It will mean war," Cohen said. "Nothing less. Now, it's getting late, and we haven't got to what Maggie and I want to tell you." He reached into his briefcase and produced yet another stack of papers.

17

"As you know," Rabbi Cohen said, "we determined fairly quickly that the numbers in the documents contained a code."

"Because," Maggie said, "while ninety-nine percent of what you originally gave me, Annie, is an accurate translation, some of the numbers are different in English from what they are in German."

"Right away," Cohen said, "we suspected we were looking at a code similar to one we'd worked on before, based on kabbalah. One element of which is a sophisticated system of numerology."

"But," Maggie said, "if you assume a connection to the kabbalistic system of *gematria*, kabbalah's numerology, you have to deal with the fact that in Hebrew there are no numeric symbols. Only letters. You have to switch from your numbers to the Hebrew letters, rather than the other way around, as happens with most codes."

Both of them seemed, Annie thought, to grow younger as they spoke. And Cohen kept putting his hand over Maggie's, maintaining the connection while he spoke. "So," he said, "Maggie and I began with what we knew, and while it was time consuming, it was not particularly difficult."

"Except," Maggie said, "that when we were sure we had the alphabetical equivalent of every one of the coded numbers, all we had was gibberish." She reclaimed her hand so she could put her glasses back on and pick up one of the papers. "If I read to you 'm-d-x-x-x-v,' it means nothing, right?" She didn't wait for a reply. "But if I show it to you like this"—she pushed a piece of paper across the table so they could see the letters *MDXXXV*—"what do you think?"

"Roman numerals," Annie and Geoff said together.

"Yes," Cohen said. "After all this effort, we come up with the Roman numerals for 1535, a date already mentioned frequently in the documents."

"The year connected to this so-called Jew of Holborn and his bequests," Maggie said. "Which we already knew."

"It's also the year when the first Carthusian monks were executed at Tyburn," Annie said. "Do you think that's relevant?"

Cohen waved away the question. "What's relevant is it's almost nine o'clock. I'll have to leave soon, so let me tell you what I can. With most codes you keep unraveling the skein, and however tangled and complex the threads may be, usually they will guide you from one thing to the next in some sort of progression. Occasionally what I call the physical logic fails. In those cases, to unlock the puzzle you need a leap of the imagination, a flash of insight."

"The sort the Pole had in 1939," Geoff said.

Maggie and Rabbi Cohen nodded in unison. Annie looked puzzled. "I'm sorry, you've lost me. What Pole?"

"Remember," Maggie said, "we talked about Bletchley breaking what they called the Enigma code?" Annie nodded. "The key to the original Enigma code was based on the position of consonants on a typewriter keyboard, q-w-r-t-p, and the rest. But in '39, after Allied code breakers figured out that much, the keyboard approach got them nowhere. Then a Polish mathematician remembered that Germans are very logical people, organized. So why presume they stayed with the illogical keyboard scheme? Why not the straightforward alphabet?"

"I take it he was right," Annie said.

"Absolutely right," the rabbi said. "The message key to the German code turned out to be the ordinary ABC's. Once they knew that, Bletchley had cracked Enigma and could decipher every coded message they intercepted."

"In fact," Maggie said, "most codes are broken by understanding the internal logic of whoever made the code in the first place. They're the outgrowth of a mind-set, a way of looking at the world. Great code breakers are able to put themselves in someone else's head. You may think, for instance, that what we were talking about before, animal sacrifice and secret tunnels holding the original Ark of the Covenant, means Jews are not logical, but you would be wrong. Grant them their initial premise, and they are supremely logical. And for Jews who believe in kabbalah, all truth circles back to the Bible. True kabbalah is a system designed to find hidden meanings in what is believed to be the word of God."

"And since we were already convinced," Cohen said, "that the quest that brought Annie to London revolves around *korbanot,* ritual sacrifices, we needed also to take that truth into consideration. Maggie and I asked ourselves what would happen if we took the Roman numerals to represent not one thousand five hundred and thirty-five but a series of individual digits."

"Our eureka moment," Maggie said.

"Because," Cohen explained, "if 1535 is to be read as one-five-three and five again, they can be referenced to the *mitzvoth* of Jewish law, the commandments to righteous behavior. And as I told you earlier, the first hundred and sixty of those *mitzvoth* are concerned with the nature of worship in the Temple, the only place ritual sacrifice can take place."

"We isolated those commandments," Maggie said, "and looked at them every way we could think of, but we still couldn't see any sense."

"Until," Cohen said, "Maggie had her moment of inspiration"— another glance at the watch—"and I really must go, so I'll be quick. In biblical Hebrew, vowels are implied but not written. A mark, like an apostrophe in English, is inserted to indicate that a vowel belongs in a particular position. Bringing us to our results. If you read the words of the specified *mitzvoth* in such a way that you pick up the first missing vowel in the first word, the fifth missing vowel in the second, the third missing vowel in the next word . . . one-five-three-five. You get the idea?"

They nodded.

"Good." Cohen stood up and began gathering his papers. "Now you know as much as Maggie and I do."

"But we know nothing." Annie could taste disappointment.

Maggie patted her hand. "That's pretty much what Simon means, darling. Wait a moment, and I'll tell you what there is of the rest."

Cohen put his papers into his briefcase. Maggie stood up and went with him to the door. He kissed her forehead. She touched his arm. He left, and Maggie returned to the table. "I might have known the cow wouldn't let go," she said. "Not even now."

"I take it," Geoff said, "the cow in question is Rabbi Cohen's mortally ill wife."

"Of course. All those years ago I told Simon I couldn't be a rabbi's wife, that it was a ridiculous idea and he should reconsider his decision. Then he met her, a rabbi's daughter. Now she doesn't just die, she lingers with bloody Alzheimer's. You wait, she'll see me out."

Neither Annie nor Geoff said anything. Maggie wiped her eyes, put on her glasses, and picked up the papers. "We were talking about the vowels. They're all we have, and each one is exactly the same. A-a-a-a and still more *A*'s. Follow the progression of the one-five-three-five code right through those first hundred and sixty biblical laws relating to the sacrifice in the Temple, and it's repeated over and over, a-a-a."

"What does it mean?" Annie asked.

"I have no idea. Simon doesn't either. We were hoping you might."

Dom Justin
From the Waiting Place

Sin destroyed my soul. For three days I sprinkled my food with ashes and wore around my thigh a cilice of spiked metal pulled so tight, it drew blood. Still my transgression hung like a millstone around my neck. I could not, however, find the courage to rid myself of my burden in confession.

God help me, I feared more the agony of the stake than the everlasting flames of Hell. And I knew there was in the Charterhouse such pollution of virtue as could compromise even the seal of the confessional. My coward's reasoning said it was better to face the justice of the Gentle Jesus than the malevolent fury of my master, who—if he were to learn I had taken for myself the prize he intended for his fetid secretary—would fly into such a rage, he would swiftly sign the order that dispatched me to a gruesome death.

I thought it possible I would go to my grave with this sin on my soul. It made no difference that Rebecca was the temptress Eve to my weak Adam and hers was certainly a worse offense. We would burn alike for all eternity. And added to that terrible truth was a second mystery. Who sent me to commit my terrible transgression? Someone surely had, for on that night nothing was exactly as it had always been before.

On the day of my downfall, I had found a speckled egg in the basket containing my midday meal. That night, suspecting nothing, I went by the ordinary route to the house of the Jew. I arrived to find his door barred and tightly shut, though it was usual that on the night of a summons, it was left ajar so I could slip inside without attracting attention. I was surprised by the change of routine, but I persisted in my innocence and knocked.

Rebecca came, not the Jew himself. Plainly I had summoned her from her bed. Her hair hung free, and she wore a looser shift than usual, and I could not help but notice that her breasts, unbound, swelled beneath it. Moreover, I could see over her shoulder the embers of a dampened fire. As for the Jew her father, he was nowhere to be seen.

"I was summoned," I whispered, looking over my shoulder, half-expecting to see the king's soldiers coming to arrest us all.

"We had no word."

I thought of the speckled egg and how every single time it appeared these last four years, it meant the same thing. "That's impossible."

"It must be possible because it is true."

She moved closer to me. I could smell her and feel the heat of her breath. She lifted her face, and because a sliver of moon had risen, I could see she had been recently beaten. I had never seen her so before. "What happened?" I asked, feeling that all these departures from customary behavior began to indicate something truly evil afoot. "Is it your father who beat you? Why?"

"We cannot talk here." She shoved me off the threshold as she spoke and pulled the door closed behind her. It was not late enough to be sure that none would be about and spy us, so I had no choice but to follow her into the copse between the house and the river.

We said nothing until we were hidden by the trees. Then she turned to me. "I am promised to Timothy Faircross. I must marry him because I cannot find the courage to burn."

"What are you talking about?" I did not recognize the name, but the way she spoke, flatly and without emotion, seemed to me more terrifying than if she shouted, which she did seconds later.

"The stinker! The stinker! The stinker!" Rebecca screamed, and I realized she was to marry the pox-faced creature whose stench preceded him by ten yards. I had always to gag down my bile in his presence, though I was never more than a few minutes in his company. Rebecca was condemned to live with him in his house, and eat her meals in his company, and share his bed, and spread her legs for him, and bear his children.

I could not help but pity her, but when she continued to shout out her misery, I became terrified lest we be overheard and stepped in close and put my hand over her mouth. I meant only to protect us both, but she seized the opportunity to pull up the skirt of the sleeping shift and push her hips against me.

Then I was gone from my senses and allowed her to pull me to the ground and did all the rest as our mortal nature drives us to do. During the moments of my madness, I even gloried at the resistance her flesh offered and the fact that I, not the poxed Faircross, was the first to have her.

Only after I pulled away and felt the crushing weight of sin descend did I do what I should have done immediately. I recognized that somehow I had been deceived and ran from the place as if pursued by demons.

❖

"In Art 101," Annie said, "you learn about the vanishing point. It's where the trajectory of two lines brings them together."

She was sitting at the granite counter of the kitchen at 29 Olde Hall Street, watching Geoff fiddle with his espresso maker so he could get the caffeine fix he hadn't had after the dinner of Chinese takeout at Maggie's. "The vanishing point," she said, "looks like this."

Annie made some quick pencil strokes on a napkin, then turned it so he could see. She'd drawn a triangle, crisscrossed and overlaid with a number of lines. "These"—she used the pencil as a pointer—"are called orthogonals and transversals. This"—she indicated the long line she'd drawn across the triangle's point—"is the horizon line, also called the distance point. And here"—the pencil tapped the place where the line and the triangle met—"is the vanishing point. Do you see?"

Geoff bent over her sketch. "I see that you've managed to create the illusion of three-dimensional depth. Clever." He turned back to the coffeemaker and retrieved a small cup of thick black brew.

Annie grabbed another napkin and switched to sketching speckled ovoids.

"Quail eggs?" he asked.

"Yes. Fascinating, but nothing to do with Weinraub." She pushed the drawing away. "Geoff, I'm starting to think I'm going to have some pretty spectacular material to write up, whatever the *A*'s mean."

"Could be. Two codes, the existence of some remarkable old Judaica—"

"But how"—Annie reached again for the napkin on which she'd illustrated the vanishing point—"does the stuff that happens at Bristol House fit in? Where does it all come together?"

"No idea," he said.

"It can't be a coincidence that all these things have happened at the same time. So where do they meet?" She grabbed another napkin, sketching so furiously, the lead in the pencil broke with an audible snap.

"Don't worry so much," he said, moving the stack of napkins out of her reach. "I get the feeling everything's in motion. That it's going to . . . sort of unfold. But not tonight." He leaned in and kissed her. "Tonight I vote we go upstairs and forget about all this for a while."

He was longer than usual in the bathroom. When he came out, he smelled of musk edged with grapefruit.

"If I knew your shaving soap smelled so delicious, I wouldn't have admired the designer stubble so much," she whispered, setting her palm against his clean-shaven cheek.

"Sometimes," he said, "smooth is better."

She had already learned he was an inventive as well as a thoughtful lover, but not how generous he could be.

At first she found it difficult to simply accept the gift he offered. Too many years of sex rather than making love. "Relax," he whispered. "Ride the wave. Unless . . . do you want me to stop?"

"Please don't." And afterward: "That was wonderful. I've never . . . thank you."

"My pleasure. Truly." One knuckle traced her jawline. "Care to go again? I know a trick with ice cubes that—"

Her cell phone rang. It was on the table beside the bed, and she grabbed it and looked at the caller ID. "Weinraub."

"Jesus, it's nearly midnight."

Annie considered for a moment, then flipped the phone open. "It's late, Mr. Weinraub. I was sleeping."

"I'm sorry to disturb you, Dr. Kendall." She angled the phone, hoping Geoff could hear as well. He leaned in, then pulled back and shook his head. Annie clamped the phone to her ear. "Did you hear me?" Weinraub was saying. "I'm calling on an urgent matter."

"What urgent matter?"

"I prefer not to discuss it by telephone. I will come and see you. I'm only a few minutes from Southampton Row."

If she said she wasn't at Bristol House, it would give him leave to have someone break in a second time. But her laptop was here at Geoff's. Besides, the locks had been changed. "I'm not at home, Mr. Weinraub."

Geoff made a face. Annie shrugged. Weinraub took a couple of seconds to reply. "I see. At least I presume I do." She could all but see his thin lips pursed in disapproval and feel those hypnotic eyes boring into her skull. "Then it will have to be tomorrow," he said. "I shall come to Mrs. Walton's apartment at precisely eight a.m. Please be there."

18

Even when her brain was pickled in booze, Annie never used an alarm clock. She could always tell herself to wake up at a specific time and hit it pretty much on the nose. She was in the shower at Geoff's at two minutes past seven.

She'd crept into the bathroom as quietly as a cat and left him sleeping, but by the time she returned to the bedroom to snatch her jeans, the bed was empty and she could hear James Blunt on the sound system. The smell of coffee led her down the stairs.

"I'm sorry to get you up so early," she said. "And I hope it's okay that I borrowed this." She was wearing one of his shirts, starched, as they all were, white, with a thin blue stripe and a small version of his three-letter monogram embroidered on the extradeep chest pocket. "My blouse," she explained, "is decorated with orange-flavored beef."

"*Saw an angel, of that I'm sure . . .*"

"That shirt looks better on you than it does on me. Keep it." He poured her coffee and left her to add her own milk. "Will you eat some porridge if I make it? Oatmeal to you."

Annie shook her head. "Much too early for food. But thanks for the coffee."

"Still no idea what Weinraub wants?" They'd kicked that around for twenty minutes after the call came the night before. Then, without answers, they'd drifted off to sleep.

"None," Annie said.

"*My life is brilliant. My love is pure.*"

Geoff gripped a mug of coffee with both hands—honoring his prohibition against espresso first thing in the morning—rested his elbows on the granite counter, leaned toward her, and deposited a quick Java-flavored kiss on her lips.

"I owe you," she said. "I won't forget." He looked puzzled. "Last night," Annie said. "You never got your turn."

"Ah, last night." Another coffee-flavored kiss. "Rule number one," he said. "No score keeping. We've got plenty of time."

"For the ice cubes?"

"Definitely time for the ice cubes."

According to Sidney O'Toole, the danger never disappeared. *You can step back from the abyss, Annie my girl, but it's always there waiting for you.* Well, Sidney did not know everything. She was not going back to hell. Four sober years were going to become five, then six, and eventually sixteen or even sixty. That Geoffrey Harris seemed as sure of her balance as she was joyed her heart, but what she said was, "It occurs to me that if the woman who wrote me from Breisach is correct, then Weinraub may not know anything about the code in the documents."

Geoff considered for a moment. "Not so. According to my mother and Rabbi Cohen, the code existed in the German documents, but it had been changed, presumably to make it more obscure, in the English translation. Even if Weinraub lifted some research papers that already existed and told you they were the work of his Shalom Foundation, it's likely he and his people did the English translations that were meant for you. He covered up the code because he wanted to. So he knew it was there."

Annie considered. "You're right. And we know for sure he has the contents of my laptop."

"Ninety-nine percent sure," Geoff corrected.

"That's sure enough. So . . . the stippled code proves there were people identified as Jews in London in 1530, and to that extent it validates the Jew of Holborn story. But according to Weinraub, he's never been in doubt about that. He wants me to find something else, the source of the Jew of Holborn's gifts. Where he got such things."

"Dare I say it again—Indiana Jones."

"Without the jungle," Annie said. "Except I'm a girl, so it has to be Lara Croft."

"I agree about the girl part." He trailed one finger down the open neck of the blue and white shirt.

Annie grabbed his hand and kissed it, then pushed it away. "What did Weinraub achieve by having someone break into my place? I still don't know the source of the loot, and there was nothing about it on my laptop."

"He couldn't have known that in advance."

"But he gave me three months to do the job. How come he took a risk—sending someone to burgle my laptop while I was sleeping had to be a risk—this early in the game?"

"Now that," Geoff said, "is a damned good question. What's the new urgency?"

"I have no idea," Annie said, "but I'm thinking about it." She got up and went around to the kitchen side of the counter to refill her mug. The large schoolhouse clock that made an analog fashion statement on the soffit above the counter said twenty to eight. "I have to go."

"Let me come with you."

"We've been all over this. Bringing you with me would be a dead giveaway that I'm onto something and you're involved. As you pointed out sometime past, you are not exactly a nonentity, Mr. Geoffrey Harris."

"But Weinraub—"

"—is not any danger to me. If he wanted to harm me, he would have someone do it, not come to where he's arranged for me to be living and do it himself. That is insane."

Geoff nodded agreement, but he did not look happy about it.

Dom Justin
From the Waiting Place

Suspended as I am between shadow and true light, I am given to understand that the sin is in the breaking of the vow. Still I shiver to tell of my misery in that time. And for the woman—I shiver also for her. She moves in and out of my sight, and sometimes I cannot find her, but on this occasion when she appears, I sense darkness and evil surrounding her. And the threat of annihilation.

❖

Annie arrived at Bristol House at five to eight. The early mail had already been delivered. Four envelopes lay on the floor. Annie stooped to pick them up while simultaneously switching on the radios in what had now become an automatic gesture. Two were advertising circulars. The others were letters bearing foreign stamps. A closer look revealed that one was from Metz and the other from Offenburg.

Bingo, she thought. The two-for-one special. Except that at that precise moment the doorbell rang. She had time only to shove the letters in her tote before buzzing her employer in.

"I realize it's early," Philip Weinraub said. "I hope this is not an inconvenient time. There is some urgency."

It was obvious to Annie he had no interest in whether his arrival was convenient. He was pretty much ignoring her, walking quickly around Bea Walton's drawing room, examining the pictures one after the other as if he were in a gallery. The art was mostly old and worthy, but Annie had made a careful inspection and found nothing special. "It's not a problem, Mr. Weinraub, but—may I ask what the urgency is?"

He ignored her question, instead continuing his inspection of Mrs. Walton's paintings and photographs. "Not these," he muttered softly once. Then, abruptly turning to her: "What is your schedule for today, Dr. Kendall? I have often wondered exactly how historians do their work. Shall you be spending hours looking at musty old documents?"

"Old documents are seldom musty, Mr. Weinraub. If they are, they don't last long enough for historians to examine them. Mostly, if they've survived, they're carefully kept in conditions that prohibit must." And if what he wanted was an hour-by-hour work log, he didn't have to arrive at Bristol House at the crack of dawn to claim it.

"Yes, I see." He had stopped beside a pen and ink sketch of an old street. "Ah," he said, leaning in to read the engraving on the small brass label embedded in the bottom of the frame, "York, 1826. That's in York-shire, isn't it?"

"I believe so."

"Miss MacPherson, my secretary, mentioned that her aunt had a re-markable sketch of London. Have you seen a sketch of old London in the apartment?"

"No, I haven't. Unless you mean the mural." She regretted the words as soon as she spoke them, but there was no way to call them back.

"That's it. I remember now." His eyes were alight, and he was bounc-ing up and down on his toes. The thought that flashed through Annie's mind was that he was dancing with excitement. "A mural of old London. That's what Miss MacPherson said."

"It's in the bedroom."

She hated taking him into the room she slept in, but there was no choice. Weinraub followed her down the hall and into the bedroom. Morning light illuminated the wall covered by the dense black and white painting. He took a step back so he could take it all in. "My word," he murmured. "How remarkable."

"Yes, it is. Sort of *Where's Waldo?* on steroids. At least that's how I always think of it."

"Do you know the period?"

"Mrs. Walton mentioned that it had been painted by a man who lived here between 1930 and 1959. I think the mural is contemporary with the city as it was over that time."

"As late as that." Weinraub sounded disappointed. "You're quite sure there's nothing from earlier times?"

"Not that I know. Did your secretary suggest it was earlier?"

"I don't remember. Perhaps I just formed a mistaken impression." Weinraub spent another few moments looking at the dense overlay of black and white scenes: backing up, then moving in closer, tipping his head back and trying to see the details close to the ceiling, moving to his right and to his left. After four or five minutes, he gave up. "Impossible," he muttered.

He clearly had not found Waldo, or whatever it was he'd been looking for.

"Remarkable nonetheless," he said. "Do you think, Dr. Kendall, any of those trees"—Weinraub nodded in the direction of the painted wall—"might be almond trees?"

"I have no idea. I'm not sure I know what an almond tree looks like." Annie's astonishment showed in her voice.

"I've seen them in southern Spain," Weinraub said. "Pink flowers. Very pretty."

"Well, southern Spain is a warmer climate than London, so—"

Weinraub cut her off with a gesture and left the bedroom.

Annie followed him into the hall. He was moving toward the front door, finished with her apparently. "Mr. Weinraub, what exactly did you want to see me about?"

"I simply wish to impress upon you the need for moving quickly to a conclusion of this affair. I suggest you see if you can uncover anything in the Tudor documents about flowering trees. Almonds in particular." He paused, fixing her with his hypnotic stare. "Flowering almond branches are often depicted on both ancient and modern Judaica. On *mezuzot* particularly."

"Weinraub is fixated on almond trees. He seemed to think they should be somewhere in the mural." She had phoned Geoff within minutes of Weinraub leaving.

"He knows about the mural, and that's what he wanted to talk about?"

"Yes, he knows about it. But he didn't just want to talk—he wanted to see it. He was looking for an almond tree."

"That's . . . the mural's all about London, right? I don't think there are almond trees in London," Geoff said.

"I don't think so either. I'll check. But there's more. I've heard from the other two congregations. The ones in Offenburg and Metz." She was clutching both letters as she spoke.

"Wow. What do they say?"

"Metz has an active congregation and an official archivist, and some-body gave her my inquiry. She says they do indeed have a small bronze *bazekh*—that's a pan for carrying hot coals—and a very early document that says it was a gift from the Jew of Holborn. Then she says that she's very curious as to how I heard about this, since no one has inquired about it in"—Annie juggled her cell and the letter so she could get the words exactly right—"'in many dozen years.'"

"Let me guess," he said quietly. "You got pretty much the same re-sponse from Offenburg."

"Yes. A rabbi wrote me. He says he keeps the records, such as they are, because they no longer have a synagogue in the town—too few Jews after the war. So years ago they sent all the treasures they managed to save from the Nazis to Israel. But he remembers the copper basin, the *mizrak,* and that it was said to be ancient and to have come from Lon-don in the early fifteen hundreds."

"And stop me if I'm wrong—he knows nothing about the Shalom Foundation's recent questionnaire."

"Exactly. 'About your Foundation I know nothing.' That's a direct quote."

According to the information department of the Royal Horticultural Society at Kew, there were no almond trees growing in any public park in London. "Our weather is not suitable for *Prunus dulcis,* Dr. Kendall. It thrives in a Mediterranean climate. Perhaps in a private London con-servatory. I could circulate a request among our fellows, if you wish."

"No, thank you. That won't be necessary." She was standing in front of the mural as she spoke. However cacophonous the jumble of vignettes, one impression was clear and overwhelming. These were outdoor scenes, public spaces. What had Mrs. Walton said? . . . Stephen Fox used to prowl the city by night and paint by day. There was no warm and humid glass house intimacy here. "Thank you," she said again. "I appreciate the help."

Rabbi Cohen's comments were considerably more apt. "In Exodus we learn about Aaron, who was the brother of Moses and the first priest. His badge of office, his rod, was an almond branch that burst into bloom overnight. Besides, in Hebrew an almond branch is *shaqed*. Which also means 'watching.' Many of the things in the ancient Temple are said to have been engraved with almond blossoms."

"Do you think that's what the *A*'s in the code stand for, Rabbi? Almond trees or almond blossoms?"

"It's possible. But it doesn't feel likely, Annie. So much intricate encoding for something so general. But what definitely doesn't make sense—you say Weinraub knew of the mural's existence before he came."

"Absolutely. That's why he came. He wanted to get a look at it."

"So maybe the mural is important to whatever his agenda may be. But if so, why did he send you to London? It was Weinraub's secretary who arranged for you to stay in her aunt's flat, wasn't it?"

Annie said it was.

"That means if Philip Weinraub already knew of the mural's existence and wanted to see it, he could easily have arranged to visit without having you move in. Instead he sends you to London for three months. That seems to me very peculiar."

"To me, too," Annie agreed. "And there's something else." She told him about the three congregations she had contacted.

"So two of the pieces are already in Israel, where according to Geoffrey, Philip Weinraub has extensive contacts with people who would know the whereabouts of such things."

"Yes. And why did he lie to me about Shalom recently discovering their existence?"

"I don't know, Annie."

"Neither do I. But I mean to find out."

When she hung up, Annie Googled up a picture of an almond tree and walked the length of the mural carrying her laptop. Repeatedly. Back and forth. After ten minutes her eyes were watering and burning, and she had to give up.

Giacomo the Lombard, known also as the Jew of Holborn
From the Waiting Place

She was reprieved.

A terrible fever descended upon the city, and the king and his court went south to Hever Castle in Kent, where the Boleyn family no doubt beggared themselves spending on His Majesty all he had lavished on them earlier. Master Cromwell was known to have taken his odiferous secretary with him. Perhaps the fresh breezes of the Weald would make his presence less troublesome than was the case in the close air of London.

What this meant for the girl my daughter, though girl she no longer was, having spread her legs for the priested monk, was a chance to avoid a life as wife to the stinker and to die more easily than might otherwise be the case.

Rebecca wrapped herself in a black shroud and thick veil and went into the city to join the plague women, creatures whose faces were half eaten away by the pox, fit for nothing but to drag the bodies of infected dead to the places where they were burned. I did not expect to see my daughter again. She had not the mark of the pox that somehow protected the others, so she must catch the fever and die. But I had to agree that such a death was preferable to marrying the stinker and infinitely better than being burned alive. Because not even the master could blame me if I told him she died of the fever, I let her go.

So does Boré Olam shape the destiny of men with what appears chance but is in reality part of the divine plan. If the fever had not come to London just then, all might have been different. If King Henry's father had not dredged the Fleet thirty years before, and in so doing drained some of the many wells that were built along its banks, the pit, which is accessible only at the bottom of one of the dry wells, would never have been found by me or anyone else. The Templars had been inordinately clever. They dug their secret chamber first, then dug the well above it, never thinking that a time would come when an English king would put at risk what the Templars had stolen from the Temple built by Solomon, King of Israel.

That much I knew, but how did it happen that on one occasion I stumbled and fell into that particular well, which had then run dry? And how was it that my fall was so cushioned by an accumulation of leaves and debris that I was unhurt? What drove me to paw through the waste until my fingers chanced on a stone that could be easily pulled aside, revealing the narrow opening through which I afterward regularly dragged myself? Beyond it was a larger space, and beyond that yet another—broader, but even less tall—where I was able to dig and occasionally uncover such wonders as I never dreamed existed. How did all that come to pass? The answers to those things only Boré Olam can know.

In the time of which I speak, when all hid in their houses for fear of the fever and Rebecca went into the city to seek a martyr's death among the plague women, I dared to go in broad daylight to climb down the well and through the antechamber into the pit itself. Once there I could not stand but had to lie full length. Over the years I learned to work in such a position, and I left the tools for digging in place. I had a small trowel and a tiny pointed dowel, of the sort smiths use when working precious metals. Also a pickax, though I resisted using it for fear of bringing the walls of earth down on my head. And always, even in those days when the rampant fever protected me from being observed, I was careful to dislodge no more dirt than I could carry away in my pockets and my satchel and sprinkle unobtrusively in the woods thereabouts.

At first during that fever time, my forays to the pit yielded no new treasure, but some days after Rebecca left, I came upon a seam of sand that occurred relatively dry in a place where everything else was sodden. I felt at once that I was close to a discovery of great importance, and I dug smaller and smaller handfuls of earth. After little more than an hour, I held in my hand a silver tube the same size as my middle finger, one end shaped to look like the precious tablets on which were written the commandments of Boré Olam, the other ridged to suggest the steps leading to the holy of holies, the place of the Ark of the Covenant in the Temple. Graven on the front was a flowering branch.

Living in hiding as Jews did in that Kingdom of England, none dared put on their doorposts the ancient symbol of our faith and of the protection of Boré Olam. Nonetheless, I at once recognized what the thing was. Indeed, if I had any doubt, it was dispelled by the Hebrew letter ש, *shin*, etched on the back. This I knew stood for *Shomer Delatot Yisrael,* Guardian of the Doorways of Israel. I held in my hand a mezuzah, and one I believed to be truly unique. Surely it had been brought back as plunder from the site of the Holy Temple in Jerusalem, else it would not be in that place.

There was a deep niche to one side of the digging place—it was not earth but stone and made not by me but by nature, guided I am sure by Boré Olam. In that place I had hidden all that I had so far found of the ancient treasure of my people. In front of those wonderful things, I had put the chest entrusted to me by the monks of the Charterhouse. Thus the bones of the man the monks claimed as a holy martyr guarded the sacred relics of we Jews whom the goyim despise. I put that most Jewish of *mezuzot* on top of the Christian's bones..

❖

19

Two nights after Weinraub's visit to Bristol House, Geoff phoned to say he'd be tied up for the evening. "I have to go to a dinner for a retiring cameraman who used to be part of my crew. I shouldn't be too late. Care to wait at my house?"

"No, thanks. I want to work on the list of cardinals." They'd come up with a source that listed every Catholic cardinal who'd died in the last year and a half. There were twenty-seven, according to Nexis, a remarkable database that allowed subscribers to search the records of every periodical with an English-language edition, including the Vatican's *L'Osservatore Romano.* Nexis could cost as much as three hundred dollars an hour to use—which was why Geoff had access to it and, in the normal way of things, she did not. But he'd given her his password, and she was working through obituaries for all twenty-seven, looking for any mention of quail eggs. If you meant to be thorough—and Annie did— it was slow going. Both Falcone and De Boer were said to have been distinguished and influential. Apart from that, the only commonality she'd discovered was that all were Catholics and dead.

She gripped her phone between shoulder and cheek and kept looking at the screen. "Come back here when you're finished," she said. "I'll wait up."

The next morning, Saturday, dawned gray, cold, and looking like rain. "Charterhouse Square," Annie said. Geoff rolled toward her. It wasn't much of a roll. The bed in Annie's room at Bristol House was an old-fashioned double, so narrow by today's standards as to seem quaint.

"What about Charterhouse Square?" he asked sleepily.

"Last night," she said, "I finished the Nexis search. No more quail eggs in any of the obits."

"You told me."

She had, just before he began waltzing her up and down the long corridor and nuzzling her neck and they went on to other things. "After the cardinals," she continued, "I signed out of Nexis, so you won't need to take out a second mortgage to pay their bill, and went back to the book about the old Carthusians. It says there's a belief in the order that the monks of Tudor times managed to save the bones of the martyred prior, but that they hid them so well, they've never been found."

"Interesting, but I don't think you're likely to find them still hanging around in Charterhouse Square."

"I know, but I want to go." Another thing she'd done before he returned was spend about ten minutes sitting in the back bedroom asking questions. She'd gotten no answers.

"Okay, we'll go. But can we have coffee first? Maybe even a croissant? I know a place that has amazing croissants." He was meanwhile running his hand along her thigh. "On the other hand, it looks like a great morning for a lie-in. With benefits."

Annie was already climbing out of the bed. "I'll make the coffee," she said. "I don't have any croissants, but I can produce some toast."

It was after ten when they got to Charterhouse Square. The weather was no better, and there was almost no one around. Annie and Geoff sat for five silent minutes facing the redbrick Tudor wall. According to the thick guidebook he'd found at Mrs. Walton's and brought along, it was the only part of the old Carthusian monastery still standing.

The rain came. It fell in lashing sheets, and even the large striped umbrella Annie had brought did little to keep them dry.

Geoff turned up his jacket collar. "I'm thinking it might be time to go."

"Can you tolerate a few minutes more?"

"The monk?" he asked eagerly.

"No," Annie said. "Looks like he left in 1537, when Henry closed down all the monasteries. Imagine being told you're not a monk or a nun anymore, and the church no longer requires your prayers."

"That," Geoff said, "had nothing to do with religion. It was pure politics. And probably the greatest land grab of all time."

Annie nodded, looking at the guidebook in Geoff's hands. "What do they say about the Charterhouse after the monks were thrown out?"

"Probably nothing you don't know." He riffled through the pages, reeling off a potted history. "Series of rich blokes owned the place until 1611. When the last one died, his will set up a foundation for eighty male pensioners who had to be either—wait for it—'gentlemen by descent and in poverty,' soldiers who 'had borne arms by sea or land,' or 'merchants decayed by piracy or shipwreck.' It really says decayed. Is that a misprint?"

"Probably not. The old meaning was to have your status lowered."

"As in 'fallen on hard times.'"

"Exactly." The rain was blowing straight at them. Annie shifted the position of the umbrella. "Is this better?"

"It might stave off drowning for a few more minutes. We're almost at the end, anyway." He looked down at the now-sodden guidebook. "The Charterhouse School became one of the cornerstones of English snobbery and thereby—"

"It does not say that."

"No, I'm saying it—cornerstones of snobbery and thereby one of the ways to oppress the worthy working class from places like Portsmouth, who will someday soon rise up and overthrow their cruel masters and—"

"And when they do, you will no longer earn three hundred thousand pounds a year."

"True. Correction: Charterhouse School became one of the finest institutions in the remarkable experiment in democracy that is modern Britain. Which school buggered off to Surrey in 1907. Thirty-plus years later the London buildings were hammered by the Blitz but are now restored and"—he read—"'house St Bartholomew's Hospital Medical School and Queen Mary's School of Medicine and Dentistry, as well as function as a home to forty male pensioners, known as Brothers.' Annie, if we don't get out of here, I shall have to go across the road and offer my pneumonia-ridden body to medical science."

"Maybe they'll let you be a pensioner," she said, standing up. "Brother Geoffrey. Since your situation will definitely be decayed."

Dom Justin
From the Waiting Place

Whilst on the other side, we do not understand that yesterday, today, and tomorrow are artificial distinctions, that time has no reality except what we humans assign to it. Neither do we recognize the meaning of place, its shadows and its links, and how what once existed never goes away but is merely layered and intertwined and made to serve what will be and what must be. We are, as has been said, all players in a single drama where, with eyes obscured and dim understanding, we play our parts on one great stage.

I cannot truly break through, but sometimes I draw the woman to me and she comes. Then, though we are so close as to be able to reach out our hands and touch our fingertips, she cannot see and will neither hear nor listen. I am ignorant as to whether this is willful blindness or simply a stop upon her senses, as seems common to those on the other side.

As I have said, her soul is not in my disposition; nor am I privy to her inmost thoughts. Still, I wait and watch and seek a way. If I can enlist her help, much may be prevented, and perhaps the great wrong of my life will in some measure be corrected. But in the way of Eternal Truth—which only now do I understand—we are none of us separate, and what will serve my good will be for the good of many, most particularly her own.

But for now I cannot find a way to reach her, and the danger grows.

❖

The rain eased off as they left Charterhouse Square. "Is it too early for a pub lunch?" Annie asked. "That toast doesn't seem to have lasted very long."

"My place," Geoff said, turning them onto St. John's Lane. "Much better. We can have a hot shower before we eat and—hang on. Have a look at this."

He was pointing to a small shop wedged between a wine bar and a café. A battered wooden sign read "Game and High-Class Provisions." Beneath it, in a window no more than a yard wide, was a display of dead birds still in full feather, and trays of speckled eggs. "Quail eggs," Jeff said.

"Really?" Annie asked. "I realized the other day that I'd never actually seen one."

A man came to the doorway, lit a cigarette, inhaled deeply, and conscientiously blew the smoke in the opposite direction; then he held the cigarette in his cupped hand. He was grizzled and gray and wore a striped apron that proclaimed him, if not the owner of the shop, at least an employee. "Are those fresh?" Geoff asked, nodding to the eggs.

"Fresh as daisies. Lady we get them from brought them round this morning."

"Round from where?" Annie asked.

"Holloway," he said.

Geoff's eyebrows rose. "You're joking." And to Annie: "That's right here in Central London, just down the road."

"No joke," the man said. "A Mrs. Grindal, she is. Been raising quails in these parts for donkeys. Small birds. Don't take a lot of space. Pack you up a dozen, shall I?" He tossed the cigarette into the gutter as he spoke and headed back into his shop. Geoff reached for his wallet and followed.

They went to his place and took the promised hot shower together. So it was nearly two before they went downstairs. "You are going to make me old before my time," he said. "Delilah, draining all my strength."

Annie ran her fingers through his damp hair, springy with short and wiry curls. "Designer stubble, yes, but I don't think I'd like you with a shaved head. As for draining your strength—that guy I was with was a real tiger. Where did he go?"

"I think he may have run off to the jungle to hunt for food. Lunch next. What do you fancy?"

"Anything as long as it's not quail eggs," she said, her throat closing at the thought.

He made grilled cheese and tomato sandwiches, and they wolfed them down at the kitchen counter, the dozen quail eggs meanwhile sitting between them in their cardboard container. A kind of lethal centerpiece, Annie thought. The shell colors ran from creamy white to dark beige, but all were splotched black in various-size dots. "You're the foodie," she said halfway through her sandwich. "What do they taste like?"

"Quail eggs?" Geoff shrugged. "Nothing special. It's the size that's the draw, I think. Little bitty eggs. Gourmet kitsch. Coffee?"

"I'd rather another of these if you have it." She waved an empty bottle of Schweppes Bitter Lemon. "So if they're not specially good, why did you buy them?"

He handed her a soda from the refrigerator. "Can't say really. It just seemed oddly serendipitous. We go looking for your ghost in Charterhouse Square and don't find him. Then we come across an entire window devoted to bloody quail eggs." He set about making espresso for one.

Annie watched his carefully orchestrated barista routine—the beans ground to just the right degree of fineness, tamped carefully into the brass filter, two thin black streams of coffee flowing into a white porcelain cup at a carefully determined rate of speed. Despite all that, as far as she was concerned, the result was undrinkable. "You must be rotting your insides with all that black sludge."

"Probably. But you're marinating yours with all that fake lemon."

"I suppose. Geoff, you think they're connected somehow, don't you?"

He looked puzzled, but only for a moment. "Your ghost and the quail eggs. Yes, I suppose that's what I've come to believe. I hadn't realized."

"Neither had I," she agreed. "But I think you're right. Somehow they are. Or they could be."

His coffee was ready, and they carried their drinks over to the black leather sofa. Annie grabbed a pencil and a sketchbook on the way. A few days earlier a quantity of both had materialized on a corner of the suspended bookshelves. He'd said he was protecting his supply of paper napkins. "This is the best guesthouse in London," she said now. "It comes with lemon soda and drawing materials."

"Along with one or two other amenities."

"Excellent food," she deadpanned. "Superior in every way."

They sat side by side on the sofa. Annie started to draw. In moments she'd produced a sketch of the old Tudor wall they'd been looking at from Charterhouse Square.

"It amazes me," he said, "how you can do that. That's exactly what we saw."

"That's the problem—there's nothing new. I hoped there might be."

"Something you'd only remember with a pencil in your hand?"

"Yes. But it didn't happen. Geoff, the quail eggs and the ghost—the connection, at least the one in our heads, is Bristol House. That's why we think of them together. Because the quail egg stories materialized while I've been living there."

"And whether or not he was once at the Charterhouse," Geoff said, with a nod to her drawing, "just now Bristol House is the ghost's theater of operation. But don't forget Weinraub. He's another connection."

"Perhaps," she said cautiously.

Geoff put his coffee on the table in front of them. Annie slid her stockinged feet along the table's edge, out of range of any kind of domestic disaster, and roughed a sketch of quail eggs in a nest.

Geoff put his hand over hers. "Stop drawing for a minute. Look at me. Weinraub's dangerous. I care about you, and I have reason to know just how horribly wrong things can go. Physical, irreversible things."

"It doesn't have to be like that," she said, gently disengaging from his grip. "I've got a really big investment in believing the past does not determine the future." She started sketching again. "About Weinraub and Rabin's assassination—how come you couldn't nail him?"

"I couldn't connect the dots. No hard evidence."

"But now," she said, "you've got more resources, and you can make bigger waves." It was something she'd thought of on more than one occasion. He was the famous Geoffrey Harris. What was she? Arm candy? Someone not afraid to need him, Maggie said. She would like to be that strong.

"I've been thinking exactly that," he said.

She was startled, then she realized he was referring to his greater resources.

"—over the ground I covered previously," he was saying. "Find what I missed. I know it's there." He drank the last of his coffee and put down the empty cup. "And we know he lied to you about the source of his information."

"That's not a hanging offense," she said. "It's a long way from planning an assassination."

"True. But . . . I trust my gut in this sort of thing. There's something there, and I want to find it."

"What about your book?" she asked. "Aren't you on deadline?" She was unsure what she was drawing until it began to materialize on the page. She used the tip of her left pinky to rub in shading.

"I don't think checking out Weinraub, at least finding out if there's something worth pursuing, will take more than a week or two. I can spare that. Anyway, I don't wear out my own shoe leather. I have people on the ground do the research." He glanced down at the sketchbook. "What's that?"

She held the drawing at arm's length, so they could both see it more clearly. Next to the sketch of the Charterhouse facade, off to the side of the nest of quail eggs and to a different and larger scale, she'd drawn a rectangular shape about two inches long. A tube of some sort. She had put a Star of David on what appeared to be a convex front.

"Looks like a mezuzah," Geoff said.

"Yes, that's what it is. But I don't know why I drew it. There's none among the Jew of Holborn relics and—wait. I'd forgotten, but I do know. Weinraub mentioned a mezuzah before I left New York for London. Then the day I met him at the Connaught, he brought it up again. I was thinking about the houses and the stippled code. The things I wasn't telling him. So the mezuzah didn't stay with me. Then there was all the business with the mural and the almond trees. He mentioned a mezuzah again when he was leaving."

"A particular mezuzah or mezuzahs in general?"

"It's a Hebrew word," she corrected. "The plural is *mezuzot*. But I think he meant one in particular. He said it would be easy to hide something so small, so it was odd none had come to light."

"They're ubiquitous among Jews even now," Geoff agreed. "Simple to hide in plain sight."

"Yes, exactly. But I don't think they have anything to do with ritual sacrifice, *korbanot*."

"What about your dissertation?" Geoff asked. "Religious symbols on doorways, wasn't it?"

"My God—you do a better background check than the FBI. It was called *The Effect of Protestant Iconoclasm on Sacred Doorway Decoration in Tudor England, 1537–1559*. How did you dig that up?"

"I had to be thorough." He looked sheepish. "I really didn't want you to turn out to be insane."

"Because you knew you liked me. Or might like me."

"Not at first. At first I thought you were one of Weinraub's evil minions. But pretty soon . . . Harris scores again." He mocked a punch to her jaw. "Tell me why you don't think there can be a connection between Weinraub's mezuzahs—*mezuzot*—and your dissertation."

"Because I wrote entirely about Christians. How the architectural habits of centuries were swept away along with established religious norms."

"But you called it 'sacred doorway decoration.' From Weinraub's point of view, couldn't that include your *mezuzot*?"

"Not if he read it. I talked about a statue of the Virgin above the gate, or a crucifix above a door. Even a door knocker shaped like a three-pointed anchor to symbolize the Trinity. All that came to be seen as supporting what was called popery, not Henry's new regime, so it disappeared virtually overnight. It was, as you pointed out this morning, about politics, not variations of belief. Anyway, no Jew hiding in Tudor England would have put a mezuzah in full view on a doorpost. That's crazy."

"Okay, but Weinraub isn't a scholar. Maybe he never actually read what you wrote. Sacred Doorway Decoration. *Mezuzot*. It could have made perfect sense to him."

"Say I grant your logic, where does it get us?"

He got up and started to pace, moving his hands as he talked. "Pretty far, I think. Try this. Weinraub tells you your brief is to find the source of the Jew of Holborn's treasures, but that's a red herring. He may be a bastard, but he's a clever one. Does he really think you're going to come over here for three months and discover a secret treasure room in London no one's found in five hundred years? That's pure Hollywood. Turteltaub, not Weinraub. Our boy's dead serious. Emphasis on *dead*."

"Sidney said pretty much the same thing," she admitted. *Sounds like a movie, not a job, Annie my girl.*

Geoff stopped walking and looked at her. "Sidney male or female?"

"Male."

"And who is he?"

"A friend. At least he was until I broke the contract with the Davis School. Sidney had gone out on a limb to get them to hire me."

"And does this Sidney know anything about Philip Weinraub?"

Annie shook her head. "Nothing. He was worried about all the bridges I was burning. Sidney's a recovering alcoholic. Has been for twenty years. We met through AA. He was my go-to guy, the number I could always call."

"How about now? Is he still your go-to guy?"

The great Geoff Harris was jealous. She wanted to whoop but managed to suppress even the hint of a grin. "Not the same way these days. I don't need Sidney to stay sober."

"Glad to hear it," Geoff said. "Can we get back on track?" And when

Annie nodded: "Suppose the whole 'source of the treasure' talk is a smoke screen. Suppose for the sake of argument that Weinraub's really after something smaller and more ordinary than a secret room you're never going to find. A particular mezuzah, for example. Doesn't that make more sense?"

"Possibly." Annie picked up her drawing, scrutinizing it from a series of angles. "But this isn't anything real. It's a composite, a mishmash of things I've seen and read about. I have no specialized knowledge of *mezuzot*. Why am I any more likely to find this than the secret treasure room?"

"I don't know," he admitted. "It's still about finding something that dates back to 1535, and—"

"Right, Weinraub said that too. Sort of."

"You've lost me."

"He was disappointed that the mural was of twentieth-century London. He kept asking if there were any scenes of an earlier time."

"And are there?"

"I have no idea," Annie admitted. "It's such a jumble. I suppose there could be."

"And if there were"—Geoff was growing visibly more excited as he spoke—"it could also be that those old scenes would identify the whereabouts of a particular mezuzah from 1535. Possibly decorated with an almond branch."

Annie shook her head. "You're really reaching. Though I admit that last part makes sense. According to Rabbi Cohen, almond branches are totemic in Judaism and are often used in sacred art. So where I've put a Star of David"—she tapped her drawing with the pencil still in her hand "there could be an almond branch."

Geoff slammed his fist into his palm. "Maybe, maybe not. I don't think that's what matters, and I don't think this is all that much of a reach. I told you, Weinraub is as wily as they come. I'm betting he thinks there's a clue in the mural—possibly something to do with an almond branch—that points to the whereabouts of a 1535 mezuzah. I think that's what he sent you over here to find."

20

Annie said she had to spend the night at Bristol House, so she could take advantage of the early-morning light and, as she put it, "spend some serious time looking for Waldo."

"With a mezuzah tattooed on his forehead," Geoff said.

"Or an almond branch."

He walked her back to Bristol House well before midnight. "Sure you don't want me to spend the night?"

"Not tonight." She kissed him on the cheek. "I need a good night's sleep in that narrow bed." The real reason, she knew, was that she had spent four years proving she could stand up without a crutch, carve a space in which to be herself. And she was scared of how important to her he was becoming.

Geoff tweaked her nose. "Woman warrior," he said. "I get it." They were standing in front of the creaky old elevator, and he reached across her shoulder and pushed open the gate. Annie backed inside. Geoff rolled the gate shut. She punched the button, and the cage began slowly to ascend. The last thing she saw was his smiling face turned up toward her.

Dom Justin
From the Waiting Place

Though we usually ate alone in our cells, it was the custom of our order that on Sundays we took the midday meal together in the Frator. On the Sabbath that followed that most terrible of my transgressions—Rebecca causing me to break my vow of chastity—I trembled for fear that one of my brothers might smell upon me the foul odor of perfidy and guess it for the unique fragrance generated between a woman's thighs; sweet at the moment of encounter and rancid forever after.

In the Frator we monks ate in silence, sitting across from one another, hooded heads bowed and our faces in deep shadow. Nonetheless I sensed attention fixed on me and prayed its cause to be only that though I was the most recently vowed and priested, the others had taken up my suggestion that Giacomo the Lombard be entrusted with the precious bones of the Venerable Father.

That thought led me to wonder how trust is generated. How does it come to rest on one rather than another, and when is it withdrawn? Four years earlier, when I came to the Charterhouse, Sir Thomas More had been lord chancellor, and none was more powerful save the king himself. Today Sir Thomas was in the Tower, and many said the king was of a mind to execute him, if only His Majesty could secure solid evidence of More's treason. My master meanwhile, despite his secret adherence to the Protestant heresy that the king despised and that Thomas More had worked so vigorously to root out of England, had now been granted yet another honor. In addition to being chancellor of the exchequer and the king's secretary, he was to become England's second-highest judge, master of the rolls.

This waxing and waning of fortune was, I knew, no great rarity in the affairs of men. But of God? Could there be doubt even of who served the true Lord of Heaven and who had been lured into false worship of the Prince of Lies? Such thoughts would not previously have exercised my mind, but in the Charterhouse each monk was given books to study to which laymen had no access. Indeed, among us were those who transcribed ancient texts and guarded secret histories of popes and cardinals long dead. I had myself recently read that little more than a hundred years earlier a number of cardinals unhappy with the sitting pope had declared his election null and chosen another who called himself Clement VII, but whom still other cardinals claimed to be the Antichrist. Thus was brought about the Great Schism, during which there was one pope in Rome and another in Avignon. Which terrible condition lasted fifty years and was not healed until 1429.

I thought then of Pilate's question, "What is truth?" and knew that we all, even when face-to-face with the King of Heaven and Earth, believe what we wish to believe.

At the very moment I was thinking such thoughts, I raised my head, and peering out from the shadows of my cowl, I saw the eyes of the saintly Dom Hilary upon me. For many seconds we looked at each other, and I was chilled by the certainty that the holy old man knew of the many times I had left the monastery, and that he waited only for one more excursion to denounce me. Then I would be driven from the Charterhouse with the curse of every Carthusian living and dead upon my head. As for my master, enraged at how I'd failed him, he would swiftly send me either to burn at Smithfield or to be butchered at Tyburn.

If, as an alternative, I took to ignoring the summons of the speckled egg and thus denied Hilary the final proof he needed, my master would know I had chosen the rule of the Carthusians over his commands. At which point he would equally quickly sign the order that sent me to an agonizing death.

And when the end finally came, I thought, what would follow? Not mercy, surely. Not for one who had committed such sins as were on my yet-unshriven soul. Be it after Smithfield or after Tyburn, I was sure I would burn forever in the fires of Hell.

❖

Annie opened the door of number eight and reached for the remote. The BBC told her the pope had been released from the hospital, and despite rumors to the contrary, the Vatican insisted he was recovering. The voice moved on to a discussion of the London water supply.

She stood for a moment as she always did, hesitating, listening not to the radio but to the sound beyond it. The flat felt empty and normal, but particularly damp. It had stopped raining a couple of hours before. Maybe she'd left a window open. She did a quick spin through the rooms, putting on all the lights as she went. Every window was closed tight. When she got to the back bedroom, she paused and took a deep breath, then went in. Nothing was extraordinary or out of place, and neither window was open. The dampness, however, was palpable. "What do you want?" she whispered. "What are you trying to tell me?"

There was no hint of any reply, and she turned away, heading for the bathroom in the long hallway.

The steam poured out as soon as she opened the door. Annie gasped. No water was running, but it felt as if she—someone—had just stepped out of a bath or turned off the shower. She stood where she was, breathing hard. In moments the air cleared sufficiently that she could see a message on the mirror over the sink. The elaborate Tudor script was handwritten in the moisture on the glass and ran corner to corner: *Seek here the Speckled Egg.*

Her heart was pounding. "How am I to do that?" she whispered. "Why? Tell me what you want."

She waited but heard nothing, then dashed across the hall to the bedroom where she'd dropped her bag and began searching frantically for her phone. It wasn't there. Moments later she found it in the pocket of the jacket she'd been wearing and ran back to the bathroom, praying the words on the mirror would still be visible. They were. *Seek here the Speckled Egg.*

The phone was an Android, a cheaper version of the iPhone she'd really wanted, but the camera was decent. Annie snapped the mirror from a number of angles, not pausing to examine her results, just moving in and stepping back, snapping as quickly as she could, always afraid the mirror would dry and the lettering would disappear. After the fourth shot, that was exactly what happened. The bathroom felt perfectly dry, and the mirror was blank. She ran back to the dining room, deciding she'd upload the pictures to her laptop, then send them to Geoff. Probably to Maggie and Rabbi Cohen as well.

Except there were no pictures. Nothing showed on her phone. Nonetheless she stubbornly went through the uploading process. The laptop screen remained blank.

"I'll come right now," Geoff said, when she called and told him what had happened.

"No, don't."

"Why the hell not? How many times do I have to say it? I care about you."

"I know. I'm . . . That matters. A lot. But the ghost doesn't mean me any harm. He wants to tell me something. I'm sure of it."

"Jesus, Annie."

"It was a message meant for me," she said. "It was written in Tudor script. I'm the only person remotely connected to this flat who could read it."

"Okay, but I can be with—"

"No," she said. "There's no need. I'll be fine. We'll talk tomorrow. Good night."

They hung up. Annie took a few minutes to sketch exactly what she'd seen, first with paleographic correctness, as by a Tudor hand, then a second time in modern lettering.

She went to bed feeling somehow peaceful. "We've got somewhere, haven't we?" she whispered into the dark. "You and I are starting to understand each other. The speckled egg. You mean the quail eggs, don't you? You're saying I'm to look for something to do with the dead cardinals. And I think you know I have to find what Philip Weinraub wants. You must know, because that's why I'm here in this flat, where you can tell me things. Geoff and I think it's a special mezuzah. That probably doesn't have anything to do with a Carthusian monk, and I don't know what the vanishing point is, where Weinraub's agenda and yours meet, but I think you do. If you want to tell me, I'm listening." There was no reply. Nonetheless she had a greater feeling of peace than she'd had for weeks.

Still, she slept fitfully—conscious of the mural and its possible secrets in the room with her—and woke at first light.

Find Waldo. Or whatever it was that Weinraub had been looking for and was hoping she would find. And probably if she did, she'd know what the ghost wanted as well.

Annie began with high hopes, but it was a daunting task. The small scale of the individual drawings made it almost impossible to pick out a detail as tiny as a mezuzah, and the sheer number of scenes was overwhelming. The wall was fourteen feet in length and eleven feet high; an unbroken expanse completely covered in infinitely detailed black and white scenes, each occupying a space no more than eight or nine inches square.

The individual views bore no geographic relationship to one another. The familiar winged Cupid of Piccadilly Circus gave way to Buckingham Palace on the right, and what she thought might be the Smithfield meat market on the left. Above both was a cobbled alley of some sort. By the time she came to it, her eyes were watering. She switched from the naked eye to her jeweler's loupe. It was an improvement, but the narrow spectrum of enlargement wasn't ideal for the job, and squinting into it for long periods was a strain.

She went down the hall and through the drawing room— past the murmur of the radios, broadcasting in unison the Sunday-morning sermon of a preacher comparing the miracles of Jesus to winning Olympic gold —into Mrs. Walton's office. There was a magnifying glass on a small table, but it was the heavy sort meant to be put on a document and slid over it. All her training rebelled at the thought of physically assaulting the old mural in that way. Neither could she make herself believe it acceptable to go through the drawers of her landlady's desk.

She was stuck with the loupe. It was all she had until she could get to a specialist optics shop and buy the kind of high-quality, hand-held magnifying glass the job demanded. London stores of that sort were closed until Monday.

By noon, when Geoff phoned to ask if she wanted to meet for lunch, not just her eyes but her neck and shoulders felt permanently damaged. And she'd covered only a section of the mural some two feet from the outside wall and as high as her head. Nothing she'd seen revealed anything remotely connected to almond trees, or Tudor times, or Jews, much less *mezuzot* or anything else that might be of interest to Philip Weinraub.

Or, as far as she could tell, her Carthusian ghost.

"Just so you know," Geoff said, reaching into his pocket, "I'm not only a pretty face."

Annie grinned. "You are, though. A very pretty face."

He did not look pleased by the compliment. "Given the circumstances, you're rather lighthearted."

"Not lighthearted, no. But I'm starting to get it. At least I think I am."

"Can I ask what 'it' is?" He was holding a folded sheet of paper, but he made no effort to pass it over.

"I'm not sure," Annie admitted. "But the ghost wants something from me."

Geoff hesitated. "Prayers for his soul, something like that?"

She shook her head. "I don't think so. Why would any ghost come to me for that? But this one . . . he's played to all my strengths, Geoff. I think he wants my"—she blushed—"my expertise."

"Tudor buildings. Doorway decorations." He did not sound convinced.

"Something like that. 'Seek here the Speckled Egg.' It was a direction. Something I'm supposed to do." She waited a moment. He said nothing. "Why do you look like that?"

"Because against my better judgment and my common sense, I'm thinking you may be right."

They were in the gastropub in Cosmo Place, the one he'd taken her to the first time they'd had dinner together. It was jammed, and apparently the big attraction was a traditional British Sunday lunch—everyone around them was tucking into roast beef and Yorkshire pudding. They'd both ordered lentil soup and ham sandwiches. "I spent some time checking after you called," Geoff said. "I've got something."

Quite a lot of time, Annie thought. The stubble was heavier than usual, and his eyes were as red-rimmed as she imagined hers to be. "Time on what?" she asked.

"Using my Nexis connection mostly." He took a folded piece of paper from his jacket pocket.

"Let me guess," she said. "You've discovered something new about Philip Weinraub."

He shook his head. "I've exhausted that avenue long since. Weinraub's secrets are too well hidden for Nexis. I was looking for Mrs. Grindal."

"Who?"

"The bloke who sold us the quail eggs said they came from a Mrs. Grindal. According to him, she raises quail in Holloway. That seemed mad to me. Holloway's in the East End, one of the most densely populated parts of London."

"But he said she'd been doing it for donkeys," Annie said. "That meant 'a long time,' didn't it?"

"Exactly. It's Cockney rhyming slang. *Donkey's ears* equals *years*. Common parlance now. Anyway, there isn't any Mrs. Grindal. At least not one living in Holloway who raises quail."

Annie didn't say anything for a few moments. Then: "That's really interesting. It sounded so convincing. Maybe he had the name wrong."

"It's not that simple," Geoff said. "Take a look at this." He finally passed her the piece of paper he'd been hanging on to.

Annie studied it for a moment, then looked up. "I'm not sure what I should be seeing."

"'High-Class Provisions'—that's what the sign said, remember?" And when she nodded: "We were in St. John's Lane. It's a short street. What you've got there is a list of every address and proprietor. There isn't any provisioner. No grocer of any sort, high-class or otherwise."

"It was a tiny little shop between a café and the wine bar," Annie said.

"And when you went back," Rabbi Cohen said, "it wasn't there."

He was looking at Annie's drawing of the tiny shop with the quail and the quail eggs in the window, and the sign above that said "High-Class Provisions." She had drawn it at the moment when the man came out the door and was standing and talking to them, holding a cigarette in his cupped hand so the smoke didn't drift in their direction.

It was Monday afternoon, and they were in Simon Cohen's study. Maggie was supposed to have joined them, but at the last minute she said she was coming down with a cold and begged off. Not even the chance to see a picture of a shop that appeared and disappeared in twenty-four hours tempted her. She'd dismissed that story instantly. "You were in a different street, Geoffrey. There's no other explanation." Annie wondered if Maggie simply didn't want to come to the house that was still, in some sense, the domain of Simon Cohen's wife.

Maggie's absence did not, however, alter the fact that Rabbi Cohen shared her opinion about the shop in St. John's Lane. "You were probably in a different street," the rabbi said, pushing the drawing back toward Annie. "It's easy to make that kind of error." He waved a dismissive hand.

Maggie's already told him about it, Annie thought. They've reinforced each other's skepticism.

Geoff apparently came to the same conclusion. He put the list of addresses and their current occupants in his pocket and didn't mention what he and Annie knew—that they had returned to Charterhouse Square and walked every inch of the surrounding neighborhood and seen nothing of the grocer or his shop.

Cohen turned his attention to Annie's sketch of the writing on the bathroom mirror. "It's difficult to read. Making it, I presume, still more authentic."

"It's written in the script common to the Tudor period," Annie said. "It's very different from ours, but you get used to it after a while. It says 'Seek here the Speckled Egg.' The 'here' stumps me. I've looked all over the flat. The only eggs are the ones I bought at the supermarket, and they're definitely not speckled. Leaving that aside, I think the ghost may have been referring to the dead cardinals we were talking about a couple of weeks ago."

"Because they both had quail eggs in their throats," Cohen said.

"More than that. It's like a dog whistle," she said. "In my brain. Something I can hear because I'm supposed to. And he's a monk, remember. So cardinals—"

Cohen nodded. "What about the police? Surely they must already be investigating the quail eggs 'coincidence'?" He surrounded the word with air quotes.

"I've got some feelers out about that," Geoff said. Annie knew he'd been waiting for days for a callback from someone at Interpol.

"And"—the rabbi began making notes on a pad—"we now know Philip Weinraub lied about the source of his information. And you and Geoff have come to the not-unlikely belief that he is seeking a mezuzah of some sort, which may be decorated with an almond branch. But"—with another of those dismissive waves—"what he actually wants, what his agenda may be—I don't see what this tells us. It does, however, indicate he might not be the originator of the *A* code. The code is embedded in the German documents, and it now seems they existed long before Weinraub got his hands on them."

"But he knows about it," Geoff said. "That's why he concealed it when he had the English translations made for Annie."

Cohen nodded. "True. Leaving us with the connection to the Carthusian monk. Which I also still don't understand. Maybe, Annie, your ghost has nothing to do with Weinraub and all the rest."

"Not so," Annie said stubbornly. "The ghost is part of everything else."

"I thought you and Maggie," Geoff said, "were of the opinion that with puzzles, there's always a connection."

"Frequently, not always," Cohen amended.

Geoff went on as if he hadn't heard. "And according to Maggie, back at Bletchley you were one of the 'clever blokes in hut three.' Supposed to be good at linking the pieces and seeing the overall pattern."

"We were dealing with Nazis," Cohen said, shaking his head. "They were more predictable than ghosts." He put down his pen. "I'm out of my element. Ghosts, mystical messages"—he looked in Geoff's direction—"even a disappearing grocer—I'm sorry, it's not my kind of mystery, and I can't help."

"But you're a rabbi," Annie said.

"A sort of rabbi. Not the sort you mean. My dear, you're asking me to revisit all the arguments I had with myself right after the war, when I was deciding whether to enter the rabbinate. I will tell you the answer

I finally came up with, but it won't satisfy you. For me, for many Jews, the issue is living like a Jew, not dying like one. Death will occur whatever we do. How we live, that's a choice. That's why I'm a rabbi."

He glanced upward, as if, Annie thought, he could see through the ceiling to his demented wife's room. "I wish you'd had an opportunity to know Esther," he said softly. "She was a lovely person." Then, before they could comment: "Go home, you two. I will think about this. Maybe there's someone . . . I'll make a call. If the man I'm thinking of will see you, I'll be in touch."

21

"Both of you," Cohen said when he called the next day. "I thought maybe he'd agree to see only Annie, but he says you can both go."

Rabbi Nachum Hazan lived in Stamford Hill. "The Piccadilly Line as far as Manor House," Cohen instructed. "From there you'll have a walk of maybe ten minutes. I'm e-mailing the link to a map. Wear a skirt, Annie. Not trousers or jeans."

"A long skirt," she said, "and long sleeves. I understand. Do I have to cover my head?"

"No, not for Hazan. He's modern Orthodox, not a Hasid. But don't expect him to shake your hand."

Annie had said again that she understood. Now, as Geoff rang Rabbi Hazan's bell, she wasn't so sure. These streets had a decided sense of otherness. They were crowded with bearded men wearing black hats, and women pushing carriages of every size and shape and shepherding what seemed like dozens of children.

The woman who opened the door was not like them. She wore jeans, for one thing, and didn't have anything tied around her head. She was also pretty in a quiet sort of way, but she looked very tired, even a bit frazzled. About forty, Annie thought, with a fat and beaming baby resting on her hip. Annie heard other children in the background, loud enough that there must be quite a few of them. "You're the couple to see my husband," the woman said. "Come in."

She showed them into what was obviously Rabbi Hazan's study. "Sit down," she said. "The rabbi won't be long."

Moments later he arrived, closing the door softly behind him. He had, Annie noted at once, dark brown eyes that smiled at them from behind horn-rimmed glasses. She and Geoff had taken seats across from the desk. Nachum Hazan motioned them to another part of the room, a couch and a couple of chairs beside the window. "Come, sit over here. We'll be more comfortable."

"Thanks for agreeing to see us, Rabbi," Geoff said.

"You are welcome. I hope I can help." He sat opposite them and Annie caught a glimpse of the fringed garment—the small *tallith* worn always by Orthodox Jewish men—beneath his dark cardigan. She'd read about such things when she began studying Judaica; it was only a couple of months ago, but it felt like a lifetime. Hazan wore as well a white shirt and a dark tie and of course a skullcap. And he had a full untrimmed beard, nothing like Simon Cohen's elegant goatee.

"The story Rabbi Cohen told me," he began, "your ... communications, Dr. Kendall. The search for the ancient Judaica. It's all quite fascinating."

"Did he mention the quail eggs?" Geoff asked.

"Oh, yes. And even a grocer who seems to have disappeared, though Rabbi Cohen is less convinced about that."

"May I ask," Geoff said, "if you've ever encountered similar phenomena?"

"Personally," the rabbi said softly, "no. Is that what you mean, Mr. Harris?"

"But you study such things," Annie said, jumping in before Geoff could answer. She'd promised Rabbi Cohen she'd keep him in line. *Nachum is not on Geoffrey's show. He should not be interrogated.* "We're hoping you can help us understand."

"I can try. But these are complex realities. I doubt I will have"—he paused, hunting for a word—"a tidy answer." He took off his glasses, leaned back, and closed his eyes. "I've heard the facts from Rabbi Cohen, but I would like to hear them from you, Dr. Kendall. Every detail you can remember, please."

Annie had been rehearsing the story in her mind for hours, rather as if she were mounting an academic defense. She reached into her tote bag. "It might help if you could take a look at these." She held out the sketchbook that contained her drawings of the monk. It was open to the one where he had his back to her.

Hazan took the sketchbook, holding it at arm's length. Then he put on the horn-rimmed glasses and drew it closer.

"There are other views," Annie said.

He turned the page. "Ah yes, the face." He looked at the drawing, then at Geoff. "Definitely your face, Mr. Harris. I'm told many people in Britain know what you look like."

"Dr. Kendall had never seen me when she drew that," Geoff said. The challenge in his voice was unmistakable.

"I don't doubt it," Hazan said mildly. "I'm only pointing out that here, too" —he looked up and smiled—"I am acting on information conveyed by third-party sources. I don't watch television." Then, to Annie: "Permit me to explain, Dr. Kendall. I realize we seem very different to you, but my family and I don't reject all modernity. We have a television. My children watch far too much, as far as I'm concerned. And my wife, who as it happens has a degree in political philosophy from Princeton, writes a column on moral governance for our community newspaper. She tells me, Mr. Harris, that you are a very astute commentator on politics. That your mother was part of the Kindertransport, as Rabbi Cohen explained, neither of us knew."

"I'm not actually—" Geoff began.

Hazan held up his hand. "You are not an observant Jew. That too Rabbi Cohen told me. Now, let us continue."

Hazan returned to studying the drawing, holding it in one hand while the other tapped a restless rhythm on the arm of his chair. "So, Dr. Kendall, from May first you are in London, living in a flat where a mysterious monk is also in residence."

"Only sometimes," Annie said. "And except for the crazy business with the store on St. John's Lane, Geoff can't—"

The rabbi stopped her with another wave of his hand. "The matter of the grocer is a different sort of thing entirely. We will discuss it later.

Now, I understand that you saw the monk when you were alone, before you met Mr. Harris. But after that?"

"The next thing was a phosphorescent glow," she said. "From under the door of the back bedroom, where I first saw the monk. Geoff had come to Bristol House, and I went into the kitchen and saw the shining and called him. He came, but even though we were both standing in the hall looking at it, Geoff couldn't see it."

Hazan leaned forward and returned her sketchbook. "How long?"

"I'm sorry, I'm not sure I understand."

"The glow," Hazan said. "How long did it last?"

Annie considered. "Thirty, maybe forty seconds. No longer. Possibly a bit less."

"You concur, Mr. Harris?"

"Well, it's hard to say, since I didn't see it. But from the time Annie called me until she said it was gone . . . about half a minute, yes."

Hazan's feet began to tap out the same rhythm that his hand was beating on the arm of the chair. "As that sort of thing goes, a long time," he said.

"What sort of thing?" Geoff asked. "That's the question, isn't it?"

"Perhaps. You are a skeptic, Mr. Harris. That is your right, of course. But in Judaism we have a saying. *Lo ra'ete eyno re'ayah.* 'I have not seen is no proof.' Because you have not seen something doesn't mean it does not exist. The world is full of mysteries. Dr. Kendall is not the first person to encounter one of them. Please"—fingers and toes still tapping in unison—"after the phosphorescent glow, then what? Tell me the rest."

She backtracked to the bell, book, and candle incident, then described the singing and the unnatural heat. That part of the story took perhaps another five minutes. About halfway through the narrative, Hazan began humming softly under his breath. The sound was so muted, Annie wasn't sure he knew he was making it.

"'Seek here the Speckled Egg,'" she said finally. "Written diagonally in Tudor script across my bathroom mirror. In moisture caused by steam that should not have been there. And when I snapped it with my cell phone camera, it didn't show up. Not on the phone and not on my computer." Then, thinking of what he'd said about television: "My cell phone has a camera, and normally I can—"

Hazan nodded toward his desk. "About that I know."

There was a sleek laptop on it, open so she could see the perky apple etched on the cover. Juxtaposed with the untrimmed beard and the fringes and the humming and tapping, the high-end computer should have seemed peculiar. The impression of a powerful intellect served to pull it all together. "A man of many parts," she said, then blushed furiously, thinking it sounded condescending. "I don't mean to—"

He chuckled. "You are expecting me to have certain attitudes and practices, and you are surprised when I do not. I am classically Orthodox, Dr. Kendall, not a member of a Hasidic sect. Today in Britain Jews such as myself are outnumbered, but I assure you we are not a dying breed. Even in America. Now . . . please . . . I have to think how to explain what I can tell you and what I cannot. And why. Please," he repeated, "have a bit of patience." He sat back in his chair and closed his eyes. The humming began again. Annie and Geoff waited. After a time Hazan said, "I think we must not be misled by the differences between supernatural and preternatural."

"Above nature or simply beyond it," Geoff said.

"Exactly. Your experience with the provisioner in St. John's Lane, Mr. Harris. That might be neither. It could be only a hoax, a clever charade. An empty store taken over for a few hours by someone who wishes for one or another reason to cause you to buy quail eggs."

"That's impossible," Annie blurted. "First of all, why? Second and even more important, no one knew we were going to be walking along that street at that time."

Geoff looked as if he'd been drowning and just caught a lifeline. "I don't know, Annie. Maybe—"

"It's absurd," Annie said.

Hazan stepped into the chasm between them. "I agree it is unlikely, Dr. Kendall. But you must admit it is not impossible. Which is my only point. Further, that was a single experience, whereas the things you have encountered at Bristol House have been recurrent and have taken a variety of forms. That makes them much less likely to be a hoax. It's a great deal more difficult to repeat a clever trick. The likelihood of being unmasked increases with each instance."

Both Annie and Geoff nodded agreement. Hazan continued: "So in the matter of the Bristol House manifestations, we will rule out some elaborate charade with a purpose none of us can fathom."

"Then you think," Annie said, "they are mystical experiences." Rabbi Cohen had told them that Nachum Hazan was the author of a number of books on Jewish mystics and Jewish mysticism.

"No," Hazan said quietly. "I do not. I suspect it is a preternatural experience. But like the supernatural, it is never easy to explain."

"I realize you're an expert on Jewish mysticism," Geoff said. "But in this instance Annie is—"

Hazan cut him off. "I know, Mr. Harris. Dr. Kendall is being visited by a Carthusian monk, most assuredly not a Jew. Trust me, it makes no difference. All mysticism is simply trying to understand as much of the One as the One wishes us to understand. It is probing what is known, not what is hidden. In Hebrew we call the attributes of what can be known *sephirot,* and ten are acknowledged. All of this is related to kabbalah. Rabbi Cohen tells me that the documents you were given by Philip Weinraub contain a kabbalistic code, but that even after he broke it with the aid of your mother, Mr. Harris, it meant nothing."

"That's right. The letter *A* repeated over and over. It makes no sense to any of us."

"And that is why I can tell you that your code, whatever it may be, was not designed by a believer in kabbalah. From the first text we can positively identify, Isaac the Blind writing in Provence in the twelfth century, the purpose of kabbalah is to enlighten so we may worship with more fervor. If the code your mother and Rabbi Cohen found does not point in that direction, it is not a kabbalistic code. Only a code designed using kabbalistic techniques. And that's why I do not think your encounters, Dr. Kendall, are to do with mysticism. Nothing that has happened, nothing you've described, indicates that you are being summoned to some greater understanding of the sacred. I suspect what is happening to you—perhaps even to you, Mr. Harris, in the matter of the grocer's shop where none is known to exist—may be a kind of wrinkle in time. Not metaphysical, simply preternatural. Beyond what we know."

Hazan got up, went to a bookcase, and pulled out a slim volume. "*Burnt Norton*," he said. "T. S. Eliot." He flicked through the pages. " 'Time present and time past are both perhaps present in time future,' " he read, " 'and time future contained in time past.' " He closed the book and slid it back into position on the shelf. "That is the insight as expressed by a poet. Einstein came at the same puzzle in a more practical way. For him the simile was that of traveling on a river. In your punt—Einstein didn't say that, but for me as a Cambridge man, always it is a punt—you can see only the part of the river you are on. The reach, I believe it's called. But where you've been, the water around the river bend at your back, and where you're going, the river bend ahead of you, those reaches are also there. They are always present. You simply cannot see them from your current position."

"Dr. Kendall thinks," Geoff said, "the monk wants something from her. She believes that's the meaning of the message about seeking the speckled egg. But if he's dead, living in some kind of afterlife, why would he want anything?"

Hazan returned to his seat. "You're asking a question about belief, Mr. Harris. That is not part of this discussion. If you wish to come and see me sometime to speak further about such things, about your personal heritage, I would be delighted."

She had, Annie realized, been effectively shut out. Not only was she a woman, she was not a Jew. She sensed Geoff about to say something scathing and jumped in. "I think you're saying, Rabbi Hazan, that belief doesn't matter. That the solution, at least in this case, is not outside nature but natural in a way we don't yet understand."

"Precisely. Looked at one way, your encounters raise questions about mysticism, about heaven and an afterlife. All of us, Dr. Kendall, want to know such things. But they are hidden. Like the name of the creator of the universe, in Hebrew, Boré Olam. That is one of the names we Jews use because *the* name cannot be known. On Mount Sinai, when Moses asks Boré Olam for this information, he is told, *e'yeh asher e'yeh*, 'I am that I am.' The nature of time is not such a mystery, only something not yet entirely understood by science."

"If it's science"—Annie could not keep the frustration from her voice—"not mysticism, why wasn't I able to take a picture of the words? Why am I the only one who sees what I see?"

Hazan shrugged. "I have no idea. Science has rules, but something this far removed from what we know . . . who can say what the rules are, Dr. Kendall? Certainly not I."

She considered for a moment. "So the bottom line . . . you're saying I'm seeing around the river bend."

"No, not exactly." The rabbi spoke slowly, as if he were weighing every word. "I think I'm saying that your monk, whoever he may be and wherever he may be—he is seeing around the bend."

22

Geoff had put the quail eggs in the refrigerator as soon as they brought them home. After they returned from Stamford Hill and after they had dinner, when they'd been analyzing everything Hazan said for maybe three hours, he took them out and put them on the counter and stared at them for a long time. "It could have been Weinraub," he said finally. "Could have been. That's all I'm saying."

"And it could have been Santa Claus paying an early visit." Annie loaded the last of the dishes into the dishwasher. "Look, I grant you Weinraub has the resources to put together such an elaborate charade. But unless he's also dabbling in mind control, he had no way to know we'd be on that street at that time."

"Hazan said it could be the explanation. It was the first possibility he mentioned."

"He said it was highly unlikely. And he can't be a fool, remember. He's a Cambridge man."

Geoff looked glum. "I will refrain from telling you how many fools can claim that distinction. But," he added, "Rabbi Hazan doesn't strike me as one of them."

Their dinner had been something he called a gratin of celeriac, which sounded healthy and boring but became spectacular when he added cream and cheese and toasted walnuts. The baking dish wouldn't fit into the dishwasher, so she put it in the sink and ran water into it. "You're latching onto that idea because it's easier to—"

The doorbell rang.

It was nearly nine. Geoff looked at her and raised his eyebrows. She shrugged. He headed for the door.

The visitor was Clary Colbert, come, he said, so Geoff could talk him down. "I should have phoned, but that bastard got me so mad, I walked out without my mobile." He looked at Annie. "See? I've been in this damp dark underworld called London too long. I'm beginning to talk like them. Without my cell," he amended.

"Sit down," Geoff said. "I'll get you a drink." Annie went to sit on the sofa near Clary. Geoff took a bottle of Dewar's from one of the kitchen cabinets and began doing something with the coffee machine. "I take it the bastard in question is Rob Franklin," he said.

"None other than."

"What happened?"

"I went into the studio to finish up some stuff and caught him going over your notes for future shows. The Nubian was with him."

"Well, well," Geoff said. He was holding the cup below the stream of coffee but turned to look at Annie. "Time to put you in the picture. The other night when we had the knees-up for the retiring cameraman, Clary told me he thought Rob was trying to undermine me. That he's been cozying up to an Egyptian newsreader affectionately known to journalistic London as the Nubian. Because of how well she's endowed."

"Best rack in town," Clay said. He did not sound happy about it.

"She was with the BBC until a couple of months ago." Geoff had turned back to the espresso machine. "Got made redundant in a belt-tightening exercise. Clary thinks Rob's trying to get her a show of her own with our lot. Maybe make me superfluous. That's it, isn't it? Nothing more?"

"She was in the office with him," Clary said. "They were going through your desk. What more do you want?"

"What advantage," Annie asked, "does Rob Franklin gain if this Nubian gets a show?"

"Not a show," Geoff said. "My show. There's a limited number of slots for this sort of thing."

"I thought Rob Franklin was your friend."

"So did I," Geoff admitted.

"He's banging her," Clary said.

Annie immediately felt sorry for Jennifer.

"Maybe," Geoff said. "Maybe not. Not germane to this scenario. My program was already established when Rob came on board. He gets no kudos for making it work. If he produces a new player, makes her a star, that counts as his goal. Goes on his side of the score sheet."

"He's banging her," Clary repeated.

Geoff came to join them, carrying a tray with a couple of cups of espresso, the bottle of whiskey, and another Schweppes for Annie. "You're not exactly a nonbiased observer," he said to Clary. And to Annie: "Clary and Rob have been oil and water from day the first. Except that our black brother here is the best techie on two continents, he'd have been gone long since."

"Except that you didn't let it happen," Clary corrected.

Geoff shrugged. "Enlightened self-interest." He picked up the Dewar's and tipped a shot into one of the cups of coffee. "I'm thinking café royale or a reasonable facsimile. If you want a proper whiskey, I'll get you a glass."

Clary stood up. "I'll get it. How come you left your notes hanging around like that, man? Right there in your desk drawer."

"Didn't seem important. I've got copies of everything here at home."

"It is definitely important. He was pawing through your stuff and telling the Nubian he could get her most of the same interviews, and he'd—whoa, what's this?"

Colbert's route to the kitchen had taken him past Geoff's desk. He was staring at something on it.

"What?" Annie and Geoff asked the question simultaneously.

"Who drew this picture of Franklin? Why?"

The chill started at Annie's toes. She knew what Clary was looking at even though she wasn't close enough to see it. "I did the drawing," she said, getting up and going toward him. "Sketching is part of my job. Sometimes I do it to help me remember things."

Geoff remained where he was, staring at her intently but waiting until she reached Clary's side and picked up the drawing to say, "I'm guessing it's the picture of the intruder."

"Yes." She'd sketched him the morning after the break-in, on a single piece of paper because it was back before Geoff had laid in a supply of sketchbooks.

Clary shook his head, impatient with their talk, certainly not understanding it. "How come you drew a picture of Franklin?" he demanded again, looking at Annie as if she had somehow crossed into the camp of the enemy.

"How do you know it's Franklin?" she asked. "I didn't do a face. I couldn't remember what he looked like. I only saw him for a second or two."

"It's Franklin," Clary insisted. "I work with the guy every day. That's how he stands. When he's at the door of the edit suite, watching what I'm doing, that's the way he tilts his head. Besides, that's his jacket. His fleece. The one with the z-shape thing on the zipper. He wears it all the time. I'd know it anywhere."

"You're saying it was Rob Franklin who busted into Annie's place and downloaded all the crap on her hard drive?" Clary asked.

He was sprawled in a chair. Geoff and Annie were on the couch. Geoff had his arm around her. She could smell the scotch he'd poured into his coffee, or maybe the glass Clary was sipping from. Her thirst was visceral. She knew she could drink enough other stuff to float the *Titanic* and still not quench it. Annie slid a little to her left, a bit farther from the alcohol-scented fumes. The drawing was on the coffee table. "If that's a picture of Rob Franklin," she said, nodding toward it, "then yes, he's the one who broke in."

Geoff picked up the drawing and gazed at it intently for a few seconds. "It's Franklin. No doubt at all, now that Clary's pointed it out. I think I said the first time there was something familiar I couldn't put my finger on."

"Sounds just like him, to fuck up at the end and yank the stick so the notice got logged," Clary said. "But why should he care what's on Annie's laptop?"

"The million-pound question," Geoff said. "And no lifelines remain."

"Crap show." Clary dismissed the quiz program with a wave of his hand. "But Franklin—there has to be an answer. He's a bastard, not an idiot. He wouldn't do something like that for no reason."

"Bringing us," Annie said, "back to the important question. Why would Rob Franklin want what was on my laptop?" She turned and looked at Geoff. He looked back.

"You two know something," Clary said. "C'mon, cut me in. I'm the one who recognized your burglar."

"Shut up a minute," Geoff said. He turned to Annie. "Clary's all right. I'd trust him with anything."

"Hold it," Clary said. "How did my trustworthiness get to be the issue?"

Annie took a deep breath. "When you came to Bristol House to look at my laptop, we didn't tell you everything."

"No lies," Geoff said. "Just not the whole truth."

"Your turn to shut up," Clary said. "The lady has the floor."

Probably, if they hadn't spent the afternoon with Rabbi Hazan, Annie would have told only the Weinraub part of the story. As it was, with the simile of the river bends fresh in her mind, she told it all.

"Holy fucking shit." Clary's first words—he'd been silent throughout her recitation—spoken while he was bent over the drawings on the coffee table. Annie had produced the full set, all the sketchbook records of the search for the treasure of the Jew of Holborn—which they now thought might be simply the search for a particular mezuzah—as well as the Bristol House phenomena. And of course the drawing of the grocery shop and the man in the striped apron. Everything she'd brought to Rabbi Hazan's earlier in the day. "This is some fucking story. You're sure you didn't just mess up about what street you were in? So there's really no mystery about the place with the quail eggs."

Geoff sighed. "Who the hell knows?"

I do, Annie thought, and so do you, but she didn't comment.

"These exact quail eggs?" Clary asked. Geoff had brought them to the coffee table while Annie described what had happened. One of the small indentations meant to hold the eggs was empty. "How come there're only eleven?"

"These exact quail eggs," Geoff confirmed. "And we cracked one to see if they were as real as they looked."

"You eat it?"

"No, we did not. You want to try, be my guest."

"Hell, no." Clary recoiled. "Some fucking story," he repeated.

"With a few missing chapters," Geoff said. "Such as why, going back to what you said earlier, Franklin would get mixed up in it."

Clary shrugged. "Maybe that's getting to sound less crazy. Your Shalom Foundation is a Jewish outfit. Franklin's half Jewish. Could be that's the tie. Could be he's working for Weinraub."

"It could be," Annie said. "Certainly the Shalom Foundation is the common denominator. They were the ones who first directed me to Jennifer Franklin, Rob's wife. Granted, she's a recognized expert in Tudor history, but she's not the only one in town. I might have looked elsewhere, except they sent me to Jennifer. And the flat I'm using belongs to the aunt of Weinraub's secretary, Sheila MacPherson. She mentioned she'd stayed with her aunt from time to time. She could easily have had a key and given it to Weinraub. He gave it to Rob Franklin, and that's how he got in."

"MacPherson doesn't sound Jewish," Clary said. "Why would she be mixed up with this Weinraub character?"

"I think," Geoff said, "she may belong to one of those Protestant sects that are so interested in seeing all the Jews return to Israel. So the Second Coming of Jesus can occur and the Jews can go straight to hell because they don't accept him as the Messiah."

Just then Geoff's computer pinged some kind of alert. They all heard it. Three heads swiveled in unison. Geoff got up and went to the desk.

"File coming"—he clicked his mouse rapidly as he spoke—"from my bloke in New York."

Annie watched him, not saying anything, taking the opportunity to tuck into one of the sketchbooks the drawing that she now knew to be an image of Jennifer Franklin's husband. Never mind that she'd never met him.

The download was apparently complete. Geoff punched a couple of keys, then whistled softly. "New info on Weinraub," he said. "Hang on, I'll print it." The printer whirred to life, spitting out pages with astonishing speed. Geoff carried them back to the couch, reading while he walked. "What New York calls the pay dirt's on page three."

"What pay dirt?" Annie asked.

Geoff was reading as he walked toward them. "Weinraub's a naturalized American citizen. Not born in the United States." He fanned the printouts on the coffee table. "These are copies of the documentation."

Annie leaned forward. "Naturalization papers for a couple named Louis and Marianne Wein who became U.S. citizens in 1958." She looked up. "You think these are Weinraub's parents?"

"Apparently." Geoff thumbed through a few more papers, found the summary, and read aloud: " 'One son, Philippe Jérémie, born in France. Age five at the time the parents became American citizens, which under U.S. law meant their son automatically got citizenship at the same time.' That's why the more cursory investigation I put together earlier didn't turn up the information that Weinraub wasn't born in America, or that his name was originally Wein."

"Okay," Annie said, "Philip Jeremiah's obviously the American equivalent, and it's not a common name. But Wein to Weinraub? Isn't that sort of counterintuitive? The less Jewish-sounding name to the one that's more identifiable. Why?"

"I imagine because they didn't want it to look as if they were denying their Jewish heritage." Geoff held up a hand to forestall another question. "Hang on." He shuffled through the papers. "Before they emigrated,

Louis Wein was a partner in something called Wein Frères et Cie., a family-controlled private equity group based in Strasbourg."

"Why am I not getting any of this?" Clary demanded. "What year are we in now? When did Wein become Weinraub?"

"In 1966," Geoff said, reading the report as he spoke. "For the first eight years after emigrating to New York, the father, Louis Wein, kept his name and worked for various Wall Street firms. Looks like he became Weinraub in '66. That's when he founded the Weinraub International Group, an open-ended mutual fund, from which grew the hedge funds and such that made our boy Philip a billionaire."

"So Wein senior was returning to the family business," Annie said. "Why change the name?"

Geoff flipped the page. "Seems there was a stench attached to the old firm. Originally because they cozied up to the Nazis during the Occupation. Then—"

"Hold it," Clary said. "Jews? Friendly with the Nazis?"

Geoff looked up. "You have no idea how frequently that happened. And rich Jews, mind. With a lot to protect. But according to this"—he returned to the documents—"*les frères* Wein appear to have been equal opportunity bastards. In the early sixties, one of them went to jail for laundering money for the French mafia. That coincided with Louis Wein going into business for himself in America. At that point changing his name must have seemed a good idea."

"It's also another layer of obfuscation." Annie sighed.

"For such a pretty lady," Clary said, "you sure do use some twenty-dollar, professor words."

"C'mon, Clary," Geoff said. "Cut the crap." He turned to Annie. "Clary likes to pretend he's a homeboy from some godforsaken Haitian slum. Actually, his father owned a large piece of the island, and Monsieur Colbert here"—he dropped the *t*, giving the name a French pronunciation—"was educated in Switzerland's finest private schools and holds an advanced degree from the University of Tulane in New Orleans."

"It's Tulane University, you English prick. And in present company, not so advanced." He turned to Annie. "I've got a master's."

"Tell her what you read," Geoff said.

"Tell her what it's in," Clary corrected. "You are some goddamned stupid English motherfucker, you know that? I've been instructing you in the proper use of the English language for almost five years now, and you still can't get it right. And I told you all that stuff in strict confidence. When I was drowning in your pissy English beer."

"Tell her."

"Medieval French literature," Clary said. Softly. As if he were confessing something shameful.

"But all the computer expertise—" Annie said.

"Picked that up on my own. On the side, sort of. How the hell was I supposed to earn a living discussing the origins of the *chantefable* and the *chanson de geste*?" Then, turning to Geoff: "Why are we talking about this?"

"Because Strasbourg," Annie said, leaning over the papers on the coffee table, "where Philip Weinraub's family's from, according to Geoff's man in New York, is the northernmost of the cities where they have the gifts from the Jew of Holborn."

"The stuff you were originally supposed to be looking for? Except now you're after a mezuzah and quail eggs."

"Sort of," Annie said, her tone betraying her discouragement.

Geoff jumped in, his eyes lit with enthusiasm. "Consider, Clary my man, that in Strasbourg, they speak French. So you can go to Strasbourg and nose around. I know a bloke there, but he's only worked for me once before. I'll put you in touch, but you run the show. Given that proper French—not some Haitian patois from a poisonous Cité Soleil slum—is your mother tongue, it shouldn't be a problem."

"Father tongue," Clary said. "My mama was from New Orleans. English is my mother tongue."

"Which," Geoff said, "does not change the point. You can function perfectly well in Strasbourg, and you definitely won't stick out as a foreigner. Will you go?"

Clary narrowed his eyes. "Are you saying that if I uncover some interesting shit, I can maybe drop Franklin in it?"

"Up to his eyeballs," Geoff said.

Clary stood up and performed an exaggerated courtly bow. "*À votre service, monsieur mon maître.*"

23

"I think," Geoff said, "it's time to take some serious precautions with all this." He'd stayed downstairs to take a phone call. Now he'd brought his printouts and a stack of her sketchbooks up to the bedroom.

Annie had already agreed to spend the night. She was in his bed, wearing only her bracelet and the crystal heart necklace, the sheet clutched two-fisted under her neck. Her libido was, however, ebbing quickly. "Why now? Who was on the phone?"

"My contact at the Connaught. Weinraub had the concierge book him a ticket to Strasbourg. He said he'd be back in a few days and asked them to hold his suite."

"That doesn't sound particularly threatening."

"I'm not sure it is. But last time I tried to trace his movements, I also found out he'd gone to Strasbourg, supposedly to a meeting of an organization that raises money for Israel. Which organization turned out to be entirely untraceable." He paused for effect. "A couple of weeks later Rabin was shot."

Then, as she made the connection between Strasbourg and assassination: "You just told Clary to go to Strasbourg. Did you tell him?"

"Called right after I hung up. Clary's champing at the bit—can't wait to get started. Makes it more interesting, he said."

Annie wasn't sure, but there seemed no point in arguing. "Okay. What about my sketchbooks?"

"I've got the one with the original drawings of the monk." Geoff flipped through them quickly. "The one with the stippled code in the drawings of the London houses, and the Tudor facade of the Charterhouse. Plus the 'old master' on the single sheet." He tapped the sketchbook in which Annie had put the drawing they'd now identified as Rob Franklin. "Is that everything?"

"I think so."

"Good. We should put them somewhere secure."

"Where?"

"How about this. Ta-da! Otherwise known as a tasteful trumpet fanfare." He touched something under the frame of the rather ordinary seascape hanging on the wall across from the foot of the bed. Frame and picture swung aside to reveal a safe.

"Jesus God Almighty," Annie said. "I don't believe it."

"I know. Pretty corny." He sounded sheepish.

"That's an understatement."

He was twisting the dial of the safe. "I was almost too embarrassed to ask the company to install it this way. But I've wanted it all my life. Since I was a kid in Portsmouth, watching old movies on the telly with my dad. Call it a form of fantasy football. Or Geoff's excellent adventure."

"And of course no thief would ever think to look there."

"I never expected to have anything really important to protect. What money I don't spend is invested, and my cash is in a bank like everyone else's."

The safe door swung open. All Annie could see were a few papers and a corner of the frame of what she took to be the picture of Emma that had been on the night table. It had disappeared after the second night they'd spent together.

He put the drawings in the safe, along with the computer printouts and the faxed copies of the Weinraub naturalization papers. "These things"—he pointed to the papers that were not part of the latest deposit—"are Maggie's Kindertransport documents and my father's death certificate. You've already met Emma." He closed the door and twisted the dial again, then swung the painting back into place. "I'll share the combination with you, just in case."

She felt the same chill she'd felt a couple of hours earlier, when Clary Colbert said the intruder she'd drawn was Rob Franklin, and she had known—intuitively, instinctively, immediately—that he was right. "Did Maggie give you her documents when you had the safe installed?"

"No. Maggie, as you have no doubt deduced, is a world-class pack rat. She gave me those things six months ago when her breast cancer was diagnosed. An early bestowal of the legacy, as she put it."

"Oh no. I thought sometimes she looked particularly thin and tired, but . . . damn!"

He'd gotten into the bed beside her by then, and he drew her close, but in a way that felt more like mutual comfort than sex. "I've done my share of cursing the Fates," he said. "Maggie will have none of it. She points out she's eighty-two her next birthday. A good run, she calls it. Particularly for a little Jewish girl born in Hitler's Germany."

"Can't they do anything?"

"They removed the lump. That's all she'd allow. A case might be made for chemo or radiation. Maggie won't hear of it. And the gods seem to be on her side—so far so good."

Annie bit her lip and didn't say that the last time she'd seen his mother, she'd looked really ill. She concentrated on Clary instead. "Are you sure about sending Clary to Strasbourg? It sounds like we're deliberately putting him in harm's way."

Geoff rolled onto his back and clasped his hands behind his head, looking not at her but at the seascape that disguised his fantasy football safe. "Am I sure? That is a question I have had to ask myself on a number of occasions. Look, frequently what I do is merely a high-class form of muckraking. Occasionally it produces useful results. That's my justification. As for the people I hire to follow the trails I can't follow myself— mostly I suppose they do it for money. It's not my business to second-guess how they choose to earn a living."

"Is Clary doing it for money?"

"Once upon a time, maybe. Not now. His father died in the earth quake in 2010. Apparently he'd been politicking in the poor part of town. Clary inherited the numbers of a couple of Swiss accounts."

"Then why does he go on working with Rob Franklin, since he obviously can't stand him?"

"It's complicated, and I suspect I don't know all the details, though

I do know Clary's spent a small fortune on Haitian relief efforts. Apart from that, he needs to be his own man. And I think the idea of teaching medieval French literature makes him gag. Not the literature, the teaching part."

"That I can understand."

"Besides, there's his wife. He adores her. She's a teacher in Brixton, cares passionately about educating the underclass. Being married to an independently wealthy scholar would ruin her image. Or so Clary thinks."

"How about being a widow?" Annie asked, half sitting, propping herself on her elbows. "What would she think of that? If you're right about Weinraub—"

"Clary can take care of himself. He spent all his summers and holidays in Port-au-Prince. Even for a little rich boy, a place like Haiti tends to concentrate the mind. Besides, it's worth doing. Can we stop talking about this business for a bit?"

He tugged her back into his arms. She started to pull the sheet up, but Geoff stopped her hand with his. "Don't. I love to look at them. You have exquisite breasts."

His fingers caressed her left nipple, but both hardened in response. So much for comfort rather than sex.

"The vanishing point," she told Geoff the next morning over coffee, "the connection between Weinraub's fanaticism and the ghost's concerns . . . I've been considering it all night."

"Really? And all the time I thought—"

"I'm serious, Geoff. Somehow the topography of Tudor Holborn is the key. There are no speckled eggs in the flat, so maybe 'here' means Holborn."

"As in, that's where you're supposed to seek the speckled egg."

"Yes."

"Fair enough. Next question. What exactly is this speckled egg? We've settled on a quail's egg because of the cardinals, but—"

"Also the man selling 'High-Class Provisions' had quails and quail eggs in his window. Don't forget him."

"I wish I could. All right, including the bloody high-class provisioner who doesn't actually exist. My point's still valid. How do you know your ghost is talking about a quail's egg?"

"I don't know. And you're right, there are probably other kinds of speckled eggs. I'll check. Then I'm going to look for some kind of specialist collection that may have more info about Holborn in the fifteen hundreds. Old maps are just the kind of thing wealthy collectors go after."

"Wouldn't Jennifer know?"

Annie made a face. "I've a mind to take a short holiday from Jennifer. At least until I get my head around the notion that it was her husband who broke into my flat and scared me half to death."

"Do a Nexis search," Geoff said. "You have my password."

"It could take some time. I can pay you back, but not until—"

He waved the offer away. "Anything that sheds some light on all these weird goings-on is fine with me. Take as much time as you need."

She hit the remote that turned on the radios as soon as she walked in the door. The BBC immediately informed her that despite today's sunshine, it was so far the coldest summer on record. Annie talked back, suggesting they tell her something she didn't know.

She glanced to her right. The drawing room looked exactly as she'd left it, cozy throw blanket slung over the couch, daisies and baby's breath in a charming Chinese vase. At the far end, the door to Mrs. Walton's office was closed. So was the one she was facing, which led to Mrs. Walton's bedroom. She always left those two doors closed, a gesture toward not violating her landlady's personal space.

She turned and walked a few steps down the corridor to the bedroom she thought of as hers. That door was open. Annie glanced at the mural, then deliberately turned her back on the mystifying art. The rest of the room was cheerful and familiar. Clear morning light poured in from the window facing Southampton Row, and lots of her stuff was scattered about, including an azure-and-gold-striped shopping bag inscribed "Give 'Em the Boot." She'd bought not boots but a pair of red patent-leather stilettos, the footwear equivalent of a Wonderbra. Fuck-me shoes. Which was why it didn't matter that she had nothing to go with them. She didn't plan to wear anything with them. The thought of Geoff's reaction caused a little shiver of anticipation.

She dropped her tote on the bedroom chair, thought about taking off her sweater, and decided against it. The flat was colder than outdoors. Annie took her laptop from its case, carried it into the dining room, and set it on the table. In seconds the tranquil flight of geese was soaring across her screen. She checked her e-mail first thing. The most recent message was from Maggie. She had not cc'd her son. "Re the disappearing cardinals," Maggie wrote, "it occurs to me the common thread could be age rather than youth. Younger people take more chances. More likely to choke to death. Check additional obits/data for the plus-seventy geezers. I think that's the anomaly."

Annie wasn't sure, but maybe it was worth a look. She added a third thing to her list of research topics. Types of speckled eggs, Tudor map collections, and death notices of cardinals over seventy. Geoff was in for an expensive morning. Maybe not the eggs, though. An ordinary Google search should work for that.

"Speckled egg" got a quarter-million results in a fraction of a second. A large percentage of them, she quickly realized, referred to businesses that went by that name. She added "birds" and tried again. That got her down to a hundred thousand hits. After a few more detours—a school project in Oklahoma, a list that included birds she'd never heard of— she typed in "speckled egg" and "history." Then, in a burst of inspiration, she deleted "history" and typed "Tudor." Twelve thousand hits. She typed "speckled egg" plus "Anne Boleyn." Twelve hits. Annie scrolled quickly through the abstracts. One was about Anne eating only quail eggs while she was pregnant. Annie was about to click on it when she spotted the seventh entry. "Heresies in Tudor Times." She clicked on that and scrolled furiously, finally coming to the highlighted words, "Speckled Egg." It was, she discovered, the name given to the leader of a schismatic sect calling themselves the True Obedience of Avignon. They originally broke with the official church in 1379 over the issue of which of two popes—one in Avignon and one in Rome—was legitimate. They "became particularly active in England," she read, "during the upheaval over the divorce of Henry VIII and his remarriage to Anne Boleyn. They were not Protestants, but rather sedevacantists." In other words, schismatics who claimed that the chair of Peter was empty. And one of the source documents for that information was a book on Christian heresies by John Kendall.

Every inch of her was tingling. This was it—she was sure of it. It was as if her father had dropped in to give her the information. This was the speckled egg the ghost meant. He was pointing her in the direction of a heresy known as the True Obedience of Avignon. She sent the link to Geoff's e-mail account and looked for her cell so she could tell him it was on its way. The phone, however, was neither in the pocket of her jeans nor on the table next to her. It had to be still in the tote she'd left in the bedroom. She went back there, grinned when she looked at the bag with the red shoes, found her phone, and started to return to the dining room.

There was an almighty shove at her back.

Really strong.

Annie dropped the phone. It skittered across the floor. She stood frozen for a moment, astonishment roiling her stomach and rising in her chest. Why must these encounters always happen on his terms, never hers? "Look, Dom Whoever, I think I know now which speckled egg you meant, but what do you want me to do about it? Where am I supposed to seek him? I live in the twenty-first century, not the sixteenth. And if we're both on some river of time, you'd better tell me how to navigate."

She spun around while she spoke, expecting to see the ghost at each turn. He was not there. The bedroom was empty. She could not see anyone, nor feel anyone, and except for the radio voices, she heard nothing.

Nonetheless, something or someone had definitely pushed her. The proof was her cell phone lying on the floor some six feet away. Its trajectory had been halted when it came to rest in the corner between the mural wall and the doorjamb.

Annie walked over and bent down to get it. Her eyes fastened on the bottom-left corner of the mural. Logic dictated that any effort to study the incredible wall of art begin at the opposite end, over by the window. Even if she hadn't given up because of the seeming impossibility of the task, it was hard to think when she'd have gotten to this section. The scenes she was looking at were in the most awkward possible position, at floor level and wedged into the corner beside the door. Only because she bent down to pick up her phone did she spot a series of unusual symbols at the top of a couple of contiguous scenes. At least that was how she first thought of them. After a few seconds, she realized the symbols were in fact letters written in some language that did not use the Western alphabet. She was pretty sure that language was Hebrew.

24

Annie lay on her belly on the floor, sketching the letters exactly as they appeared. When she finished each sequence, she ripped off the sheet and handed it up to Simon Cohen, who stood next to her. Geoff was in the dining room, meanwhile, looking for information on the Stephen Fox who had lived in this flat from 1930 to 1959. The man who, according to Mrs. Walton, had been a reclusive eccentric who prowled London by night, and by day made painting this mural his life's work.

"That's all," she said, her finger hovering a quarter inch above the mural's surface, tracing the section that included the Hebrew characters and searching for anything she might have missed. "The rest is trees beside a river. I think it's the Embankment, over near Chelsea Bridge. No more words. Except . . . wait. Maybe I'm wrong." Annie looked more closely, screwing the jeweler's loupe back into her eye. "Here," she said, pointing to the leafy branches of one tree. "More letters, but not in Hebrew. I think it's a set of initials. *E.R.*"

Cohen was more interested in the Hebrew. He was studying the five pieces of paper she'd handed him. "I'm not sure," he murmured, "but it may be gibberish."

"No!" Annie practically wailed the objection. "I didn't drag you all the way here for gibberish! It can't be! Besides, what about the shove, and my cell, and—"

Geoff appeared in the doorway. "What's going on?"

"Rabbi Cohen thinks it's gibberish."

"Hebrew gibberish?" Geoff asked. "At least that?"

"Definitely Hebrew characters," Cohen said. "And I said maybe it's gibberish. I'm not sure."

"I also found the letters *E.R.* written in a tree," Annie said. "Western alphabet, not Hebrew."

"Time for a cup of tea," Geoff said. "You must be getting cross-eyed." He extended a hand and helped Annie to her feet. The three of them went back to the dining room.

Geoff disappeared into the kitchen. Cohen spread Annie's papers on the table and stared intently at them. After a few minutes he said, "The radios, Annie, if you wouldn't mind . . ."

"Of course. Sorry. Mostly I don't hear them anymore." She went down the hall, found the remote, and switched off the stream of sound. On her way back she stopped in her bedroom and spent another five minutes with the loupe. When she returned to the dining room, Rabbi Cohen was still shuffling the papers, and Geoff had just carried a tea tray in from the kitchen.

"I've got something else," Annie announced. "Extraordinary."

"Okay," Geoff said, "drop the other shoe. What?"

Annie pushed away an image of red stilettos. "I've found another few trees with letters in them. I think there may be more. It's always *E.R.* written in the leaves."

Number eight Bristol House was as quiet as a library.

Annie had returned to the mural.

Geoff was working at her laptop, paging through one after another of the seemingly limitless pages of information his Nexis connection made available.

Rabbi Cohen continued to shuffle papers, a mug of tea going cold at his elbow while he filled a notebook with various notations. Every once in a while he glanced at his watch. When she first called him about the Hebrew in the mural, Annie had suggested she draw what she saw and bring the information to him, or maybe take a picture with her cell and send it as an e-mail attachment. Cohen insisted he would come to her. "I can leave the house for a couple of hours," he'd said. "Perhaps seeing what you've found in situ will be important." She didn't argue. Even a man as devoted to his ill wife as Simon Cohen had a right to jump on an occasional excuse to get out of the house.

After half an hour Annie returned bleary-eyed to the dining room. "No more Hebrew that I can see. But look at this." She put her sketchbook on the table, moving it so both Geoff and Rabbi Cohen could see. She'd done a stylized drawing that showed the position of the trees with the initials in the leaves, and put in random lines to indicate the parts of the mural between them. "So far the pattern's absolutely clear," Annie said. "The occurrences of *E.R.* form a chain that creates capital letter *A*'s."

"Holy shit," Geoff said softly, "the code—excuse me, Rabbi."

"I can," Cohen said, "think of some stronger expletives. It appears Maggie was right. There is a connection between the phenomena in this flat and Philip Weinraub. But so far I can't see what it is."

None of them could. "The artist's name was Stephen Fox," Annie said. "So it's not him. Could E.R. be a relative? A woman? Maybe a lover or a wife or—"

"No one survived him," Geoff said, "and no reason to think he'd ever been married."

"How do you know that?"

"Come take a look."

Annie went to where he was sitting and leaned over his shoulder, studying the screen of the laptop. Geoff didn't wait for her to read the information. "According to the General Register Office," he said, "three people named Stephen Fox died in London in 1959. One is definitely our man. His residence at the time of death was this flat. He was killed during one of the last of the great London fogs."

"That's him. I remember Mrs. Walton saying he was run over in a pea-souper. I can't imagine green fog."

"Yellow fog," Simon Cohen said, still playing with his notes and Annie's sketches of Hebrew characters. "English pea soup, made with yellow split peas."

"There's almost no other information." Geoff hit a couple of keys, then shook his head. "Fox's date of birth is given as approximately 1900, but there's nothing else. Not even where he was born."

"Mrs. Walton told me he moved here in 1930."

"Fair enough. Where was he the thirty years before that? I've nothing on that, and I can't find a single obit anywhere. I'm thinking maybe he wasn't born in England. Maybe he—"

"Aha!" Cohen looked up. He was beaming. "I'm sorry," he said. "I interrupted. You first, Geoff."

"No, please. Go ahead. The Hebrew's the main event."

"Indeed. But it isn't Hebrew."

"But you said it was." Annie sat down between the two men.

"I mean Hebrew is used only for the alphabet. A way to confuse. Hebrew," Cohen said, "is written from right to left. Not just the words, the letters as well." He picked up a pen and scribbled something on a sheet and passed it to them.

"T-a-h e-h-t n-i-t-a-c," Geoff read aloud.

"Gibberish," Cohen said. "But read it the other—"

"The other way it says 'cat in the hat,'" Geoff said.

"That's what Stephen Fox wrote?" Annie demanded incredulously. "His mural's not Waldo, it's Dr. Seuss?"

Cohen laughed. "No, it's what I wrote, to demonstrate. I began by reading these words in Hebrew the way Hebrew is written. Right to left. That way they made no sense. Then I realized our Mr. Fox used Hebrew characters to write in Western alphabetic sequence, left to right. And to make it more difficult he mixed up the letters in each word, made them anagrams. But what made this bit of code breaking take over an hour," he sounded apologetic, as if a world-class professional had made a rookie error, "is that he capped his little puzzle by writing not in English but in—"

"French," Geoff said.

"No. Why do you think that?"

"Later," Geoff said. "Sorry to interrupt. Please go on, Rabbi."

"Fox was writing in Latin." Cohen tore another sheet out of the sketchbook. "And here is what he wrote."

"'*Collus Aventinus,*'" Annie read aloud. "The Aventine Hill. Then the single letter *a*. Then '*Arco,*' which is arch, of course. Followed by"—glancing once more at the note—"'*Vespasianif.*'"

"Vespasian's Arch?" Geoff asked. "I never heard of it."

Annie shook her head. "That's not what it means. This inscription occurs on one of the most famous arches in all of Rome. The Romans didn't separate words in lettering of this sort. The *i* and *f* at the end of *Vespasian* stand for 'son of.' His son was Titus. Stephen Fox was using a crude bit of code to describe the Arch of Titus."

"It's a long time since I cracked a book on Roman history," Geoff said, "but if memory serves, that's the same Titus who commanded the Roman legions during the Jewish War."

"The very same," Cohen said. "And pictured on his arch are the sorts of things Philip Weinraub supposedly sent Annie to find here in London. Ancient Judaica. A menorah and trumpets from the Second Temple, which the Romans pillaged and destroyed. And of course your de rigueur addition to any Roman celebration of victory, captives in chains. In this case, enslaved Jews." He looked again at his notes. "And between the two phrases—'Aventine Hill' and 'Arch of Titus'—is our old friend, the *aleph* symbol. Hebrew's silent and frequently unwritten letter *a*. In this instance I have no idea what it means."

"I think I do," Geoff said. "In fact, I'd bet money on it. It stands for *à*, the word 'to' in French. In English, therefore, the message reads 'Aventine Hill to Arch of Titus.' Note that the key words begin with the letter *A*. So you could write *A-A-A* and that might signify exactly what we have here. *Aventine à Arc.*"

"And to emphasize that connection with the code," Cohen said, "he made a graphic map of initials that form still more letters *A*." He thought for a moment. "It doesn't explain everything, but it's definitely possible."

"The Aventine Hill is one of the legendary seven," Annie said. "So in that sense it was always there. I'm pretty sure the Arch of Titus was dedicated around the year 84. So the message could mean from the founding of Rome to then, but why the sudden introduction of French?"

"I suppose," Geoff said, "since he wrote Hebrew letters, Stephen Fox was a Jew, but his native language was French."

"How do you know that?" Rabbi Cohen asked.

"I don't—I'm guessing. But I'd wager a fair sum I'm right. I think the reason I couldn't find any birth info on the man who died in this flat is because I was searching British records, and he was born in France."

"Why France?" Annie demanded. "Why not Tibet, or Australia?"

"Because in French," Geoff said, "the English name Stephen is Étienne."

"But the initials are *E.R.* His last name was Fox, so—"

"Exactly," Geoff said. "Fox in French is Renard."

"Ah," Rabbi Cohen said softly and with satisfaction. "He was signing his painting, his obsessive mural, with his true initials."

"In a pattern," Annie said, "reinforcing the significance of the letter *A* as found in the code that's hidden in the documents I was given by the Shalom Foundation."

"Which code," Cohen said, "is based on kabbalistic numerology, so I'm guessing Geoffrey is correct and our Mr. Fox or Mr. Renard was Jewish. But the meaning of the letter *A*," Cohen said. "That I am not yet sure we completely understand."

Annie let out a little gasp. "There's something else. I was so excited when I found the Hebrew letters, I forgot about it. I think I know what the speckled egg refers to. In Tudor times it was the person who led a group of schismatics who called themselves the True Obedience of Avignon. Church scholars, my father among them apparently, lump them in with a group called sedevacantists. People who, for one reason or another, insist the pope isn't legitimate and the chair of Peter is empty."

Geoff was typing things into the computer. Rabbi Cohen was scribbling in his notebook. "The True Obedience," he said. "And what was the word you used?"

"Sedevacantists," Annie repeated. "It's a generic term for a type of schism that has occurred within Catholicism any number of times."

"Nothing in Nexis about any True Obedience," Geoff said. "Doesn't surprise me. History's not what they're about."

"Dominicans," Annie said.

Geoff looked puzzled. "You're not talking about the Dominican Republic, are you? Nexis would have plenty on that, but—"

"Dominican priests," Annie said. "They were founded in twelve-something to hound heretics and schismatics. Originally the Cathars in southern France, but they extended their reach."

Rabbi Cohen made a face.

"I don't think," Annie said, "they've been presiding over any inquisitions of late, but they used to be real pros."

"Not lately. You're right. In fact, you should excuse the expression," Cohen said wryly, "some of my best friends are Dominicans."

Annie made a note on the corner of one of her sketchbooks. "I'll pursue the True Obedience thread."

Cohen stood up. "Each puzzle is more intriguing than the last," he said, "but now I must go. Thank you for a fascinating time. And for the memories. It was good to see my old stomping ground again."

"You've been in Bristol House before?" Annie's tone betrayed her astonishment. "Do you know Mrs. Walton?"

Cohen laughed. "My dear, you must think me London's secret Lothario. Not true, I'm afraid. I meant only that years ago this part of Holborn was very familiar to me. Lately, as you know, I don't get out much." It was obvious they were waiting for more. "There isn't time now," he said. "Someday perhaps. But since we're dealing in mysteries, I'll leave you with one clue. Have you noticed the barred gates in the middle of the junction between Southampton Road and Kingsway?"

"Looks like an old underpass," Geoff said. "It's been out of use at least since I've lived in the neighborhood."

"Much longer than that," Cohen said. "Since the fifties. What you're calling an underpass was built in the nineteenth century. It was a tram tunnel that ran from Kingsway to Waterloo Bridge. But that's not all. Take a good look the next time you go out. You're seeing history."

25

They took Maggie to dinner that evening. "You can debrief us," Geoff said by way of persuasion when he phoned to set it up, and his mother said she didn't feel like going out. "You can't live on soup, Maggie. We'll have an early meal at that Greek place you like down the road."

When they arrived, Maggie was at a choice table, sipping a glass of white wine. The restaurant, a Primrose Hill standby, was called Lemonia. Even at quarter to six it was busy, but the waiters obviously cherished Maggie. Each time one of them passed, he would leave a small temptation in the form of olives, or stuffed vine leaves, or tiny morsels of feta cheese. Maggie pretended to nibble each offering. After Geoff and Annie arrived, he ordered shashlik and pilaf and tsatsiki for the three of them. When the food came, Maggie pronounced it delicious, but mostly she pushed things around on her plate. Nonetheless, as the meal wore on, her spirits and her color improved.

Annie banished thoughts of cancer and concentrated on telling the story of Rabbi Hazan and his river of time, and the discovery that it was Geoff's former producer who had broken into her flat, and how five hundred years ago there had been a schismatic group who called their leader the Speckled Egg. Then Geoff explained about Weinraub having been Wein and the family emigrating to America, and he said he'd sent Clary Colbert to France to try and get more information. By that time they were sipping larger-than-usual cups of insanely strong Greek coffee—Lemonia's staff apparently knew Geoff as well as they did his mother—and Maggie was flushed and laughing, and her eyes sparkled. "Then today," Geoff said, "Annie found writing in that mural we told you about."

"Hebrew writing," Annie said, and went on to the tale of Rabbi Cohen's visit and what he had deciphered, and how they were trying to figure out the relevance to the Shalom Foundation of the years between the founding of Rome and the erection of the Arch of Titus.

"So that's all?" Maggie said. "We haven't talked for an entire forty-eight hours and nothing else happened? What have you been doing with yourselves?"

"There is one more thing," Geoff said.

"Oh my God. Very well, Geoffrey, tell me."

He explained about the initials *E.R.* occurring in the pattern of the letter *A*.

"So there's a connection between the flat and the code," Maggie said, her voice triumphant. "I knew there had to be."

"Rabbi Cohen agrees," Geoff said, "though he doesn't think we've got it all figured out. And I think Stephen Fox's real name is Étienne Renard. I can't prove it yet, but I'm right."

"When will you be able to prove it?" his mother asked.

"Soon. I've arranged for someone in Paris to look for corroboration."

"Your friend the computer technician? Clary?"

Geoff shook his head. "No, he's gone to Strasbourg. This is simply an ordinary investigating bureau I've used before."

Maggie shrugged her elegant shoulders. "My son and his legions of drones, all busy ferreting out the world's secrets."

"Speaking of secrets," Geoff said, "what's the story behind the barred gates at the end of Southampton Row? In the middle of the junction between Theobald's Road and Kingsway."

"It has a connection with Rabbi Cohen," Annie said. "He referred to the neighborhood as his old stomping ground."

"The tunnels," Maggie said quietly. "I think we'd better talk about something else."

"C'mon," Geoff said. "How many state secrets can you still know, Maggie? It's been more than sixty bloody years."

Maggie laughed and called for another cup of coffee. "Greek coffee, but my way," she told the waiter, who smiled and asked what other way he would possibly consider.

"Her way," Geoff told Annie, "is that they cover the bottom of the cup with half a teaspoon of coffee and top up with hot water. Tell us about the tunnels," he said, turning back to his mother.

Maggie hesitated, then said, "You have a point. All these years—why not? There is a system of very deep, once-very-secret tunnels below some of the Holborn streets."

Geoff sat up straighter. "Which Holborn streets?"

"I'm not sure. But I know you could get in from a spur off the Kingsway Tunnel. So during the war you could just take the tram and slip off at the right place in the dark and simply disappear. Poof. Down the rabbit hole, and no one the wiser."

Annie knew her jaw was dropping. Geoff's as well. Maggie took no notice of their astonishment. "There's supposed to be another entrance from the basement of a building on Furnival Street. Possibly a third, but I don't know where it is."

Geoff reached for his iPhone. Seconds later he had conjured a Google Earth image of the area and handed the phone to Annie. "Note that a straightish line from Furnival Street to Theobald's Road runs close to Bristol House," he said. "Not as close to Orde Hall Street."

"It is certainly not a straight line," Maggie said, "and you're never going to pinpoint the exact location with fancy technology. They started with an abandoned nineteenth-century tube line, so there was no reason to attract attention by breaking ground at street level. Also, the laborers were brought in from somewhere in Eastern Europe. People who didn't speak English and didn't know London."

"My God—Maggie, you're making this up. It's right out of a book."

"Annie darling, I swear, everything I'm telling you is true."

"Let me guess," Geoff said. "The secret tunnels turned out to be another incidence of government making a hash of it."

"Not a bit of it." Maggie sounded indignant. "The point was that they were beyond the reach of the Blitz, so a number of very dedicated people spent huge amounts of time down there. I know the spy stories and the movies make it seem easy. Take my word, it was not. There was a very long time when we really didn't think we were going to win. Meanwhile the higher-ups were worried about the troglodytes working underground being overwhelmed by tension, and of course claustrophobia." She smiled at her son. "You'll appreciate this. They fixed them up with a five-a-side football pitch."

"Five-a-side is a kind of soccer," Geoff explained in a quick comment to Annie. "You can play indoors."

"They also had a restaurant," Maggie said. "With South Sea Island scenes painted into trompe l'oeil windows. Their own telephone exchange as well. What we used to call 'all mod cons.'"

"A five-a-side pitch for the spooks," Geoff said, apparently still fascinated by the notion of spying footballers. "You're sure?"

"Yes. I remember Simon telling me about it. He worked there for a time before he came to Bletchley."

"Did he play?"

Maggie shook her head. "I doubt it. Simon was never the athletic type. Not like your father as a young man."

And having quashed any hint of dubious DNA, Maggie said she was tired and wanted to go home.

Giacomo the Lombard, known also as the Jew of Holborn
From the Waiting Place

In the late morning of a hot summer's day, I stood beside the kiln forging a small portion of silver into a brooch to take into town to sell. It would make an opportunity to inquire as to the whereabouts of my daughter who, I would say, had allowed an excess of Christian charity to cause her to come into the city and nurse the sick. Doubtless my questions would lead me to a plague woman, who would attest to Rebecca having come down with the fever and died. Then I could mourn my daughter properly as was my duty, and I need tell Master Cromwell only that she was buried in a plague pit and put an end to the matter.

The scheme had been in my mind for some time, but it had become a matter of urgency. There had been no new cases of the fever in a fortnight, and it was rumored the king and his court were making preparations to return to Westminster. Thomas Cromwell would soon be again in London and would likely send immediately for the wench he intended to make the wife of the stinker—if for no other reason than to remind me of who between us held in all things the upper hand.

The heat of the kiln was nearly insufferable beneath the blazing sun, and when I turned from the anvil to wipe the sweat from my brow, I saw what I thought must be a vision from beyond the grave. Rebecca stood before me. I was speechless with astonishment.

"No word of greeting, Father? Are you not joyful to see me?"

"Are you come from the Semayim above the earth or Gehenna below?" I remember that I whispered the words and that my voice was hoarse with fear. Also that Rebecca laughed, but it was not a mirthful sound.

"Neither, I promise. I am alive, though I kissed every corpse I carried to the pit. See how the Creator of the Universe plays with me? I am not permitted even to choose my own death."

She wore the black shroudlike garment she had put on three weeks before and carried the heavy black cloak with the hem that ends in four points to which bells are attached to warn of the approach of a plague woman. That and her shrewish tongue persuaded me it was the Rebecca I knew who spoke, not a ghost. "You blaspheme." I spat upon the ground to wash the words from my mouth, though she had spoken them, not I. "And you smell almost as bad as your intended. Go and wash. Then bring me those terrible garments, and I will burn them."

I was so astonished by her return, I stayed in my place beside the anvil, the smith's hammer limp in my hand and the sheet of silver before me growing cooler and less malleable by the moment. Ten minutes later she appeared, carrying most of her plague clothes, though not the cloak, and wearing a shift made of undyed homespun. I had seen it many times, it being her ordinary dress, but I noted at once that the garment seemed to fit her more tightly than before she departed on her ghoulish errand. How could it be that she would spend over a month in the filthiest, most disease-ridden corners of London and return fatter than when she left, her cheeks pink with health and her eyes sparkling? It came to me most forcefully how ill prepared I was to understand this creature who defied not just me but, it seemed, the very laws of life. Perhaps, if her mother had lived . . . For my part, I saw no way to save her from the stinker while not dooming us both to the stake. Moreover, I knew that even such a torturous death would come for me only after I had been made to suffer such agonies as would cause me to betray the whereabouts of what remained of the patrimony of my people.

I did not speak my thoughts aloud, only picked up a long iron poker and lifted the latch on the door of the kiln and swung it open. Rebecca tossed the black garments onto the brick floor, and I slammed the door shut. The escaping heat sent us both staggering back, despite that having been prepared to fire silver, not gold, the blaze was not at its most intense. I added more charcoal and pushed open the dampers, encouraging a roaring flame. "They will be ashes in minutes," I said. "Then we may both forget this madness. All will be as before."

"I think not, Father."

I sighed at the recurring defiance in her tone. "Have you learned nothing?"

"I have learned a great deal. It is you who are ignorant."

I still had the poker in my hand, and I raised it as if to strike her. Rebecca stepped back out of my range, but she was not afraid. Indeed, she laughed that hollow laugh a second time. "You are a man," she said, "so you do not see what to a woman's eyes is immediately apparent. Look at me, Father." Her voice rose when she spoke, and she cupped her hands under her breasts and lifted them and thrust them toward me as if she were a whore soliciting custom. "Look at my swollen teats. Do they not remind you of how my mother's breasts looked after you had planted your seed in her belly and made me?"

For the second time that day, I was startled speechless. I dropped my arm and stood numb with terror.

"See," she said, drawing the skirt of her dress tight behind her and flaunting her curved hips and rounded stomach, "do you not think the babe already makes its presence known?"

Her boastful tone told me she thought she could punish me without condemning us both to the Smithfield fires, but I knew better and my blood ran cold. "His?" I asked. "Are you telling me the cursed monk's bastard is in your belly?"

"His," she agreed, as coolly as if she did not know she brought news that signed our death warrants.

She did not ask how it was that I guessed the father of the child, and I wondered if she knew I had watched them the night he lay between her legs in the copse beside the river, but I set the thought aside in favor of others more urgent. I was swiftly making a plan to save us, but before I could speak of it, I heard a stranger's voice. "Goldsmith," a woman called. "I have come to give you a commission."

Rebecca and I turned to the sound and saw the wife of Juryman the silk merchant in the clearing in front of our house. She sat on a donkey, and beside her stood an oafish servant carrying the drawing materials she took everywhere. The woman fancied herself an artist, though all who saw what came from her brush knew that to be a joke worthy of the best jester in the kingdom. "You made me this ring three years past," she said, holding up her hand. "I would have another just like it for my daughter who is to be married."

The Juryman woman spoke to me but looked at Rebecca, as did her servant, and his toothless grin told me all I needed to know. We had been overheard.

"Indeed, mistress." My voice betrayed none of the fear I felt. "It would give me honor."

Rebecca hurried away, and Mistress Juryman and I spent a quarter of an hour discussing the nature of the commission she proposed. (The ring was to be exactly as the one I had made for her before, but at the same time entirely different. Such being the usual manner of all rich customers of my experience.) In the end she gave me some coins that represented half the agreed price and rode away.

It had been in my mind to tell Rebecca we must go at once to Drury Lane in the town and find the woman known to make a drink that would force her to expel the child from her body. Now it was too late for such a remedy to save us. Mistress Clare Juryman, for all her foolish pretensions to artistry, was the wife of an important man in London. Like others of his station, he gathered information and used it to his advantage. His wife was sure to be his helpmeet in this regard.

Whether the silk merchant knew I was associated with Master Cromwell, or that Master Cromwell might find interesting what Juryman's wife had overheard, did not matter. If Rebecca was to marry the stinker, they must do so in a Christian church. The banns would of necessity be posted, and being as the odiferous Timothy Faircross was connected to the court, all the city would take note of them. Juryman would swiftly know whose favor he might curry by sharing knowledge of a bastard child in the belly of the bride-to-be.

I went inside. Rebecca sat beside the cold fire, not having bestirred herself to poke the embers into enough life to allow her to cook me a meal. Her body was bent forward in such a way as to make it apparent she was thinking the same grim thoughts that tormented me.

I grabbed the hair of her head and forced her to look me in the face. "Whore," I said. "Jezebel. Do you see now what you have brought us to?" Once more her mother's voice echoed in my mind and I fancied she was pleading on the girl's behalf. I ignored such thoughts and sent my fist crashing to her mouth, and though her lip immediately poured blood, it gave me no relief and no satisfaction. I let her go and dropped Mistress Juryman's coins on the floor in front of her, for they seemed to me tainted with such evil as to be things of terrible foreboding.

⚓

26

After their meal at Lemonia, Annie insisted on going back to Bristol House for the night and staying there alone. "I think the ghost wants to talk to me, but he's not as likely to come if you're there."

They were in the back of a cab. Geoff looked at her for a long few seconds. Annie saw the play of light from the street passing over his face in a dappled exchange of brightness and shadow. "Okay," he said finally. "I have to admit, I think you're right."

And that, she realized, was the point of the apparition—she knew no other word for it—of the old-fashioned provisioner on St. John's Lane. The ghost had neutralized his only real opponent. Originally Geoff had tried to get her to leave Bristol House and avoid the phenomena that took place there. Now he'd been co-opted. He'd become the ghost's ally.

He came up to the flat with her, stayed only long enough to look around, then kissed her softly and left.

Annie walked around for a while, waiting. Nothing happened. Eventually she went to bed. The Carthusian did not appear. It was very late when she fell asleep and she woke to bright sunlight and her cell phone ringing on the table beside the bed. She fumbled for it and caught the call just before it disappeared to voice mail. "It's Jennifer. Sorry to call so early, but I've got something I think you should see. Can you come to the museum?"

Annie said she'd be there within the hour.

The British summer had made a tardy but welcome appearance. It was a gorgeous day, warm and sunny, and tourist hordes from every corner of the world had sprung up like multicolored flowers and taken over the museum. Annie made her way through the throng to a security checkpoint and flashed the orange-bordered pass that identified her as an independent researcher. The guard nodded in the direction of the staff-only elevators, one of which descended to Jennifer Franklin's temporary quarters in the subbasement.

The room was always chilly, a function of the climate control that protected the treasures. Today, by contrast, it felt positively cold. Jennifer wore a heavy dark green cardigan that Annie had seen a number of times. The archivist had pushed the sleeves up and left the front unbuttoned. Underneath she had on a spaghetti-strap gray knit top over wide-legged black linen pants. The knit top was stretched over a decided bump.

"Wow! Congratulations. When's the big day?"

"Not until November." Jennifer caressed her rounded belly with one well-manicured hand.

"Well, I must say it becomes you. You look wonderful. Is your husband excited? Rob, isn't it?" And do you know he has a sideline in breaking and entering? she wanted to say. Then she remembered that according to Clary Colbert, Jennifer's husband was also banging some Egyptian woman with great boobs and felt terrible.

Jennifer apparently picked up no negative vibrations. "Yes, Rob's over the moon. We've been trying for a while. I can't believe you two haven't met. We must go out together sometime."

"We definitely must," Annie said. That was one of the things she'd planned to get done today—maneuver a meeting with Rob Franklin. He was a player in her very private drama; she wanted to get a look at him. "Better be soon," she said. "I've only a little over a month left in London."

Jennifer did not react with a specific offer. "Definitely soon," she said. She nodded toward the far end of the table. "I've pulled something for you. I think it may be useful."

Annie sat down in front of a paper portfolio tied with the ubiquitous cotton ribbon beloved of archivists. "You know," she said while she slipped on white gloves, "I'm prepared to nominate you the source of all wisdom in the matter of Tudor London. I hope you're not planning to stop work after the baby comes."

"Probably not an option. We can't afford it. Being a television producer sounds glamorous, but the big money is reserved for the on-air stars. Geoffrey Harris, for instance." Jennifer paused. "The grapevine has you two an item. True or just a rumor?"

It had to happen. Geoff was far too well-known for it to be otherwise. "I've seen him a few times. Does that make us an item?"

"Absolutely. Not to mention the envy of every unmarried female in London. Don't blush—you must know that's the case."

"The blushes go with being a redhead. I can't control them." How many times in her life had she said that? "And Geoff's great. We're having fun together. Thanks for introducing us."

Jennifer shrugged. "As I recall, it was entirely accidental."

That was true, but it did not alleviate Annie's sense of . . . what? What exactly had she meant when she told Geoff she wanted a vacation from Jennifer? Despite the fact that it was the Shalom Foundation that recommended the archivist, Annie had been clinging to the notion that maybe Jennifer didn't know her husband had broken into Annie's apartment at the behest of Philip Weinraub. After all neither Geoff nor Clary had said anything about the possibility Rob's wife was involved. On the other hand—Annie had no time to pursue the thought.

"Take a look." Jennifer had pulled the special gray cushion into position. Annie reached for the portfolio and untied the ribbon. Inside was a sheet of parchment covered with nonacid tissue paper, which Jennifer whisked away. Annie slipped her hands beneath the document and very gently transferred it to the cushion. She was looking at a landscape of sorts, done in browns and greens with touches of pink and red, and splashes of blue meant to convey the sky. One corner was badly torn, and all the edges were frayed.

"It's one of the earliest English watercolors in existence," Jennifer said.

The technique—suspending colored pigment in water—had been around since cave painting, but as a medium for art, it hadn't been widely used in the West until the early 1600s. Before that the great masters employed watercolor only for what were called cartoons, preliminary sketches of a planned work in oils. This painting was not a cartoon. There was no understanding of perspective for one thing, and the draftsmanship was poor. Nonetheless, the painter took some pride in the work. It was signed in the lower left with the initials "C.J." and dated "Ann. Dom. 1534."

"It's believed to be the work of Mistress Clare Juryman," Jennifer said. "She was the wife of a prominent London silk merchant and an enthusiastic amateur painter. Three of her sketches survive. This one happens to be a scene of exactly the area you're interested in." She pointed to the torn corner where the title of the scene had once been written. What remained were the letters l-e-t and, below them, b-o-r-n; both were rendered in a wavy attempt at what would be, even for Tudor times, elaborate script.

"Hamlet of Holborn," Annie said. "At least that's my guess." And how come you waited until now to show me this?

"Has to have been Hamlet of Holborn," Jennifer agreed. "See, here's the Charterhouse. And over here the monastery of the Knights of St. John."

The artist's lack of skill meant that both establishments were flat and two-dimensional, but the unique sprawl of the Charterhouse—the rows of small houses for hermit monks built around a number of open courtyards—was recognizable, as was the round dome of the church of the Knights Hospitaller of St. John. Next to the dome were the letters p-r-e-c-e-p. "Preceptory?" Annie asked.

"I would think so. It wasn't one by then, of course. In 1534 it belonged to the Knights of St. John, not the Templars, but there's evidence the locals went on using the old name." Jennifer pointed to the sketch. "And everyone knew the round church was modeled on the Church of the Holy Sepulcher in Jerusalem. Which, of course, was linked to the Knights Templar."

"I thought the Templars were linked to the ancient Jewish Temple." Annie made sure to keep her tone neutral. "Didn't they build their first monastery on the Temple Mount?"

"They did," Jennifer agreed. "Over the ruins of the Second Temple, according to legend."

Annie looked up. Jennifer was looking at her. Annie no longer required a mental dog whistle—she was certain. She was being prodded, manipulated, and indeed robbed. And not just by Philip Weinraub but—no doubt at his behest—by both Rob Franklin and his wife. A few seconds passed. Neither woman blinked. Finally Annie looked away and traced a line in the airspace above the parchment. "These circles aren't labeled, but they seem to follow the course of the river."

"They're wells," Jennifer said, "dug near the banks. One theory says that's why the Fleet silted up so quickly each time it was dredged. There are nine wells shown in that relatively small space. That implies the existence of many others, and all of them were, in effect, siphoning off river water and impacting the Fleet's flow."

Annie picked up a magnifying glass and bent forward over the painting. "Doesn't seem to be any mention of the Jew of Holborn, does there?"

"Not a whisper," Jennifer said. "I thought of that too. Went looking for it a week or so ago. I'd have called you if I'd spotted anything."

No, you would not. You have been following a careful script all along. First the Scranton map, then the Juryman watercolor. Keep Annie intrigued. Make sure she continues to look for . . . what? A mezuzah. In the Bristol House mural. Maybe. But what did Mr. and Mrs. Robert Franklin stand to gain from that?

Annie kept her head down, still poring over the old and crude attempt at landscape art. "Thanks for showing it to me now," she said evenly.

"I knew you'd be interested." Jennifer carefully replaced the protective tissue over the watercolor. "Would you mind putting this back in its portfolio? I need to run to the loo. I'm peeing every half hour these days. I suppose you remember that."

27

Annie hurried up Great Russell Street toward Bristol House with her cell phone pressed against her ear.

Geoff answered on the first ring. "I was just thinking about you."

"Listen," she said with no preamble, "it's not just Rob Franklin. Jennifer's part of it."

"Part of what? Working for Weinraub?"

"Yes."

"How do you know?"

"She produced something incredible today. She should have shown it to me the first day. It's absolutely relevant. Oh, and she's pregnant."

"Good for her. Is that relevant as well?"

"Probably not." Except she knows I once was as well. Annie couldn't say that to Geoff. Or, to put it more accurately, she didn't want to.

Not far away a crowd of mostly gray-haired women in saris descended from a tour bus and headed for the British Museum. Annie stepped out of their path and leaned against the wrought iron fence that skirted Bloomsbury Square. "I mentioned the Temple Mount, and she didn't react, but I know she was thinking things."

"How did the Temple Mount get into the conversation?"

"We were talking about the Templars."

"Curiouser and curiouser. Happens I'm at Middle Temple. Part of the old Templar monastery."

"Why?"

"Because these days it's where we lock up our lawyers. I've been talking to a barrister who's an expert on the Palestinian issue. For the book."

"Geoff, about Jennifer, I think she's been manipulating me all along. She—"

A chubby little woman in a bright green sari shot with gold ran past

Annie, knocking the phone out of her hand. Annie caught it in midair. The woman turned back and offered a *namaskar* in apology. Annie smiled and produced a half wave as a sign of forgiveness, then pressed the phone back to her ear.

Geoff was still on the line: "—lunch," he was saying.

"What? I lost you."

"I said I'll take you to lunch and we can talk about it. Meet me at the Temple in half an hour."

"Where the lawyers are?"

"No, the Templar church. It's right across the road, and it's open."

"Okay. What's the tube stop?"

"Temple, but don't do that. It's at least three changes from where you are. You can get a bus, I think the one sixty-nine or the fifty-eight, but you have to walk over to Theobald's Road and—forget it. Take a taxi. I'll see you there in about thirty minutes."

The traffic was ghastly. It took Annie the better part of twenty minutes to get to the corner of Fleet Street and Inner Temple Lane. "Near as I can get you, love," the cabbie said when he pulled over. "The Temple's just across the pavement and through that arch. About thirty yards."

She paid the driver and passed beneath the archway and along a brick path toward a church that, according to the small pamphlet she picked up outside the door, had been consecrated to the Blessed Virgin Mary in 1185. His Majesty Henry II, first of the Plantagenets, had been in attendance. He bestowed that mark of high favor, Annie knew, because in the sixty-seven years between the creation of the Knights Templar and the building of this church, the Templars had become Europe's bankers. The order had grown incredibly wealthy by making themselves the custodians of the fortunes of noblemen marching off to the Crusades.

Staggering amounts of money made for immense power, and medieval monarchs suffered no rivals. By the early 1300s, the Knights Templar had been disgraced, their leaders burned at the stake, and the rest disbanded; but 1185, when they built this church and the adjacent monastery—now the Inns of Court where, as Geoff said, London locked up its lawyers—was the moment of the ancient order's greatest splendor.

A small entry had been cut into the huge double doors. Annie walked through it into the eight-hundred-year-old round church. The knights at once surrounded her.

In the Templars' world, being buried beneath the dome of one of their preceptories was equivalent to achieving the cherished goal of resting forever in the holy city of Jerusalem. The knights buried eight hundred years earlier in this corner of London had been granted this great honor, and to this day the prone effigies above each grave indicated the role of each within the order. Some lay still and stiff; they had been administrators of the Templar fortune. Others, the fearsome warrior monks, were depicted in the act of drawing their swords.

Originally the effigies, like the church's stone walls and the grotesque heads that topped its huge marble pillars, had been painted in bright reds and yellows and oranges. Over the centuries the paint had flaked away, leaving a symphony of stone clothed in a numinous paleness that seemed to reflect all the light coming through the tall arched windows and channel it through the opening to a rectangular nave. Pews ran along both walls, not one behind the other, as in an ordinary church, but facing each other in monastic fashion. Everything, the dead knights as well as the play of light and shadow, led the eye to the altar at the far end.

The church was silent and mostly empty. A lone official in a bright red cassock was doing something near the altar. Two middle-aged men knelt side by side in the left rearmost pew. They were holding hands. Annie felt like a voyeur and looked away. Behind her, footsteps echoed on the stone floor, and she turned to see Geoff approaching.

He was so good-looking he made her heart stop, and when he put his hands on her shoulders and kissed her forehead, murmuring an apology for being late, she wanted to cry: because it had been so long since she'd let anyone in this close; because she'd never thought grown-up, responsible, sober Annie would be allowed to feel this way; but most of all because part of her didn't think she deserved him.

* * *

"Medieval European maps," Annie said, "were all drawn with Jerusalem at the center. And the center of the center was the round Church of the Holy Sepulcher, supposedly built over the tomb in which Jesus was buried. Ground zero for the Templars, as Jennifer called it. So, she said, all their churches followed that model."

They were in a small restaurant and wine bar on Fleet Street called Temple Rest. Geoff, who knew the chef-owner, had insisted they both have the brawn accompanied by parsley salad. According to a menu that made provision for American tourists, brawn was headcheese. Authentic old British food, Geoff insisted, appropriate to the setting.

"And I take it," Geoff said, "you reminded Jennifer that, Holy Sepulcher notwithstanding, the Templars are supposed to have built their first monastery over the ancient Jewish Temple."

"On the Temple Mount. Yes. She didn't bat an eye, but I could practically feel her vibrating."

"It's not conclusive, Annie."

"I know, but—" Their food was delivered. Annie studied her plate. She'd thought headcheese would be—well, cheese. It was instead bits of meat and onion suspended in aspic. "Am I to assume this meat comes from some creature's head?"

"Yes. It can be pig or calf or even cow. Jon uses prime steer. Black Angus from Scotland. One reason his brawn is so good. Try it."

"I take it Jon is your buddy the chef." Geoff nodded. Annie poked at the aspic with a tentative fork. "I have a prejudice against food that moves."

"Try it," he said again. "One bite. If you don't like it, I promise you can have something else."

"You sound like my father."

"I assure you, my feelings for you are not at all fatherly. Go ahead—one bite."

She put a small portion of the brawn in her mouth. The aspic instantly dissolved on her tongue, leaving behind the essence of steer. The meat itself was both meltingly tender and full of flavor, its beefiness fol-lowed by a burst of spicy, vinegary tang. "It's delicious," she said, scoop-ing up another mouthful.

"Told you so. Now stop eating long enough to tell me the rest of what happened."

"Jennifer showed me a watercolor from 1530, a primitive Holborn landscape painted by an amateur. In itself that's remarkable, but hell, the whole archive's awesome. That's to be expected. Only I've been here al-most two months, and my focus is incredibly narrow—Holborn in 1535, and she waited until now to show me that?"

"Professional jealousy," Geoff said immediately. "Publish first. All that well-known academic vitriol."

Annie shook her head because her mouth was full of parsley salad. The slightly bitter green was a perfect foil for the rich brawn. It had never occurred to her that parsley could be eaten pretty much on its own. "No. She was manipulating me. She has been from the first. It's never been about the research. Not for her. She took a few days to produce the Scranton map, when you'd think it was the first thing she'd have shown me. Then she went away for a couple of weeks and left me to stew on my own. It's all been deliberate."

"Annie, you don't know that."

It was obvious that while Geoff had had no hesitation in attributing evildoing to Rob Franklin, he was less sanguine about putting Jennifer in the same category. "I do know it," Annie insisted. "She knows personal things about me that only Weinraub could have maybe found out. So—"

She broke off because a large man with a long white apron tied firmly around an expansive waist appeared at their table carrying two glasses of wine. "I hope you weren't planning to slip in and out without saying hello, Geoffrey my man. You can't keep this ravishing redheaded crea-ture a secret. My spies are everywhere."

"Annie, this is my friend Jon Atkins. He's responsible for the deli-cious food you have just inhaled. Jon, this is Annie, an American who objected to anything in aspic—what she called 'food that moves'—until she had her first bite of your brawn." He pointed to Annie's empty plate. "You can see she changed her mind."

The chef put down the two glasses of wine, murmuring that they were compliments of the house, and extended his hand. "Pleased to meet you, Annie."

"Annie doesn't drink," Geoff said, moving her wine to his side of the table. "Bitter Lemon's her thing."

Jon motioned for someone to bring Annie another soda. The three of them exchanged a few more pleasantries. Jon said Geoff must bring her to their next dinner—referring, she guessed, to some kind of club. Geoff said the next dinner was in fact scheduled to be at his house, and he definitely would invite Annie. Jon repeated that he was pleased to have met her and left.

"I gather the meeting is a cook-along," Annie said. "Like a sing-along, but with pots and pans."

"Something like that. But tell me what you meant. What kind of personal things does Jennifer know about you?"

Her stomach dived toward her heels, and she felt dizzy.

"What is it?" Geoff asked after a couple of seconds. "You look, forgive the term, ghostly pale."

"Never a good blush when you need one," Annie said. "Can we go somewhere more private?"

Geoff walked her back to the Temple precincts, to a small jewel of a park, empty despite the glorious summer day. "It's not open to the public," he explained. "One of the porters gave me a temporary pass while I was waiting for the barrister."

They were sitting side by side, on a stone bench that rested on the heads of two openmouthed lions, looking at a fountain whose waters sparkled in the sunlight. "I told you about Zak Johnson, my ex-husband, being a biker," she said.

"Yes, you did."

"What I didn't tell you . . . I—we—have a thirteen-year-old son."

She was gripping the bracelet with her right hand. "His name's Aaron, for my twin, and he's called Ari as well. At least he was when he was little."

There was a long pause. She could see him processing the implications of why, in nearly two months of growing intimacy, she had never mentioned having a child. "I'm guessing," he said finally, "you have no relationship with the boy."

"None. His father has sole custody. I haven't seen Ari since he was three." What kind of mother loses the custody of her three-year-old toddler? A very bad one.

He reached out and put his hand over hers. "Annie . . ."

"Please don't suggest that time will change things. Or that you know how I feel. Or that you understand." The words were forced out of a throat choked with misery. "You don't. You can't."

"You're right," he said. "I've never been anyone's parent. I wanted kids, but Emma didn't. Back when what became toxic assets were huge money-spinners, Emma was a senior trader at Goldman Sachs—and, according to her, much too busy to be pregnant. That's what started the Christmas row that led to her storming out of the house."

An explanation of the heavy baggage he'd mentioned weeks before, when he said being sorry went with the territory. "As in," Annie said, "storming out and getting killed."

"Exactly." And when she didn't say anything. "I've stopped beating myself up over it. The what-ifs take me all the way back to what if we'd never met. The whole line of thought is useless. I guess what I'm trying to say is not that I know how you feel, but I do get it."

"I've tried," Annie said. "I keep trying. Right after I got sober, I found Ari on Facebook. He refused to friend me. A few days later he took down the page. Until about a year ago I wrote him long chatty letters twice a week, trying everything I could think of to open a conversation. Each one came back unopened. These days I send postcards. At least you can't send them back."

"Maybe it's your ex-husband who returned the letters."

"I don't think so. Zak never was vindictive. Besides, I tried calling once. I'm pretty sure Ari answered the phone, but he hung up as soon as I said who I was."

She got up and walked over to the fountain, a cherub riding the back of a dolphin spewing water. Geoff came to join her. "Perfect innocence," he said, nodding toward the sculpture.

"I'm not sure I remember what that felt like. Presuming I ever knew. Geoff, you might as well know the rest of it."

"Only if you want to tell me."

"In AA," she said, "one of the things we promise is to confess to our Higher Power and to at least one other person absolutely the worst thing we ever did when we were drinking." She hesitated. "I've never told anyone this story."

"Not even Sidney?"

"Not even him."

He didn't say anything after that, only waited for her to speak with that listening patience that made him so good at his job. "I was barely eighteen when I married Zak," she began. "But I was already a drunk and long past innocence. I told you we didn't live together because I was still in school, didn't I?"

He nodded.

"Thing is, no matter how much I was drinking, I was always able to go to class and study, even get top grades. That part of my life—it was as if I walked through a looking glass into another world. Zak couldn't disconnect that way. He had a small trust fund, and he picked up odd jobs, but pretty much he just drank and biked. We went on like that for a couple of years. Then when I was twenty, he announced he was leaving. Temporarily, he said. He was going to get sober or get dead. I told him I was two months pregnant. Zak said that was all the more reason to do what he had to do."

She stopped speaking.

"It's okay," Geoff said after a time. "You don't have to tell me any more."

"Yes," she said, "I do." Deep breath. "I had no idea where Zak was when Ari was born, and I didn't make any effort to find him. Didn't see the point. As long as you set the bar pretty low, we were getting along. I was doing a combination master's and Ph.D. program at BU, and I had a fellowship with a stipend. It was enough for a tiny walk-up apartment in what was a crummy part of Boston called Jamaica Plain. Back then the best thing about the neighborhood was that the woman next door loved Ari. Mostly she looked after him when I had to go to class. And I had backup babysitters. At least I think so. Frankly, I don't remember a lot of how it was, because I was drinking so much by then."

The hard part.

"Came the day I was supposed to present the defense of my dissertation. I know I had to be at the university at ten a.m. Apart from that . . . I don't remember if the woman next door wasn't there, or if some babysitter had let me down. I only know I went to my orals and did my usual brilliant job. But when I came home, my door had been busted down, and there were cops waiting for me, and a woman from Boston Social Services."

No tears, but for a few seconds she couldn't speak. Literally could not. The words were choking in her throat.

"I take it," Geoff said quietly, "the social services people found Zak."

She swallowed hard a couple of times, then found her voice. "No. He'd called them. He'd gone to Chicago and got off the booze, and he had a radio program, and he was writing articles for lots of biking mag azines. And having found out where his wife and child were, he'd come back to get us." She was crying now. No sobs, but big tears were rolling down her cheeks. "Zak Johnson walked right up to that stinking little apartment with his arms full of flowers and a teddy bear. Hollywood couldn't have done it better. Only no one answered the door, and he could hear a baby bawling inside, so he broke in."

She stopped speaking, wondered if she had to tell him what Zak told the judge, and decided she did not.

After a time Geoff said softly, "I'm guessing there was a subsequent hearing and Zak got custody."

"Yes," she said.

"Okay."

"It's not okay."

"I know. That's not what I meant. Okay as in 'I understand.'" He didn't try to touch her, just handed her his handkerchief and waited until she had blown her nose and wiped her eyes. Then: "Do you want to talk more about it? Maybe get some legal advice? I know a bloke in New York who—"

"No," she said. "I don't want to fuck up Ari's life any more than I already have. A big legal battle—it's the last thing he needs. And I definitely don't want to talk about it anymore. Can we please move on?"

"Yes, of course we can. This all started with Jennifer. Tell me what the link is."

"She made a remark about peeing all the time because she's pregnant. Then she said she supposed I remembered that. But there's no way she should have known I ever had a child."

"Public records," Geoff said. "CVs . . ."

Annie shook her head. "It's not listed anywhere obvious. I've never used the Johnson name. You'd need to find the birth records, and where would you start? When? Hell, you put the famous Geoffrey Harris spyglass on me, and you never discovered it." She paused. "You didn't, did you? You're not just pretending this is a surprise?"

"Scout's honor," he said. "I didn't know. You're right, it certainly wasn't obvious. And I dug pretty deep."

"So do you think it's likely Jennifer Franklin came up with that information on her own? Or that she had any reason to look in the first place?"

He hesitated a moment. "Not likely," he admitted.

"But we know Weinraub set me up for this"—Annie waved her hand—"for whatever he's after. And as you said from the first, he picked me because he figured I could be manipulated. So it was in his interest to find out everything about me. And he could pay to dig as deep as he wanted to."

"You're saying Weinraub is the one who found out about your son. And because Jennifer is working for him, he told her."

"Yes," Annie said. "That's what I'm saying. But working for him how? Doing what? And why? What in God's name does Jennifer Franklin want with some piece of ancient Judaica, mezuzah or otherwise?"

"She doesn't have to want what Weinraub wants. It could just be about money. If she—hold it. Text coming." He pulled his phone from a pocket. "It's from Clary."

"Is he still in France?

"Yes." He was staring intently at the message.

"What does he say?"

"That he's come up empty on the connection to the Rabin assassination. But he wants us—or at least me—to come to Strasbourg right away."

"Us," she said instantly. Then, seeing his face: "It's not negotiable, Geoff."

"Okay." He was scrolling through the message again.

"Why does he want us there?" Annie demanded.

"According to Clary, so he can demonstrate that Philip Weinraub is not a Jew."

28

Dom Justin
From the Waiting Place

I woke in the still blackness of a summer's night to a whisper in my ear: "It is over. Rise and follow me."

A creature sat beside my bed, hooded and hunched over. Death had come to claim me, and my stained soul would go straight to hell. I opened my mouth to scream. Instantly a bony hand was clamped over my lips.

"Are you mad? Noise will finish us. Come, we must hurry."

The creature moved to the door of my cell, and I got up and went with him, following him down the stairs and out to the cloister walk and then into the courtyard, along the very route I had traveled nights without number: my secret way out of the Charterhouse. I heard no sound, and nothing moved around us. The night was black as pitch and close with the heat that had so far marked this strange July. Sweat poured from me, but still I shivered and trembled. "Who are you?" I demanded, thinking I should not go so willingly to eternal damnation.

He paused, still with his back to me, and said softly, "Do you not know me? I am the Speckled Egg."

I opened my mouth to ask the countless questions that had so long preoccupied me, but they clogged in my throat and none could find a voice.

In moments we were in the small courtyard that led to the door that was never locked. "Go," he said. "Hurry to the house of the Jew and his daughter and warn them. She is known to have whored herself and conceived a child. The order has been signed. You are all three for the fire."

"Wait," I protested, the quandaries of the past few years once more asserting themselves in my mind. "How do there come to be quail's eggs in this place where there are no quails? And how did one come to me on a night when Master Cromwell did not summon me, and—"

The one who claimed to have such authority as to send me from this place where I was vowed to spend my entire life sighed a deep sigh and said, "Ah, Justin, you are still not able to give up your will to your Creator, but instead trouble yourself with the things of this world rather than those of the next. Thomas Cromwell knows nothing of how you are directed to do his bidding, only that you are. As for the eggs, they come through the generosity of a woman in the town, a Mistress Grindal, who keeps the small birds. She is one of us. And it was I who sent you to the Jew that particular night. A voice came from heaven and told me to do so."

More important than the answers to my questions was a far more extraordinary truth. Though the figure yet kept his back to me, I was certain I recognized his voice. "What is meant by 'one of us'? And in the name of Almighty God, if you are the man I think you are . . . how can you be holy enough for heaven to speak in your ear, yet align yourself with a scheme that for four years has made a mockery of the integrity of this place?"

Just then, as if my guardian angel would perform one last task of his assigned custodianship, a ray of moonlight showed me in the distance the cloud of dust raised by a number of oncoming horsemen.

"Hurry," the shrouded figure said.

I did not move. I knew by then it was not the angel of death who stood near me, though he still hid himself in the shadows of the night, but I required confirmation if I was ever to make sense of all that had transpired since I came to the Charterhouse. "I shall not go until I know who you are."

My companion raised his hand and pushed back his cowl, and I saw the old and saintly Dom Hilary standing before me.

"You are the Speckled Egg—I would never have believed—"

"The unexpected hidden in the ordinary is the surest disguise, Justin. It is a point worth remembering."

I had no interest at that time in his philosophy of secrets. "Dom Hilary, hear my confession. Otherwise, if I die, it is with deadly sin on my soul, and

I will burn not just once but for all eternity. The girl, the Jew's daughter, I gave in to—"

Hilary raised his hand and cut off my words. "There is no time." He made the sign of the cross above my head. "Make an act of contrition and accept that I give you absolution in the name of Christ. And know," he said, after the blessing was done and his hand had dropped, "that five years ago when I began this business that made me Master Cromwell's accomplice, I thought to protect all we have here. And to protect the Truly Obedient Priesthood, as I am sworn to do. Instead I have brought the peril on us more quickly. May God have mercy on us both, though perhaps you will need it more than I. If you survive this threat, Justin, you must quit England. Your journey will be fraught with danger, though I will try to send you help along the way. Mistress Grindal for one, in the place east of here known as the Hollow Way, will hide you if she must. There are others—I will arrange it. Now hurry, take this and go."

He thrust a parcel toward me, but I did not take it. "Wait—" Despite the obvious menace indicated by the oncoming horsemen, I could not resist the new question his words raised in my mind. "What is the Truly Obedient Priesthood? How does it differ from the ordinary sort?" Even then, newly shriven of my terrible sin, though I had not confessed it—or so Dom Hilary had said, though that strange way of gaining absolution would come to weigh heavier on my conscience than had the sin itself—it was in my mind that there might be a sort of priest not bound to a lifetime of celibacy as are all the rest. In the face of death by fire, my thoughts yet turned to the notion that I might licitly possess the Jew's daughter. Such is Jezebel's power when a man turns from righteousness to lust.

Dom Hilary smiled, knowing my thoughts, as it seemed he had so often in the past. "You are a priest forever, Justin. And a Carthusian sworn to celibacy and obedience, as are we all. But you, my son, are more. You are a priest in the True Obedience of Avignon."

All at once I remembered what I had read in one of the many books I had studied in the Charterhouse. How in 1378 there was a dispute among the cardinal electors at the conclave to choose a new pope, and some broke away and set up in Avignon a man they called Clement VII, who became the first antipope of the Great Schism that lasted for fifty years. "Avignon," I said. "You speak of the antipope?"

Hilary's hand shot up, and he slapped my cheek with more force than I could have imagined such an old man to have. "I speak of the true papacy. The antipope is he who today sits in Rome and all who come after him. *Sede vacante*," he said, speaking the Latin words for empty chair, "*sede vacante*. Peter's throne is vacant, and the church of God has no true pope. But thanks to you and to me and to others of our obedience, someday a true pope will return to Rome. Now go—already I fancy I can smell the bubbling fat beneath your charred skin."

By this time we could hear the pounding hoofs of the king's soldiers. Once more Hilary thrust the parcel toward me. It was wrapped tightly in an old piece of sacking and tied with rope. "Practical things," the old man said, "but look carefully, and you will find within a rare and blessed secret. It will protect you from even dangers such as this." The sounds of the approaching horsemen grew louder. I took what Hilary gave me and ran.

Giacomo the Lombard, known also as the Jew of Holborn
From the Waiting Place

And so the time in Holborn ended in the shadow of a cloud of greasy smoke and the echo of agonized screams. One night the monk came and roused my daughter and myself from our beds with the words I had so long dreaded: "We are for the fire! Even now they come to arrest us. We must hide!"

Mistress Juryman had done her work well and swiftly. No such announcement as I had imagined was required. The banns proclaiming the coming marriage of Timothy Faircross to my daughter had not yet been posted, but at Henry's court news flowed like water, filling every crevice and cranny of its own accord. The Juryman woman had only to whisper what she knew—perhaps to her husband, perhaps to another—and Thomas Cromwell heard it. That day, the same day the court returned to

London, he signed the order. We were to burn. All three of us. His lackey the so-called Dom Justin included.

When that midnight summons came, my first thought was that there was no place in all the kingdom where we could hide from such a fate as awaited us and from such power as had decreed it. Then I thought of the pit. It had protected the Templars' hoard for three hundred years. Perhaps it might shield us for a few days.

In that moment and at that place, I did not ask myself what might happen afterward.

❖

"He's definitely not a Jew," Clary said.

He and Geoff and Annie were sitting in a dingy, low-ceilinged establishment that was part grocery and part café, in a blink-and-you'll-miss-it village west of Strasbourg. "Tell me again how you know that," Geoff said.

Clary held up two fingers, folding them down as he made his points. "One, it turns out the Wein family of financiers were Catholics, pillars of the church. Two, and most important, Philippe Jérémie as he was originally didn't have the whack job. They didn't cut off the end of his prick when he was a baby."

"It's not the end," Geoff said. "It's the foreskin. No loss."

Annie shook her head impatiently. "That's hardly the point. Clary, how can you know whether Weinraub's circumcised? And even if you do, it's not definitive. Plenty of men who aren't Jews are circumcised, so—"

"In the United States, maybe," Clary said. "Rest of the world, not so much. Not in Europe. Not in the Caribbean either. First time I stood at a urinal in New Orleans, I was freaked out by all the whack jobs either side of me. Muslims do it. And definitely Jews. If you're a member of the Chosen People, you get the whack job when you're eight days old. Definitive as anything can be. Weinraub, or Wein as he was then, didn't get it at that age and he's not a Jew."

Annie shot Geoff a quick glance, felt the blush start, and looked as quickly away. It hadn't occurred to her that his being circumcised might be unusual for an Englishman. Maggie's choice probably. Maybe one more thing she'd fought with her husband about.

"Okay," Geoff said, ignoring Annie and speaking to Clary. "I'll bite. How come you're so sure about all this?"

"Because I talked to the woman who did the whack job on Weinraub forty-four years ago, when he was fifteen." Clary smiled, enjoying their openmouthed stares. "She's right over there," he added, nodding toward the woman standing behind a beat-up wooden counter.

The woman was leaning on her elbows and staring at them. They stared back. She smiled—not, however, at the three of them. Geoff had her primary attention. "*Est-ce que vous voulez un autre gris, monsieur?*"

According to Clary, *un gris* was local parlance for the Riesling that made up most of the region's wine production and just about all the everyday *vin de table*. He and Geoff had agreed that the stuff being poured here—there were three unlabeled bottles of white on a shelf behind the counter—was one step above cow piss. Nonetheless he motioned to his glass and Geoff's. "*Deux autres,*" then, nodding toward Annie, "*et un autre citron pressé pour madame.*"

The woman poured a glass of fizzy mineral water from a green plastic bottle, squeezed half a lemon into it, and added a spoonful of sugar. She put the drink on a small, round tray, chose one of the half-full bottles of wine from the shelf, and carried everything to where they sat. The table, also small and round, was the only one in the place. The zinc top was scarred with the rings of God knows how many cups and glasses.

The woman took Annie's glass and replaced it with the fresh *citron pressé,* then waited until both men drank the last of their wine before uncorking the bottle and refilling their glasses. "*Neuf euros,*" she said. The hand she held out was perfectly manicured. Her makeup was flawless, her short silver hair was expertly shaped, and she wore a good-looking linen blouse cut to flatter a shelflike matronly bosom while drawing the eye to slim hips, a short skirt, and decent legs and ankles accentuated by high heels. *Vive la France.* The phrase was maybe the only French Annie knew.

"*Neuf euros*," the woman repeated. And when Geoff had counted out the coins: "*Merci, monsieur.*" Then, to Clary: "*C'est lui votre riche Anglais, non?*"

"*C'est le riche Anglais, oui*," Clary said, then turned to Geoff. "You brought the money?"

Geoff nodded.

It was hot—France had what Annie thought of as normal summer weather—but Geoff was wearing his black leather jacket. He hadn't taken it off because he had eight thousand pounds in small bills secreted in the jacket's various pockets. Another two were in Annie's shoulder bag because they had pushed the jacket into the category of attention-getting bulk. "See," she'd said that morning when he gave her the money, "you do need me." That had followed a telephone call during which Clary had explained to Geoff that he and Annie needed to bring a big chunk of cash to France.

The woman again held out her hand. "*Très bien, c'est vous le riche Anglais. Donnez-moi l'argent.*"

"*Pas trop vite.*" Clary said. "*D'abord les documents.*"

Geoff had reasonable French, but they'd agreed that Clary would do all the talking. The woman, Clary assured them, spoke no English. "I called her a fat slut, and she didn't blink."

It was as good a test as any Annie could think of. Being called fat would definitely have gotten under the woman's skin. "What are they saying?" she asked.

"She wants the money," Geoff said, "and Clary wants the papers."

The negotiation had apparently ended. The woman reached into the front of her blouse. The shelf yielded a single piece of paper, much folded. "*C'est tout ce dont vous avez besoin*," she said.

"All we need, according to her," Geoff said. "I have to see for myself."

He was sitting back, sipping his wine, looking as if he did this sort of thing every day. Which, Annie realized, might be a bit of an exaggeration, but not much. They paid him well enough that he could put his hands on a substantial wad of cash in half a day—and not break a sweat at the idea of handing it over to a Frenchwoman whose name he didn't know, in some out-of-the-way place neither Google nor Map-Quest could come up with, though it showed on the infinitely detailed Michelin *carte d'Alsace*. Which, of course, Geoff had produced as soon as it was required.

Clary and the woman had resumed their argument. She still clutched her scrap of paper, and she'd taken a step back, as if afraid he might try to snatch it out of her hand.

Geoff reached into one of his pockets and brought out a stack of ten-pound notes secured with a rubber band. "There's a thousand pounds here. *Mille livres.* The rest after I examine the document."

Clary translated rapidly, but the woman seemed to have understood. She was staring at the money. Annie could actually see her trembling. After a few seconds, she snatched at the pile of bills. Geoff allowed her to take it. "*Neuf mille de plus,*" he said. "Nine thousand more, after I see what you have." He held out his hand.

"*Après l'examination,*" Clary said. "*Pas avant.*"

The warning wasn't necessary. The woman had already given Geoff what he wanted.

The paper had been folded to a four-inch square. Open, it was standard European A4. The heavy stock, almost cardboard, was ruled with a series of lines and columns. From where she sat, it looked to Annie as if each column were headed with a date. That was all she could make out.

The woman said something to Clary.

"She wants me to explain what it is," he said.

The woman meanwhile was staring at Geoff as if she had discerned the bulging pockets of his jacket. If so, she was the first to do so. Annie had worried about getting such a large sum over the border. Geoff had reminded her that these days there was virtually no border between England and France. They'd gotten on a train at London's St. Pancras Station a little after five in the morning, made one change at Paris, and soon after noon French time—call it six hours' travel time, as France was an hour later than Britain—Clary had picked them up in Strasbourg and driven them here.

Geoff continued to study the unfolded paper. The woman kept talking.

"She wants me to tell you," Clary said, "that she risked her life to keep this document."

"What is it exactly?" Annie asked.

"She's a nurse," Clary said. "Used to be a nurse. She was paid a small stipend by the government for offering basic health care in a rural community. To get the money, she had to fill in a monthly form stating what services she had performed. In March 1967 Louis Weinraub arrived at her door with his fifteen-year-old son. He wanted her to circumcise the kid. Because, he said, they were living in America where all the other boys were circumcised and young Philip was embarrassed because he was not."

"Why didn't they just go to an American doctor?"

"That puzzled her as well," Clary said. "And she also wondered how it was, since Weinraub sounded like a Jewish name, the son hadn't been circumcised when he was an infant."

"Maybe," Annie said, "he was going to convert to Judaism. He'd need to be circumcised in that case."

Clary shook his head. "I checked. If that was it, he'd have been circumcised by a rabbi. That's the only way it's official."

Geoff stopped looking at the paper the woman had given him and raised his head. "He's right about that." Then, nodding toward the woman: "What answer did she get when she asked?"

"None," Clary said. "Her husband told her not to poke her nose where it didn't belong—just do what she was supposed to do. He said they were being paid well." He broke off and turned to the woman and asked something in French. She responded with a stream of impassioned talk accompanied by many gestures. "She says she never saw a penny of whatever Weinraub paid and doesn't know exactly how much it was. That's why she didn't file her report that month, so the monthly stipend wouldn't be paid. She did it to spite her husband. She never saw any of that money either."

"Where's the husband now?" Geoff asked.

"Died eleven years ago. And soon after that the government ended the program she was working for. Transportation had become good enough so it wasn't needed. Even from out here in the sticks, anyone can get to a hospital. These days this place is her only income."

"*S'il vous plaît*," the woman said, nodding toward the paper. "*S'il vous plaît. Ça suffit? C'est l'information que vous voulez, non?*"

Annie thought she might be crying.

"She wants to know if it's what you're after," Clary said.

"Tell her it is." Geoff took the rest of the money out of his pockets and put the stacks of bills on the table. Annie added her stash. "Let's get out of here," Geoff said. They started for the door, but the woman wouldn't let them leave until she formally kissed each of them on both cheeks.

Clary's rented Peugeot was parked a few feet away. "Just the car to have when you want to keep a low profile," Geoff said.

"Hey man, you're paying. Besides"—he gestured to the lifeless single street with its array of small stone houses, all of which appeared to be empty—"this place is a corpse that doesn't know it's dead. Not even a bakery anymore." There was a shop across the road with a faded sign that said "Pain et Pâtisserie," but it was shuttered and looked as if it had been for some time. "Who's going to see us?"

"Why do you think she's stayed here all these years?" Annie asked. Both men knew she meant the woman in the bar.

"Because she had no money to get out," Geoff said. "At least here she had a roof over her head."

Something, Annie realized, he knew without being told, because it was different from Maggie's story, but not that different.

As if her thought had somehow conjured the connection, Geoff's cell rang. He grabbed it and put it to his ear, mouthing "Maggie" in Annie's direction. And after a few quick words, "I have to get back right away. My mother's in hospital."

On the train taking them back to London, he got a text from Agence Investigations Mme Defarge. When she first heard the name, Annie insisted it was a joke. Geoff wasn't sure they read Dickens in Paris. This time she let it pass without comment. "What does she say?"

"A man named Étienne Renard was born in Avignon in 1900. Sounds like he could be the bloke we want. She's checking for more."

29

We had neither food nor water in the diabolical hole to which the Jew brought us, that pit which had so long exercised my curiosity. By the second day I would have given anything I possessed—more accurately, since I had nothing, any treasure in the poxed place—never to have encountered it.

The pit was at the bottom of a dry well, through a small opening into which we had to crawl on our bellies. We were then still in an antechamber too small for even Rebecca to stand upright, with barely enough room to contain the three of us. And all the while we huddled there in misery, we heard sounds above that made it apparent we were hunted like rats in a hole, which we indeed were.

I could see no evidence of any treasure where we were, nor any sign of digging, but sometimes the old man crawled through a second narrow opening. At such times the Jew never fully disappeared. I could see always the toes of his boots, and when he extracted himself from that hellish tunnel, his white hair was streaked with dirt. I guessed what he found in that cramped and filthy place to be the treasures of the Templars, exactly as he was originally sent to discover, but I had little curiosity about them. What worth did gold or silver have for us as we were then?

For my part, I wanted only more space. In what we had, my legs and the girl's must intertwine when we were alone, and when her father rejoined us, she was squeezed full length against me. So I discovered Dom Hilary's final blessing to have changed me in a way beyond my imagining. He had cured me of my lust for the Jew's daughter. I felt only cramp and thirst, which was far worse than hunger, though I suffered that as well.

Clearly the Jew was beset by the same misery. "The girl must go and find drink and food," he said. According to my calculations, which were based on the light that came from aboveground, he spoke those words on the morning of our third day in hiding, adding, "We will all die here otherwise."

It was no fair reproach to say we were fools for providing ourselves with nothing when we came to the pit. We were not three minutes in our cramped hiding place when we heard the first troop of horsemen thundering overhead. Had we stopped to gather provisions, we'd have been caught. Besides, at that time it was in my mind that Dom Hilary might have supplied necessities for a time of hiding. But when we were safe in the pit and the horsemen had passed, I opened the parcel he had given me and found it to be the clothes I had worn the day I first came to the Charterhouse. (And one other thing I will speak of later that, though as rare a treasure as may be found in Christendom, did not ease our bodily needs.) The clothes served as a pillow for my head but added little to my comfort.

"We must have something to quench our thirst and fill our empty bellies," the Jew told Rebecca. "Go."

"Why do you send me on this perilous errand?" she asked. "Will my flesh not singe and burn as readily as yours? Or do you imagine that when Master Cromwell learns of my condition he will relent?"

She touched her belly, which seemed to me to have swelled more in the few days we'd spent hiding, and looked not at her father but at me. It was however Giacomo the Lombard who said, "A woman has a better chance of passing unnoticed."

"And you," Rebecca said, turning to me, "do you also think it my place to go for what we need?" I nodded, and she again put her hand on her belly. "You do not fear for the life of your son, or perhaps your daughter?"

"The child was conceived in mortal sin," I told her. "It may be fated never to be born." I wanted to be kind, so I did not add that her role as temptress meant she bore the greater responsibility for the evil and thus should suffer the worse consequences.

She said nothing to that, only managed to disentangle herself from her father and me and crawl through the hole that led to the well. Soon we heard her using the ancient handholds to climb to the world over our heads.

I do not know how long she was gone. It seemed many hours, but perhaps not. However long it was, it passed with terrible slowness. Even though there was now a little more space, I could not sleep for thirst. As for the Jew, he did not say a word to me. Instead he stared into space, occasionally muttering to himself in some Jew's-language I could not understand.

It was, I think now, the worst of the time we passed in the pit, but eventually it ended.

We heard her return before we saw her. Both of us, I think, feared for the first few moments that perhaps it was not Rebecca but the king's soldiers who were clambering down to where we were. There was little logic in such suspicions. As soon as the child had started to grow in her belly, the girl had given up any bargaining power she might have possessed while she was a desirable virgin. Had she wanted to trade our whereabouts for her freedom, it's unlikely she would have been able to do so. Still the thought crossed my mind, and I was sure it also occurred to her father.

Our fears were groundless. Rebecca crawled through the hole to where we were, then dragged a small bundle in behind her. It contained ale enough to quench our thirst, and bread and cheese to calm our hunger. Only when we had drunk and eaten did I see in the dim light that she had carried our sustenance in the distinctive black cloak worn by the plague women. I drew back and crossed myself, but Rebecca laughed. "Which do you fear more? Mortal illness or the flames?" she taunted, shaking the cloak to ring the bells that hung from its jagged hem. And when I did not answer, she said, "Never mind. Neither my father nor I sickened in the presence of this cloak, and I doubt you will either. It is many days since I clasped a victim to my chest while wearing it, and the plague women say the curse wears off after a time. Besides, the cloak is the means of our salvation. When I wear it, no one comes near me. I can go again to get what we need."

"No," her father said.

I was astounded that he would protest now, when she was not commanded but volunteered to serve us in this way, and when she had contrived the means to do so in some safety. He'd shown no reluctance earlier when she was without the protection of the cloak. "She speaks sense," I said.

The Jew laughed. "You are as shortsighted as she is. How long do you think we can remain here, even with a bit of food and drink? A week? Two weeks? A month perhaps? Will we not then have lost the use of our legs for not having stretched them? Or might not the stink of our dung rise up and attract the attention of another troop of soldiers who are riding by and summon them to examine the dry well and so to find us?"

I could find no fault with his argument. "Then we have no hope," I said.

"That is not true. There is a way, though I must rely on you to take it, and I do not know if you have the courage or the skill required."

"I have both, Father," Rebecca said.

The Jew nodded. "Yes, you do."

I said nothing, waiting to hear his plan. But when I thought he would speak, he instead once more crawled into the next chamber, and for some time we heard him rooting around in his secret place. I asked Rebecca if she knew what he had in mind, but she shook her head and did not answer me; instead she arranged the plague woman's cloak behind her head as a pillow, in the same way I had been using Dom Hilary's parcel, and kept her hands clasped over her belly, as if the unborn child required protection more than we did.

At last the Jew pulled himself back to where we were. This time he too had a bundle, made I saw from his kirtle. Even our breath seemed to find no place in our cramped quarters, but he managed to squeeze the thing he carried into the space we occupied. "In here," he said, "are treasures that will buy you hospitality and safety."

"The master will not be content with whatever you have in there," I said. "He will simply have us tortured until we reveal their source. Then we will burn as he intended right along."

"You are a bigger fool than I imagined," the Jew said, and turned from me to look at his daughter. "Rebecca, I will tell you a series of names and places. You will remember them?"

"Yes, Father."

He nodded. "I trust you shall. And you"—he looked at me—"will go with her because as a woman alone, even with the protection of the cloak, she cannot travel so far without incurring suspicion or worse."

"Go where?" I still did not understand the daring of his plan.

"First to the coast of Kent. Then you must get across the channel. There are plenty of boatmen who will take this"—he pulled a gold plate from his parcel—"as fare."

"No need," Rebecca said. "I have Mistress Juryman's coins."

Her father laughed, and I had no opportunity to ask what they were talking about because he immediately went on. "I should have expected you would. Very well, but you may use this if need be." He again brandished the gold plate. "It is not a treasure like the rest." He patted the bundle he had made. "These go only to our people."

"To Jews," I said, beginning finally to see the outline of the scheme he had in mind. Then I remembered Dom Hilary's words: *If you survive this threat, Justin, you must quit England.* "To Jews living in places far away," I added. "That is what you mean, is it not?"

"It is. There are thriving Jewish colonies in the Rhenish towns of Metz and Strasbourg, and across the Rhine in Offenburg and Breisach. I have clansmen in each. Even you"—he looked at me—"will be received for my sake. And because of what you bring." He gestured again to the hoard in his kirtle.

I had heard stories of how Jews had blood contacts everywhere and thus maintained and grew their wealth. I never thought the notion to be of more than passing interest. Now I was learning that my life depended on that spiderweb of connection.

But what life? I began all this seeking a reward that would make me rich enough to claim as my wife the daughter of Giacomo the Lombard. It had instead led me to become in truth what I had pretended to be. "I am priested," I said, "and vowed to remain so until I die." In my mind I added the extraordinary intelligence that Dom Hilary had shared with me, that I was a priest of the True Obedience of Avignon, charged with the task of returning a real and bona fide pope to the church. Though I believed utterly in what Dom Hilary had said—was not the Jew's scheme further proof that God spoke through Hilary?—I did not say the words aloud. Because I could not imagine how I would discharge my obligation, it seemed best not to boast of it. "I am vowed to be a monk of the Charterhouse. I cannot change that now."

"I do not ask that you marry her," the Jew said. "Only that you see these treasures safely to our people. The girl as well," he added, though it was plain to me, and I suspect to Rebecca, that the contents of his pack mattered to him more.

"I can promise that," I said. Getting out of this dilemma by any plan, however unlikely to succeed, seemed to me far better than remaining where we were and starving or being discovered.

"Swear it," he said, "by the Almighty Creator of the Universe."

I swore.

He looked content. Rebecca was not. "Do neither of you ask what I wish in all this?"

"Do you have a choice?" her father asked. "You are my flesh and your mother's daughter, and for those reasons I might forgive you what you have done. For other men you are simply a whore."

"Not," she said quietly, "if he"—she nodded in my direction—"escorts me as a widow."

The Jew nodded. "It is a story that will be believed," he said. "And you will be welcome because of what you bring."

"If," she said, "you have in there what I believe you have, I will be more than welcomed, I will be revered."

Her father looked not at her but at me. Then he seemed to make up his mind. "Treasures stolen from the Temple in Jerusalem," he whispered. "Do you understand?"

Such things, I realized, as might have been touched by the hand of Jesus

Christ himself, for the Gospels tell us that when Our Savior was in Jeru-salem, He went to that very temple to offer worship to His Father in heaven. I could not speak for the enormity of the thought, but I nodded and so did the Jew.

So was our bargain made.

It was necessary to wait until my hair had grown sufficient to cover the tonsure, which meant Rebecca must make one further excursion into the countryside to fetch us food and drink. "Go," I said, "to Mistress Grindal in the Hollow Way and ask for help in the name of the Speckled Egg. She will give you all you need." Rebecca donned the plague cloak and went and did as I had told her, and returned with meat and cheese and ale enough to last us until my tonsure was grown out and my beard full enough to serve as some sort of disguise should any who sought us know what I looked like. Then, after nightfall of a day when we had heard no patrols of searching soldiers, Rebecca and I climbed out of the pit.

I left my habit behind and dressed in the clothes Dom Hilary had given me, as he had obviously intended I should do. Hidden beneath them, close to my heart, was the other thing I had found in the parcel: an Agnus Dei. It was little bigger than my thumbnail, and I recognized it at once as that rarest and most precious of holy relics, a scrap of wax—this one encased in red silk—blessed by a pope. I was sure, given the source, it commemorated the reign of Pope Clement VII, whom I then believed to be the true successor to Saint Peter—a conviction based on the word of Hilary, and on all the remarkable things that had happened to me since first I entered the Charterhouse.

"Do we now again call you Geoffrey?" the Jew asked, eyeing my change of clothing.

"Call me what you will. In my heart"—I touched my hidden and blessed treasure—"I remain Dom Justin." And, I added in my mind, a priest of the True Obedience of Avignon.

"Geoffrey is dead," Rebecca said. "I loved Geoffrey, but he disappeared a long time ago."

She spoke more truth than she knew, so I did not contradict her.

In all the time of our preparation and planning, we had not asked the

Jew her father why he was not coming with us, or what he intended to do when we were gone. It seemed an unnecessary question. In the final moments before we left, he said, "Wait four days, Daughter, then begin to say the mourning prayer for me. As I have no son, I rely on you."

"It is a sin," I said, obligated by simple charity in the face of such a blatant confession of wicked intent, even on the part of a Jew.

"Not always," he told me. "Not to protect what remains from further desecration." He turned to his daughter and showed her something that was in his hand. "This is for you," he said, "not to be gifted to the others. I pray you will pass it on to my grandchild."

"I promise I will do so," Rebecca said.

He did not immediately give her the treasure he had deemed to be a personal gift, only looked at her for some few seconds, then said, "For your mother's sake, indeed for your own, I wish it had not been thus. It means little now, but I am sorry for what you have suffered because of me." Then he grasped the two ends of the thing he was giving her, a silver tube of some sort, and twisted them in opposite directions. One end came free in the manner of a stopper pulled from a jug. I knew from the way he angled his body he thought to keep me from seeing what he did, but so close were our quarters, it was not possible. And though he whispered, I heard him tell her the thing inside was never to be removed. "You must swear you will not replace the original *klaf*. And that you will make whoever you give this to swear the same thing." And when she had done so, he replaced the part that had come loose and gave her the thing, and she did as women always do and secreted it down her bosom.

Giacomo the Lombard, known also as the Jew of Holborn
From the Waiting Place

I intended to wait the full four days until, following my instructions, my daughter would begin saying the prayer of mourning. But the second day after they left, I heard above my head more patrols than ever before, and I suspected that something or someone had given the soldiers a clue as to where I and my treasure might be found. Had they captured Rebecca and Geoffrey and forced the information from them? Perhaps, but perhaps not. There were many other possible explanations, from chance to coincidence. Having for so long refused to allow grief for my daughter to take precedence over what I knew to be my duty, I could not dwell on that riddle. My intention was not changed.

I crawled into the second chamber.

The tools I used to dig were where they had always been. I ignored the trowel and the small smith's mallet, which I sometimes used to break up stubborn clods of earth, and took in hand the much larger pickax. Instead of tiny, careful strokes moving a few inches of soil at a time, I swung it wildly, using as much force as I could summon while lying on the ground at full stretch. Indeed, I exerted more strength than I should by nature possess. After a time great lumps of clay fell on my head and all around me. I struggled to my knees, fearing I might smother myself without bringing about what I intended.

Then, after a few more strokes, thin cracks began traveling the length and breadth of the wall of earth in front of me, widening even as I watched. All at once, the wall crumbled, as if a child's hand had pushed over an edifice built of sand. Miraculously I was not buried by the shower of dirt and stones but was instead able to drag myself over the rubble into the cavern that was newly exposed.

I was in a chamber that was wider and taller than either of the two I had so laboriously uncovered over the space of nearly five years, and everywhere I looked were wondrous things.

I staggered to my feet, my eyes dazzled by the glory of the treasure I had discovered and turned every which way, hungry to see it all, not knowing where to look first. But even as I stumbled toward the nearest marvel a golden menorah as tall as a small child and as wide as the span of both my outstretched arms—the water began rising at my feet. In seconds it was at my knees, and moments after, waist-high. The Fleet was rushing toward me, ready to claim the stolen treasure of the Templars. And me with it.

The flooding river rose as high as my chest, but I struggled toward the thing that shone before me, hoping to survive long enough to touch it with my own hands. Finally I was close enough to see the almond blossom shape of the menorah's nine candleholders and so to convince myself of the likelihood that once it had burned in the Holy Temple in Jerusalem. Here was truly the most ancient symbol of my people. I grasped it and lifted it above my head and shouted my final words: *"Shema Yisrael Adonai Eloheinu, Adonai Echad."* Hear, O Israel: The Lord Our God, the Lord is One.

And so I came to the Waiting Place. I am told my wife and my daughter have preceded me here, and that both spoke for me before moving on. Moreover, I am promised that having told my story, I too will soon be allowed to depart this way station between time and eternity. I am joyful.

❖

30

Maggie looked lost in the hospital bed, small and wizened, only her sea-blue eyes showing any sign of vitality. Geoff had told Annie what to expect; nonetheless she was shocked by the physical deterioration wrought in what seemed a few days.

"Apparently the cancer's everywhere," Geoff had said, repeating the verdict of the oncologist in a flat monotone that for him was more expressive than hysteria. "All the vital organs are involved, and she's got a lump the size of my fist on her rib cage. Exterior, or it would have killed her by now. As it was, the thing started hemorrhaging, and that's what drove her to get help. She said it was ruining her pink chair."

Maggie's way of putting it was more direct. "I made an agreement with my cancer. I wouldn't bother it if it didn't bother me. It was a temporary truce, and the time ran out. Sit down, Annie darling, and stop looking so glum. No poking and prodding and vomiting and losing my hair. My choice, and I'd do it again." She patted the thick white braid that hung over her shoulder. "Now, tell me what you found in Strasbourg. Geoff started to explain yesterday, but I was too doped up to understand. And it made a great excuse to have you come and visit."

"I want to come," Annie said. "Every day if you'll have me."

"We're not talking about a lot of days," Maggie said. Geoff started to protest, but she went on as if she hadn't heard. "Tell me everything now. Once I start 'kicking old Buddha's gong'"—she nodded toward an apparatus at the side of the bed, one of many sporting a tube that led to some part of her body hidden by the blankets—"nothing you say will make a bit of sense."

Annie looked puzzled.

"Morphine, darling," Maggie said. "They've got me hooked up to dope-on-demand. 'Buddha's gong,' according to the old Hoagy Carmichael song." She hummed a few notes. " 'Hong Kong Blues.' More of my Bletchley music. Geoff knows it—get him to play it for you sometime. He's to have the piano, by the way. I'm trusting you to make sure he keeps it and practices once in a while."

The way she said it—the utter seriousness of her tone—was a small surprise. As if . . . Maggie and Annie, partners in a conspiracy to keep Geoffrey Harris on the straight and narrow. Annie choked back tears.

Geoff was standing near the head of the bed, a vantage point from which he could see his mother and avoid looking at the paraphernalia of her illness. "Maggie, there are still things they can try. I don't—"

"Hush, darling. It's not going to happen, and I do not have the strength to argue with you. Now, tell me everything about Strasbourg. I haven't taken a hit for an hour so I'll be sensible enough to understand, but I won't be able to resist much longer."

For long seconds Geoff didn't speak. He was, Annie realized, struggling with tears of his own. She pulled her chair a bit closer to Maggie's bed. "Philip Weinraub's name was originally Wein," she said. "And the family were Catholics. He wasn't circumcised until he was fifteen."

Maggie's eyebrows shot up.

Geoff had regained control. "There's more," he added. "They were living in New York by then, but his father brought him back to France to have the deed done by a sort of public health nurse in a tiny village in Alsace."

"Meaning," Annie chimed in, "that it couldn't have been because young Philip planned to convert to Judaism. If that was it, he'd have had the circumcision done by a rabbi."

"What the father planned," Maggie said, "was for the record to disappear down the sinkhole of French bureaucracy. Than which nothing is deeper. Otherwise, unless he was going to be a monk, the deed itself would prove hard to hide." She managed a weak smile, but it only lasted a moment. "How sure are you about this Alsatian caper?"

"Entirely sure," Geoff said. He explained about the woman in the bar and her record of the procedure performed in 1967. "She was absolutely genuine," he said. "The document, as well. My tried-and-true bullshit meter didn't budge."

"Tell me again how you found her?"

"My friend Clary Colbert," Geoff said. "Remember, I sent him to Strasbourg to do some sniffing."

"I remember. But just like that he uncovered this evidence?"

"Not just like that. I have a Strasbourg source. I put Clary in touch. He chased down a couple of leads the other bloke never bothered with because there didn't seem any reason."

"Anyway," Annie added, "I think the woman, the nurse, would simply have turned away anyone who came asking questions. Until now."

"Why now?" Maggie's voice was getting weaker with each word, but her mind appeared to be as sharp as ever.

"Because," Annie said, "we happened along at the right time. She was desperate."

Geoff explained about the woman's life behind the counter of the café-cum-grocer's shop.

"Like Portsmouth," Maggie said, "with Riesling."

"Exactly," Geoff said. "And trust me, the Riesling was barely drinkable. She'd reached the end of her tether."

"So she opened her heart to my boy."

Maggie reached out the hand that wasn't intravenously connected to the supply of morphine. Geoff took it. "Your boy," he said, "and ten thousand quid."

"Maybe," his mother said, "it's a good thing you're not a musician." Then: "Jack Harris should never have got mixed up with me."

"On balance," Geoff said, "I think he was glad he did."

"On balance, probably," Maggie agreed. "Your father was a mensch, Geoffrey. A good man. It wasn't his fault I was bored out of my skull."

"I know."

Maggie turned her head and looked at Annie. "Will you give us a minute, darling?"

"Of course." Annie stood up and leaned over and kissed Maggie's cheek. "I'll come back soon."

Maggie smiled but didn't comment. Annie saw her disentangle her hand from Geoff's and reach for the button she'd called Buddha's gong.

"I'll be in the visitors' lounge down the hall," Annie said.

Geoff joined her there in about a quarter of an hour. "She's sleeping," he said.

"I'm so sorry, Geoff. Truly."

"So am I. But Maggie's always done it her way. Dying as well as living, it seems."

"Staying in Portsmouth until you were grown up and your dad died," Annie said. "That was her way, too."

"Definitely. Maggie was no quitter. And she still never fails to surprise." He took something from his pocket. "I've had another installment of what she calls the legacy. The last important bit, she says, except for the bloody piano." He handed over a small object folded into a piece of worn blue silk-velvet. "Have a look at this."

Annie unwrapped it. "A mezuzah."

"Apparently something that has been in her family for donkeys. Sewn into her knickers, my mother tells me."

"Knickers? You mean her underpants?"

"Yup. When she was sent out of Germany with the Kindertransport."

"My God . . . it's beautiful." The mezuzah was silver, some four inches long, including the finials at either end. "Geoff, I think this is very old." The idea, the possible connection, was swimming out of her gut and rushing for her brain. It seemed too preposterous, particularly in this setting where the harsh realities of life so frequently overpowered the dream.

"I know what you're thinking," he said. "I can't get my mind around it. Besides, Jews always have these things. Everywhere. Why not Maggie's family?" He took the mezuzah from her and held it in the palm of his hand. "This is a Hebrew letter," he said, pointing to the single character engraved in the metal. "Maggie knew that much, but not what it means. Obviously, neither do I."

"She never asked Rabbi Cohen?"

"Apparently not." Geoff turned the mezuzah back over so they were both looking at the front. "What do you think this engraving represents?"

Annie studied the delicately wrought image. "It's a flowering branch," she said. "I'm not saying it is, but it could be an almond branch." She was hearing it again, that dog whistle that went off in her mind. No sign of the ghost, only a conviction that did not require additional evidence. "This is the vanishing point, Geoff. You and the monk, and Philip Weinraub, who's only masquerading as a Jew but has a powerful interest in almond trees and *mezuzot*."

"I think you're saying, to use Rabbi Hazan's analogy, we're approaching the bend in the river."

"I think we may be," she agreed.

Geoff looked back toward his mother's room. "I wish," he said, "Maggie could come along for the ride. She'd love it."

A man and two young girls came into the lounge. Both girls were sobbing. The man looked ready to join them.

Annie felt a great melding of grief: theirs, Geoff's, and even in some measure her own. She wanted to say something about letting go and accepting the things you could not change. In this place, absent an audience of recovering alcoholics, it seemed banal. They left.

Rabbi Cohen produced a small black skullcap and put it on. For him, Annie realized, what was about to happen was holy.

The mezuzah decorated with the almond branch—Annie had found a horticultural illustration that confirmed her guess about the engraving—lay on his desk. More accurately, on the piece of silk-velvet in which it had been wrapped. "Very old," Rabbi Cohen said quietly, repeating the judgment expressed by Annie and Geoff.

"We believe," Annie said, "it's one of the treasures of the Jew of Holborn. Which would make it at least from 1535."

"An idea," Geoff said, "that obviously never occurred to Maggie. I had mentioned to her that whatever Weinraub told Annie he wanted, he seemed to be looking for a particular mezuzah. She never told me she had that." He nodded toward the mezuzah on Rabbi Cohen's desk.

The rabbi shrugged. "There is no more common piece of Judaica. Many families have one that's been passed down through generations. There's no reason Maggie would have made the connection."

"And maybe she was right," Geoff said. "I'm starting to wonder if we're all going off the deep end. We don't have any proof."

"None," Cohen agreed. "But—" He was interrupted by a loud thud above their heads. He looked up and waited. Silence. The nurse apparently had everything under control. He returned his attention to the mezuzah. "This"—he pointed to the Hebrew character—"is the letter *shin*. In this context it stands for *Shomer Delatot Yisrael,* 'Guardian of the Doorways of Israel.' The mezuzah fulfills the commandment—the mitzvah—to write the words of the Lord 'upon the door-posts of thy house and upon thy gates.' "

"Not all the words, surely," Geoff said.

The other man shook his head. "All these years she kept this, but she didn't teach you even the *Shema*." He reached into a desk drawer and came up with another skullcap. "Here, put this on."

"Look, Rabbi, I told you, I'm not—"

"I know what you told me. But your mother is a Jew, and you're circumcised. So—"

"How do you know that?"

"Who do you think did it? Put on the *kippah*."

Geoff looked at Annie, shrugged, and put it on.

"Better," Cohen said, and turned back to the mezuzah. "The design is classic." He pointed to one silver finial, the one that looked like an open book with a rounded top. "This represents the tablets Moses brought down from the mountain. While this"—he indicated the opposite end, a series of narrowing ridges that created the illusion of depth—"stands for the stairs leading to the holy of holies, the place in Solomon's Temple where the Ark of the Covenant rested. We call the entire thing a mezuzah. In fact, this is a mezuzah case. The piece of parchment inside, the *klaf*, that is the mezuzah, so—"

"Inside?" Geoff asked.

Cohen looked up. "Yes. Why?"

"Maggie told me the mezuzah was never to be opened. That's all she knew, the only thing she remembered. The last time she saw her father, on Kristallnacht, when the gentile friend came to get her, her father gave her this and whispered she must keep it hidden but always with her. That she was never to open it and never to tell anyone she had it."

"And she never did?" Annie asked. "That doesn't sound like Maggie."

Geoff shrugged. "The last request her father made . . . yes, in a way it does."

Rabbi Cohen had listened to all this in silence. "It's a very strange request," he said. "Usually the *klaf* is checked every seven years. You remember, Annie, I told you about a cracked word in a Torah making it not kosher?" Annie nodded. "Inside a mezuzah case, on the *klaf*, are written the holiest words in all of Judaism. Our raison d'être, if you will, our message to the world and perhaps the reason we continue to exist."

"All that," Geoff said, "in something no bigger than my middle finger."

Cohen sighed. "Listen to me, Geoffrey. *Shema Yisrael Adonai Eloheinu, Adonai Echad.* 'Hear, O Israel, the Lord our God, the Lord is one.' That is fundamental. You have to know at least that. For your mother's sake."

"I don't see how that follows," Geoff said, looking, Annie thought, extremely uncomfortable.

"When the end comes for Maggie, I will probably not be there. Please God, you will be. You must say the *Shema* with her. Or for her. For a Jew, those must be the last words."

"I won't remember it," Geoff said. "And Maggie's not a religious Jew."

"She was separated from her parents and forced out of her country by people who wanted to put her in an oven. That's Jewish enough. I'll write out the words for you. Promise you'll do it."

He gave in. "I'll do it."

"Thank you. Now, what about the mezuzah? Am I to open it?"

"Yes," Geoff said instantly. "If Maggie were here, she'd say the same thing. Jew or not, I think Weinraub and his crowd want to start a third world war over some supposedly holy hill."

Cohen's head shot up. "What does that mean? Jew or not? Who, Weinraub?"

"Jesus." Geoff ran his hand through his hair. "I'm sorry. So much has happened so fast. I meant to tell you on the telephone earlier. But . . ." His call had been to say that Maggie's cancer had returned, and she was in the hospital, and it was not expected she would leave. And to ask if they could come and see him and bring a maybe extraordinary bequest.

"But we had other things to talk about," Cohen finished for him. "So tell me now."

"I sent someone to Strasbourg," Geoff began. "Because as I think I told you earlier, that's where Philip Weinraub was actually born. When the family's name was Wein."

After that they told it in tandem. Annie finished up with how desolate the village where they'd met the nurse was, and how happy she seemed to be to have gotten the wherewithal to leave it.

Cohen listened to the recitation in silence, then tented his fingers below his chin in that way he had. "So," he said softly, "we have another wrinkle. The Jewish fanatic is a goy."

Annie thought of Nachum Hazan's comment that the disappearing provisioner might represent a wrinkle in time, but she dismissed it. This wasn't of the same order. "Maybe not so much," she said. "There are all these Protestant groups in America who claim to be devoted to Israel. Maybe Philip Weinraub is just taking that a step further."

"Identification to the point of lunacy," Cohen said. "The very clever Philip Weinraub . . . I'm not sure."

"Nor am I," Geoff agreed. "But we know the people he's mixed up with, the restore-the-Temple crowd, wouldn't hesitate to start a war over the Temple Mount."

"Some of them," Cohen said. "Not all. But this—" He gestured to the mezuzah still lying on his desk. "It might have some particular meaning."

"Open it," Geoff said.

31

The finials of the mezuzah appeared to have been forged separately from the body, but neither was easy to pry away. Cohen tried repeatedly, albeit very gently. "Solid silver is soft, they tell me," he murmured. "And something this old . . ."

Annie was holding her breath. She thought Geoff might be doing the same, but as usual, he was the practical one. "For it to open," he said, "you need to find the proper torque. The fulcrum."

"An engineer," Cohen said, "I am not." He looked up. "Here, it's yours. You try."

Geoff kept his hands in his lap. "You're suggesting a genetic propensity? For opening *mezuzot?*"

Cohen smiled.

"Don't look like that," Geoff said. "Annie taught me the word."

The rabbi's smile grew broader. He continued to hold out the mezuzah.

Geoff took it. Tiny silver knobs topped off both ends. Geoff grasped each one and turned them clockwise. Nothing happened. Nor did counterclockwise produce a result. When he turned them in opposing directions, however, the section carved to look like the tablets pulled out and came free.

Both Annie and Rabbi Cohen jumped as if they'd been startled by a loud noise, though there had been no sound. Cohen half stood and leaned over his desk, trying to see inside the hollow case. "The parchment—" he began.

Geoff held the mezuzah up to the light coming from the window behind him. "No parchment," he said, squinting into the interior. "At least, that's not what I think it is." He handed the mezuzah back to Cohen. "Your turn," he said. "This part is your speciality."

Rabbi Cohen took the silver case and squinted into the interior. He frowned. "I don't . . ."

Annie waited, but Cohen didn't say anything else. Instead he produced what looked like a pair of tweezers, also silver, probably meant for the task.

What he extracted looked like a very small sachet. It was made of red cloth—silk, Annie guessed—and was roughly heart shaped. But not like a valentine—it was more elongated and anatomically accurate than anything done by Hallmark. There was an embroidered design on one side, and the heart appeared to have been made by stitching two pieces of cloth together. The thread used to do the sewing had rotted away. As soon as Cohen laid the thing on the piece of velvet in which the mezuzah had been wrapped, the heart divided, revealing a small flat something. About the size of a dime, Annie thought. Or a British twenty-pence piece.

"I have no idea what this is," Rabbi Cohen murmured. "But it's certainly not a *klaf.*"

"I think I know." Annie picked up the silver tweezers and used them as a pointer. "If I'm right, the embroidery on the front of the heart tells the whole story." The tweezers traced a pattern in the air. "I think this is meant to be a lamb." Both men nodded. "What's inside"—she moved the tweezers to indicate the small flat disk—"is what Catholics call an Agnus Dei, a reference to Saint John the Baptist who said of Jesus, 'Behold the lamb of God.' It's an ancient sacramental. Made from—"

"Whoa," Geoff held up both hands. "You're going way too fast for me. I thought a mezuzah was Jewish. And what, pray, is a 'sacramental'?"

"I can't tell you what an Agnus Dei is doing in a mezuzah case, but a sacramental . . ." She hesitated. "It's a symbol. Something that's supposed to remind you about God and religion. Like rosary beads or pictures of saints."

"Holy tchotchkes," Cohen said.

"Exactly," Annie agreed. "But an Agnus Dei is a really old tchotchke.

They were first made back in the third century. Only a pope can create them, and he only does it during the first Easter after his election."

Annie held the tweezers over the strange little something that had been inside the silk heart. It was an uneven lump, grayed as if by touch. A long time ago, Annie thought. The tweezers slipped a bit in her fingers. Nerves, she thought, and held them tighter. "This is made of wax that comes from an Easter candle blessed by a new pope." She looked up. Both men were watching her. "The drippings are gathered up and shaped into a number of little round disks of this sort. Then each one is stamped with the name of the pope who blessed it in the first year of his reign."

Geoff bent over the circle of wax. "I can't see anything written here. Maybe it's on the other side."

"Do you want me to turn it over?" Annie asked. "It may disintegrate if I do."

He shrugged. "I'm interested in what it means, not that it's a holy tchotchke."

Annie touched the wax disk with the tweezers. They vibrated in her fingers. "Something . . ." she said.

"What?" Geoff asked. "Something what?"

She was aware of Rabbi Cohen watching her. "Nothing. My imagination." She grasped the tweezers more tightly and flipped over the tiny lump of wax. It held together.

"Ah," Geoff said. "We're away. There's definitely some writing impressed on this side." He bent closer. "Damn. I can't read it."

Cohen used a magnifying glass, but he had no luck either. "It's still too small for my old eyes."

Annie put down the tweezers. They stopped vibrating as soon as she moved them away from the disk. She reached into her tote, came up with her jeweler's loupe, and screwed it into her eye. "Let me try." The men backed off so she could crouch directly over the wax and study it from barely an inch away. "Clement VII," she said finally. "And something else . . . Starts with an *A*, but I can't see . . ."

The loupe was warm. Getting warmer as she bent closer.

"*A, A, A,*" Geoff said softly.

Cohen nodded.

"This time it's A-v-i-g . . . Avignon," Annie pronounced in triumph, standing up and taking the loupe out of her eye. The loupe was almost hot to her touch. Nerves, she told herself again. Because she was starting to get this. "Clement VII," she said with a restrained note of triumph. "Pope in Avignon."

"When?" Geoff asked.

She thought for a moment. "One of the Medicis became Clement VII in 1523. But in Rome, not Avignon. So . . ." She hesitated, then: "I think this has to be the much earlier Antipope Clement VII."

Cohen swung around to his computer and executed a series of rapid keystrokes. "Exactly. Antipope Clement VII elected in Avignon in 1378."

"And that's the connection," Annie said. She tucked the loupe away— it was cool now, normal—concentrating instead on the release of the knot of tension in her belly. She wasn't speculating any longer, she knew. "The Antipope Clement VII was the first pope of the fifty-year Great Schism. And the splinter group in Avignon who elected him gave rise to the sect known as the True Obedience."

"Whose leader," Geoff said, staring at the deconstructed mezuzah on Rabbi Cohen's desk, "was known as the Speckled Egg."

"I don't know about the egg, but the Catholic Encyclopedia"— Cohen was peering at the screen—"agrees with Annie. Later there was a legitimate Clement VII in Rome, but the one elected in Avignon was an antipope. 'Supported by a strong faction of cardinals,'" he read aloud. "'Said to have created a cult of persistent sedevacantist schismatics convinced that since his death the chair of Peter has been vacant because the popes in Rome no longer come down in a straight line from Saint Peter.' Your father was John Kendall, Annie, was he not?" When she nodded, he added, "One of his books is cited as a source document."

"I'm not surprised. Apparently he was something of an expert on the subject. But the book's out of print, and so far I haven't managed to find a copy."

"And the Dominican priests," Cohen asked, "the experts on hounding heretics?"

"I'm told," Annie said, "the man I should see is on retreat. Meaning he's totally incommunicado. He's due back in a few days."

"So," Geoff said. "Exactly what have we got?"

"Étienne Renard was from Avignon," Annie said. "Did we tell you that, Rabbi?"

Cohen shook his head.

Geoff explained about Agence Investigations Mme Defarge.

Annie only half listened. She stood up, stretched, began pacing the perimeter of the crowded room. Like Maggie's Primrose Hill flat, it was so jammed with things you never seemed to see them all. God knows what some place the two of them lived in together might have looked like.

The bookshelves that lined the study walls were stuffed to overflowing. Pictures and various *objets* were slipped in and around the books. A gilt frame held a series of tiny watercolors displayed together in a line.

"That was a gift," Rabbi Cohen said, noticing her focus. "From a friend who's interested in heraldry. It's supposed to be the coats of arms of the twelve tribes of Israel. As they would have been if heraldry existed in biblical times."

Heraldry.

Dog whistle.

No, better than that. There was a siren going off in her mind. Annie made a conscious effort not to shout. "Geoff, remember Maggie telling us your grandfather, her father, was a silversmith in Freiburg?"

"Yes, of course. I knew that anyway. That's why her maiden name was Silber, German for silver."

"Heraldry on the other hand," Annie said, still keeping her tone neutral, "uses French words to describe the official background colors of the field in a coat of arms. *Or* is gold and silver is *argent*." She turned to face the two men. "What if the mural and the code tell where the mezuzah Weinraub's after is to be found, just as we suspected? What if *A, A, A* means the mezuzah can be found among the Silver or Silber family?"

Dom Justin
From the Waiting Place

Rebecca and I traveled mostly by night and did not speak much, and the farther we got from London, the safer we felt. She continued to wear the plague cloak. Beneath it her father's treasures rested over her belly. He had wrapped the thing so it was a smooth and rounded parcel and enhanced the image of a woman swollen with child. It was not the most clever of ruses, but we could think of none better. And while it was undoubtedly true that robbers would have risked the fever to see what booty they might snatch from two such unprotected wanderers, we met none. I came to believe that we were led by some unseen angel sent by Almighty God.

That first night we went to Mistress Grindal, and she at once knew us and sheltered us and sent us on our way with provisions for two days. She said it was for love of the Lord, and the Speckled Egg. On three subsequent occasions during that early part of our journey, Rebecca hid in the woods while I went alone into a village, choosing always one where it was market day. It was easy at such times to pass unnoticed among the crowds, and I used the money Rebecca doled out to purchase enough bread and cheese to keep us alive. For drink we had the streams of the forest. Occasionally there were berries, and once we came across a clutch of goose eggs and ate them raw, fearing to make a fire.

After ten days we reached Dover and secured passage across the channel, and so without incident we found ourselves in the Pale of Calais, where many spoke our English tongue, Henry was king, and Thomas Cromwell's writ ran. But here England's claim was disputed by both the Emperor of France and the Dukes of Burgundy, and the locals had learned that to be desired by the powerful does not make for a peaceful life. We remained fugitives, but none paid us much mind. For us, Calais felt like safety, a foreign hurly-burly of new smells and sounds and sights that clothed us in anonymity. Rebecca and I sensed we were following a destiny beyond our understanding. We were like the Children of Israel wandering in the desert and being led to the Promised Land by a pillar of fire. We could not, however, rely on manna from heaven to feed us.

"Have you coins left?" I asked. Years before, when I called Cromwell master and lived beneath his roof, I had seen a map of the Frankish lands hanging on the wall of his study. To get to Metz—the first of the cities where the Jew of Holborn said we would find sanctuary—we faced a trek across almost the whole of the kingdom's border with the Low Countries. "We shall need money, for we have still a great distance to travel."

"Only one coin," she said, "but it does not matter."

"Why not?"

"Because, Geoffrey"—she spoke my former name as if to taunt me with it—"while you gazed at the sea or slept on the deck, I made provision for our future." She had met a man, she said, another Lombard. He and his servants were also on their way to Metz. "They are well armed," she said. "And we are to travel with them."

"Why does he make us this offer?" Dom Hilary had promised to send assistance for my journey, and he had been proved right in the matter of Mistress Grindal, but Hilary could not have known which boatman would carry us across the channel, nor even which was the port from whence we would sail. It could as easily have been Rye or Hastings as Dover. "Is this Lombard also a Jew?"

"I do not know, but I think not."

"Then why should he offer us assistance?" Even as I asked the question, I knew the most likely answer. Despite the peril and travail of our flight from the pit, Rebecca's incredible sea-colored eyes sparkled, her black hair gleamed, and her cheeks were rose pink. She had even found somewhere a silver clip with which to fasten closed the black cloak, making it look less like the livery of death. (And in any case, in these parts the uneven pointed hem of the plague cloak did not seem to have the same meaning, whilst Rebecca had long since removed the bells.)

"The Lombard told me," Rebecca explained, "that his wife died a month past, and his two motherless daughters are in need of a woman's comfort." She patted her belly. "And since I am also widowed, he thinks it wise we journey on together."

"And what did you tell him of me?"

"The simple truth," she said, and seeing my expression, added, "that you were my servant and would be content to travel with his, being as rough and unlettered as are they."

However much her manner displeased me, I saw the plan as canny and fell in with it, saying as little as possible to our traveling companions so as to maintain the deception she had created for us. I was nonetheless surprised by one thing. In front of the others, she called me Justin, making that the name I was known by the entire time we were together with the family and servants of the man known in his own tongue as Diego di Mantova.

While we were still in Calais, the Lombard procured a horse and three donkeys and arranged for us to join a caravan of merchants traveling together for mutual protection. And so, without incident, after three weeks we arrived in Metz. It proved to be as great a city as any we had seen along our route—and all seemed to me more splendid than London—but also one in turmoil.

Metz stood at the place where the Moselle and Seille rivers met and was surrounded by a great wall. It was neither Frankish nor Rhenish but independent, though that was not apparently an easy condition to maintain. When we arrived, war was expected at any moment. The townspeople turned this way and that, unsure of what would happen or how to behave. They did not welcome strangers at such a time, but we were allowed through the gates because here as everywhere else, the Lombard merchants were princes of trade who paid such enormous taxes and tributes to the city's rulers that no one questioned too closely what went on behind the doors of their houses.

Rebecca had told Diego she had relatives in the city—a grain merchant, according to her father—and he had agreed to take her to them as soon as we arrived. He did indeed escort us to the place where, according to the Jew of Holborn, the man lived. After tearful farewells between Rebecca and Diego's daughters, who had grown fond of each other during our journey, we found ourselves standing alone at the door of a modest establishment. Even there on the street the yeasty smell of fermenting grain was apparent, and the dust of chaff filled the air and caused us to hide our mouths and noses behind our hands. "Hurry and knock, or we shall choke," I said.

"Do you imagine, foolish Geoffrey, that it will be less unpleasant inside than it is out?"

I could not argue with her logic, so I said nothing.

And still she did not knock, only stood for a few moments, then said, "Now, come quickly and do exactly what I tell you. Whatever happens, contradict me in nothing." Thereupon she set out at a pace so hurried, I could do nothing but follow her.

I was in no doubt she was following a plan she had previously made—a judgment confirmed when we came out of the maze of alleys of the Jews' Quarter. Free of that tangle, we found ourselves on a broad street where it was possible to see the spire of a great church rising on a hill directly in front of us. "There," Rebecca said, pointing to the spire, "is where we are going. We seek a house across from what they call the Annunciation door. It is the home of Diego's brother and where he will stay while he is in Metz."

I knew then that she had discarded the whole of the scheme of her father and put one conceived by herself and Diego in its place, and I wondered if Diego had understood her intentions and provided answers to her questions with full knowledge of how she would use the information, or if he was simply disarmed by her beauty. That seemed to me entirely possible. Even with the artificial belly she had created to disguise her parcel of treasures—she looked six months with child rather than three—the sight of Rebecca would take the breath and twist the thoughts of any man.

Where such thoughts led, I already knew. And, God forgive me, it had sometimes given me secret pleasure to remember that what every man who looked at her lusted after had already been mine. Indeed, it was the constant awareness of my sin that made me proof against repeating it. I had come to know such charms as Rebecca possessed to be the gift of the devil, and to understand that women are put on this earth to tempt men to sin exactly as Eve tempted Adam.

But of the cleverness of females, at least as exemplified by the one I followed that day, there could be little doubt. "Watch for this so-called Annunciation door," she said as we traveled down an ancient alley that led to the great church at the heart of the city. "You should find it more easily than I, should you not? Or have you forgotten all they taught you in that place?"

This harking back to the life we had left behind, which now seemed so distant it might not have existed, brought me enough to my senses to cause me to put out a hand and seize her arm. I gripped it tightly, not thinking of whether I hurt her, and would not let her free. "What about that?" I asked, and pointed to her belly.

"Do you suddenly have care for the child you once told me was so steeped in sin it probably was not meant to be born?"

"The child is in the hands of God, as are we all. It will live or die as He chooses. But if you do not intend to do what your father meant you to do, what is to become of his legacy?"

"Exactly what he planned," she said. "I will accomplish his intentions in a way better than he imagined. The only question remaining, Geoffrey, is whether your intentions are still what they have been." With that she looked around, and having seen that we were for the moment alone in the narrow divide between two high walls, she reached down and drew back her cloak.

The parcel of treasures wrapped in the old Jew's kirtle hung over her belly as before, but her intention was not to assure me of that fact. While I stared, she lifted her underskirt, causing the treasures to be raised above her waist and exposing her plump thighs and the thatch of curly black hair that decorated the cunny that had caused me to risk my soul.

God help me, I could not look away.

"Take a last look, Geoffrey. And be certain you prefer your monkish state to what you tasted and found sweet."

I would like as not have taken her where she stood—thrusting her against the brick wall and driving my swollen cock into the place it craved to be—except that somewhere a church bell rang and summoned me to my senses. Rebecca heard it as well, knew its meaning, and let her garments fall back into place, though she did not once take her eyes from my face. "Ah, Geoffrey," she said, her voice without that lilt of mockery I had lately come to expect from her, "I loved you so. Now I have lost you, and my rival is no creature against whom I might fight but your almighty church."

I hesitated, remembering how in days past she had whispered to me of her struggles and schemes to see to it that her father did not promise her to one of the other Lombards before I would be quit of the Charterhouse. All for naught, once I was priested and the future was out of our hands.

Rebecca saw the memories that overtook me—no doubt they played upon my face as they did my soul, drawing me away from the things of God to the lures of Satan. "Geoffrey," she said, speaking my name with such a depth of feeling. "Geoffrey."

"I have no choice," I said. "I am a priest, indeed a priest of the True—"

Praise God, she stopped my words with her fingers before I had a chance to utter them and betray Dom Hilary's secret. "Listen to me, Geoffrey. It is all lies, everything they tell you. All this talk of holiness and prayer and men denying themselves the very things that make life worth living—it's lies to further their dreams of power and their bloodlust. What God is this who asks such things? A savior worth following? I think not."

Her blasphemies brought me to my senses, and I was overcome with fury and pulled her close to me that she might better hear every word I spoke. "That you are Satan's whore I have known for some time, but if you cause me to break yet another vow, the one I made to your father concerning the treasures he gave us to carry here, I swear I will be happy in hell knowing you are suffering worse torments as you must."

"You left your good humor behind, as well as your sweet nature, when you were priested, Geoffrey. Very well, know this—I will do what I must to find protection for my father's patrimony, but also for myself and my child. And for the love I once had for you, and because you are that child's father, I will shield you as well—but only so long as you do exactly what I tell you. Diego is on his way to a Rhenish town called Freiburg, in a place of mountains and forests. I have wheedled from him the knowledge that it is some four days' walk from a Charterhouse. You chose the monks over me, Geoffrey who has become Dom Justin. Now come with me and do as I tell you, and before too much longer, you will be back among them."

"And the treasures of the ancient Temple of Jerusalem, which may have been touched by the hand of the Savior Himself?"

"They will be distributed along our route, precisely as my father intended."

"How can you arrange such a thing? If the Lombard or anyone else knew what you have there"—I nodded to the hiding place beneath her cloak—"he would take it from you by any means necessary."

"Of course," she agreed. "But in the dark, Geoffrey, and sometimes, as now, even on a bright sunlit day, men do not think with their heads but with their crotch." Then her manner softened toward me, as if she saw my anguish and regretted being the major cause. "Do not fear," she said. "I gave my word to my father. I will not break it. The gifts of the Jew of Holborn will go to those he meant to have them."

I knew that for some time she had each day said the mourning prayer for the man who had given her life. It was a duty she solemnly observed, and I did not think she would be faithful in that obligation and ignore the other. As for me, my duty seemed to be twofold: to keep the vow I made to the old Jew, and to bring word to my brother monks of all that had transpired at the Charterhouse in London. Perhaps when I was once more with my Carthusian brethren, I would find others of the True Obedience of Avignon and learn what Almighty God meant for me. So it seemed yet again that doing as Rebecca planned was the wisest course to follow. Only one thing still troubled me: "How have you explained to the Lombard the reason for your journey? Does he not wonder at a woman traveling with a single servant setting out on such a trek as you have undertaken? By now there is doubtless a price on our heads. What if he—"

"You are such a fool! I told Diego what he wished to hear, and he told me what I needed to know. But if we spend more time in argument, everything I have done will be wasted, and we will truly be alone and penniless in this foreign place."

After that I knew she was more likely than I to find solutions to our problems—as much on account of her beauty as her intelligence—and I did what she asked without complaint.

Soon we were walking the perimeters of what turned out to be a great cathedral dedicated to Saint Stephen—Saint Étienne as he was known in the language of the place—and when we came to what I thought to be the west facade, I saw above a set of doors a series of carvings that made music out of stone. An angel hid his shining face behind his wings lest the young girl beside him be blinded by his glory, and she stood listening intently, head bowed and hands clasped in an attitude of prayer and acceptance. It was as if, seeing this thing, I heard aloud the words of scripture: *Behold the handmaid of the Lord. Be it done unto me according to thy word.* "Here," I said, "is your Annunciation door."

As she had no doubt previously arranged with Diego, as soon as the door of his brother's house was opened to her, Rebecca spun a tale of having been turned away from the home of her relative the grain merchant and in desperation come here instead. The result was that not only Diego and his daughters but also his brother Giuseppe greeted her with open delight and invited her to stay as long as she liked. As for me, they took me in for her sake. Would they deprive a widow in such straits of the one servant she possessed?

It transpired that this Giuseppe of Metz was not a wandering trader but had been many years in the city. His household was large and well established, and numbers of merchants visited to arrange the receipt or the shipment of goods. For that reason there was a constant coming and going

of people in and out of the house, and no one took note of the arrival of a
beautiful young widow and her servant. As for Giuseppe himself, he
seemed to count our presence no hardship.

So were we settled in exactly the manner Rebecca had predicted.

I, however, was not at peace. I was prepared to take it on Dom Hilary's
word that the sins of my comings and goings in and out of the Charterhouse had been in the service of the priesthood of the True Obedience and
as such not sins at all. But the time in the woods beside the Fleet, when I
had given in to the lure Satan sets between a woman's thighs, yet felt to me
like a millstone that would press me into the bowels of the earth, there to
burn forever. Never mind that Hilary had given me absolution. How could
that suffice when I had not told him the terrible truth of what I had done?
It could not, I determined. Rather it was a parody of the very forgiveness I
so desperately required. And how could I go to some strange priest at the
cathedral, when telling my story as I must meant exposing who I was and
what Rebecca had carried with her out of England, and perhaps sending
everyone in the Lombard's household to the stake along with Rebecca and
myself? Nothing in my experience of the past few years gave me confidence
in even the sworn secrecy of the confessional.

These thoughts threatened to overcome me, except that I clung to the
notion of the Charterhouse in the Rhenish forest. I made myself believe
that when I reached it, I would be like gold tried in the fire and permitted
to tell my sins and be absolved of them. I could not know that everything
I had been through was merely prelude.

What followed came about because, like all men, I had sometimes the
need to piss.

❖

32

If Annie was right about the code of the *A*'s—and both Geoff and Rabbi Cohen thought she likely was—they knew a lot more than they had before, but not what it all meant.

"Weinraub's agenda," Geoff said. "We still don't get that."

Annie and Rabbi Cohen had to agree.

Dead end.

Had Geoff been given the mezuzah a week earlier, Annie would have gone to Jennifer Franklin and gotten proper archivist supplies. As things stood that was out of the question. Turned out a fancy stationer in Southampton Row had some handmade acid-free paper. It was pale lavender, satisfyingly thick but still flexible. "Since we're so close to Bristol House," Annie said after they left the shop, "let's go up to the flat and get this done."

Geoff was carrying the mezuzah and the deconstructed pieces of the Agnus Dei in a large brown envelope provided by Rabbi Cohen. He was holding it carefully in both hands, as if conscious of the extreme fragility of the contents. Once, when they were buying the paper, Annie had started to take it from him, then pulled back at the blast of warmth. She hadn't said anything then; now, as she turned the key in the lock and held the street door open so he could go ahead of her into the lobby, she again put out her hand and felt the radiant heat emanating from the envelope. She pulled away. He seemed totally unaware of the phenomenon or her reaction to it. "Do you feel anything?" she asked.

"A lot of things," he said. "I haven't sorted them out yet."

"I don't mean that. Physically." Nodding toward the envelope.

"No, of course not. It barely weighs anything. I— That's not what you mean, is it?"

They were at the door of the flat by then. "Wait," she said, maneuvering the double lock, then reaching automatically for the remote and switching on the radios. She had reduced the volume recently, but the drone of the BBC had become part of her world when she was in the flat and even now, when she was no longer afraid, she could not give it up.

They said no more until they were in the dining room and the newly bought paper and the envelope with the treasures lay side by side on the table. "Wait," Annie said again.

"I am waiting. What's happening?" Looking around as if he still hoped he would see whatever she saw. "Is he here?"

"No, it's not that. When I put my hand anywhere near the Agnus Dei it feels warm. Hot even. But that doesn't happen with you, does it?"

He shook his head. "Do you feel it only with the Agnus Dei, not the mezuzah?"

"I think so," she confirmed. "At least that's how it was before. But maybe whatever it is, it's contagious." She stretched her hand over the envelope to test the phenomenon. It was like an old-fashioned radiator—almost too hot to touch. Annie held her hand in place for a few seconds, then pressed her palm into Geoff's.

"Jesus," he said. "It's like you've got a fever." He spread his other hand, the one she hadn't touched, over the envelope. "Nothing," he said. "Let's separate them. See if that has any effect."

Moments later the mezuzah and the pieces of the Agnus Dei were spread on the table, a few inches apart. None of them produced any sensations in Geoff. The mezuzah induced no reaction in Annie, but she felt the heat as soon as she got near the tiny lump of wax or the red silk in which it had been contained.

"Any ideas?" Geoff asked.

"It's much stronger here than at Rabbi Cohen's. There was some vibrating there as well. The tweezers sort of buzzed in my hand. I wasn't absolutely sure I wasn't imagining all of it. That's why I didn't say anything. But now—there's no doubt."

Geoff thought for a moment. "Confirms what you said about the two lines coming together. The mezuzah Weinraub is after, and all the Bristol House carry-on . . . I'm the Silber descendant, but the ghost and his manifestations, that's down to you." Then, before she could contradict him, "I know I saw the bloody grocer and his bloody quail eggs, but I still don't think that's the same."

She did not share her conviction that he'd been allowed that vision only because the Bristol House ghost needed him as an ally. "Let's get this done," she said instead.

The mezuzah was back in one piece, with a new *klaf* inserted by Rabbi Cohen, and still wrapped in the piece of faded blue velvet. Geoff deferred to her expertise and Annie carefully enclosed it in acid-free paper, then handed it to him. "This should probably go in your safe."

"Yes," he agreed. "What about the other bit?" nodding toward the Agnus Dei.

Annie put a single finger over the disk, then very carefully, actually touched it. "What's really peculiar," she said, "is that despite how much warmth I feel when I go near it, the wax is no softer. It hasn't melted a bit."

Geoff shrugged. "That's no more peculiar than a great deal else that's been happening." Then, as if he'd been reading her mind, "I think that should stay here, Annie. I think it may have belonged to your Carthusian."

"Yes," she agreed, and after she'd folded the fragment of ancient red silk and the wax disk into the protective paper they carried it into the back bedroom—empty of any sign of the monk—and lay it on top of the small chest that stood beneath the window that looked toward the old charterhouse.

A day went by.

Rabbi Cohen made some discreet inquiries among rabbis he knew in New York, trying to pin down more details of Philip Weinraub's practice of Judaism. So far he discovered nothing conclusive.

Maggie's deteriorating condition was Geoff's overwhelming concern.

Annie spent the best part of her time at Bristol House.

A couple of hours were occupied with Web surfing, looking for information on sacramentals in general and the Agnus Dei in particular. "Protects from all malign influences," she read, "and from the perils of storm and pestilence as well as fire, flood, and sudden death." Pretty potent stuff. She went into the back bedroom and stretched her hand over the package. The warmth was muted but definitely present. "Are you here?" she asked. "Was this yours?" There was no reply.

She spent more time in front of the mural and found a few more of the E.R. clues. They reinforced the graphic representation of the capital letters *A*. But as to why Weinraub might want the mezuzah—she wasn't able to connect the dots.

She tried writing an article based on her findings concerning the Jew of Holborn. It never jelled. It seemed to her that the story of Maggie's mezuzah did not count. It was the stuff of television drama, not academic journals. Besides, the mezuzah story, like the object itself, was Geoff's, not hers. This was not the time to discuss what he wanted to do with it.

Sidney O'Toole's final verdict—the one he'd pronounced last April, when she'd called him to say she'd taken up Philip Weinraub's offer to go to London—played in her head. *Jesus fucking Christ, Annie my girl. What are you thinking?*

For two days nothing changed. Eye of the storm, Annie figured. She didn't say that to Geoff because of what waited for him when the winds began again to howl.

He seemed pretty calm and accepting of the facts, but he'd definitely dropped more weight. Late Wednesday afternoon Annie headed for a small specialty butcher in Theobald's Road, hoping to find something that would induce Geoff to cook a meal he'd actually eat.

These days the entrance to the old tram line and Rabbi Cohen's secret tunnels functioned as a pedestrian island in the middle of the extrawide crosswalk between the broad and busy streets. Annie started to cross when the light was flashing—and predictably got caught when it changed. She stepped onto the safety of the island, and as she always did since she'd heard the story, she looked into the tunnel.

Usually the only things to see were the old cobbled road, the cinder-block walls, and a collection of wind-blown rubbish. On this occasion, three men were emerging from the darkness and walking toward her.

Two wore business suits; the third was a workman with a large ring of keys. He swung one gate open, and the suits came to stand beside her, waiting like Annie for the light to change. When it did, they crossed the road in tandem. The workman stayed behind and relocked the gates.

One of the suits seemed to be brokering a deal. "Secure as the catacombs, you said. Hard to imagine anything that would come closer than this."

"Difficult. You're right there." The second man spoke with an American accent. "It will depend on the price, of course. Though as I said, money isn't my client's first consideration."

"I'm sure we can—"

Annie didn't hear any more. They were outstriding her, for one thing, and for another she'd come to the butcher shop. She considered following the men, then decided it was absurd.

"Some U.S. something-or-other is making a move on the secret tunnels," she said as soon as she let herself into 29 Orde Hall Street.

Geoff didn't respond.

"I was going to the butcher's on Theobald's Road, and I— Geoff, what's the matter?"

"I just got off the phone with the hospital. They're moving Maggie to a hospice unit."

End-of-life care. A clear statement that nothing more could or would be done.

He was sitting at his desk, and she went to him and put her hand on his shoulder. "They'll make certain she's comfortable. That's a good thing." It was all she could think of to say.

Geoff put his hand over hers. "Yes, I know they will, and it is. What have you got there?" He gestured to the package from the butcher.

"Steaks," she said. "Two small but luscious-looking bits of filet mignon. I thought you might—" He did not look as if cooking a meal was high on his immediate priority list. "Will you trust me to cook them? I'm not in your league, but I can make a salad and broil a couple of steaks."

"Fine," he said. "But if they're fillet steaks, you should panfry them in butter, not grill—broil—them. They said I'm permitted to visit anytime and stay as long as I like. I thought I'd go over now and see how she's doing."

"Good, but have something to eat first." Annie headed toward the kitchen. "The American said—"

"What American?"

"The one who was negotiating to take over the tunnels. A broker type. He said his client was looking for a modern-day equivalent of the catacombs."

Geoff shook his head. "Well, you've got a good few religious crazies in America. Oh, I nearly forgot—Rabbi Cohen called right after you left. Weinraub is a member of an Orthodox synagogue near his apartment on"—he glanced at a note on the desk—"West End Avenue. Where's that?"

"Upper West Side. Very nice."

"Thing is, according to Rabbi Cohen's contact, Weinraub isn't active in the congregation. Doesn't show up even for the major holidays."

"Makes more sense now than it would have before Strasbourg," Annie said.

Geoff didn't pursue the subject.

The steaks came out fine, but neither of them did justice to the meal. After they stopped pretending to eat, Annie cleared the table. "Leave the dishes," Geoff said. "I'll do them when I get back. Only fair, since you cooked."

"Don't be silly. Just go." She started to say he should give Maggie her love, then realized how unlikely it was that his mother would be conscious.

Geoff got as far as the door, then turned back to her. "Will you wait for me?" he asked. "Maybe stay here tonight?"

"No place I'd rather be," she said.

*　*　*

He came home soon after ten, and they went to bed, and Annie held him tight until finally he fell asleep. When she woke, it was barely dawn and she was alone. She got up and went to the top of the stairs. Geoff was at his desk, working at his computer. Annie went back to the bedroom and pulled on jeans and went down.

"Sorry," he said. "Didn't mean to wake you. I woke up to check my phone." It was something he did many times each night. "Nothing from the hospital, but I couldn't get back to sleep, so I came down here."

"You didn't wake me. I was slept out. Shall I make some coffee?"

"I'll do it." He got up.

Annie took his place at the desk and opened her own e-mail account. "Something from Timothy O'Hare, O.P.," she said. "He's the Dominican priest I've been waiting to hear from, the expert on schismatics and heretics. He's back in London."

"What does he say?"

She clicked through and opened the message. "He'd be happy to talk about the True Obedience of Avignon, and I should call him and make an appointment."

"Good. Do it." His words were punctuated with the sound of the coffee grinder and the hiss of the boiling kettle. A few minutes later the scent of brewing coffee drew her to the marble counter.

Geoff poured mugs of coffee for both of them, then left her to add her own milk and went back to the desk. He was, Annie thought, attached to his electronic gadgets as if by a bungee cord. He hit a couple of keys, then said, "Bloody hell. Looks like the technology stars are properly aligned. Here's another interesting message. From Madame Defarge in Paris."

"C'mon," she urged, "what does she say?"

He leaned back. The Aeron, the only office chair sold by butt size, tilted to the perfect angle for his height and weight. "You're not going to believe this."

"Believe what? Tell me."

"We were wrong about Étienne Renard. Just as we were about Wein-raub. Renard's not Jewish, either. He was a Carthusian monk at La Grande Chartreuse from 1923 to 1929. At which time he was dispensed from his vows and left the order. Defarge says the trail dies after that."

"You're right. I don't believe it."

"It's true. *La* Defarge sent *le* proof."

"Is there a description of Renard? Maybe he looked like you."

"He didn't."

"How can you be sure?"

"There's a picture. Come see."

The image on his screen was a scanned illustration from *Le Journal Illustré d'Avignon, 30 Mars 1923*. Black and white and grainy, it showed Renard as a fair man, short and considerably overweight, with pudgy cheeks and a number of chins. He was wearing what looked like a home-made attempt at a toga. The caption was in French. Geoff translated. "It says Étienne Renard was Pontius Pilate in the Good Friday Passion Play of the League of Penance."

"Hence the toga," Annie said.

"Hence. But apparently the league wasn't penitential enough. According to Defarge, Renard hightailed it to La Grande Chartreuse a few weeks later."

"Geoff, it can't be a coincidence that the Bristol House mural was painted by an ex-Carthusian."

"Doesn't seem like it."

St. Dominic's Church was an imposing yellow-brick building in a non-descript section of North London called Haverstock Hill. "Come to the priory," Father O'Hare had said. "It's the wing to the left of the main entrance. There's a sign."

He opened the door himself, immediately offering his hand. "Tim O'Hare, and you must be Dr. Kendall." He had white hair and a big, open Irish face with a ready smile, and he wore the white habit of his order. In keeping with the Dominican tradition, heavy wooden rosary beads swung from a black leather belt at his waist. "Any relation to John Kendall, the church historian?" he asked, adding that he hoped she hadn't been inconvenienced by meeting him at the priory.

Annie said she was John Kendall's daughter and that it was not in the least inconvenient to come to Father O'Hare's priory. She was grateful he'd been able to see her so quickly.

"Not at all. I admit to being quite curious. The True Obedience of Avignon was a bizarre and persistent group of schismatics, but their heyday's been over for some time. I was astounded to get an inquiry about them. We can talk in here," he added, opening a door and waiting for Annie to precede him.

The room was small and comfortable. There were a couple of leather chairs on either side of a fireplace, a few tables, and many, many books. Father O'Hare motioned her to one of the chairs and took the other. A thick cardboard folder lay on the table beside him, and he picked it up and held it on his lap. "I'm afraid I haven't got around to entering much of this into the computerized files. I've been concentrating on more modern sedevacantists. Since Vatican II, they've sprouted like mushrooms after rain."

"And these days they all seem to have Web sites," Annie said. "Which I suppose makes it easier."

"Somewhat," he agreed. "Moreover, modern schismatics are more likely to form independent religious communities, not burrow into an established order the way the True Obedience did with the Carthusians six or seven hundred years ago."

"But the Carthusians still exist."

"Indeed they do. In fact, they discovered the remnant of the True Obedience schismatics and expelled them in the twenties."

"That," Annie said quietly, not allowing the buzz in the back of her mind to surface just yet, "seems like an exceptionally long run."

Father O'Hare agreed that it was. "But," he pointed out, "it ended nearly a century ago. May I ask the nature of your research, Dr. Kendall?"

"At the moment I'm simply investigating, without being sure exactly what academic value all this may have. What I do know is that a man calling himself Stephen Fox painted an extraordinary mural in a flat I'm renting. I have reason to believe Fox was French, originally from Avignon, for a time a Carthusian at La Grande Chartreuse, and that his birth name was Étienne Renard."

O'Hare looked surprised, then began paging through the papers in his folder, finally withdrawing one. He looked at it for a moment. "Yes, I thought I remembered that. Étienne Renard was expelled from the Carthusians in 1929 and officially defrocked soon after. He was a biblical scholar, fluent in Hebrew, apparently made a great study of kabbalah, and"—he looked up—"he was reputedly the last leader of the True Obedience of Avignon, the man they called the Speckled Egg."

Hallelujah! She could not, however, stand up and dance a jig. "That's particularly interesting, Father. May I ask you something else?"

"Certainly."

"Do you know any reason Étienne Renard would have been interested in a particular mezuzah? One that was exceptionally old."

The Dominican didn't seem to find the question in the least unusual. "Of course. It's a vital part of the True Obedience legend. There's been a Jewish element in their story for centuries, though no one is quite sure why. And there's a rumor that a mezuzah that's supposed to have come from the Second Temple by way of the Knights Templar is somehow involved."

She tried to get Geoff as soon as she left the priory. He didn't pick up. So he was probably with Maggie. Annie left a brief message—no details, just that he should call her as soon as he could.

It was a beautiful day, sunny and warm, with just enough of a breeze to keep things comfortable. The Belsize Park tube stop was nearby, but she ignored it, choosing instead to walk, glad she'd worn comfortable flats, lengthening her stride and letting the movement—even though it wasn't actually running—soothe her, help to organize her thoughts.

Seek here the Speckled Egg.

The ghost had written that on her mirror not because there was a quail's egg in the flat. And not just to say she should be looking for the Speckled Egg who led the True Obedience in Tudor times. Her visiting Carthusian had been trying to tell her that the Stephen Fox who painted the mural in the early twentieth century was the Speckled Egg of his day. And probably that the mural held the key to the code of the *A*'s. Which, in fact, stood for *argent* in French and meant the Silber family had something that Weinraub wanted.

Why? Why was the Bristol House ghost so determined to get Annie Kendall to do what he wanted?

She was heading south toward Southampton Row, though even for her it was too far to walk. Now she looked up and saw she was on Primrose Hill Road, skirting the park. Maggie's place was nearby. Empty now. She and Geoff had gone together to clean out the kitchen right after they got back from Strasbourg. They'd only thrown out things that would spoil, indulging themselves in the mutual fantasy that Maggie might come home from the hospital.

There was a café on the corner of Sharpleshall Street. Annie took a seat at a small sidewalk table and put her tote down beside her. A young woman in a waitress uniform appeared. Annie asked for *citron pressé,* not too sweet. She was prepared to settle for a Schweppes, but the girl took her order without comment and went inside. Annie reached for her sketchbook and a pencil.

She had not brought any of the important drawings to her meeting with Father O'Hare. This was a new sketchbook, pristine and smaller than she usually used. Her pencil moved rapidly on the page. She drew the door to the priory. Then the Dominican in his white robes with the swinging rosary beads. Next the little book-lined room where they had talked and he had provided the startling information that the True Obedience of Avignon had been active until the early part of the twentieth century.

Holy shit! As Geoff would say.

Her insight was so stunning, she'd have tried again to reach him, but she didn't have to. Her cell rang just then, and it was Geoff returning her call. Annie blurted her revelations the moment she heard his voice. "There's a special mezuzah tied to the True Obedience legend. And Étienne Renard was a kabbalah scholar and the last Speckled Egg. In fact, that's why he was expelled from the Carthusians in 1929. So the True Obedience was around as late as that. The Dominican I talked to thinks they must have died out after that last Carthusian purge, but they didn't, Geoff. I'm sure that's the connection. That's what the ghost has been trying to tell me. Weinraub is part of the True Obedience. In fact, he's the current Speckled Egg. It explains everything. Do you see?"

"I'm not sure."

His voice seemed flat and kind of overcontrolled. "Geoff, I'm sorry. I didn't ask . . . Maggie?"

"No change," he said. "But I've got some news as well. I just heard from my contact at the Connaught. Weinraub's back in London."

She sucked in a long breath. "That means he's getting ready to do something."

There was no reply.

"He is, Geoff. That's what you said happened before. Once Weinraub left Strasbourg, Rabin was assassinated by someone who wanted to make sure the Israelis wouldn't make peace with the Palestinians and possibly give up their claim to the Temple Mount."

"That's what I think, yes."

"And there's a good chance you're right. Now he's looking for the mezuzah because it's part of the True Obedience legend, and he's going to make a move."

"On the Temple Mount?"

"Where else can it be? Geoff, it's time. We've got to tell someone."

33

Geoff's hair was still damp from the shower. He was buttoning his shirt. Annie sat on the bed watching him get dressed. "You're going to say it's something you've been researching for some time, right?"

"Exactly."

"Do you want these suspenders?" She held out the pair lying beside her.

"Braces," Geoff said. "Yes, thank you."

His appointment with the prime minister was at four-fifty. *Do please be punctual, Mr. Harris. The PM will be leaving for a reception at the Dutch embassy promptly at five.* Annie, they'd agreed, would be superfluous. Ten minutes was not enough time to explain about an obscure heresy active since at least the fifteenth century, much less the ghost in the back bedroom.

Geoff picked out a paisley tie in shades of rich royal purple. "What I'll say is, it's a story I've been researching for weeks, based on work I originally did in '95." His suit, navy with a faint pinstripe, was one she'd never seen before. It fit as if it had been made for him, which probably it had. "I'll point out it's pretty straightforward. We believe—"

"You believe," she corrected.

"Right. I believe Philip Weinraub's Shalom Foundation to be a front for a Christian fundamentalist group—possibly Catholic fundamentalists and possibly with a connection to the Carthusian order. I won't give them any more than that."

"Maybe not even that," Annie said. "The Carthusians may be a bridge too far. It complicates the story."

"Could be, but when I knew him, the PM could definitely walk and chew gum. So possibly I'll say a group connected to the Carthusians, but definitely people with an interest in restoring the ancient Jewish Temple in Jerusalem."

"And why would Christians care about the Jewish Temple?" They had been over this. Her question was a prompt.

"So the ancient biblical prophecies are fulfilled and Jesus can return. Which necessitates blowing up or otherwise getting rid of the Islamic holy sites on the Temple Mount. And I have reason to believe this group is getting ready to make their move."

They'd agreed he wouldn't say how he knew. He'd use the American defense of journalists' right to protect their sources. It wouldn't stand up in a British court, but Geoff figured it would do for his old friend the prime minister. At least temporarily. "You're not going to mention Bletchley or the code, or even the mural?" she asked.

"All that," he said, "is definitely too complicated for a ten-minute presentation. I just want to persuade him to contact the Israeli authorities. Put them on alert so that whatever Weinraub is planning can be stopped before it happens." He gave the tie a final tug. "I haven't worn clothes like this in months. It feels like putting on a straitjacket."

"However it feels," she said, "you look good enough to eat."

"Later," he said. "I'll remind you."

They both laughed.

Laughter, Annie realized, was the nicest kind of intimacy, and it only happened when you were sober. Then, because she couldn't continue to avoid the subject: "Still no word from Clary?"

"None. I've been trying to reach him, but he's not answering."

"Geoff, I want him to come back to England. If we're right about the timing, Clary's nosing around now could be perceived as a threat. I'm worried."

"So am I. A bit at least. But I keep reminding myself that compared with Port-au-Prince, Strasbourg is Disneyland. Clary can take care of himself."

"That's what you keep saying."

"It's what I believe."

It was not quite two. "Are you going to the hospital first?" Annie asked.

"Yes. It makes me feel better, even when she doesn't know I'm there."

They were keeping Maggie heavily sedated all the time now. Which meant he'd had no opportunity to confess that he'd opened the mezuzah despite the prohibition, or to ask what she knew about what it contained. His guess was his mother would have nothing to offer. "If there was an explanation, Maggie would have told me when she gave it to me. She knew there weren't going to be many more lucid conversations." That's what he'd said the night before, and he had not faltered over the words, but looking at him now, Annie realized that without the suspenders, the trousers of the custom-made suit wouldn't stay up. Fortunately the jacket looked fine. She watched him load his gear—wallet, keys, business cards, iPhone—and add a pen to an inside pocket, then pat himself down in that way men did.

"What are you going to do with the rest of the day?" he asked.

It was nearly three weeks since she'd been to AA—too long. Part of her did not feel comfortable saying that to Geoff. *It's drunks who get why AA works, Annie my girl. Civilians think it's peculiar.* But Geoff Harris was not just another civilian, and letting him in was part of the easy intimacy that only thrived with sobriety. "I'll probably go to an AA meeting," she said.

He didn't flinch. "Great. Don't forget your mobile. I'll call you when I leave Number Ten, but I expect I'll go to see Maggie again afterward. That's always presuming they haven't called me to come earlier."

"So you definitely think the prime minister took you seriously?" Annie asked.

They were at the pub in Cosmo Place. Neither of them was eating much, both just playing with their food. "Absolutely," Geoff said. "Particularly once I said I'd come up empty after I tried to get Interpol to check out the deaths of two old but influential cardinals—both involving quail eggs—that I thought might involve Philip Weinraub. Which was why I didn't want to go back to them with my suspicion that he was planning an imminent move on the Temple Mount. That's the point where I was hustled into a two-hour meeting with blokes in dark glasses and trench coats."

"Really?" She opened her eyes wide. "Dark glasses at that hour?"

"Metaphor," he said. Then: "You're winding me up, aren't you?"

"Pulling your leg. Maybe a little."

Anything to make him smile. It was after ten. Most of the evening he'd spent with his mother. Maggie was in an oxygen tent. First time. Geoff stopped talking about MI6 or whoever the spy types had been, pulled inevitably back to his own reality. "According to the nurse, the oxygen's only so she's more comfortable. It won't prolong anything."

"Did they say how long she—" Annie broke off and wished for the words back.

He shrugged. "The only thing they can tell me is that she's stable, and it may still be a number of weeks." The place they'd put her, he added, was crawling with grief counselors and bereavement gurus and various other people eager to talk about death and dying. Geoff wanted no truck with any of them. He was sure if Maggie were conscious, she wouldn't either.

Annie tried some gentle hints about the value of support groups, "a subject on which I am something of an expert," but he looked as if she'd grown a second head.

"Change of topic," he said. "I take it you haven't heard from Clary? I've had my mobile off all evening. I thought if he couldn't reach me, maybe—"

Annie shook her head.

"Shit," he said. Then: "Let's get out of here. Unless you're still hungry." He indicated her half-eaten pork chop.

"Past it," she said.

Geoff motioned to the waiter.

He marched them back to his place at a virtual trot and for once didn't head for the espresso maker the minute they closed the front door. Instead he pulled her close for a hungry, demanding kiss, at the same time shrugging off his suit coat and tugging at his tie. Sex as an antidote to terminal cancer. Annie got it. She dropped to her knees and reached for the zipper of his fly. A couple of explosive minutes later she said, "Let's go upstairs. I've got a surprise."

He was sitting up in bed waiting for her when she came out of the bathroom. The lights were on but dimmed. Natasha Bedingfield was singing about needing some inspiration . . . *It's who I am, it's what I do . . . gonna lay it down for you.* Annie was wearing the red stilettos and nothing else, except her Ari bracelet and, nestled in the hollow of her neck, the crystal heart on a golden chain.

Geoff grinned. "Love the shoes," he said. "New?"

"Yes."

"I hope you were thinking of me when you bought them."

"I was." The two words came out husky because there was a sudden lump in her throat.

"Me and no one else?"

"Positively no one else. These are strictly 'for Geoff' shoes."

She walked closer to the bed, and he reached up and traced the outline of the necklace. "I heart you, Annie Kendall."

She opened her mouth, but before she could say anything, the iPhone on the night table played "Soul Power" and drowned out the thudding heart in Annie's chest.

He grabbed for the phone.

It wasn't the hospital, as it turned out. It was Clary. Geoff put him on speakerphone. Clary said he'd been incommunicado for a couple of days because the woman in Alsace, the one who had produced the record proving Philip Weinraub wasn't circumcised until he was fifteen, had been murdered. "Her throat was slit ear to ear. Seems it happened a couple of hours after we left, but her body wasn't found for a couple of days."

Annie felt her bile rise and dashed for the bathroom. She could still hear their voices.

"So how come," Geoff asked, "no one in that entire godforsaken village reported a black criminal type driving a late-model Peugeot? How come you're not in the Bastille? How come we're not screaming for our solicitors? Do they take a vow of *omertà* in Alsace?"

"At least three people reported seeing us," Clary said. "Your man in Strasbourg took care of everything. Had to be cash money right away, so there'll be an extra three grand on my expense sheet. He says he'll bill you for the ordinary services."

"What about the money we gave her? Where's the ten thousand quid?"

"Either the killers took it or the cops did. Near as we can tell, there's no mention on any official record."

Annie lost whatever came next because she had to flush. And run the water to rinse her mouth. She got back to the bedroom in time to hear Clary say, "One more thing. Really weird. They found a raw quail egg in her mouth. The whole egg, shell and all. Has to have been put there after she was dead."

34

Dom Justin
From the Waiting Place

On the July morning when Rebecca and I, along with Diego di Mantova and all who traveled with him, left the home of his brother Giuseppe, the church bells of Metz pealed joyous sounds to announce a feast of the Blessed Virgin. I set out on the next leg of our journey placing myself and all of us under her protection.

We were on our way to Strasbourg. It was a city some distance away, but our journey took many days more than it might have, because we stopped frequently to allow Diego to visit one or another town along the route and make trades or arrange for others in the future. On most of these excursions, he took with him a servant whose job was to seek out a market and buy provisions for our journey while Diego did his more important business.

While I had heard the names of the towns that the Jew her father listed for Rebecca to commit to memory, I could not have recited them back to him as she did. But frequently I would recognize a name along our route. In such instances, I noted, Rebecca was the one to accompany Diego into the city. I had no doubt she quickly obtained the wine or cheese or bread she had been sent to find, then used her father's instructions to go among the Jews of the place and deliver one of his gifts. But I had sworn an oath, and I required to be certain.

When we first traveled with the Lombard, on the journey from Calais to Metz, Rebecca had walked as did most of the party. The horse carried Diego, and the donkeys were loaded with the goods that accompanied us. On this shorter journey, Rebecca was sometimes permitted to ride one of the donkeys. I suspected that to be a mark of her changed status in regard to Diego—he seemed to prize her company and sought out occasions to be with her. But it was not in my mind to speak of that when I managed to place myself in the position of holding the donkey's halter, a task usually performed by one of the boys who looked after the Lombard's animals.

I hung back until no one was near enough to hear, then asked the question that was troubling my conscience: "We swore to place the treasures with Jews. Do you—"

"Silence!" Rebecca leaned forward and spoke directly in my ear: "Take care, or priested monk though you claim to be, you will never see the Rhenish Charterhouse."

"Why? Are these not all Diego's servants? Which one do you fear?"

"The bald one called Josef," she whispered, speaking of a man who had joined our party when we left Metz.

"Giuseppe said he belonged to the household we go to in Strasbourg," I said. It had seemed an innocent enough explanation for placing this Josef in our midst. "You think he lied?"

"I do not know, but he watches me, and I do not trust him. Diego and his brother are Mantuans," Rebecca said. "I do not think this Josef is even a Lombard."

Just then the boy who usually led the donkey approached with the message that he was again to take the donkey's halter, since we were falling behind the others. I had no choice but to yield my place.

After that I watched Josef more closely. I soon realized he did indeed keep a sharp eye on Rebecca. As a result, I too began to watch her more closely. Thus I discovered that during the night, when all but the guards were asleep, she slipped between the folds of Diego's tent and remained with him until nearly sunrise.

Her own father had called her a whore. I could not bring myself to think of her so. Her beauty—in no way diminished by being nearly four months with child—was the only weapon she possessed. She had used it to procure a measure of safety for herself and for me, as well as the unborn babe, and to execute the charge her father had laid upon her. God would judge her. I could not.

Perhaps the Holy Virgin viewed Rebecca's sin with the same indulgence, for it seemed to me the Mother of God certainly had taken us under her protection. After a fortnight and without incident (gradually carrying fewer and fewer of the secret treasures while Rebecca's belly swelled to conceal their loss), we arrived at our destination of Strasbourg.

Whatever I have said about the other great cities we had seen, and whatever praise might be heaped on the splendid churches frequently found at their center, nothing could compare to the exquisite Cathedral of Notre Dame that was the heart of the most beautiful city I expected ever to see. Only a poet could describe either or both. As I do not have that gift, I will not attempt the task.

The Lombard with whom we were to stay was called Jacopo. He was a cousin of Diego and the owner of a number of boats. That was a fine thing to be in a city sitting beside the mighty Rhine. The household of Jacopo of Strasbourg was if anything grander than that of Giuseppe of Metz.

As soon as we arrived, Rebecca, who had been feeling poorly the last days of our journey, was put to bed, while I was dispatched to live among the servants. The man who had previously been in charge of polishing the household plate had recently died, so I was to perform his duties. "That task will be yours," the majordomo of the household told me, "until some labor can be found that makes better use of your muscles." In Metz I had been given the job of emptying the chamber pots and cleaning the latrines. Shining silver and gold was a far more agreeable task.

I soon learned whom I had to thank for my assignment. In Jacopo's household, the bald-headed Josef was assistant to the man the Lombards called the *scalco*, he who purchased the household foodstuffs. Being thus so close to the control of the kitchen purse gave Josef influence, and though he had ignored me while we traveled, in Strasbourg he appointed himself my friend and protector. Soon he began to seek opportunities when we could speak together in English, a language he claimed to have acquired years before while in service in the Pale of Calais. On one such occasion, with no prodding from me, he told the story of a bloody massacre of the Strasbourg Jews. "Cut hundreds of 'em into little pieces," he said, waving in the air the cleaver with which he hacked apart carcasses of beef when they were brought to the kitchen. " 'Cause they was bringing the plague down on the city and causing good Christians to die in agony." At this he piously made the sign of the cross. "Was the butchers and the tanners what brought justice to the Jews. Killed every one they could find in the city."

"I take it," I said, "that means there are now no Jews in this place."

Josef smiled. "Ever killed a rat?" he asked. I said I had. "Me as well," he said. "Plenty of 'em. But if we go down to the cellars now, I warrant we'll find plenty more to kill."

It seemed his intent was to engage me in a discussion of Jewish perfidy and Christian virtue. As this was a conversation I did not wish to have, I merely listened, making as few comments as possible. Thinking on it later, I wondered why the assistant to the *scalco* in a household of such affluence as this should concern himself with Jews, who in Strasbourg as elsewhere occupied a section of their own, separate and apart from Christians. I was to learn the answer the following Sunday, when we had been two weeks in Strasbourg.

A celebrated preacher of the Dominicans, known for both their oratory and their learning, was come from Mantua to preach at the cathedral. After the midday mass and the much-anticipated sermon, Jacopo would give a feast for many noble and important visitors. Preparations for the occasion went on all week. We were told that most of the servants might attend the service, and I expected to be among them, but the day before the event, the majordomo told me I was not to go to the cathedral with the others. I must stay behind and polish the plate. I used what little of his tongue I possessed to say I had already done the job, but it availed me nothing. I had my orders, and there was nothing I could do but obey them.

As the noon hour approached, masters and servants alike left for the cathedral, and the house grew eerily quiet. For a time I thought I might be entirely alone. Then I heard noises in the kitchen, which was near the small room where I worked. I went to see what was happening and found Josef. He had also been left behind. His task was to tend the many kettles hanging above the hearths, the spitted fowls done to a luscious turn being kept warm beside banked embers, and the two whole pigs suspended high above a fire that occasionally sputtered from the fat dripping off their crisp and golden skin. "Come, Justin," he said when he saw me. "Let us celebrate our luck in not having to listen to talk of life in the hereafter. What about this one, eh?"

"What about it?" I asked.

"Come closer," he said, beckoning me forward. "What are you afraid of?"

I could not safely ignore the invitation. I took a few steps deeper into the kitchen, all the while suspecting they led to my doom.

Among the Lombards, even the servants ate food such as I had neither seen nor tasted in years, but since joining them, I had struggled to secretly adhere to the diet of a Carthusian. (It seemed to me that if I could be faithful in small things, I might be forgiven for betraying more important ones.) I could not any day eat only bread and water lest I attract undue attention, but I managed to shun meat and much of the time ate no fish. Now I had been lured into the place of ruination. The smell of sizzling fat and melting flesh nearly overwhelmed me.

"Here, take this." Josef hacked off a portion of the crisp and fragrant meat of one of the pigs, speared it on a sharpened stick, and offered it to me. "It is good, I promise you. I just had some myself."

I shook my head. Josef thrust the meat closer, wafting it under my nose. "Just taste it," he urged. "I think it needs more cinnamon. The master insists we use enough so everyone knows how rich he really is. Why not? This isn't Lombardy, and here there is no sumptuary tax." With this he threw back his head and laughed, showing a mouth with only three teeth, as yellow as buttercups in an English meadow.

Josef held the skewer with its cap of luscious meat so close to my mouth, the fragrant grease dripped down my chin, though I tasted nothing of it. "I am not hungry," I said. "Besides, I have work to do." With that I fled the kitchen and returned to my little room and the stack of silver trenchers that already shone, but which in obedience to the command of the major-domo I was polishing again.

A few minutes later Josef appeared at my door. This time he carried a jug and a beaker made of fired clay, though we were surrounded by the golden goblets that would later be offered to Jacopo's guests. "A drink, Englishman?" He nodded to the piles of plate. "You do thirsty work."

I took the wine he offered—that being the usual beverage of this place where ale was reserved for the masters of the establishment—and drank it down, grateful for refreshment I was not forbidden to accept. When my cup was empty, Josef refilled it, and I drank again as greedily as before. "Thirsty work," I agreed. "The wine is good."

"Good enough for these Lombards," he said, refilling my goblet yet again.

Thomas Cromwell had trained me well. No opportunity to gain information was ever to be ignored, because what you learned might someday serve a purpose you did not yet imagine. "I take it you are not a Lombard?"

"Me? Indeed I am not."

"A man of Strasbourg perhaps?" I asked.

Josef shrugged. "Yes and no. My mother's people come from here, but my father's people are from Avignon far to the south. I was born there."

"And do you then prefer Avignon to Strasbourg?"

"Truth," he said in a manner suddenly turned solemn, "is to be found in Avignon."

The hair rose on the back of my neck, but however desperate I was to probe his meaning, by now my bladder was brimming full and I could hold back no longer. I had to piss or burst, and as there was in my workroom no hearth or chamber pot where I might do so, I rushed to the small courtyard just beyond the door. I had still my cock in my hand when I realized that Josef had followed me outside. "And there's the proof," he said, coming close to the wall at which I directed my stream and looking as intently at my member as might any whore. "You may travel with a Jewess, and you may refuse to eat pork, but you are not disfigured as they disfigure their sons, so you are not one of them. Forgive me, Dom Justin. I had to be sure." Then he fell to his knees beside me.

I was by then rearranging my garments and secreting my member, but for a moment I thought he was a cursed pervert about to perform an unnatural act upon my person, and I jumped back. Then, as it were, his words spoke themselves again in my mind. "You called me Dom Justin," I whispered, almost overcome with surprise.

"We were told the Jewess traveled with a priest of the True Obedience of Avignon, but we had to be sure." He had not risen from his knees. "I beg you, Dom Justin, give me your blessing."

I could refuse no man a simple benediction, and I raised my hand and traced the sign of the cross above his head. Then, before either of us could speak further, we heard the sound of the returning household.

It was nine o'clock and a full summer moon had risen by the time all the guests departed and the servants went to their beds. I was ready for mine, as much to think about what had happened earlier as to sleep. In the hubbub of the feast, I'd had no time to try and piece together the many parts of the puzzle. It seemed I still would not be able to do so. I was just putting away the last of the goblets when Josef again appeared at the door of my workroom. He did not speak, only beckoned to me while looking right and left as if to be sure he was not observed.

I opened my mouth to tell him the next day would be time enough for talk, but he immediately turned and went into the small courtyard where we had spoken earlier. My curiosity prevailed, and I followed him.

Diego waited for me. As soon as I appeared, he fell to his knees, saying, "Pray God, a blessing from a priest of the True Obedience."

"You too know this?" So great was my astonishment, I all but stammered the words.

"I was not sure. We knew only to look for a woman, a Jewess of uncommon beauty, and a man traveling with her. But we were given no distinctive way to recognize the man. It seemed possible that the perfidious Jews might have murdered our priest and substituted one of their own kind."

I did not ask him whether, on the many nights he lay with her, he thought Rebecca perfidious, but asked instead, "Who is this 'we' of whom you speak?"

"Myself and a few others who are loyal. All were dispatched to wait and watch at different ports."

"Dispatched? Who charged you with this errand?"

"The command came as do all others among our brotherhood, accompanied by the egg of a quail, thus from the one who, failing a proper pope, we think of as Christ's voice on earth and call the Speckled Egg."

Diego had remained on his knees throughout this exchange, waiting for my blessing. Finally I raised my hand and gave it to him, and only then did he stand up. At which point I asked, "Where is Rebecca?"

All pretense between us had been dropped, and the Lombard did not remark on my abandonment of the fiction that she was the mistress and I the servant. "She sleeps soundly," he said. "I arranged a special draught in her last goblet of wine, but in the morning she will wake none the worse for it. Though if I had given her half again as much . . ."

His words trailed away, but I did not need to hear them to know what he meant. "Why would you consider such a thing? What has she done to you that you should speak thus?"

"Nothing," he admitted. "And in the normal way of things, I bear her no ill will. But if it served the interest of the Speckled Egg . . ." Again he ended without finishing his words, though his thought was plain between us.

"Listen to me," I said. "I know well the one you call the Speckled Egg." When I said that, both he and Josef signed themselves with the cross. "It was never his intent to have any harm befall Rebecca."

"As long as she knows nothing of who we truly are—indeed, who you are—then she has nothing to fear from us," Diego said.

I did not bother to tell him how much Rebecca knew, for I was sure it would not make her future any more secure, a thing that was in my mind because I was starting to realize how uncertain it truly was. I knew she had entertained the hope that because Diego was widowed and because his daughters loved her and she them, Diego might marry her and so assure her and her child food and shelter in the years ahead. But the fact that Dom Hilary, in laying his charge upon Diego and whomever else he had sent to watch the ports, had labeled her a Jewess had apparently put that possibility out of reach. Diego was the sort of Christian who might use a Jewess as a whore but never consider her as a wife. "I go to the Charterhouse near Freiburg," I said, aware that knowing me to be a monk and a priest of the True Obedience, these men had yielded to me a certain measure of authority. "I wish to be sure the woman and the child she bears will be taken care of after that."

I blamed her for much, but I owed her more. And the child was—God have mercy on me—flesh of my flesh.

Diego nodded. "I will think of something," he promised.

❖

35

The woman in Alsace had her throat slit from ear to ear, and a quail egg placed in her mouth. Every time Annie thought of it, she shivered: "We killed her."

"No, we didn't." Geoff held her tighter and nestled the down quilt closer around both of them. "She knew the risk and decided to take it. She had lots of choices, Annie. Most of them she made before we ever came on the scene."

"But if she hadn't talked to us, she wouldn't have died."

"Look, she understood that staying in that wretched village meant the people her husband warned her about knew where to find her. It was a bad choice, but it had nothing to do with us."

"You're saying she died because of where she was?" Annie made it a question. "Death by real estate? Location, location, lo—"

She stopped speaking. Countable seconds went by. Geoff was good about things like that. He waited. "Whenever you're ready," he said after a time.

"Location," Annie said, finishing her original thought. "Geoff, why do we assume that *Aventine à Arc* is a reference to time? What if 'Aventine Hill to the Arch of Titus' referred to coordinates on a map?"

"Jesus fucking Christ." He grabbed the iPhone from the night table. Annie squirmed into a position where she could look over his shoulder. He brought up Google Earth and located the Arch of Titus. "That's the easy part," he said, manipulating the image with two fingers. "Shit. Aventine Hill's too vague to be useful. It's a section of the city, divided into a number of streets. We need an address. Any ideas?"

"I'm not sure. Let's go downstairs. I need to see this on a bigger screen. And I need a sketchbook." The red stilettos were by the bed where she'd kicked them off. Annie ignored them and shoved her feet into sneakers.

Geoff sat in front of his desktop computer. Annie was at the kitchen counter, sketching furiously, starting one drawing after another, frequently closing her eyes in frustration, then ripping off a sheet of paper and trying again. "I can't get it."

"Any chance you can tell me what 'it' is? I'm not having a lot of joy here myself."

"I don't know. But if I'm right, and location matters more than time, then the geography in the mural is important. But the thing's screwy—nothing is where it really is in London. I've looked and looked, and there doesn't appear to be any pattern or logical sequence. It's all random." She was still sketching at a breakneck pace. "I'm trying to get a handle on the little piece of the mural that has the Hebrew letters. When I was copying them for Rabbi Cohen, I said they were above a sketch of the part of the Embankment. Trees beside a river."

"There are a considerable number of places in London with trees beside a river."

"Exactly. I'm trying to remember the details, why I made that assumption, but they won't come. I think it's because I know what the Embankment looks like, and I'm trying to make that be what I saw, but I'm getting the feeling it's not. Geoff, I want to go to Bristol House. I've got to see it again."

"Now?" He glanced at his watch. "It's one o'clock in the morning."

"Can you go back to sleep with all this hanging out there?" And when he shook his head: "Neither can I. So we might as well go now."

"Wait," Annie said as soon as they walked in. She had automatically picked up the remote, but so far she hadn't switched on the radios.

"He's here?" Geoff asked. "The monk?"

"I don't know." Then, after a long few moments: "No, I don't believe he is. But if he means to find me, he will."

"Jesus. Do you mind if we put on some lights? And the radios."

Seconds later they were listening to the BBC telling them the Vatican had made public the fact that the pope was gravely ill and not expected to recover. Catholic dignitaries were beginning to gather in Rome.

"*Sede vacante*," Annie said. "The chair really will be empty."

They went into Annie's bedroom, and Geoff dragged over a lamp so the lower-left corner of the mural was better lit. Then they lay on the floor, side by side on their bellies. "Right below here," Annie said, "just underneath the Hebrew. That's what I've been trying to get my mind around."

Geoff peered at the section she indicated. "That," he said, "is definitely not the Embankment."

"You're sure?"

"Positive. The bridges are wrong. You'd be looking at—" He stopped speaking but squirmed into a position where he could look still more closely at the mural.

"What?" she demanded. "What are you seeing?"

"That I'm a fuckwit. I should have thought of it right away. Look, over here." He pointed to a grand-looking building in the middle of the scene. "This part of the mural isn't London. It's Rome. And unless I'm badly mistaken, this is the headquarters of the Knights of Malta on the Aventine Hill."

Annie drew a long breath and held it. When she let it out, she said, "The Knights of Malta are officially known as the Knights Hospitaller of Saint John. In the fourteenth century, the pope gave them all the property of the disgraced Knights Templar."

"And the Templars," Geoff said, "were the blokes who established their first monastery on the Temple Mount. Leading to that ever-popular conspiracy theorists' myth that they brought a shitload of treasure from the ancient Jewish Temple to London and stashed it somewhere yet unfound."

"We've been over all that," Annie said. "Right now it's not the point."

Geoff was running his hand along the mural, searching for more clues hidden in the close-packed, overlapping scenes. Annie smothered the impulse to tell him not to actually touch the work.

"What about this tree here?" he asked after a few seconds. "It could be an almond tree, couldn't it?"

"Maybe. I'd need to find the horticultural drawings again to be sure. But it's definitely different from the others, so it could be."

"Any odds you care to name," Geoff said.

Annie didn't take the bet. "Okay," she said, pointing to the vignette with the Hebrew letters. "If you're right about this being the Knights of Malta building on the Aventine Hill, then this is the entrance to their gardens." She wagged her finger at the scene to the right of the lettering. "Which means this is the Piranesi gate, which happens to be one of the best-known tourist destinations in Rome. Because when you look through the keyhole, you have a perfectly framed view of the dome of Saint Peter's and—" She broke off.

Geoff was following her nonetheless. "So it's Rome that leads to the code of the *A*'s," he said, sweeping his hand toward the window on their right to indicate the progression. "But then what? What do you get after you have Maggie's mezuzah?"

Annie scrambled to her feet. There was a sketchbook on the night table beside the bed. She grabbed it and a pencil and sat down and began drawing.

Geoff got up and went to sit beside her, watching as a quick-stroke suggestion of the mural appeared on the page.

"Here are the Roman scenes," she said. A few dark lines appeared on the lower-left corner of the impressionistic drawing. "They lead to the *A*'s, which are pretty much like this." Annie added a few black dots, glancing up once or twice to confirm her memory of the placements of telltale *E.R.* initials.

"No," Geoff said. "That's wrong."

"How so?"

"It's not the order of things. We're looking the wrong way. With the wrong mind-set. My mother would say we need to think like the person who made the code." He stood up and walked the length of the mural, moving from the door to the window. "Renard was a Hebrew scholar steeped in kabbalah. Our instinct is to read this way"—a wide sweep of his hand indicated left to right—"from the Roman scenes to the window. But if we're supposed to read his message like Hebrew"—another wave of his hand—"it goes right to left."

"So it's reversed," Annie said. "Meaning the *A*'s lead to Rome and Saint Peter's, not the other way around."

"Exactly."

"And right now in Rome," Geoff said, "the chair is about to be empty, and the Catholic Church is going to elect a new pope. So what if—"

Annie held up a hand to signal for silence. "Shush. Listen."

The BBC was explaining that the word *conclave* comes from the Latin *con clavis*, "with a key." "The cardinals," a woman's voice told them, "will be locked in until their meeting in the Sistine Chapel elects a pope and we see white smoke coming from—"

"The two most influential old cardinals!" Annie shouted the words. "Maggie was right about that as well. Those two old cardinals who were murdered by the quail egg crowd, by Weinraub and his people—they're the key."

"You've lost me."

"It's canon law," she said, "at least for the last thirty or forty years. No cardinal over eighty is allowed to vote for a new pope. So the old ones don't attend the conclave. But what if the ones who do go were somehow eliminated?"

"As in," Geoff said softly, "the Sistine Chapel is set on fire or blown up or gassed or something with all of them in it."

"Yes. Then the old cardinals would probably be called in as backup. And respected men like De Boer and Falcone would have a lot of influence. History shows silverbacks of that sort to be unforgiving about ancient schisms."

"So if you wanted to manipulate that second emergency conclave, maybe you'd take out what you're calling the silverbacks first." Geoff was working his iPhone as he spoke.

"What are you doing?"

"Looking for the number of the spook I met yesterday. The MI6 bloke. He said to call any time if I thought of something. Seems like sending him chasing the wrong wild goose is someth—"

The phone rang in his hand.

It was the hospital. There had been a sudden change in his mother's condition. She was no longer stable. Mr. Harris should come immediately.

36

"You're sure you're going to be all right?" Geoff asked.

"Of course I am. I'll close up here and go back to your place."

"Do that, Annie. Don't spend any more time with the mural. We'll come back together later and—"

"Stop worrying about me." She kissed him quickly. "Just go. Don't forget to call the spook from the cab." She closed the door behind him and turned right to the drawing room. They'd put the lights on in there when they came in, and she had to—

Jesus! What was she thinking? She was letting him go by himself to do the maybe hardest thing he'd ever do in his life! If it was the other way around, if she were the one facing a similar crisis, what was Geoff likely to have done? Annie whirled round and ran out of the flat, pulling the door shut behind her. She could hear his footsteps pounding down the stairs and running across the lobby. "Wait! I'm coming with you!" It was not quite a shout, rather a super loud whisper—all she could summon in the inhibiting nighttime hush.

He didn't hear her, and there was no reply.

Annie tore down the stairs. She'd reached the landing of the next floor down when she heard the front door of the building close. By the time she was on the street, his taxi—she could see Geoff's profile in the rear window—was heading south toward Kingsway. Annie shouted and waved both arms, but he seemed to be talking on the iPhone and didn't turn his head.

Another cab pulled up to the front of the hotel a few doors away. The curbside door opened, and a man got out, taking a few moments over it because he was hauling a couple of suitcases. Annie dashed toward him, then ran into the road and opened the cab's opposite door. "Guy's Hospital!" she shouted, hurling herself into the backseat. "Hurry." She was fishing in all her pockets meanwhile and—thank God for the longtime habit—came up with a ten-pound note.

The man with the suitcases closed the door on his side. The driver pulled away. Annie sat forward, trying to see the taillights of Geoff's cab up ahead. There wasn't a lot of traffic at this hour, so she thought it might be possible. Then the light caught her cab at Theobald's Road and banished any hope of catching up. There was, however, no better hour to speed through London. In less than ten minutes they were crossing London Bridge, and she had calmed down enough to begin wondering if Geoff would think it presumptuous of her to have come. Wouldn't he have said, if that's what he wanted? Too late. She didn't have enough cash to tell the cab to turn around and take her back to Holborn. Besides, they had arrived.

The cabbie reached behind him to open the Plexiglas screen. He thrust the back of his head in her direction. "What entrance do you want, love? Casualty?"

That's what they called Emergency here. "No, not Casualty. I want . . . damn, I'm not sure." She knew where Geoff had taken her when they visited, but Maggie had been moved since then. And despite having been founded some nine hundred years earlier, Guy's and the nearby, equally old and venerable St. Thomas' were amalgamated into an enormous ultramodern teaching institution that sprawled over a number of city streets. A variety of buildings accommodated various departments and schools and faculty and student living accommodations. Threaded among them were the small bars and restaurants and shops that invariably attached themselves to any such urban campus.

The driver slowed down, as if to give her time to get her bearings, but offered no guidance. Annie patted her pockets again, this time looking for her cell. No luck. Because, she remembered, she'd left it at Geoff's, when they first headed out to Bristol House. The cab's screen was still open. She leaned forward, speaking in the direction of the cabbie's ear. "Look, have you got a mobile, and can I use it for a moment?" The meter already showed seven pounds fifty pence. She couldn't offer him a big tip as inducement. "I have to get to someone who's dying, and I need to call and find out exactly where I'm to go."

The driver pulled to the curbside. He held up a phone but didn't hand it back to Annie. "What number do you want to call?"

"I don't really know. I need the number for the central reception or switchboard or whatever they call it. Information . . . directory inquiries."

"You don't know where this dying person you need to be with is?"

"No. I told you, I—" Two young women were walking toward them, both wearing green scrubs. Annie rolled down the window and leaned out. "Please, can you help me?"

The one closest to the curb, a brunette who looked as if she might be Middle Eastern, stopped and leaned in. "If you want Casualty, it's—"

"No, not that," Annie said. "I need to know where someone is moved to when they're dying."

The girl looked skeptical.

"My boyfriend's mother," Annie said, praying for female solidarity. "He got a call saying she wasn't stable, and he should come. I just want to be close by for him." The girl nodded and looked a bit more understanding. "She's dying of breast cancer," Annie added, "and last week they moved her to what I guess would be called a palliative care unit. Does that help?"

The young woman turned to her companion, and the pair of them conferred for a moment. Then the one who hadn't spoken to Annie offered the driver a series of directions, while the maybe–Middle Eastern brunette wished Annie good luck.

The cab sped away once more, this time taking a number of turns and cutting across a maze of small streets before pulling up in front of an unmarked redbrick building. The fare was ten pounds and twenty pence. Annie did what Geoff always did, got out on the driver's side and proffered her ten-pound note through the window. "I'm sorry, this is all I have." The cabbie rolled his eyes, took it, and drove away.

* * *

Inside, another woman—this one graying and short and round, and wearing jeans and a loose multicolored smock as well as a stethoscope around her neck—took Annie by the hand. "Mrs. Harris is down here," she said. They walked along a short corridor to a room with an open door.

Geoff's back was to her. He was sitting beside the bed. Holding Maggie's hand, Annie thought, though she had no precise view of Maggie herself. All she could see was the bottom half of what appeared to be a small and inconsequential disturbance beneath the sheets. An intravenous setup had been shoved into a corner. The only equipment still hooked up to Maggie's wasted frame was a monitor mounted on the wall to one side of the bed. Annie could make out a series of small up-and-down squiggles and hear the low and constant beeps.

There was a couch against the wall opposite the door to the sickroom. The woman with Annie, a nurse she supposed, gestured toward it, and Annie sat down. The woman went into the room and murmured something to Geoff. Annie saw him nod, but he didn't turn around. The woman went to the other side of the bed, put the ends of the stethoscope in her ears, and bent over Maggie. After a few seconds she straightened and said something Annie didn't hear. Then she came out to where Annie was waiting. "I don't think it will be long. I told him you were here."

Annie thanked her, then added before the woman could walk away, "Is Mrs. Harris in pain?"

"No. I'm quite sure she's not. She was conscious until a short time ago. I don't think she is now, but she's very peaceful."

The woman left.

Annie didn't have a watch, and there were no clocks anywhere she could see, but she didn't feel any urgency about time. She was with him, and he knew it, and apparently it was okay that she had come to share this vigil, even if from a distance. At least he didn't come out and tell her to go away.

On the other hand, neither did he turn around and acknowledge her. For a long time the only thing that happened was that occasionally

Geoff lifted Maggie's hand to his lips. Then at last the monitor switched from beeps to a soft steady hum, and the little peaks and valleys flattened to a single and steady straight line. The nurse or whatever she was appeared at the end of the corridor and gazed in Annie's direction, then went away.

More time passed. Maybe only a few minutes—Annie wasn't sure. She wasn't sure either if she should go in and say something or maybe do something. Offer some comfort beyond mere presence. She was on the verge of making that decision when Geoff stood up and bent over and kissed his mother's forehead. Then he came out to the corridor.

Annie got up off the couch. "I'm so sorry, Geoff."

"I know. So am I. Really sorry. But I don't think Maggie was. I think she figured it was time."

He was holding a small, folded piece of paper. He took his wallet out of his hip pocket and put it away.

"Rabbi Cohen's prayer?" Annie asked.

"Yes. But it turned out Maggie didn't need a cheat sheet. She knew the prayer off by heart. I said the first word, and she took over and ran through the Hebrew like a pro."

"The nurse said she was conscious when you got here. I'm glad about that."

"Me too."

There was not much emotion in his voice, but he was deathly pale. And they were still standing apart from each other. Like strangers. Or maybe just like English people. Annie nodded toward the room he'd just left. "If you want to go back, it's okay. I'll wait."

Geoff shook his head. "No need," he said. "Maggie's not there any longer."

Annie nodded toward the couch. "How about we stay here for a minute." They sat down, side by side but still not touching. There were a few small bottles of water on a side table. Annie opened one and handed it to him.

Geoff took a long swallow, then handed it back to her. "It was as if she'd been waiting for me," he said. "After I came in, she opened her eyes and smiled, then closed them again. I thought she was sleeping, but I started the prayer anyway. That's when she chimed in and spoke every word clear as a bell."

"You did good," Annie said. "According to Rabbi Cohen, that prayer is supposed to be every Jew's final words."

"In the matter of Maggie Harris née Silber, not quite. Shall I tell you my mother's last words?" He didn't wait for agreement. "Maggie said, 'I told you that cow Esther Cohen would see me out.' It was wonderful." He was chuckling as he spoke. Annie couldn't help but chime in.

"It was pure, unadulterated Maggie," Geoff said. Then, without warning, his laughter became quiet tears.

Annie put her arms around him and held him while he wept. Eventually he pulled back a bit and looked at her and stroked her hair and kissed her softly on the lips. "Thanks for coming," he said. "It means a lot."

"As soon as you walked out the door, I realized how much I wanted to be here with you. Only for support. I didn't mean to intrude."

"You're not an intrusion," he said. "You could never be that. And one thing about all this . . . the timing could have been a lot worse. I am so damned glad Maggie got to meet you."

"Not as glad as I am to have met her. Your mother was unique."

The nurse appeared again; this time she walked down the corridor to where they were. Annie and Geoff stood up. "If you've finished your good-byes," the nurse said, "I'll take care of things." She nodded toward Maggie's room. "And there are some papers we need you to sign, Mr. Harris. You can come back and do it tomorrow if you prefer."

"I'd rather get it over wi—" Geoff broke off. He murmured an apology and drew Annie aside. "The spooks," he said. "I called them from the cab. They were heading over to my place. I told them you'd meet them there and explain everything. I said you could do it better than I."

"I'll go to your house now," Annie said. "As long as you're sure you're okay."

"I'm fine," he said. "I expect I won't be when it hits she's really gone, but for now . . . I'm okay."

Annie stepped in and hugged him hard. He hugged her back. Eventually they broke, but she took his face between her hands and stood on tiptoe for one last kiss. When it ended, she started to turn away and leave, then stopped. "I forgot. I don't have any money. I didn't take my bag when we left your house earlier. Fortunately I had a ten-pound note in my pocket and that paid for the cab here."

"Annie's hidden treasures," he said.

"You've noticed," she said, holding out her hand.

Geoff found his wallet and gave her a couple of bills and all his coins. They kissed again and he held on to her for a long few seconds. "Thanks again for coming," he whispered. "Thank you so much."

There was a red telephone marked "Taxi" inside the building's front door. Annie used it to summon a cab. "Twenty-nine Orde Hall Street," she told the driver, then leaned back and tried to shut off the thoughts of Maggie's death and how Geoff must really feel and switch to academic mode. She needed to organize a ton of facts that might seem random and unbelievable, and do it well enough so the MI6 guys were persuaded to shift their focus from Jerusalem to Rome. Otherwise—oh my God.

She had left number eight Bristol House unlocked.

At least she was almost sure that's what she'd done. She'd pulled the door closed behind her, but she hadn't locked it.

All Mrs. Walton's precious possessions, her pictures and furniture and china, much of it in her family for generations . . . *I know Auntie Bea would love to let her flat, as long as she was sure the tenant would look after her things.* The very first London obligation she'd assumed.

And what about the mural? What if somehow Philip Weinraub knew Annie and Geoff had figured out its significance? Maybe Weinraub would send someone to deface it. Why would he do that? She had no idea, but he'd burgled the place before. That's why she'd changed the locks. What good was that if she didn't use them?

On the other hand, maybe she had.

No, she had not. The more she thought about it, the more sure she was she'd left the flat unlocked.

The cab had crossed the river and was heading up Cannon Street. Annie leaned forward and knocked on the screen. The driver slid it back. "I've changed my mind," she said. "Take me to Bristol House on Southampton Row."

37

Dom Justin
From the Waiting Place

A short time after Diego di Mantova and I had revealed to each other that we both served the Speckled Egg, all of his party, including myself and Rebecca, left Jacopo's household in Strasbourg. In two weeks we crossed the Rhine, and a few days later we were in Freiburg.

I expected Diego would keep Rebecca with him as nurse to his children and companion to his nights for some time more. Instead, no sooner had we arrived in the town than he deposited her at a fine house in the Jewish quarter. "The master of the place was once a renowned silversmith. Now he is old and ill and waits to die," Diego told me. "He is a widower, and his wife of many years was barren. He is alone except for those he pays to stay beneath his roof. Swollen belly or no, he will gladly take Rebecca to his bed to warm his ancient bones. And she, clever girl that she is, will probably prevail on him to marry her before he dies and give her and the child his name. In the end, I have no doubt, he will leave her his fortune."

It seemed to me a good solution to the problem of Rebecca. Despite the sinful nature of our lust, I had many times found myself agitated by the thought of what awaited her and my unborn child. Now, with Diego's suggestion, I felt at peace regarding their future. I had, after all, already made her a secret gift of the most precious thing I possessed and the most effective protection I could offer.

While we were yet in the house of Jacopo, I hid one night near where she slept and waited until she went to Diego's bed, then searched among her things for a place to hide the small and precious Agnus Dei given me by Dom Hilary the night I last saw him. It is well-known that this particular sacramental has immense power. Like the blood of the lamb that marked the doorposts of the Israelites so the angel of death might pass over them, the blessed wax protects against all evil, all fear, and all enemies. It quiets the wind, prevents shipwreck, and guarantees safe passage and a happy death. There was nothing better I could do for Rebecca or the child.

I thought sure my gift was inspired by the Holy Spirit because when I looked for a safe place to hide the Agnus Dei, somewhere Rebecca would have it with her but perhaps not know she did, the silver tube that the Jew of Holborn had bestowed upon her came miraculously to my hand.

Rebecca had cleverly made a place for it in the heel of a boot, one of a pair that Diego's brother Giuseppe caused to be fashioned for her while we were in Metz. (What Rebecca had done to merit the gift, I never allowed myself to ponder.) That night in Strasbourg, while I searched for the perfect hiding place for the most precious sacramental in all Christendom, the heel of one boot parted from its body, and I saw in its hollow core the bequest given Rebecca by her father. For a time I trembled to touch that which perhaps Jesus Christ had touched, and I went on my knees before it and prayed for forgiveness for my sins, and even hers. Then the Spirit spoke within my mind, and I remembered what I had seen the old Jew do. I twisted the two silver knobs in the fashion he had. One end of the thing came free.

I recalled as well what he had said about the parchment inside the tube—that it was never to be removed or exchanged for another. That, however, was a Jew's thing, while what I wished to give her was a powerful talisman of the New Dispensation, the salvation come through Jesus Christ. Without hesitation, I removed the tightly rolled bit of parchment and put in its place the bloodred Agnus Dei. Then I closed the tube and returned it to the hiding place Rebecca had made in the heel of the boot. Ever after I had a sense of profound peace about her and the son or daughter—flesh of my flesh—she would bear.

Later I unrolled the parchment, curious to know what might be written on it, but the thing was in the language of the Hebrews, which I could not read, so I put it on the kitchen fire.

A week later we were in Freiburg, and a few days after that I was at last high in the mountains of the Black Forest, in the Rhenish Charterhouse where, finally confessed of all my sins and unburdened of the terrible story of the travails of our brethren in London, I would spend the rest of my earthly days.

There, as in all other Charterhouses, every Thursday I walked with my new brother monks, changing partners each quarter of an hour. On one such occasion not long after I arrived, I took my place beside the monk called Dom Felix and greeted him in Latin, since in those early days we had no other common language. He smiled and took my hand and pressed into it the speckled egg of a quail.

It was a year before I had enough of the Rhenish tongue to ask Felix if there were other priests of the True Obedience of Avignon in the monastery, and to learn that there were not, though a few others of our allegiance could be found in the area. Indeed, it was because Diego di Mantova had accompanied me to that Charterhouse that Dom Felix had known I was of their number. Eventually I told him of my remarkable journey and how, having been priested by the Speckled Egg himself, I received from his hand the Agnus Dei blessed by the last true pope. I offered as well an explanation of sorts as to why I could not show him that precious relic. "It is where Almighty God meant for it to be," I said. But at that time I said no more.

A few years later, after we knew of Henry's having seized all the monasteries of England, including our Charterhouse in London, I learned that the tale of the precious relic I had brought with me out of England had made its way beyond the walls of the monastery. It occurred to me to wonder if indeed the story had first been circulated by Dom Hilary himself. It seemed possible because Henry had not dared send this former bishop, so popular with the ordinary folk of London, to Tyburn but had instead arranged that he should "escape" to France, to La Grande Chartreuse. But whether through Hilary or someone else, a legend had come to surround the Agnus Dei of Clement VII, the last true pope. Among the adherents of the True Obedience, it was said that when the blessed wax was found and taken back to England, the imposters in Rome would be overturned, England would be once more a Catholic land, and a pope of the true succession would ascend to the vacant chair.

As for Rebecca, it had gone with her almost exactly as Diego had predicted. She had been taken in marriage by the old Jew of Freiburg, and a month later he was dead and Rebecca had become a wealthy widow and heiress to a business—the smithing of silver—that she well understood. Sometime later, as if to give me comfort for never seeing the child who was flesh of my flesh, I heard that in her widowhood Rebecca had given birth to my son. (Though that I was his father was a secret she and I would take to our graves.) He was called by the Rhenish name Gottfried, which in English is Geoffrey.

That such information reached me in the silence and solitude of the Charterhouse seemed to me another mark of how closely the good God watches over all our affairs. It was a sign I never forgot, and a memory that stoked my faith during the more than forty years I spent on earth after the adventures I have told of here.

Seven years later another Thursday walk changed everything. After the first hour of the customary three, the rotation brought Dom Felix and me together. We took a few steps in companionable silence, then he said, "I am now the Speckled Egg." I remember I paused, thoroughly surprised, and he touched my arm and urged me on lest we attract unwelcome attention.

"Dom Hilary went to his reward some months past," my companion said. "The leadership of our small band has passed to me."

I wished to kneel before him and offer my allegiance, but I dared not do so in that setting, so I murmured that I would be his good and faithful servant in all things. "That I have come to this peaceful place to live out my vows after the great turbulence and upheaval of my time in London and my perilous journey," I said, "is for me proof that Almighty God looks with favor on the True Obedience of Avignon."

Felix once more touched my arm, this time to show his acceptance of my oath of fealty. Then he said, "Now you must tell me the whereabouts of the Agnus Dei blessed by the last true pope. Where God means it to be, you said. Where is that?"

I did not hesitate but explained at once that the treasure was hidden in a silver case come from the Jewish Temple of Jerusalem before the Romans destroyed it, and as such likely had been touched by the hand of Our Lord and Savior Jesus Christ when he went to that Temple to pray, as scripture tells us he did. "That precious artifact is called in the tongue of the Hebrews a mezuzah. This one belongs to the Rebecca who came with me as far as Freiburg. It was given her by her father, and she solemnly promised to pass it to her firstborn and charge him to do the same, always with the admonition that the contents of the thing must never be disturbed."

"And is this Rebecca," he who was now the Speckled Egg asked, "she who is the widow of the Jewish silversmith of Freiburg?" I nodded agreement, and he added, "In those circumstances it would not, I think, be easy to get the thing back. She has become a powerful figure in the town, known to all, and the mistress of a thriving business that she grooms her only son to take over someday."

"Perhaps we are not meant to get it back." I blurted out the words without thinking, then realized my presumption, given that the man who walked beside me was now, in the eyes of us of the True Obedience, the Vicar of Christ on earth. "Though if you wish, I shall of course leave this place and try—"

He interrupted me with a quiet but forceful admonition. "You have wandered enough, Dom Justin. There will be no more adventures. Take the discipline an extra time every day for a week for having considered such a thing."

It was almost time for us to switch partners, but Dom Felix asked me one more question: "How will we know this mezuzah from any other?"

I explained exactly what the thing looked like, including the engraving of the almond branch on its face and even the special way in which it opened.

"Very well. For now we shall leave the mezuzah where it is, but the description and the secret of its whereabouts will be passed from Speckled Egg to Speckled Egg, and we will strive always to watch the sons of the sons of the Jewish silversmith of Freiburg. Be at peace, Dom Justin. You have played your part."

And so it was until, in my sixty-sixth year and on a Thursday walk, I stumbled over a broken branch and fell and broke my neck and came here to the Waiting Place.

Giacomo the Lombard was here. I saw him for a moment only, his face suffused with glory. I stretched out my hand, but he did not see me and walked toward the effulgent light that sometimes glows in the distance and then disappeared. I am aware of many others, though most I cannot see. I asked after Rebecca and learned she had already come and gone. "To the light?" I inquired.

"Ah yes, to the light."

I asked then after Dom Hilary and the others who were in their lifetimes called the Speckled Egg, but my guide turned away and did not answer.

There are a deal of unanswered questions here. Apart from that glow which sometimes appears but always hurts my eyes, causing me to turn away, it is a place shrouded with many dark clouds—the cumulative fog of our ungoodness, I am told. But as I have explained, there is here nothing of time as we know it on the other side of the divide between death and life. It is always now in the Waiting Place. Despite that, it is cold and dark, and a place of great and sorrowful deprivation, where I and others like me strive to make reparation so we may cross to the other side where bliss is assured.

Now I have told my story. What next I ask?

I am told I must break through and right the gravest of my wrongs. The Agnus Dei will help me, and the woman has been made ready, harrowed by the sharp teeth of the prelude to true life that in our ignorance we call living.

I stretch out my hand . . .

❖

38

She'd made the right call. Number eight Bristol House was unlocked. The door to the flat opened as soon as Annie turned the knob. She hadn't turned off the radios either. It was nearly four in the morning, but the relentlessly informative BBC talked on. At the moment they were extolling the virtues of regular exercise, whatever your age. "Even a brisk walk of ten minutes a day can make an enormous difference if . . ."

The remote lay in its customary place on the hall table. She snatched it up but allowed the radios to continue to play. She would turn them off last thing, after she put out the lights.

She started from the back bedroom. She switched on the lamp and stood for a moment looking around. "If you're here," she said aloud, "I hope I've done what you want. I mean about finding the Speckled Egg. I'll do my best to convince the MI6 people to stop Weinraub. I promise."

She turned off the lamp and in the darkness stepped into the short hall. A sudden glow stopped her. And a low melodic sound; not so much chant as the prelude to chant. As if a long intake of breath. She turned slowly back to the room, already pretty much sure what she would see.

The ghost however was not there. The source of the light was the small package she had carefully wrapped in lavender-colored acid-free paper.

Agnus Dei, qui tollis peccata mundi . . . Not so much chant as an echo of a chant she'd heard countless times. The Latin phrases spoken or sung at every Mass hovered in her mind. Words repeated day after day, week after week. Every Mass everywhere. *Repeated somewhere every minute of the day and night.* At least that's what she'd once been told. Lamb of God, who takest away the sins of the world . . . *miserere nobis.* Have mercy on us.

Annie half whispered, half sang the words. "*Agnus Dei . . .*" The glow intensified and she was surrounded by warmth. She stretched out her hand. "What do you want me to do?" Even as she spoke, she knew. She took the small parcel from the top of the chest and tucked it in her bra, next to her heart. That was wanton disregard for the physical integrity of an ancient artifact and violated every rule of her professional world. Nonetheless it felt exactly right.

She experienced no particular heat, only that of her own body and also a sense of satisfaction. Or perhaps, after the sadness of Maggie's loss and Geoff's bereavement, a better word was *comfort*.

There was no mess to clean up in the kitchen—they hadn't stayed long enough to make one. Annie took a bottle of Bitter Lemon from the refrigerator, unscrewed the top, and took a drink; then she pulled the cord of the overhead light in the kitchen and went into the dining room. They'd spent no time there either. It was pristine. She flipped the switch on her way out. That left only her bedroom to deal with. Then she could go to Geoff's.

God, he must be feeling like shit. Would he take any comfort from Rabbi Hazan's notion of the river? In terms of death, what exactly did it mean? Had Maggie gone to some other reach, as Hazan had called it, and was it a difficult journey? Maybe it was Maggie speaking to her from wherever she was, saying Annie should take the old Agnus Dei that had been so long in Maggie's apparently unwitting possession. Maybe they were supposed to put the thing back in the mezuzah, remove the *klaf* Rabbi Cohen had put in its place. She'd have to talk to Geoff about that.

Annie switched off the bedroom lights.

Only those in the hall remained to be dealt with, and of course the radios. A woman was now discussing a museum exhibit, illustrations of the old Pale of Calais.

She took another swig of her soda, screwed the top back on, and wedged the bottle into the pocket of her jeans so both hands were free. She would first open the front door, then simultaneously turn off the hall lights and the radios, using one hand for each task. It was a practiced routine. The final requirement was to stretch out her arm and put the remote back on the table.

Done.

The lights in the outside corridor operated on time switches, one beside each flat. The stairwell lights, however, were on permanently. The reflected light they cast was enough for Annie to see to lock the door. She fitted the key into the first lock and turned it.

Coming here had been a good thing. Responsible. And the whole business had taken only a few minutes.

She found the special key that operated the second lock, then inserted and turned it. One problem remained. Even before this detour, she'd been late enough that maybe the spooks had given up and left Orde Hall Street. She didn't know the number to call to get them back. She'd have to get hold of Geoff and—

Footsteps.

Measured and deliberate and mounting one step at a time. Annie held her breath and listened. The footsteps grew louder.

Breathe, she told herself. This is an apartment building. Someone is coming home.

Or maybe someone with a quail egg wanted to climb up a couple of flights and pay her a visit.

She pressed her hand over her heart, over the ancient Agnus Dei. *Protects from malign influences and even sudden death.*

The corridor was without any architectural features, no nooks or crannies, just closed doors. There was nowhere to hide. Why should she need to hide? Someone who lived here was returning. That was a perfectly ordinary—

The footsteps stopped.

Annie drew another long breath and held it, straining to hear whoever it was unlocking a door on the floor below. She began counting the seconds. When she got to six, the footsteps resumed. They were still climbing. Really close now.

The stairs had become a trap. She could go back into the flat. But how long would it take to undo both locks? And what if whoever it was somehow had duplicate keys?

She ran toward the elevator. It was on her floor. She could see the cab through the small window in the outside door. Annie ran to it, yanked it open, and pushed aside the accordion grill. It opened with a loud clang. The footsteps stopped.

Annie flung herself into the elevator and pulled the outside door closed behind her, cursing the fact that it was heavy and had one of those air-brake systems that prevented it from shutting quickly. Finally it clicked into place. She shoved the grill closed and punched the button marked "Ground."

Nothing happened.

Annie banged every button she could see, over and over. The elevator did not move. The mechanism was old and creaky and didn't always work the way it should. She opened the grill a few inches, then slammed it shut a second time. The ancient elevator began a slow descent.

She passed the floor below. In the elevator she could hear nothing and had no idea if whoever it was had turned around and started down the stairs. You could go down a lot faster than you could go up. Please, God, let her get to the ground floor before the footsteps did. If she could get out of the building and onto the street, she'd be fine. Southampton Row was never entirely empty. There was bound to be—

The elevator slid past the entrance lobby and continued down.

She was in a basement of sorts. Lit fairly well. Through the window in the elevator door, Annie could see a small section of the main staircase. It made a sharp turn so she couldn't actually see where it went, but it had to rise to the lobby because there was nowhere else for it to go. Running up those stairs would be faster than using the damned elevator. She pushed open both doors and stepped into a narrower and shorter version of the corridors on the floors above. A door on her right looked as if it led to another flat. Probably a super. She could—

She heard the footsteps starting down the stairs. Not hurrying—slow and deliberate, as they'd been right along. Because her pursuer knew exactly where to find her and knew she was trapped.

Jesus God Almighty . . . *Agnus Dei, qui tollis peccata mundi* . . . She banged on the maybe-super's door. Nothing happened, and no one came. There was another door on the left. Annie hurled herself at it. The door gave way, and she flung herself forward and into complete darkness.

The door closed behind her, and Annie pressed against it, trying to catch her breath, feeling behind her for some kind of a lock or bolt. There was none. Against the small of her back, she thought she felt the knob start to turn. She knew tears were running down her cheeks, but they were not really connected to her. That was some other Annie, a woman who was about to give way to terror and despair. The real Annie, the one who had clawed her way out of a bottle, was not going to be trapped by some lunatic with a quail egg in his pocket.

"Not this time, you son of a bitch."

The whispered words disappeared in the darkness. She put out a tentative foot. Stairs. Annie went down. When the stairs came to an end, she stretched out both arms as wide as she could. She was in a narrow space. A corridor of some sort. Her right hand touched a stone wall, her left rough wood. Planks maybe. She moved forward, keeping her fingertips in contact with both the stone and the boards. After a few steps, her left hand touched a padlock. Then more of the unfinished wood and another padlock. Storage bins, she realized, probably assigned by flat; places in a subbasement where the residents of Bristol House could keep things they didn't need every day. Probably built originally to store coal for the fireplaces. Before pea-soup fogs ushered in the law that made everyone switch to inefficient smokeless coal and eventually install central heating, individual coal cellars had been a prized amenity in London buildings.

Figuring that out changed nothing, but it gave her courage. She walked a little faster, always listening for the opening of the door at the top of the stairs behind her. She heard nothing. And her eyes were adjusting to the dark, picking out a faint glimmer of light ahead. If she could—

Her left hand lost contact with the wall of wood. A few steps more, and the stone wall ran out as well. She was facing a junction of some sort, the entrance to a corridor that ran horizontal to the aisle in front of the storage bins. Annie stood still, trying to sense the building around her, using all her skills to mentally retrace the directions she'd come and the logic of the construction. Best guess, she was under Southampton Row looking west toward the museum, about to step into a north-south-running passage. Which at one time must have provided access for delivering coal, so it wouldn't be trucked through the public lobby. Meaning that somewhere this below-street-level passage was connected to the outside world.

Annie squinted to her left. In the direction, she thought, of Theobald's Road. She was pretty sure the faint light she was seeing came from there, but a good ways distant. It seemed that what she now thought of as the coal passage didn't serve only Bristol House. It extended along the neighboring buildings all the way to the corner. At that point there had to be a gate of some sort, probably opening into an alley. She stood still long enough to listen for the sound of anyone following her, heard nothing, and set off.

She was walking on uneven cobbles, which confirmed her idea about the age and purpose of the original construction. Thank God she had on sneakers. Still, for the first minute she went gingerly, always continuing to listen for sounds of pursuit. Nothing. How come? There were only two doors on the basement level and one was locked. Why had whoever was after her given up?

Maybe because there was only one way out of where she was, and her pursuer knew where she'd end up. Even so, she'd rather face whoever it was in an above-ground-level alley. Somewhere she could shout and be heard. And if she got there first, maybe she could get out of the alley and onto the street before there was any kind of confrontation. Annie broke into a trot. The sneakers helped to keep her footing on the treacherous cobbles, but a couple of times she stumbled and thought of what could happen if she tripped, maybe broke something. Don't think about that, Annie. Run.

The dark was becoming more gray than black, and the air felt different, as if she were outside. She could make out stone walls to either side. Lots of moss and damp patches. No sun here ever. Run, Annie. She saw a gate up ahead, and a few stairs leading up to it. Her heart was pounding. The adrenaline drench had revved her up, undermined her training. She had to draw deep gasping breaths to keep herself going. Run, Annie. Run.

She was there. She hurled herself up the stairs and flung herself at the heavy iron gate that barred her exit from the coal passage. It did not budge.

Locked.

Of course. That was sensible. The buildings didn't want to invite strangers. But it must open from the inside. No reason it shouldn't. Salt sweat was pouring into her eyes, and she couldn't see clearly. She felt up one side of the gate and down the other and found a metal box-type closing. There had to be a latch. She couldn't find it.

She found instead a keyhole.

The gate to the alley was locked from both sides. The residents of the buildings, the ones with legitimate reasons to be down here, had keys. She had none. Mrs. Walton had never given her a key to the storage cellar.

Annie pressed her face to the grillwork. She was looking at what she'd expected to see, a narrow service alley between two buildings, lit by the false dawn of the early English morning, and to the right the subdued nighttime glow of Southampton Row. She could make out a line of rubbish bins. Nothing else. No one. Annie opened her mouth to scream for help. Then she closed it. The guy with the quail egg—she'd decided it had to be a man—was probably out there. Waiting for her, maybe coming for her.

The smart thing to do was go back. Go all the way back as fast as she could and up to the lobby and out the front door. She'd be yards away from him then. Even if he saw her leave and came after her, she could outrun him. She swallowed her despair at the thought of retracing her steps and turned around.

Run, Annie. Run. Don't think about—

A hand grasped her shoulder.

She screamed and thrust her body toward the deepening darkness ahead. "No! No! No!" Her feet skittered on the cobbles, and she fell against the stone wall to her left.

It gave way, crumbling as if it were sand, and she tumbled into blackness.

Annie came to slowly, with no idea how long she'd been out. She was lying on her back, on something she could not immediately identify, looking up at a curved wall that became a curved ceiling that . . . she was in a tunnel, and she could see because there was low-level overhead lighting, tiny bulbs set into evenly spaced narrow recesses.

She tried to sense her body. Nothing hurt particularly. She flexed her fingers and felt grit beneath her hands. That's what she was lying on, a huge pile of sand.

She heard nothing. No one was clambering down from wherever she'd been to wherever she was. There were no footsteps racing through the tunnel. And no one, thank God, was touching her.

Slowly, gingerly, Annie got up. Both arms and both legs— everything—worked. She peered to her left and to her right. The most likely explanation had to be that she was in some kind of subway, probably out of use. Except if that was so, why were the lights still working? And how come there were no tracks and no provision for them? The space was some nine feet across and level, without the customary dropped bed for subway car tracks.

A passage then. Between one station and another. Part of the old tram tunnel possibly.

What help was that? She already knew the exit on Theobald's Road was barred. Also, that the nearest exit out of the coal passage above her head was locked. A moot point. She couldn't get back up there if she wanted to. The wall that was now some ten feet above her head had collapsed into a pile of sand. That's how come she hadn't broken her neck when she fell, but it was much too unstable to support a climb in the opposite direction. And something up there had tried to get her. The killer with the quail egg or . . . something. Better to take her chances on the Kingsway Tunnel. So what if the gates were locked? She could climb over them, or shout until someone heard her.

Annie paused long enough to work out her bearings, then turned to her right and started walking. In a few moments she realized it was easier than she wanted it to be. She wasn't climbing up toward Theobald's Road—she was traveling along a gradual descent, deeper into the hidden world below London. She pressed her hand over her heart and felt the paper-wrapped Agnus Dei, still in place. Lamb of God, *miserere mei.*

39

She was thirsty, but she'd lost the bottle of soda somewhere along the way. Probably when she fell into wherever she was. And because she wasn't wearing a watch, she had no idea how long she'd been walking. It seemed to make little difference. Nothing changed. The tunnel was the same height and width, the lights spaced at the same distance, the descent steady. She should have been able to estimate how deep she was, but she couldn't make herself concentrate on that kind of calculation. She was too busy fighting back terror. How long could she be lost down here? How long before Geoff—dealing with no less than the fact that his mother had just died—realized Annie was missing? How long before anyone was able to figure out she'd gone down to the subbasement, then trace her route to where the wall caved in and puzzle out where she was?

Too long. She could die down here before—

She told herself not to be melodramatic. There had to be maintenance crews of some sort, and this tunnel was a connector to somewhere else. That, after all, was the only reason anyone built a tunnel. When you get to wherever it's taking you, she reminded herself, there'll be an opportunity to reassess the situation.

More time passed. She walked farther and farther from where she had started, always going deeper into the bowels of . . . what? She no longer had a theory that fit the facts. There were no signs of tram tracks or anything that might link where she was to where she'd thought she might be.

Fear was a physical thing, she could feel it expanding in her belly and rising into her throat. She forced it down, burying it under an equally instinctive commitment to survival. One foot in front of the other and the other and the other, until . . . there was an opening to her left, leading to an even steeper descent, but at the end, brighter light. Annie began to jog toward what seemed a beacon of hope.

"*Benedicite, omnes.*" A blessing on all.

Annie heard the words before she saw anything. The monk? Down here?

The passage in front of her made an abrupt right-angle turn. The sound was coming from somewhere beyond that bend, while on this side of it she thought she saw a slight deepening of the shadows that might indicate the opening to another spur. Slowly, very tentatively, Annie took a single step. And then one more.

"*In nomine Patri, et Filio, et Spiritui Sancto, Amen.*" Then, immediately following the chant, Annie heard a startlingly familiar voice. "We must talk."

Jesus God Almighty. The person handing out the blessings was Philip Weinraub.

Annie inched forward. She'd been right about the opening to another spur. She was level with it. She could head in that direction, away from Weinraub's benedictions and commentary. Or she could take one more step and edge around the corner and see what was happening.

Two steps in fact. A few feet of dim passage lay between her and a large, brightly lit room. Wooden folding chairs were scattered about, and there were tables stacked in a corner, as well as South Sea Island scenes painted into trompe l'oeil windows. Maggie said the old spy tunnels had had a restaurant with fake windows. This had to be it. Now, however, the spies were gone, and it was a gathering place for crazy people.

Weinraub was maybe ten feet in front of her. He was dressed entirely in black but with a white clerical collar. He was speaking to Jennifer Franklin and a man who had to be her husband. They both wore white. Jeans and a T-shirt for the guy Annie thought must be Rob. Jennifer had on a gauzy, long white skirt that fluttered around her legs, and a white T-shirt pulled taut over her swollen belly. Her golden hair and her bronze tan shimmered beneath the blue-white fluorescent light.

"As soon as the imposter dies," Weinraub said, "and the Conclave begins, I shall fly to Rome. The time will at last be right, and shortly thereafter the entire Christian world will be ready for the truth."

"But the Agnus Dei," Jennifer protested. "We still don't have it, Holiness. If—"

Weinraub cut her off with a raised hand. "You cannot yet call me that. Not until everything is revealed and I am pope. Now I remain only the Speckled Egg."

"But you're supposed to be the real authority," Rob said. "The true Vicar of Christ on earth. You've been saying so right along."

Weinraub nodded. "By the grace of God, I am."

"Then it seems to me you should have the answer to Jen's question. How come we don't have the mezuzah and the Agnus Dei? They're supposed to be in our possession when the true pope returns to Rome."

"They are supposed to be in England," Weinraub corrected. "I believe they are. And if the Speckled Egg before me had not died suddenly, we would know exactly where among the Jews we were to look for it. He would have left instructions for how to decode his mural. I hoped there would be enough time for the Kendall woman to uncover its secrets. As it is, the hand of God has struck sooner than we expected, and the Antichrist is dying. Our moment has come, and I must be ready to take my rightful place."

Annie saw Jennifer shake her head. "I think we should wait until we have the mezuzah. We can't do . . . do something so drastic, unless we're sure." She sounded genuinely upset. Tears were muffling her words.

Something drastic. Gas, Geoff had said. Or maybe a fire or a bomb. Jesus God Almighty . . .

The Franklins might have doubts; Weinraub clearly had none. "We can't delay any longer. Everything is ready, and as I said, this is our time. Rob, you shall accompany me to Rome. Jennifer, you will wait in London to welcome the others. The true believers will come from all over the world as soon as I send the word. You're to bring them here to our twenty-first-century catacombs and wait for my instructions."

Annie had heard enough. All she had to do was get out of this god-damned tunnel and talk to someone who could not just put the pieces together but do something. Slowly, very carefully, she drew back.

Weinraub said something about a blessing before they left.

"Hang on—" Rob cocked his head in the direction of the door. "I thought I heard something."

Annie caught her breath.

"*Benedicite, omnes, Pater et Filio*—" Weinraub began.

"Hang on, I said! I'm sure I heard something."

Annie stopped moving. The little paper-wrapped parcel in her bra was burning hot. It felt as if someone were holding a lit torch to her flesh. She reached in and tore it away from her breast, but kept as tight a grip on it as she could. She mustn't drop it. She mustn't.

"*Agnus Dei, qui tollis peccata mundi*"—the chant that filled the tunnel did not come from the direction of the old restaurant—"*miserere nobis.*" The sound reverberated off the walls and the ceiling. It was as if a hundred monks were singing, a thousand

She heard the slap of a hand against a wall. Someone had hit a switch and the passage was flooded with bright light. She froze. So did the others. But they were staring straight at her. Two heartbeats. Three. Annie spun around and ran. The chant had stopped, but she could hear pounding footsteps coming after her.

There was no point in going back the way she had come. She dived into the spur. Moments later she confronted a dead end flanked by a pair of exits to one side and a single one opposite it. With nothing to go on but instinct, Annie picked the leftmost exit and raced forward.

Behind her the pursuers reached the same need to choose. A moment of indecision, then a flurry of footsteps, resulting in just one set remaining clear enough to be heard. They had split up to follow all three options. Only one of them was now behind her.

Annie looked around, searching for some sort of advantage, desperate to overcome the fact that Weinraub and Jennifer and her husband had some familiarity with this maze. She spotted a niche up ahead, identified by a break in a shadow of the sidewall's expanse. If she could squeeze into that crevice, hide there until whoever was following her had passed, then double back, she could . . .

Better still, there was a breaker handle in the niche. It was painted bright red. Her pursuer's footsteps had grown louder and closer. Annie was still clutching the Agnus Dei, but with her other hand she grabbed the handle and yanked it down.

The lights went out.

The darkness was absolute. Her eyes could not adjust sufficiently to make out even shadows. As for sound, she heard nothing. Whoever was in the tunnel with her was waiting and listening as well. The Agnus Dei was no longer hot. She slipped it deep into her pocket, then held her breath, sucking in her stomach and folding her arms in front of her, making herself as small as possible so she could wedge herself deeper into the niche. Five seconds went by. Six. The footsteps started again. Slow and cautious this time. She tried to decide if it was Weinraub or Jennifer or Rob, and which one she stood a better chance against. She had no good ideas about either question. In a few more seconds, whoever it was passed by her, close enough that she could hear the soft sounds of breathing, and went on.

Annie waited until the echo faded, then let out her breath, climbed down, and pressing her body against the wall for guidance in the total darkness, went back the way she'd come.

Some ten feet along she felt a break in the wall. It was so narrow she hadn't noticed it when she passed this way the first time. She had to turn sideways to get through. Another dead end probably. If she got caught here, she'd be trapped. But after a few steps the tiny passage widened. Only a little at first, then a little more. Then she had to blink a couple of times because she was in an area where the lights were still on, in a small square room that housed only an old-fashioned switchboard. And beside it, on the floor, a relic from that same long-past age: a telephone with a rotary dial.

Annie bent down and grabbed the phone. Please, God, let it somehow be working. Please, please, please. She pressed the receiver to her ear. There was a dial tone.

It wasn't 911 in England, she reminded herself. It was 999. She put her finger in the dial, but she didn't move it. How could she explain who she was? Where she was? Who was threatening her? A second went by. Two. She made up her mind and began dialing. Each clattering return of the old-fashioned wheel sounded thunderous in the silence. She stretched the telephone cord to allow her to get as close as possible to a short flight of steps leading up to a door. It was closed, but she had to hope for the best. That door was the only way out of here, other than the sliver of a passage that led back into the darkness. She finished dialing and waited. Nothing happened for what seemed like an eternity. Then it was ringing.

Pick up. Pick up. Pick up.

"Geoff Harris here."

"It's me. I'm—"

"Annie, where are you? I've been—"

"I'm in the spy tunnel. Not far from the restaurant with the painted-on windows. In a switchboard room. Weinraub's down here. And Jennifer and—" Voices. Coming toward her. "I've got to go. They're coming."

"Try and get to those gates!" Geoff shouted into her ear. "The ones at the top of Kingsway!"

The voices were louder. Annie dropped the phone and dashed for the door at the top of the stairs. She reached for the handle. It turned. The door opened, and she pelted down yet another tunnel.

Running, running, running. No sense of direction left. Get to the gates, Geoff said. So he'd know where to find her. They were locked and chained. Never mind, he would find a way in. Geoff was coming for her from the direction of the old gates. But Theobald's Road might as well have been in Tibet. She had lost any ability to figure out where she'd been or where she was going.

It seemed to Annie she had been fleeing for a lifetime, running in a nightmare that was stuck in an endless loop: tearing down one passage after another, always pursued, always coming up against a dead end, never finding a way back to a world she understood.

That wasn't true. She'd found the phone and called Geoff. Help was on the way. And she hadn't heard anyone coming after her in some time. Maybe five minutes. Maybe ten, maybe twenty—she didn't know anymore. It didn't matter. She had to keep running. She turned yet another corner and half-ran, half-staggered down a short passage. Her sneakers felt like lead boots, and each step echoed in her ears. The tunnel ended in a door. There was nowhere to go except back the way she came. She opened the door on yet another room. This one was large, with bright lights, and a wooden floor covered in a film of dust, but it still looked like what it had once been: a gym of sorts. A pair of disused soccer goals were pushed against the far wall, with a stack of balls lodged between them. The place they'd played the indoor football Maggie talked about. What good did it do her to know that? None.

The blood was pounding in her ears. Her chest was on fire. Annie leaned against the wall and bent over and clutched her knees, gasping as she tried to suck in enough oxygen to keep from passing out. She had to stop somewhere long enough to catch her breath. Try and figure out where she was. But not here. There was no way out of this room except the way she'd come in. If she were caught here, she—

"So, Dr. Kendall, I believe you may at last have a report for me."

Philip Weinraub was standing in the doorway smiling at her. There was something in his hand. It was very small, but Annie knew at once it was a gun.

He moved the weapon, as if to be absolutely sure she saw it. "Tell me, please. Then you can go."

She knew he was lying, that she was slated to have a quail's egg put in her mouth, but there was no point in saying so. "I don't know what you're talking about."

"But you do, Dr. Kendall. I congratulate you on a remarkable feat of scholarship. It is apparent to me that you have discovered the whereabouts of the mezuzah I have been seeking for most of my life. And I suspect you know it contains the Agnus Dei consecrated by the last true pope. That was the meaning of the chant we heard. It was a message from Almighty God, not just alerting me to your presence, but signaling that now, at this most opportune moment, the mystery has been solved and I am His anointed. Tell me everything, please. Then we can conclude our business."

"You're insane. You killed the old cardinals and that poor women in Strasbourg because of your obsession. I'm not going to—"

"I sincerely regret the need for anyone to have died, but to save the Holy Catholic Church . . ." Weinraub was staring at her. His arm came up. She was looking straight into the barrel of the gun.

Protects from all malign influences . . . pestilence, fire, flood, and sudden death.

Annie shoved her hand into her pocket and clutched the sacramental.

In that instant he knew. His face glowed with triumph. "God be praised. You have it with you. I should have had more faith. Of course the prophecy was exact. When the time comes, we will have the most precious Agnus Dei in the world. Give it to me, Dr. Kendall. It is meant for me. I think you know that as well. Give me what you have."

"No, I won't. You—"

"*Agnus Dei, qui tollis peccata mundi, miserere nobis.*" Once more the ancient petition echoed through the tunnel; sung, it seemed, by the voices of the entire world. "*Agnus Dei, qui tollis peccata mundi, miserere nobis.*"

Annie heard as well another voice, this one whispering in her ear. Or perhaps only in her mind. *Fear not. Give him what you have. He will never possess what he seeks.*

The chant, meanwhile, rose to make a great crescendo. "*Agnus Dei, qui tollis peccata mundi, dona nobis pacem.*" Lamb of God who takes away the sins of the world, grant us peace.

Annie withdrew the paper-wrapped sacramental from her pocket. The singing cut off without an echo.

Weinraub was still pointing the gun directly at her. His arm was remarkably steady. He stretched out his other hand. "*Deo gratias*," he murmured. Then, more forcefully: "Move very slowly, Dr. Kendall. Nothing sudden. I assure you, I serve a cause much greater than the life of any individual. I will not hesitate to pull the trigger. Now, put what you have in my hand."

She did so.

Weinraub started to close his fingers around the small parcel. It burst into flames. He screamed and jumped back. Ashes drifted from his clenched fist. "Whore of Babylon! What pact with Lucifer have you—"

When she was a teenager growing up in New York, Annie had taken a self-defense class. *If you're looking down the barrel of a gun, your best chance is to present a moving target.* She propelled herself off the wall, headlong toward the only possible weapons, the goals and the soccer balls. Weinraub swiveled in place, growling in fury, following her with his eyes and with the hand holding the weapon. Annie darted to her right and then her left. She felt rather than heard a bullet pass by her cheek. He made another low growl, then took a few steps in her direction. For the length of perhaps two heartbeats she had the advantage she was after, the one where she was younger and many times more athletic.

She sprang for the nearest goal and pulled the metal post toward her. The netting came with it. Weinraub was running toward her. Unable to pull just the post free, Annie tried to shove the whole apparatus into his path. The balls were jarred loose and rolled in every direction. Annie kicked one out of the way, trying to aim for the madman who wanted to shoot her, but failing miserably. Instead her foot became tangled in the goal's side netting and when she tried to twist free she tripped and fell. Weinraub was standing above her now, the little gun raised and pointing at her heart.

"What fiendish thing did you give me? Where is the real—"

A soccer ball sailed across the room, lifting high before it dropped in an improbable swerving bend. The strike was perfectly on target. The ball smacked into Philip Weinraub's head and knocked him sideways. Then Geoff was on top of him, wresting the gun from his hand.

Two men were behind him. Guys with much bigger guns.

Typical boy stuff, Annie thought. Mine's bigger than yours. And she knew they were spooks, even though they weren't wearing sunglasses or trench coats.

40

She slept in his arms for twelve hours, then came gradually awake over a "breakfast" he brought her in bed—his—at what turned out to be seven p.m.

"So how are you?" he asked, handing her a second cup of strong tea laced with milk.

"Okay," she said. "Grateful." Maggie's voice played in her head: *Geoffrey requires someone strong enough to need him.* She had not expected such a graphic demonstration. "Thank you for rescuing me." Then she remembered not just the hell in the tunnel but everything that had gone before. "I'm sorry, I didn't think . . . how are you?"

"Holding up. I keep reminding myself of what Maggie said, that she'd had a good run."

"I think if you'd pressed the point, she'd have said a great run. She had you." Annie drank the last of the tea.

Geoff took the mug out of her hands. "What now? Are you ready to talk?"

"Not a lot, but there's something I have to tell you. I took the Agnus Dei from Bristol House. After the hospital, when I was locking up, I went into the back bedroom and . . . I was supposed to take it. I knew."

"Okay. I get that. Are you trying to tell me you lost it down there? We could—"

"I didn't lose it. I gave it to Weinraub. Even though I knew he'd shoot me anyway. The monk—at least I think it was him—told me to."

Geoff had been standing, now he sat on the edge of the bed and took her hand. "It's okay. Weinraub's going to stand trial and—"

Annie shook her head. "He doesn't have it. It burned up in his hand. I saw the ashes."

Geoff didn't respond for a few moments. Then: "Just like that?"

"Just like that." She wanted to tell him about the chant as well, but she was too tired.

"I need to sleep some more," she murmured, turning over. The last thing she remembered was his pulling the covers up to her chin.

The next morning he said he had to deal with funeral arrangements. "More papers I need to go and sign. Will you be all right on your own for a while?"

"I'm fine. Truly. I may go for a run." And when he raised his eyebrows: "A short one. Just so I don't seize up."

The truth, she realized an hour later, was that she needed to walk into Bristol House alone and confront any lingering demons.

There were none. She avoided the elevator, but she seldom took that anyway. Instead she climbed the two flights of stairs with no sense of pursuit, certainly not fear. When she opened the door of the flat, for the first time ever, she felt no compulsion to reach for the remote.

"Hello." She spoke the word aloud in the silence and waited. Then, after a few seconds: "You're not here, are you? I thought you might not be."

A few pieces of mail had been pushed through the slot. Annie reached down to claim them, shuffling quickly through three advertising circulars, then pausing at an oversize postcard with a glossy picture of a motorcycle in front of a large sign that said "Harley-Davidson Chicago." She was almost afraid to turn it over. *This is the Sportster 883. Dad says maybe for my sixteenth birthday. I take art too.* The words were neatly printed, almost drawn, and carefully spaced. He'd not left much room for his signature, however. *Ari* was squeezed in at the bottom, as if it were an afterthought.

Annie wept.

"Oh, Annie." Geoff flipped the card a few times, looking at the picture and rereading the message. "Fantastic. I can't imagine how you must feel."

"I'm not sure myself," she said. "I have to keep remembering that it's real. Contact. Finally. Despite everything."

He'd come to Bristol House after completing the funeral arrangements, and they were eating a late lunch she'd brought in ready-made from the nearby supermarket—chilled sorrel soup and beef and horseradish sandwiches. Geoff drank the last of his soup and looked at Ari's postcard yet again. "He knows who you are, you know. That's what he was trying to say when he mentioned studying art."

Annie knew she was beaming and couldn't stop. "I know."

"Have you decided on your next move?"

"Already made it. Sent a card saying I thought the eight eighty-three was a terrific choice. And that summer seemed finally to have arrived in London."

"Slow and easy," Geoff said.

"Exactly. All the hard things I need to say, to tell him, they'll come later."

It was called *Seudat Havraah,* a meal of condolence, traditionally prepared for the family by friends and neighbors, food to await their return from the cemetery. In this case, it was a crematorium, and Geoff was the only blood relative. His house, however, was crowded with people who had loved Maggie and now mourned her.

Annie knew few among the guests. Clary, of course. He gave her a big kiss, then introduced his wife. She was gorgeous, a young Lena Horne, Annie thought. And she recognized two of the waiters from the Greek restaurant in Primrose Hill. They were casting a professional eye over the impressive buffet spread out on Geoff's dining room table. It was the work of the friends who met for what Annie had likened to a sing-along with pots and pans. One—a tall skinny guy with a shock of blond hair—was a big-time soccer star as well as an amateur chef. He was also Jewish. He'd alerted the group to what should be done. "I was going to have a local restaurant send in a meal," Rabbi Cohen told Annie, holding tight to her wrist as if she might try to get away. "But Yossi here was way ahead of me. Who knew he could cook as well as, thank God, put Spurs into the final of the FA Cup? Or that he and Geoffrey were friends. The world"—the rabbi smiled in Annie's direction—"is full of wonders. Like Maggie," he added. "Maggie was one of the world's wonders."

"I wish I'd known her longer," Annie said. "But I'm glad for the time I had."

"In the Talmud it says—"

Cohen didn't have an opportunity to repeat what some ancient rabbi had said about the duration of friendship. Geoff nudged past Yossi the footballer so he could stand next to Annie. "You two are not permitted to steal my girl." He put an arm around Annie's waist. "There's no special offer for strikers or clergymen."

"Annie," Si Cohen said, "is a bargain at any price."

Someone called Yossi's name from the kitchen, and he excused himself and left. "Just as well," Geoff said. "Otherwise I'd have to kill him. Because of that header."

"He means," Cohen explained to Annie, "that Spurs, the team I support, played Portsmouth, the team Geoff supports, in the cup semifinal. And it was Yossi who put Portsmouth out of the competition with a goal in overtime. The absolute best header of last season. Everyone agrees."

Annie had no idea what the FA Cup was. But she was definitely developing opinions about English football. "Not in my view," she said. "Someday I'll tell you about the greatest header in this or any other season."

Geoff grinned and hugged her closer. "It's not a header because of where it lands. It's a ball you hit with your head rather than your feet."

The sports banter dried up and blew away, as such talk always did at funerals. "Geoffrey," Cohen began, "I don't want to pry, but . . ."

"We said the prayer," Geoff said. "Not five minutes after I got there." He explained about Maggie knowing the words. Si Cohen smiled when he heard that. Geoff skipped what Maggie had said about Cohen's wife.

Yossi returned, carrying a plate he held out for the rabbi's inspection.

"I told the group simple food and that hard-boiled eggs were traditional. So Atkins"—he nodded in the direction of the big man Annie had met before, the one who owned the restaurant across from the Temple— "brought hard-boiled quail eggs in, and I quote, 'champagne aspic layered with ribbons of parsley and a balsamic vinegar reduction.' A *goyisher kop*, but the guy can cook."

You didn't have to be Jewish to get it. Even Annie laughed.

"Quail eggs," Simon Cohen said after Yossi left, "we will talk about later. Whenever you have time, Annie darling. Maybe Sunday for tea."

The spooks were not so accommodating. Under the circumstances, they were willing to wait until after the funeral, but the next day Dr. Kendall and Mr. Harris were expected at the ordinary-looking high-rise on the South Bank side of Vauxhall Bridge. The building, as all London knew, where the spies were.

Annie and Geoff were debriefed separately. Annie got someone who, according to the brass plate on the desk of an otherwise featureless room, was called Malcolm Fallsworthy. "Please sit down, Dr. Kendall."

She did so. And smiled and waited. Her plan was to answer his questions as honestly as she could without volunteering anything; the goal being to avoid discussing the Carthusian in the back bedroom of Bristol House. If the monk came up despite her best efforts, she would depend on Rabbi Hazan and Einstein and T. S. Eliot and the river. Play the academic card and drown him in speculative analysis. Make it sound absurd for him to say *You're a drunk and you've been hallucinating and I have your rap sheet right here, so tell me why I should believe a word you say.*

"Now," Fallsworthy said, "please tell me how you became involved with Philip Jeremiah Weinraub."

Annie went through the approach from the Shalom Foundation, ending with the fact that she had made arrangements to arrive in London the beginning of May.

"Canceled your contract, you mean." Fallsworthy was stating a fact, not asking a question. "With . . . the Davis School." That last after a glance at his notes.

"Yes."

"I see. I presume that was because Weinraub was particularly eager for you to start on his project immediately. Any idea why that might be, Dr. Kendall? The haste, for one thing. You in particular, for another."

They had come immediately to a slippery slope, but she saw no possibility of avoiding it. "At the time I had no idea why the need for speed. I now believe it was because Weinraub had insider knowledge. I think that's why, after I'd been working in London three weeks, he showed up at the Connaught Hotel and began to apply real pressure. It makes sense only if he'd become aware that the pope was much sicker than the Vatican was publicly admitting. So there was going to be a conclave sooner rather than later." They had found Weinraub's packed suitcase in the tunnel, ready for his trip to Rome. It contained a perfectly tailored white cassock and matching beanie, along with the last word in modern-day Vatican chic, pointy-toed red shoes. His papal delusions were thus a matter of record.

"As for why me . . ." Annie bit her lip, then plunged. "I haven't managed to do anything important professionally in some years. I think Philip Weinraub believed he could manipulate me and that I'd be so grateful for the opportunity to do possibly noteworthy research, I wouldn't ask awkward questions."

"Which did not, however, turn out to be the case."

"It did not."

According to the *International Herald Tribune* and *L'Osservatore Romano,* the carabinieri used bomb-sniffing dogs. The explosives had been planted in the crawl space over the ceiling of the Sistine Chapel, directly above the pointing finger of God. The papers reported that a Swiss Guard and a senior member of the Vatican Secretariat of State, a Croatian priest, were being held for questioning.

"Can you explain, Dr. Kendall, exactly what this 'noteworthy' research was supposed to be?"

She told him about the Jew of Holborn and the Judaica scattered across Europe in his name. And she had the feeling he already knew a good deal about both. "I was to discover the source of the treasure."

"Which Mr. Weinraub believed to be here in London."

"Yes. I've come to believe he thought there was a Templar connection." Every conspiracy theorist with an Internet connection wound up with the Templars. She was tossing him a well-chewed bone.

Fallsworthy did not take it. "Was there not one particular piece of Judaica in which Weinraub was particularly interested?"

"I can't say exactly. He was demanding and insistent about a lot of things." She was not going to give him Maggie's ancient treasure. Nor would Geoff. *I never asked for it or expected it, Annie. But if we're right and after five hundred years, maybe longer, I'm next in line . . . I'm not going to be the one to break the secret chain.* She wouldn't mention the Agnus Dei either. Weinraub might talk about it, but what could he say? She gave it to me and it burned up in my hand. Without searing his flesh no less. Screw Weinraub. He could say whatever he wanted and it would simply be put down to the fulminations of a madman.

Fallsworthy tented his fingers and held them below his chin. Just like Rabbi Cohen—maybe they taught the gesture in spook school. "We have been watching Philip Jeremiah Weinraub for some time," he said. "We were asked to do so by our counterparts in Israel. When Mr. Harris came in a few days ago, to talk about your suspicions concerning the Shalom Foundation and the Temple Mount, they fit with the thesis we had been formulating. Turns out, however, we were all wrong. Mr. Harris, the Mossad, the FBI, our associates in France—all of us were guarding, so to speak, the wrong barn. Meanwhile the horse was galloping off in the opposite direction. But you and Mr. Harris, Dr. Kendall, managed—one might say in the nick of time—to get it right. Can you tell me how you came to the conclusion that the target was Rome rather than Jerusalem?"

Because a ghost shoved me in the back so my cell dropped, and when I bent down to get it, the evidence hit me in the face. No way she'd say that.

Not if he took her to a dungeon and applied thumbscrews. "A lot of the clues played to my particular historical expertise," Annie said. "And Geoff Harris has excellent political contacts. In the end, I expect we got lucky."

"Luck does seem to have played a part." Fallsworthy managed a thin-lipped smile. "Let's move on. The PJ have also been watching Weinraub, and they—"

"The PJ?"

"The Police Judiciaire, our opposite number in France. Like us they surveil dissidents as a matter of course. Weinraub's followers are, however, a very small group—at most a few dozen people worldwide. All are in custody now. They call themselves"—Fallsworthy looked again at his notes—"the True Obedience of Avignon. Any light to shed on that, Dr. Kendall? As an historian."

She explained about the disputed conclave in 1377, and the Clement VII who was the antipope. "But that there would still be people willing to kill over that argument seems insane."

The cardinals had refused to leave Vatican City as long as their conclave remained in official session. They were kept under guard in St. Peter's while the search was conducted. Once the bomb was defused, they went back to business. White smoke from the Vatican that very morning. The Catholic Church had a new pope, a French cardinal as it happened. But from Paris, not Avignon.

"So it might seem," Fallsworthy said. "But there were those two odd deaths of elderly cardinals, both of whom were left with quail eggs in their mouths. And a woman who was murdered in Alsace. It's not immediately clear why she was killed, but she too was left with a quail-egg calling card. I'm particularly interested in what you can tell us about that, Dr. Kendall." Fallsworthy shuffled the papers on his desk. "According to what you said when you first came out of the tunnel, that's what Weinraub called himself—not the pope, rather the Speckled Egg."

She'd been a blathering, burbling idiot, and she couldn't now remember exactly what she'd said, only the feel of Geoff's arms around her and the ferocious way he'd fended off the questions the two guys with him were hurling at her. *Later. She's in no state to talk now. Unless of course you want to give me material for a great show about MI6 harassing a visiting scholar . . .* "That is what Weinraub said, Mr. Fallsworthy. That he was the Speckled Egg."

Fallsworthy looked at him for a moment, then went on. "Two clerics," he repeated, "and one rather ordinary Frenchwoman in a tiny Alsatian village. I know what you told our people about the old cardinals, but the woman . . ."

"I don't know." Annie stared him down. And hallelujah, she didn't blush. Maybe because she was keeping quiet about the little she did know to protect Clary and his unorthodox arrangements with the French police, Judiciaire or otherwise. "You said Weinraub had only a small group of followers. Do you know who actually did all this killing?"

"Assassins for hire mostly," Fallsworthy said.

"But not in my case," she said quietly. "I promise you. He was definitely prepared to kill me himself."

"Fired and missed at least once. We know that, Dr. Kendall. It is precisely why we were immediately able to charge him and put him in prison. As for the change in modus operandi, you arrived with no warning and he perceived you as an existential threat. In the main, however, he outsourced his killing. Not surprising, since we now know he had longstanding connections to tap into. Mr. Harris was quite right, incidentally, Weinraub was born Philippe Wein."

Annie did not say that she'd never doubted Geoff's information, or point out that he obviously had better sources than the world's cops. Either that or he tried harder. She nodded and didn't comment. Fallsworthy went on speaking. "The Weins are an old Alsatian family. Financiers of many generations. But they were tarnished by associations with the Nazis in the forties, and a decade later they were connected to money laundering for a notorious French criminal ring operating out of Marseilles. Apparently soon after that scandal broke, Philippe Wein's parents moved to

New York. Ten years later Wein senior was making a great deal of money on Wall Street. We believe that provoked him to change his name."

Annie contrived to maintain a blank expression. He was ignoring Weinraub's years of masquerading as a Jew and associating himself with the Temple radicals—to the point of attracting the attention of the Mossad—but she didn't want to go there either.

"Apparently," Fallsworthy was saying, "the channels between French organized crime and the Wein family remain open. Given that plus his wealth, it wasn't difficult for Mr. Weinraub to find his contract killers, even some with bomb-planting expertise and a reach into Rome."

At last, an explanation for the trips to Strasbourg. Geoff had been puzzling about that. Annie did not intend to explain it to MI6—they could do their own police work. "This surveillance you tell me was on-going," she said. "How come it never turned up the fact that Weinraub was hiring hit men?"

"I doubt anyone watching him made exactly that connection." Fallsworthy was doing his best not to sound defensive. "It was, after all, two Roman Catholic cardinals who died, and the proprietor of an Alsatian grocery shop. In the case of Weinraub, the danger was supposed to be of an incident at the Temple Mount. As I understand it, you thought that as well, Dr. Kendall. Until something changed your mind. Can you tell me what that something was?"

"Pure happenstance, I dropped my cell phone and had to bend down to get in." She blurted out the words and realized she had walked right into it. Nothing to do but keep going. She explained how the clue in the mural made them realize the focus of the Shalom Foundation was Vatican City, not the Temple Mount. "According to what I overheard, Weinraub knew the clue in the mural existed, but not exactly where it was or what it meant."

"Ah yes, the mural. That seems to be at the heart of your involvement in this affair, doesn't it, Dr. Kendall?"

"It seems so." Maybe she could learn to control the blushes. Think of something else, like a guy trying not to have a boner.

"And you were living in the Bristol House flat as a result of a suggestion from"—he consulted his notes—"a Miss Sheila MacPherson, Mr. Weinraub's secretary in New York."

"Yes. The flat's owner, Mrs. Walton, is her aunt. I've been wondering about the two of them. Are they members of Weinraub's group?"

"No. Weinraub reached out to Miss MacPherson as he did to you. In her case, he brought her to New York from Edinburgh. It seems Sheila MacPherson is one of those people who believe the Jews must return en masse to the Holy Land so that the Second Coming of Christ can take place. She thought she was helping speed that day by working for the Shalom Foundation. What she was actually doing was enabling her employer to place you in the Bristol House flat. Presumably"—he looked up—"Mr. Weinraub believed your skill set to be what was wanted there."

"Presumably." Annie tried for another deflection: "About Bea Walton—"

"No reason whatever to connect her to Weinraub. I expect she will find your story quite a surprise. Dine out on it for years."

It sounded like a dismissal. Annie started to get up.

Fallsworthy waved her back to her chair. "Just another question or two, Dr. Kendall. It is not unthinkable that your professional expertise should have taken you to the point where you recognized the real intentions of Weinraub and his followers, but how did you know they were using the old tunnels as a meeting place?"

"I didn't."

"Then why did you go down there?"

"It was accidental. I already explained—"

He cut her off. "We are, of course, aware of the activities of Mr. Harris's late mother, her connection with Bletchley in the 1940s. And those of Rabbi Simon Cohen." Fallsworthy looked again at his notes. "I believe you are acquainted with Rabbi Cohen. So perhaps he told you—"

"Rabbi Cohen would never do anything that violated any kind of government secret. You cannot believe—"

"I assure you, Dr. Kendall, we are not accusing Rabbi Cohen of anything. The existence of those tunnels has been public knowledge for the last few years, reported in at least one newspaper. My question relates to your . . . adventure the other night. As I understand it, Mr. Harris left you"—another glance at the papers on the desk—"at ten to two in the morning because he'd been called to the bedside of his very ill mother. A minute or two later you impulsively decided to follow and ran after him, leaving number eight Bristol House unlocked."

Annie nodded, sure her misery showed on her face. Even the impulsive part sounded accusatory.

"Subsequently," he continued, "you returned to close up Mrs. Walton's flat, with the intention of afterward going to 29 Orde Hall Street and meeting with our people. Why didn't you do that?"

"I intended to. But as I was leaving the apartment, I heard someone coming up the stairs."

"Quite late for a weeknight, wasn't it?"

"I thought so. I became frightened. I got into the elevator, but it wouldn't start. I forgot that the gate is temperamental, and I pushed all the buttons before I thought to fix it. As a result, once I got it going, the elevator didn't stop at the lobby. It went down to the basement."

"And then?"

"Then I thought I heard the footsteps again. So I ran through the nearest unlocked door. It led to the old coal cellars. I believe they're used for resident storage these days."

"And from there"—Fallsworthy was looking at his notes again—"to a service passage that opens into an alley near the junction of Southampton Row and Theobald's Road."

"Yes, but the gate was locked."

He looked up. "You're quite sure of that?"

"I am entirely sure. I was desperate to get out. I couldn't because, as I said, the gate was locked." A little knot of panic was starting to form in her stomach. She tried to ignore it.

"Dr. Kendall, according to the building management, that gate is never locked from the inside. The fire laws don't permit it."

Fallsworthy was giving her what she thought of as his spook look. An intense, unwavering stare. This time she couldn't suppress the blush. "I'm not lying. I tried every way I could to get the gate open. It was locked."

"Yes, well, suppose we let that pass for now. Next point." He consulted his notes yet again. "Please tell me how you managed to get from the service passage to the much deeper tunnel that led to . . . the prior installation."

"I didn't actually 'manage' anything. It simply happened. The wall collapsed as I was running back to try and get out through the lobby." She was not going to mention the hand on her shoulder.

"Collapsed," Fallsworthy repeated. "Am I to take that to mean with no help from you?"

"Of course with no help from me. I didn't bring a pickax down there. The entire thing was unplanned. And frankly terrifying."

"Climbing down a slide of rubble of that nature in the dark, Dr. Kendall. A small woman like yourself—it must indeed have been terrifying."

"Rubble?" There was no rubble, only sand. That's why she didn't break every bone in her body.

"Rubble," Fallsworthy repeated. He took an iPhone from his pocket, tapped the screen a few times, and passed it to her. It displayed a picture of jagged boulders below a gaping hole in a stone wall. "This was taken soon after you were brought out of the tunnels, Dr. Kendall."

Annie couldn't summon a response. She had slid down a slope of sand. She only had to close her eyes to feel it again exactly as it had happened.

". . . structural engineer's report," Fallsworthy was saying, "only two months past. The wall was judged entirely sound."

She had to say something. "I can't help that."

"You insist, however, that you got into the tunnels by accident. Because a wall collapsed?"

"I do."

Fallsworthy reached down and brought up a plastic bottle of Schweppes Bitter Lemon, three-quarters full, but the top was screwed on tight. "One of our people found this at the base of the collapsed wall. We're told you drink a lot of this particular beverage, Dr. Kendall."

"Yes. I had a bottle in my pocket when I fell. Afterward it was gone."

"This bottle?"

Annie shrugged. "I suppose it could be."

They were both silent for a few seconds. Then: "Very well," Fallsworthy said. "One last point if I may. How did you manage to get your mobile to work from that depth? Calling Mr. Harris the way you did—that was extraordinary."

"That part's easy." Annie felt the knots in her stomach relax a tiny bit. "I didn't have a phone with me. I stumbled into the room with the telephone switchboard. I suppose it was part of what you call the prior installation. There was a phone there, an old one with a dial, and I used it. I called Mr. Harris rather than emergency services because I didn't know how I could expl—"

"Just a moment. Are you telling me you made the call to Mr. Harris's mobile from a landline in the tunnel? A phone you discovered in the old telephone exchange room?"

"Yes, exactly."

"Dr. Kendall, there has not been a working landline in that installation in over forty years."

41

"So maybe," Rabbi Cohen said, "Einstein and my old friend Hazan are right. Maybe time bends."

"And it bent enough for me to call Geoff," Annie said.

"And snapped back into position immediately thereafter," Geoff added. There was a certain amount of derision in his voice, despite the fact that the call log on his iPhone had no record of the call Annie knew she'd made and he knew he'd received.

"Have either of you a better explanation?" The question came from Timothy O'Hare, who, it transpired, served on an interfaith board with Simon Cohen and had been invited to join what Geoff was calling the wrap party and Cohen Sunday tea.

"I wish I did have a better explanation," Annie said. "Since I don't, I expect I'm going to be on the MI6 watch list for the next hundred years. Or at least until I go home next week."

"We can't prevail on you to stay?" Cohen asked.

She could feel Geoff's eyes on her. They had been circling the subject for three days, neither of them saying anything definitive about what was between them or what the future might look like. It was not something likely to be settled in Rabbi Cohen's study. "I would love to stay," she said, "but I can't afford it. I don't think Philip Weinraub is going to be paying my salary from his jail cell. I'll have to come back at some point to testify at his trial, but meanwhile I have to go home. I think I can get a job at MIT."

Sidney had e-mailed about a slot at the university's humanities library. *Doesn't pay a whole lot, but don't forget rent is considerably cheaper around here than in New York.*

When she told him, Geoff's only comment was that he'd heard it was bloody cold in Boston.

"I'm also going to write a couple of articles about my work here," Annie added, "but that will take a while. Meanwhile, a girl has to eat."

"Exactly so," Rabbi Cohen said. "Try one of the scones. I baked them myself." The room was as cluttered as always, but on this occasion Cohen had produced a tea tray—sturdy mugs, not Maggie's fragile flowered cups and saucers—and a plate of scones, as well as a bowl of thick cream and another of strawberry jam. "The one thing that was always down to me," he said. "Even before Esther got sick, I baked scones every Sunday."

"I'm impressed, Rabbi," Geoff said. "You'll have to consider joining our food group. We'll be short a member after I poison Yossi."

"Scones, I'm afraid, are the extent of my repertoire. So, Annie, where do we start?"

"I'm not sure. Maybe with the question I've been asking myself since this all started. Where exactly is the monk I've seen? And how come he could reach out to me?"

Rabbi Cohen looked at the clock on the mantel. "We've got an hour or so, Timothy. You can explain the nature of the universe in sixty minutes, I'm sure."

"I think," the priest said, "Dr. Kendall already knows as much as I could tell her about that. Heaven, hell, and purgatory. Page one of every Catholic catechism. Believing it is a good deal more difficult than knowing it."

"I interviewed a Protestant minister once," Geoff said, "who in between breathing flames and shouting about the Catholic whore told me there is no mention of purgatory in the Bible."

"None," Father O'Hare conceded. "It's a theological construct. Because our human ideas of justice demand it, and because what we believe of God's mercy makes it likely. An opportunity for the soul to be cleansed of sin. Personally, I believe in a God who gives second, third, and fourth chances. Probably more. Whether purgatory is an actual place . . ." He shrugged.

"I like lots of chances," Annie said. "But a place . . . I'm still working on Rabbi Hazan's explanation of the nature of time."

"If you mean Nachum Hazan, Dr. Kendall, he's a good man."

"Please, just Annie is fine. And that's who I mean. You know about the river?"

"Einstein and T. S. Eliot," the priest said. "I know."

"Apparently," Geoff said, "all you clerical types study the same primer."

"I've heard Rabbi Hazan speak," the priest said. "But the river and its bends is a metaphor for time, exactly as Annie said. It doesn't speak to that which is eternal and outside of time."

"Or," Annie said, "how a solid wall collapsed into a pile of sand, which somehow became stony rubble by the time it had its picture taken. Or how I got a dial tone on a telephone that hadn't been connected for forty years."

"*Ex nihilo nihil fit,*" Father O'Hare quoted.

Annie supplied the translation: "From nothing, nothing comes."

"Precisely," the Dominican said. "The idea of the river is immensely attractive and I would say logical, but where the river came from, and whether we're all going to simply float on it forever in some endless journey, are questions the theory doesn't address. Nor why, from wherever he is, your Carthusian monk decided to conduct what appears to have been a crisis intervention."

"Perhaps I must reconcile myself to not knowing," Annie said. "But Geoff does have something to add to our limited understanding of this business."

"A bit," he agreed. "I've had someone doing further checking in Strasbourg. It appears that on each of his trips there, Weinraub visited some old bishop. In his nineties now. According to my source, he was drummed out of the Catholic Church forty-plus years ago."

"Ah, yes," Father O'Hare said.

"You know of him?" Annie asked.

"Sorry"—the Dominican looked sheepish—"my lot are still expected to keep tabs on the dissenters. As for the bishop in Strasbourg, he was excommunicated in the late sixties because he insisted the Second Vati-

can Council taught heresy. He was one of the most vocal of the Sedevacantists for a few years. Then he just seemed to fade away."

"K'ching," Geoff said. "Another piece of the puzzle slots in. My New
York sources tell me Weinraub's parents became Sedevacantists in the
sixties, also as a result of what they saw as the liberalizations of the Second Vatican Council. I'm guessing that either the bishop found them or
they found the bishop. And between them they unearthed this largely
defunct True Obedience outfit, including a number of its old documents, and declared it alive and well and themselves its head."

"So," Annie said, "the ex-bishop was probably the Speckled Egg for
a time, during which tenure, I'll bet he ordained Philip Weinraub."

"And," Father O'Hare said, "made him the Speckled Egg when the
bishop felt he was too old to do the job. It's a short jump from there to
claiming Weinraub to be the next legitimate pope in the line established
by the Antipope Clement VII."

"According to Weinraub," Annie said, "your old spy tunnels, Rabbi
Cohen, were to be his twenty-first-century catacombs. I heard him tell
Jennifer that his followers were going to flock to London and she was to
lead them all down there. I'm not sure what they were supposed to do
when they got there. Maybe wait for the Second Coming."

"MI6," Geoff said, "has been liaising with the Vatican. The conclusion is that it's not much of a flock, just a couple of dozen nutters." No
one asked him how he happened to know what MI6 was thinking. "But
what about Weinraub being circumcised in France?" he continued. "Was
that to become a new requirement of the Catholic Church?"

"Unlikely," Rabbi Cohen said. "That argument was settled a couple
of thousand years ago. As soon as the Jewish Christians began allowing
gentiles to join their church. Insisting on adult circumcision is not a
good plan for growing your fan base. Timothy and I think it was a
wrinkle added by Weinraub's father uniquely for his son—part of
grooming Philip Jeremiah to take over."

"Precisely." Father O'Hare helped himself to a second scone. "But
anything that's been around for hundreds of years—a whole mythology

develops. Wein, or Weinraub if you will, and later his son, latched onto a number of its facets. Including the fact that there was supposed to be a mezuzah decorated with an almond branch, that it was of enormous importance, that some Jews somewhere in the old Rhenish Palatinate once had it, and that according to legend it would make its way back to England as a sign the true pope was about to be installed."

He stopped speaking and looked at the three others for a few moments. No one said anything. The Dominican nodded.

He knows we're not going to tell him anything more, Annie realized, but he suspects. About the mezuzah certainly. Maybe even the existence of the ancient Agnus Dei. She was aware of an almost palpable current between herself, Geoff, and Rabbi Cohen. They had become the secret-keepers. A good deal more benign than the True Obedience, however.

O'Hare stepped into the awkward silence and diffused the tension. "So in order for Philip Weinraub to maybe someday find the special mezuzah, and fulfill what he and his parents had decided was his destiny, he needed to be able to move freely in the Jewish world."

"For which reason," Annie said, "he put himself forward as a Jew and became involved in all kinds of Jewish fringe groups. That's why he set up the Shalom Foundation. It was useful as a front and allowed him to conduct a search for the Jew of Holborn. And since he knew about Étienne Renard's mural in Mrs. Walton's flat, he looked for a way to get close to that and found Sheila MacPherson, Mrs. Walton's niece, in Scotland. The MI6 guy told me Weinraub went to Edinburgh to invite her to come and work with him in New York."

"No stone left unturned," Rabbi Cohen said. "Have some cream, Timothy."

The priest's scone was already spread with strawberry jam. He waved away the additional indulgence. "Installing Annie in the flat where Renard spent the last years of his life must have seemed a stroke of brilliance. She had what Weinraub saw as perfect credentials."

"He knew I was motivated by a rather large need to establish professional bona fides," Annie said. "And that I have what the MI6 guy called the right skill set. And he needed the mezuzah for validation. That night in the tunnels, I heard the Franklins say their main objection to what Weinraub was planning was that he hadn't located it. I guess the archivist in Jennifer wanted all the *t*'s crossed and *i*'s dotted before she sanctioned mass murder. Weinraub had decided it didn't matter."

Geoff shrugged. "My guess is he figured this conclave was his last best shot. Popes seem to have longer and longer reigns these days. Benefits of modern medicine."

"And," Annie said, "he had the perfect setup, since he had a couple of people in place in Vatican City. What do you spy types call them, Rabbi?"

"Moles," Cohen said with a smile. "And now you must allow me a change of subject." He reached beside his chair and picked a book off the top of one stack. "This is for you, Annie. I have a quite wonderful used-book dealer, and I asked him to locate it for me." He handed her a copy of *Schismatics in the Late Middle Ages* by John Kendall.

Annie was speechless for a few seconds. Then, after she'd hugged him and put the book safely in her bag: "I've been wondering about something." She looked at the pair of clerics. "Do you think it was Étienne Renard who pushed me the day I dropped my phone and who followed me down to the coal cellar the other night? Or perhaps my father? Just how haunted is number eight Bristol House? One ghost or two, or even three?"

Cohen and O'Hare spoke at the same time: "One."

"Religious unity at last," Geoff said. "Annie and I have been talking about this all day. How come you two are so certain?"

"I expect," O'Hare said, "we're both thinking of some variation of the philosophical principle known as Occam's razor. 'Entities should not be multiplied unnecessarily.' The simplest answer, in other words, is most likely to be the one that's true. Why posit two or three ghosts when one will do?"

"I like it," Annie said after they left, while they were holding hands and walking for a bit, because it was a beautiful and balmy summer evening and they were in no particular hurry. "We don't need a second or a third ghost, so why try and fit my dad or Étienne Renard into the picture?"

"Renard fit himself in," Geoff said. "He lived in the flat and painted the mural."

"But he probably never knew about little Maggie Silber arriving with the Kindertransport. So he didn't know the mezuzah was already in England."

"Probably not," Geoff agreed.

The sound of children playing floated over their heads from somewhere in the grassy expanse of Hampstead Heath to their left. "What I think," she said when they'd walked a bit farther and the kids' voices had faded, "is that Étienne provided a glide path. Part of one at any rate. Along with the straight line of sight from the old Charterhouse to the back bedroom. Those things plus being related to you—that's what gave my monk, your zillion-times-great-whatever, a way in."

"You're still sure he was somehow my ancestor?"

"Geoff, you look just like him. There is no other explanation."

He was silent for a few moments, then: "Presumably that glide path existed when your Mrs. Walton was in residence as well. When you said you were reconciled to not knowing why the ghost chose you, did you mean it?"

"I meant . . ." She hesitated. "I'm reconciled to not being able to prove my theory."

"Which is?"

"I think he picked me because . . . I had space for him. I'm more hollowed out than most people. AA does that. I've had to learn to discard a lot of things that don't matter. And a lot more that matter enormously but that I can't do anything about."

"You mean the bit about the serenity to accept what you cannot change," he said.

She heard that flicker of derision again. Geoffrey Harris, important man of affairs, celebrated pundit. No time for feel-good nonsense like twelve-step programs. No time—at least no more time—for a charming but very damaged piece of goods. *I'm truly sorry, Annie, but it's a lot of baggage, a lot of risk* . . . Let it lie, part of her said. She couldn't do it. "That is what I meant. I think it's because of AA that I was psychically available."

"Fair enough."

She could read nothing in his tone of voice.

"Tell me something," he asked. "Do you think your ghost will come back? Pay regular visits, that sort of thing."

"Somehow," Annie said, "I do not. I think he's done with me."

Dom Justin
From the Waiting Place

Judgment comes not in thunderous tones but in a whisper spoken by the Word in the quiet of my soul: "And so, Geoffrey who became Justin, have you now forgiven yourself?"

"I, Lord? But it is for You to forgive me."

"And still you do not understand? I forgave you long since. Hanging on the Tree. What else did I mean when I said it was finished?"

"*Consummatum est.* I remember, Lord."

The light invites, and I start forward. Then I think of one last thing to do with this world of time and no time, which I now understand to inhabit the same space, a place I am about to leave. "The woman, Lord. Will she—"

"*Consummatum est,* Justin. Fear nothing."

I go where I am beckoned.

❖

"Hampstead's great," Geoff said after they'd been walking for nearly fifteen minutes, "until you want to get somewhere else. The tube's a mile away, and none of these buses are going where we want them to." About then he spotted a cab and flagged it.

Annie held on to his hand in the back of the cab and kept looking out the window. She wanted to absorb London through her pores, memorize every scene so she would never forget. Earlier that morning she'd said something about coming back at Christmas. Geoff had seemed . . . noncommittal. No doubt women all over London were lining up to take her place. Make that all over Britain. He might be getting the schedule in place right now. For the last ten minutes of the cab ride, he'd been using the hand she wasn't holding to work his iPhone. "Can I ask what you're doing?"

"Checking my mail. I've got something important coming."

"On a Sunday afternoon?"

"Yes."

They didn't say a lot more. Talked out, Annie thought. Both of us. We'll go back to his place and we'll make love, and I will not cry. Not once for the next seven days. At least not until I get on the plane.

He was still checking the phone when he unlocked his front door. "Blimey!" he said as the door swung open. "At last. Deal with the alarm, will you? I want to print this."

Annie punched in the code while he went straight to the desktop computer. Curious as she was, she really couldn't go and stand over his shoulder. She went into the kitchen and got a soda. "Coffee?"

"Not just now, thanks."

She wandered over to the couch.

At the opposite end of the room, the state-of-the-art printer whirred into life.

"You will not believe," Geoff said, "how many favors I had to call in to get this damned thing released on a Sunday. And that's leaving out the bit about them not wanting to issue the grant of representation for another week." He was collecting the pages the printer spat out while he spoke. There seemed to be quite a few of them.

"What," Annie asked, "is a grant of representation?"

"Tell you in a second." He gathered the last paper from the printer tray and came to sit beside her. "Maggie's estate," he said. "The executor's a Portsmouth solicitor. Not very convenient, but very Maggie. I'm guessing he might be an ex-lover. Anyway, here's what I wanted to show you."

He'd been thumbing through the sheaf of documents until he found the page he wanted. He handed it to Annie, saying, "Third paragraph from the top."

. . . my flat at number one Sharpleshall Street in Primrose Hill . . . to Dr. Annie Kendall, fully furnished with the exception of the piano which . . .

She couldn't speak for a few seconds. Finally she managed, "Geoff, I had no idea. I'll make it over to you right away. Before I go ho—"

He chuckled. "Do you for one minute think I didn't know about this? Maggie and I discussed it while she was in hospital, the same day she gave me the mezuzah. I told her it was maybe the best idea she'd ever had. And over the years"—he was stroking Annie's cheek with one finger—"she'd had some great ones."

"But . . . it's worth a fortune, Geoff. At least to me it seems like a fortune."

He waved that away. "Not important. But you've got to realize—it's not an obligation."

The blush came with such a whoosh of intensity, it made her feel weak. "I would never . . . Geoff, I'm not going to pursue you. I don't—"

"Not even if I say please?" he said.

It took her a couple of seconds to process that. Even then she wasn't sure. *I heart you, Annie Kendall.* "Please what?"

"Please pursue me. At least a little."

She wanted to respond in kind but couldn't. She had dreamed it, but the reality was overwhelming. She gestured instead to the paper with the announcement of Maggie's incredible generosity. "I can't accept—"

"Don't be an idiot. Of course you can. Maggie wanted you to, and so do I. I just don't want you to think of it as an obligation to me. But that shouldn't mean you have to move back to New York or Boston or wherever—and I understand it's not because of O'Toole—"

"It's nothing to do with him. I need to be where I can see Ari. When he's ready. The job at MIT means I can earn enough to live and visit Chicago once in a while."

"How about a variation on that plan?" he said. "I'm trying to get the probate done in time so you can let the flat for the summer. That's where the grant of representation comes in. I think we'll have it tomorrow, Tuesday at the latest. Then you'll be able to proceed. Even though it's the last minute, you can probably find some takers. So you'll have a bit of working capital. And I took the liberty of talking to my agent about getting you a book deal based on the Jew of Holborn and your research. She thinks it might be possible."

Annie sat very still, staring at him, allowing the flood of information to wash over her, shaking a bit.

"Jesus, Annie, I wish you'd say something. No? Fair enough, I've got more arguments. A book deal is bound to be more lucrative and get you more attention than a couple of articles in professional journals. If you give Elizabeth—she's my agent, I know you'll like her, American but been in London for years—if you give her a good proposal, she can get you a decent advance. Maybe enough to live on for a year or so. The working capital I mentioned will tide you over until the advance is paid. The two together can certainly be stretched to include a few flights to Chicago. Eventually I'm presuming Ari can come and visit you here. What teenager wouldn't jump at a trip to London? Annie, talk to me. What do you think?"

Someone strong enough to need him, Maggie had said. Was she really that strong? Ready to cede so much of herself? "I would love to do a book. I think I could. But—"

"But what?" And when she didn't immediately answer: "I want a life with you, Annie. A future, maybe a family."

I heart you, Annie Kendall. Apparently not just because of the red stilettos. She stood up. "I'm sorry, I'm not sure how to . . . I need some air."

She headed for the door.

"Annie, wait."

She could not wait. She was afraid to wait. She pulled the door open and ran into the street.

A car came around the corner from Great Ormond Street on two wheels and raced down the road. A woman was crossing, pushing a baby carriage. There was the screech of brakes and the smell of burning rubber as the car—a bright red Maserati—squealed to a stop inches from the woman and the child.

"Jesus! No! Annie!" Geoff ran out of the house screaming her name.

Annie stood where she was, watching the man clamber out of his car and pull a wallet from a breast pocket and push a wad of bills at the woman.

Geoff was behind her—his hands were on her shoulders. "Annie . . ." This time he whispered her name, and she felt the warmth of his breath on the back of her neck.

"It's all right," she said. "I'm all right."

"Yes, you are."

In the street the man and the woman were shaking hands. The woman shoved the wad of bills into her pocket and walked on, smiling. The man turned to them, shrugged, then swung himself back behind the wheel of the Maserati and drove away.

"Come inside," Geoff said. "Please."

They went into the house, and he closed the door and leaned against it. He was, Annie noted, very pale. "I thought . . ." He could not seem to speak the words.

"You thought Emma," she said.

"No, I didn't. I thought Annie. I thought this time, because of my big mouth, I'd lost Annie, my best shot at . . ."

"At what?"

"At being happy."

"But you want a family. I'm thirty-three. It may not happen."

He shook his head. "I want the possibility of a family. But only because I want you. I heard those brakes squeal, and I knew. I want Annie. The rest, if it happens, great. But it's a bonus, not the main event."

"Before," she said, "with Ari—I wasn't a very good mother, Geoff. I have to make that right. Whatever happens, Ari must be my first priority."

He took a few seconds over that, then led her to the couch. "I know he must. I'm not trying to shut your son out of your life, Annie. Out of our lives. Far from it. I'll do everything I can to help you make it okay. But you told me once that the past did not have to determine the future. You said you had an investment in believing that was true."

"A big investment. Yes."

He jerked his head to indicate the upstairs, the room with walls. "The stuff in my rather silly little safe . . . The mementos of Maggie's life, my family's past."

"The mezuzah and her Kindertransport papers."

"Yes. And the other things as well. Your drawings. This whole experience . . . I've been thinking about it since my mother died. Looking for a word. I think I've got it now. Your monk, the provisioner with the quail eggs, all the rest of it . . . I think I'm ready to believe in the forgiveness of sin. So the word is absolution. You for Ari. Me for Emma. Is that too Christian a notion for the son of Maggie Silber?"

"You'll have to ask Rabbi Cohen, but I think that's what Yom Kippur is about. The Day of Atonement. There's not much point in atoning if you don't believe in forgiveness."

"Point taken, Dr. Kendall."

"Geoff, are you sure?"

"If you mean about your Higher Power, or Rabbi Cohen's God of the 'Jewish enough,' or the Catholic version that makes men—including perhaps some ancestor of mine—become penitential hermits—no, I'm not sure. But if you mean us, you and me and Ari and perhaps a child of our own, whether we're worth a shot, whether we deserve another roll of the dice—yeah, I'm sure."

Annie smiled.

Afterword

Pace supporters of Portsmouth and Tottenham Hotspurs, I tell stories—I do not have a crystal ball. The teams win and lose and face relegation in a reality that exists only in these pages. And if I could actually dictate results, Liverpool would win every game in every competition.

The tunnels beneath the Holborn section of London, on the other hand, exist both in this book and in the parallel universe we call reality. The story of how and why those tunnels were built and used during World War II—down to the onetime restaurant and the old telephone system—is accurate. I made up the five-a-side football pitch, but I'd bet a fair sum that if someone somewhere had chronicled absolutely everything about those heroic and terrifying long-ago days, the odd game of indoor soccer might occur in the record. For those wanting to know more about the spy tunnels, at the time of writing this URL will get you to an article in the *Guardian* newspaper that details much of the story: http://www.guardian.co.uk/uk/2008/oct/18/london-underground -secret-tunnels.

Finally, the out-of-print book about the London Carthusians that Annie downloads from Google Books really exists. It's *The London Charterhouse: Its Monks and Its Martyrs,* by Lawrence Hendriks (K. Paul, Trench and Co., 1889). Dom Lawrence was himself a Carthusian and he includes in his history a story apparently well-known in the order: how the quarter part of the carcass of the martyred Venerable Father was tacked up over the Charterhouse gates by Henry's soldiers in 1535, and how, once they fell, those precious bones were so well hidden by the monks that they have never been found.

Acknowledgments

This story could not have become the book in your hands without the help of many people. I am enormously indebted to: the real Waltons, Margaret and Jennet and Tim and Anna, who years ago introduced me to number eight Bristol House, and have always made me welcome there; to Karen Ross, who allowed me to riff on her mother's story, met Annie and Geoff when they were shadows on the horizon, and was clever enough to buy a flat on Sharpleshall Street; to Maily Rusoff, Michael Radulescu, Danny Baron, and Heather Baron Shapiro, literary agents extraordinaire whose belief made it happen; to my editors at Viking Penguin, Carole DeSanti, who pushed me to the edge of the cliff and insisted I jump, and Beena Kamlani, who wields an editing emery board with the delicacy of a brain surgeon's scalpel; to David Halperin, whose expertise in Judaica and Jewish mysticism is matched only by his writerly generosity; to Elizabeth Statmore, true Renaissance woman, who combined her Latin skills with the imagination of a novelist to produce one of the key elements of the Speckled Egg code; to Shymala Dason, who repaired a broken link and fitted Annie for running shoes; and finally to Audrey Von Balluseck, my favorite Parisienne. Heartfelt thanks to all.